*Sorcery and the Single Girl*

Also by Red Dress Ink
and

# MINDY KLASKY

GIRL'S GUIDE TO WITCHCRAFT

# MINDY KLASKY

# Sorcery and the Single Girl

RED
DRESS
INK
™

SORCERY AND THE SINGLE GIRL

A Red Dress Ink novel

ISBN-13: 978-0-373-89563-2
ISBN-10:     0-373-89563-1

www.RedDressInk.com

**Printed in U.S.A.**

## ACKNOWLEDGMENTS

No book enters the world without the support of many, many individuals. Thank you to everyone who helped me as I researched and wrote and revised and edited and ranted and raved about Jane Madison's life. Most especially, though:

Thanks to the "book" people: my agent Richard Curtis (who continues to define professionalism, phone conversation after phone conversation) and all the folks at Red Dress Ink (Mary-Theresa Hussey, Adam Wilson, Margaret Marbury and the armies of behind-the-scenes folk who make everything possible).

And thanks to the "library" people, as well: my colleagues in the libraries at KDCS and SNR, and especially Judith Leggett, who provided endless information about herbs and flowering plants.

Of course, my family has stood by me as well—Klaskys and Timmins and Maddreys and Fallons (with a special shout-out to my nephew Jake, who didn't get a choice about having a crazy Aunt Mindy). As for my husband, Mark—there aren't enough words to thank him for his endless support, celebrating the highs and comforting the lows.

With this book, I continue to support First Book, a national nonprofit organization with the single mission to give children from low-income families the opportunity to read and own their first new books. For more information about First Book, please visit their Web site at www.firstbook.org.

To correspond with me and keep track of my writing life, please visit my Web site at www.mindyklasky.com.

For the Greenhill Girls,
who fought the battle against the Popular Snobs

Once upon a time, I thought that being a witch would make everything easier.

Yeah, right.

There I was on another Friday evening, leaning against the counter in Cake Walk, the Georgetown bakery owned by my best friend, Melissa White. Over the summer, I'd started helping Melissa close up every Friday night, after I left my job at the Peabridge Library. My assistance gave us a chance to catch up on our weeks, and then we conducted always-needed mojito therapy.

I was just waiting until we could turn the sign on the door from Walk On In to Walk On By. I could already taste icy lime juice and rum, mixed with mint and nearly frozen seltzer water in a chilled tumbler. Summer in Washington was always hot, and this late August day was no exception.

I held a glass of iced tea against the pulse point in my right wrist and tried to forgive the bakery's air-conditioning.

After all, it was doing its best to beat back the swampy heat. My red-shot curls frizzed against the back of my neck, and I was pretty sure that my kohl liner had smeared around my eyes. So much for drawing out the emerald glints trapped inside my hazel irises. Anyway, did that stuff *ever* work outside of fashion magazines?

I probably should have taken a page from Melissa's book and ignored makeup altogether—after all, it was just the two of us girlfriends. The two of us, and a pitcher of icy mojitos.

Since therapy had not yet commenced, however, I took a deep swallow of mango-lime iced tea and tried to explain to Melissa. Again. "I know that it shouldn't matter. I dated Scott for twelve years—twelve *years!* And I only saw the I.B. for twelve weeks."

I.B. That used to stand for Imaginary Boyfriend. Now, it stood for Idiot Bastard. Or Ignorant Boor. Or Irritating Boil. Get us going, Melissa and me, and we could continue the game for hours.

The I.B. The man I'd set my heart on. My friends and family had all agreed to refrain from using his name. He didn't deserve a name.

I sighed. "It's been ten months. Ten months, and nothing. Not a glimmer of a hint of a scintilla of a possibility on the romantic horizon. I'm never going to date again."

"Jane Madison, never is a very long time," Melissa said.

"I don't think that I can seriously take romance advice from a woman with fifty-two first dates under her belt in the past year."

"Don't exaggerate," Melissa said with a good-natured shrug. "There were only forty-one."

I shuddered. Forty-one. Forty-one nights of sitting at a table for two. Forty-one nights of coming up with witty and compelling Conversation Topics, five per date. (Okay, I knew that Melissa reused many of them, but still!) Forty-one nights of putting on perfect dating clothes, of combing out perfect dating hair, of squelching down perfect dating jitters.

And what did she have to show for it? A Friday evening with me. Me, a DVD of *Casablanca,* and microwave popcorn.

As if she'd read my mind, Melissa brushed her palms together, a businesswoman ever in charge. "We'd better turn on the air conditioner upstairs, or it will be hot enough to make the popcorn without getting anywhere near the microwave."

Melissa lived in a comfortable apartment above her bakery. Her little home was perfect in every way—except it didn't have central air. In fact, it had a wheezing window unit that was probably Carrier's prototype. You know. Willis Haviland Carrier, the inventor of the air conditioner. I *said* I was a librarian. We accumulate a ridiculous amount of trivia.

Actually, Melissa's contraption could get the job done, if we gave it enough time. The only problem was braving the oven of an apartment long enough to turn the rattling thing on. She waited for me to volunteer to step into the swamp that was her living room, but I merely shifted my wrist against my icy glass.

"Come on," she finally said. "Rock, paper, scissors."

Melissa and I settled all our disputes with the childhood game. We might be immature, but we'd never had a serious fight, not in the twenty-five years that we'd been best friends. Now, we counted to three, tapping our right fists against our left palms, and then we displayed our choices—paper for me, rock for Melissa.

"Paper covers rock," I said, trying not to gloat.

"Yeah, yeah," she said good-naturedly. She turned to the steps in the back corner of the bakery. "Keep an eye on things while I'm upstairs. And don't do anything I wouldn't do."

Well, that just opened up a huge realm of possibilities, didn't it?

I turned to the gigantic stainless steel sink at the back of the bakery, ready to wash a few dishes and get Cake Walk shut down for the night. It was the least I could do, since Melissa was braving the air upstairs.

In fact, I'd been practicing a water spell; I thought that it would be perfect for a little kitchen cleanup. I'd worked through it with my familiar, Neko, three times in the past week, trying to get my mind around the controlled whirlpool that the magic required.

Not that Neko excelled at helping out with water magic. When I'd first met him, he'd been frozen into the form of a black cat statue. I'd awakened him with my very first spell. He still retained a lot of his feline features, even though he'd remained a flesh-and-blood man for ten straight months. Okay, not *straight* months. Not precisely.

Neko had turned my little home upside down more than once with his parties and his exploits and his boyfriends-of-the-week, but when magical push came to enchanted shove, he'd been there for me, helping me to focus my powers and learn new ways to use my gifts.

Even when I wanted to work on water spells.

After a week of practice, I'd succeeded in gathering up

water from the faucet, and I could consistently get the miniature windstorm spinning in the center of my old farmhouse sink. Each time I tried to factor in dish soap, though, my concentration fell apart, and I was left cleaning up a froth of bubbles. Or a slick river of soap. Or an ocean of foaming water, ankle deep on my kitchen floor.

I bet that the Weird Sisters in *Macbeth* never needed to worry about these things. They just hired some sniveling apprentice to scrub their cauldrons clean. Eye of newt, wing of bat....

I decided that it was wiser to use conventional cleaning methods in Melissa's bakery. No reason to endanger pastries and pottery alike. Shaking my head and promising myself that I *would* master the spell, I reached for a sponge.

Before I could add soap, though, the bell over the door jangled its jaunty greeting. I turned around with a ready smile; I knew how to treat Melissa's clientele when I was at the counter.

And I almost sat down in the sink.

The man who stood in the doorway was drop-dead gorgeous. I couldn't compare him to a particular movie star—he was like the best of them rolled into one.

He seemed utterly unperturbed by the August heat; there wasn't a hint of sweat on his brow, on his lip, anywhere about him. His short blond hair lay perfectly, each strand cooperating to set off the strong lines of his cheekbones, his jaw. His eyes glinted in the early-evening sunshine, a blue so light that they seemed like glass. He wore a crisp white shirt that looked as if it had just left an ironing board, and his jeans fit well enough that Levi's should pay him for the advertising. His shoulders were broad, and his waist was narrow.

He had to come from the Midwest—corn-fed, small-town, a football quarterback if I'd ever seen one. There were country songs written about this man. He'd dated the head cheerleader; they'd been the prom king and queen. He had wanted to stay on the farm, take over for his daddy, but his mother had presented him with egg money she'd saved through the years, begging him to leave Kansas, to move to Washington for college, for a business degree.

He had broken his father's heart, even as he'd made the old man wipe away a surreptitious tear of pride. He still called home every Sunday afternoon at four, to catch up with his parents after church, after the mid-afternoon meal they called dinner. He tried to describe the big city to them, to fill them in on his life on Capitol Hill, but they never truly understood.

"I say, are you still open?" he asked.

A British accent.

Okay, so maybe I got a little carried away. It could happen to anyone. A Brit, though… That was even better than a Future Farmer of America.

I knew that I was supposed to be a levelheaded woman. After all, I had two graduate degrees—in library science and English. I was supposed to know better than to swoon over a man's good looks, to melt because he smiled at me, to fall at his feet because he spoke the Queen's English.

So shoot me. I was a fool. I'd always had a soft spot for a British accent.

Obviously, plenty of Englishmen were jerks. I knew that,

too. But my track record wasn't so great with the standard American issue. And if you asked me to define my perfect man, to write up a quick summary of what I was looking for and place it in an online-dating profile, those crisp consonants and plummy vowels would be near the top of my list.

"Um, yes," I said. Brilliant. Witty. Yeah, that's me.

"Have you any Lust, then?"

"Excuse me?"

He winced and then smiled ruefully. "A friend sent me. She said that you sell Almond Lust, and that I couldn't walk by without trying a piece. In fact, I'm to buy up all you have and bring it to a dinner party this evening."

Oh. Almond Lust. One of Melissa's specialties.

Well, maybe in some cultures a stinging crimson blush was considered attractive. After all, those British women were all fair skinned. My dream man was probably used to a gentle companion who blushed the color of a summer sunset. I could hope.

"Of course," I managed to say. I pointed to the pottery plate of shortbread confections, their thick chocolate layer covered with toasted, sliced almonds. At least my Code Red nail polish was smooth and unchipped. Chalk one up for the colonial team. "We have four left."

"Splendid!"

Again, that flush spread to my face. Pastry, I reminded myself sternly. He was only commenting on the pastry.

I found a paperboard box beneath the counter and began to transfer the Lust. "Do you work around here?" I asked, intent on drawing him out before he walked through the door, before he disappeared from my life forever.

"I do now. I've just accepted a new position in Arlington."

Arlington. Just over the river. Not in my backyard, but close enough for me to imagine seeing him again. "What do you do?"

"I'm in acquisitions."

Acquisitions. A lawyer, then. My skunk of an ex-fiancé, Scott Randall, had been a lawyer. I felt my shoulders stiffen, but I ordered myself to take a deep breath, to smile, to act like lawyers were my favorite people in the world. After all, if I was going to hate all lawyers, I'd have to move out of Washington.

I punched a few keys on the cash register and announced the price. My British friend reached into his pocket and pulled out a money clip. A money clip, with stylized art deco lines that made me think of the statue of Prometheus in Rockefeller Center, the golden god delivering the torch of knowledge to all mankind. I'd never seen an American man use a clip. I bit back a heartfelt sigh.

"Blasted American bills," he muttered with good humor.

Blasted! He said "blasted"! You couldn't get any more British than that!

He shook his head as he slipped off the clip. "You Americans don't have the sense to make your money different colors. Force a poor sod to sort through every last bill to find the right one."

He'd complicated his task by forcing the money clip into double duty; he had at least a dozen slips of paper tucked next to his cash. He smiled at my quizzical look. "Receipts. I'm terrible about filling out my expense account."

I smiled, anxious to keep even this stilted conversation

going. "Receipt!" I exclaimed, like a parrot that had mastered a new word. "Do you need one?"

"That would be lovely, actually." I pressed a button on the register, and it spit out a curl of paper. By then, my Brit had finally found the appropriate bill. I calculated his change, wishing that I could think of something else to say.

Monty Python. *Upstairs, Downstairs. Pride and Prejudice.* Bridget Jones. I didn't think that any of those was likely to spark a deep and meaningful conversation. Certainly not enough of one to get him to ask for my phone number.

And so, I collected his change from the register. I counted it into his palm, and no one could really blame me if I let my fingers slip against his. The touch lingered only a moment, just long enough for him to curve a smile and say, "With these coins?"

I had no idea what he meant, but I was eager to prolong the conversation. "Pardon me?"

"It's an old nursery rhyme. Mother Goose, I think. 'With these coins I find you. With these words I bind you. Keep our secret, silent be. Speak to no man, not of me. Diddle dum, diddle dee, fi, fo, fum.'"

When all I managed was a puzzled smile, my mysterious Brit laughed and shrugged at the same time, saying, "I suppose our nurseries had different rhymes." He shot his cuff and glanced at his watch, clearly eager to be heading out to his dinner party. Reluctantly, I made a show of tucking in the lid of his paperboard box. I took a printed sticker from the roll that Melissa kept by the register and pressed it onto the box for good measure. At least all the guests at his dinner party would know the source of the delectable treats he carried.

"Good Lust," I said in a cheery voice, and cringed when I heard how stupid I sounded.

"Many thanks." And then he winked at me.

He. Winked. At. Me.

From a lot of guys, a wink would be sleazy. It would be sly. It would be a pick up line that wasn't a line, a hip-and-happening exclamation that managed to stay silent-and-silly.

From my Brit, though, it was a shared joke. A private conversation. An entire future, all wrapped up in one fortuitous twitch of an eye.

And then the bell jangled, and he was out the door, heading back into the steamy D.C. evening.

"Oh good!" Melissa said, coming back down the stairs. "You killed the Lust."

"What?" I was still staring after the customer, willing him to remember something, urging him to come back, to ask for my name, my number, anything.

"The Lust." Melissa pointed to the empty pottery plate. "It doesn't keep well at all."

I sighed and licked my lips. "Then we would have been forced to eat it all by ourselves."

"What's that?" Melissa reached around me and picked up a white slip from the counter.

I craned my neck and looked at the item in her fingers. It was a card. Like a business card, but with different dimensions—more square than rectangular. It had a dark silver lining, dully reflective, and words embossed in bold, black letters.

GRAEME HENDERSON
ACQUISITIONS

And beneath it, as discreet as a priest in a confessional, a telephone number. 703 prefix. Arlington, Virginia.

I remembered him shuffling through his money, juggling the receipts. He had seemed to take more time than he needed, made the paper more of a production than was strictly necessary. He had wanted me to have this card.

That was what he'd meant by his wink, by the tiny smile on his perfect lips.

Melissa sighed and turned toward the trash can. Her wrist cocked; she was treating the card as garbage. "No!" I exclaimed. She looked at me as if I had two heads. "No," I repeated in a quieter voice. "I think he meant for me to have it."

"Acquisitions?" Melissa read again. "How pretentious is that?"

"Not pretentious at all!" I rushed to Graeme Henderson's defense. Even as I protested Melissa's dismissal, I realized that he couldn't be a lawyer. Not with a card like that. A law firm would have sucked out any spark of creativity, would have bled dry the smooth polish of the silver-lined card. "I mean, it's not pretentious if that's what he does."

"But what does he acquire?"

"Lust," I said immediately.

Melissa gave me a strange look, but she passed the card across the counter. I slipped it into my pocket, vowing to phone him the very next day.

After all, didn't the dating gods help those who helped themselves?

If I'd known the havoc that one little phone call would

wreak, I would have thrown away the card right then and there. Lust and everything, I would have just tossed it.

Or at least remembered that witchcraft never made anything simpler. Never, ever, ever.

Melissa and I were well into our second pitcher of mojitos, almost soused enough to join the patrons of Rick's club in singing their rousing rendition of "La Marseillaise," when we were interrupted by a knock at the door. For just a moment, I thought that Graeme might have returned to Cake Walk, intent on finding satisfaction beyond Almond Lust, but I realized that I was being ridiculous even before Melissa had paused the DVD.

As she opened the door, she sighed her disgust. "Oh," she said, in a tone that let me know exactly who stood on the landing. "It's you."

"And what a pleasure to see you, too, my dear," Neko said, slinking into the room with the aplomb of his Egyptian feline ancestors.

"Well, girlfriend," he said to me, gliding across the living room. He kissed me on both cheeks—his latest affectation—and sat in the middle of the couch. "I thought I'd

find you here. You really should let me know where you're
going to be, so that I can pass on urgent messages. And
while you're at it, you shouldn't look quite so disappointed
to see me."

He pulled his legs onto the couch, sitting cross-legged
and stretching back, as if to show off his spinal flexibility.
When he settled onto the overstuffed cushion, he looked
for all the world like a cat occupying a particularly spectacular sunbeam. After studying his immaculate fingernails, he reached into the bowl of popcorn I'd been sharing
with Melissa and extracted a generous handful. He held his
cupped palm to his lips and extended his tongue, delicately
gathering up a single puffed kernel. He chewed slowly, then
cocked his head to one side. "What? You're not even going
to offer me a drink?"

I shot Melissa a pleading glance, but she started to shake
her head in the negative. She and Neko had scarcely been
on speaking terms for the past three months. I mouthed,
*Please!* and she recanted, stalking into the kitchen to retrieve
a glass. She filled it with our magical concoction of rum,
lime and mint before passing the drink to Neko. "Thank
you, darling," he purred, raising the glass to toast her before
tossing back a healthy swallow. "Mmm. Could use a bit
more mint, but any port in a storm, as they say."

Melissa bristled. "*We* thought that they were just fine,"
she said through gritted teeth. "We made them just the way
we like them."

I leaned forward to separate them. "Neko, if you'd rather
*go home,* I have some chardonnay in the fridge."

He beamed a smile at me. "Not anymore. Jacques and I

finished it last night." He dragged out the foreign name as if it were a delectable appetizer. Lowering his eyes and looking up at me through lashes that were longer than any boy deserved, he went on, "Or should I say, this morning?"

Melissa huffed in disgust and hustled down the hallway, slamming the bathroom door behind her. I glared at my familiar. "Neko, was that absolutely necessary?"

"What? It was only a bottle of Turning Leaf. Hardly anything to get upset about." A small frown creased the ageless arch between his eyebrows, and his mouth opened into a startled O. "I'm sorry! Did Melissa give the wine to you? Was she upset that I drank a gift?"

"You know why she was upset." I took the bowl of popcorn away from him before he could devour the rest of our microwaved bounty. "You didn't need to mention Jacques. You know she still isn't over him."

"And once again, I have to say that isn't my fault! I can't help it that Jacques liked me more than he liked her!"

I took a deep breath, ready to explain, again, that Neko wasn't helping matters. I was ready to tell him, again, that Melissa had found Jacques first. I was ready to state, again, that Jacques was the one who had posted on FranticDate.com. I was ready to remind Neko, again, that Jacques had said that his ideal date was a woman—a *woman*—who could bake like his *grand-mère* and who looked like Brigitte Bardot, circa 1960. I was ready to scream at Neko, again, that Jacques was the one who had thought that he could cajole himself out of his gayness, that he could "heal" himself, that he could start playing for the other side, if only he found the right woman to lead him onto the straight and narrow path.

But we'd crossed that ground before, back and forth, countless times in the past three months. Neko had come into Cake Walk just as Jacques arrived for his second date with Melissa (a rare second date, I might add—Melissa was pickier than Jacques's sainted *grand-mère,* but she'd been feeling desperate). The attraction between the men had been instant. Jacques had wandered off with my catlike familiar, barely remembering to say goodbye to Melissa, scarcely taking the time to cancel dinner plans with her that night.

And Neko and Jacques had been inseparable ever since.

I'd tried to tell Melissa that she hadn't even *liked* Jacques all that much. She'd been bored by his conversation (all about fashion and designers and life on the haute couture circuit in, um, Gay Paree). She had thought that he was self-absorbed and more than a little snobby. She had found it odd that he had not even tried to kiss her good-night, despite a first date that lasted until nearly midnight.

But her pride had been injured. Her pride, and her sense of security. There she was, turning over every stone that she could find as she searched for the man of her dreams, and Neko had been able to waltz in and pluck the plum from her dating tree, with scarcely a pause to catch his breath.

And I was left in the middle, trying to bridge the gap between my best friend and my familiar. "Neko, would it kill you not to mention him here? Just until she finds someone else. Until she's focused on another guy?"

He frowned. "It's not like Jacques and I were engaging in hot sweaty man-sex on her sofa." I immediately thought of the cracked leather couch in my basement, Neko's bed every night that he spent in the cottage that we shared. I did *not* need that image flickering in front of my eyes, thank you very much.

With a precise moue, Neko leaned forward and touched the remote control, unfreezing the DVD. The rousing French anthem began to pour from the television once again, filling both Rick's club and Melissa's living room with the stirring strains of Gallic patriotism. Before I could decipher the buttons on the remote, Melissa stormed out of the bathroom. Her fingers flew over the electronic gadget, and the television crashed into silence. The laboring air conditioner made the only sound in the room. The air conditioner and my pounding heart, as I waited to see if this storm was going to pass.

"Enough!" she said. "We all know how the movie ends."

Okay. So maybe the French national anthem wasn't the best soundtrack at the moment. I guessed we were through watching *Casablanca*. I gulped down a large swallow of mojito, searching for a new conversational course to guide us into a safe social harbor. Before I could divine one, Neko said, "Any new men come by the bakery?"

I started to say something, anything. I fumbled for words about the golden stranger, Graeme Henderson, but was stopped by Melissa snapping, "'Friendship is constant in all other things.'"

I stared at her, utterly confused. I knew the rest of the line—it was from *Much Ado About Nothing*. "Save in the office and affairs of love." Melissa and I played the Shakespeare game often enough, quoting snippets of the Bard to each other. We'd used his plays like our own private code since we were absurdly precocious teenagers, gaga over the romance of Romeo and Juliet.

Nodding when she saw that I remembered the rest of the line, Melissa said sweetly, "Jane, could you help me in the kitchen?" She slopped the dregs of mojitos from the pitcher into Neko's glass and practically dragged me out of the room.

"What?" I asked her, as she began dismembering limes with a knife that was large enough to make me take a step back.

"Friendship Test."

"What?" This time, I let my voice reflect my utter confusion.

"Friendship Test. You know."

Well, I knew all about Friendship Tests. I knew that you could call "Friendship Test" on your best friend any time you needed to confirm your relationship. You could Friendship Test the last slice of chocolate cheesecake, for example, calling out those two words and freezing the treat on its way to your best friend's plate. You could Friendship Test packing for a trip, dragooning your best friend into staying up till the wee hours of the morning, deciding whether the stone-washed jeans or the overdyed jeans were more likely to make your great-aunt have conniptions at Thanksgiving dinner. You could Friendship Test a movie, shoving out the latest blockbuster romance for an action flick that everyone *knew* would be terrible, but it starred Brad Pitt, so you just had to go, no matter what the critics said.

But Friendship Testing an entire topic of conversation? Especially one as innocuous as Graeme Henderson, Acquisitions, and my dreams of British romance?

Melissa rolled mint leaves into a careful pile before employing her knife with the unshakable rhythm of a trained professional. The sharp scent mingled with the rum that she glugged into the pitcher, melded with the citrus tang of the limes. She fumbled in her freezer for ice cubes, and when she turned back to me, unshed tears glittered in her eyes.

She wasn't crying for Jacques.

She was upset about all the other First Dates. She was saddened by her endless quest for happiness, her constant searching for completeness. And, truth be told, she was probably just a little jealous about *my* relationship with Neko, about my mysterious bond with my familiar. She knew I was a witch, and she understood that I had new powers, new abilities, a new life that was separate and apart from the years we'd known each other.

If she'd be happier knowing that we kept a few secrets just between the two of us, well, that was actually fine with me. After all, it wasn't like anything had happened with Graeme Henderson. It wasn't like I really had anything to tell Neko at all. I'd keep the confidence, just with Melissa.

"Friendship Test," I said, and I shrugged. I lifted the pitcher as Melissa rinsed her hands, taking a moment to press her fingertips against her eyelids. "Okay?"

She smiled, and her lips were only a little shaky. "Okay."

Neko had switched the television to the Game Show Network, and he was gleefully shouting out answers to an ancient avatar of Alex Trebec. He bombed out at Final Jeopardy!, though, and sat back on the couch with a pout. "Stupid game."

"You'll get no argument here," I said.

He started to surf through stations, bypassing anything

that hinted of education or drama and stopping for agonizing minutes on any station featuring large rhinestoned objects for sale at ridiculous prices. "There," he said, waving the remote at a "Classic" peacock pin. "You should have one of those."

"It would clash with the embroidery on my brocade petticoat." My job at the Peabridge Library included a colonial wardrobe—rich taffeta and linen, hoops to make my waist look tiny, and delicate embroidery that made my fingers ache every time I looked at the stitches. All right. I wasn't such a big fan of the costumes, but they did give me an extra fifteen minutes of sleep every morning. I never needed to decide what to wear to the office.

The costumes had been part of my boss's last scheme to keep the Peabridge budget in the black. She required all of us librarians to dress like colonial matrons, in hopes of bringing in local library traffic. The same desperate measures had led to my living in a cottage on the Peabridge grounds—I had exchanged twenty-five percent of my salary for a fully-furnished cottage. A cottage that just happened to contain a collection of books on witchcraft. Books—and Neko, whose fashion sense (at least in jewelry) seemed twisted from the years he had spent enchanted as a statue in the basement.

From the corner of my eye, I saw Melissa shudder at the hideous rhinestone disaster. "Come on, Neko," I pressed. "Why did you come over here? What did you need to tell me?"

"Oh!" He put down the remote. "Clara phoned."

Clara. My mother. "And?"

"She wanted to remind you that you're both having brunch with your grandmother, a week from Sunday."

So now Clara was my calendar tickler? Brunch was more than a week away. I guessed she just didn't want to disappoint Gran.

Monthly brunch meetings had been my grandmother's idea. She thought that if the three of us got together on the first Sunday of every month, then we'd get to know each other better. We'd learn to trust each other more, to share with each other like mothers and daughters are supposed to.

Most of the time, we managed to make it through the meal without any outright argument, but I had to admit that I'd taken to ordering Eggs Benedict, so that I could take out some of my frustration on the English muffin base. I didn't think I'd ever be able to eat a simple breakfast of Special K and skim milk with my mother. There wasn't enough of a subtextual battle there to get us through the meal.

I attended our monthly get-togethers religiously, though, seeing them as a sort of penance for my grandmother's complete recovery from the pneumonia that had sent her to the hospital the year before. While it had taken months for her to regain all of her proverbial vim and vigor, she was finally entrenched in her volunteer work again, helping out the D.C. concert opera guild.

She was also wholly devoted to the cause of strengthening my bonds with my mother. There were now entire weeks when I didn't sulk about Clara abandoning me for two and a half decades. (I could recite Gran's explanations in my sleep by now. Clara had needed to defeat her own demons. She had needed to grow up herself. She had needed to find the spiritual anchor of her life in the whirl-wind world around us. Yeah, yeah, yeah.)

I glared at Neko. "And that reminder couldn't wait until I got home?"

My familiar plucked at an imaginary thread on his black jeans. "There was another message."

I caught Melissa rolling her eyes, and I had to admit that I was getting annoyed with my familiar as well. "Yes?" I prompted.

"Teresa Alison Sidney called."

I couldn't keep from catching my breath.

"Who's that?" Melissa asked.

Neko cocked his head, clearly asking if I wanted him to elaborate. I fortified myself by filling my lungs and said, "The head of the Washington Coven. The leader of the local witches."

I hadn't met Teresa Alison Sidney yet, but I'd heard her name often enough in the past ten months. She'd been invoked, like a saint or a sinner, every time I strayed from my studies with David Montrose, my warder. Teresa Alison Sidney and the Coven had the right to control all witchcraft in their territory. If I passed the Coven's in-spection, if I learned enough witchcraft to satisfy them, then I would be permitted to join their secret circle. I could keep all the arcana in my possession—spell books, crystals, runes.

And Neko. My familiar was part of the package. Part of the package I would lose if the Washington Coven deemed me unworthy of membership. I pictured Teresa Alison Sidney as a forbidding woman, wise, waiting—like Whistler's

Mother in modern dress. I knew that I'd have to meet her eventually, but I'd been perfectly content to put off that reckoning. Put it off until I'd learned more about my powers. Until I'd gained some confidence. Some courage.

Melissa, not being up on the witchcraft celebrity watch, failed to register the importance of the call.

"What did she say?" I asked, trying to sound nonchalant. After all, she might be calling for any number of reasons. She might…she might have realized she had a sudden need for colonial American recipes. Or she might…she might have been looking for advice on locally grown herbs and aromatics. Or she might…

I couldn't really think of any *good* thing that she might.

"She wants to meet with you. Next Friday. At midnight."

Despite the summer heat, gooseflesh rose on my arms. Midnight. The witching hour. "A—" I needed to clear my throat. "Alone?"

"She'll have the entire Coven gathered," Neko said helpfully.

That did nothing to ease the sudden fear that whispered down the back of my neck. I thought of Gran's old-fashioned expression: someone had walked across my grave. "I mean," I managed to say after thinking out each word, "do *I* have to show up alone?"

"Of course not." Neko's smile was sympathetic, and I could tell that he was trying to make his answer light. "I'll be there. And David."

My familiar and my warder. To help me work magic and to protect me. I didn't really feel any safer, though.

"Is this it, then?" I folded my arms around my belly, suddenly wishing that I hadn't downed the last couple of minty mojitos. I wanted to rock back and forth, find some comfort in acting like a rebellious toddler. "Are they going to test me?"

"Of *course* they're going to test you," Neko scoffed. His casual dismissal converted my apprehension into annoyance. "You've known that all along. No, this isn't the time for the testing itself. They'll wait for some big important day to do that. This meeting is just to lay the groundwork. To tell you the rules."

I nodded. Neko's words made sense. All except for… "Big important day? What sort of big important day?"

"You know. One of the Witches' Sabbaths. Imbolc. Beltane. Lughnasa. Samhain."

I'd read enough in my collection of witchy books that I recognized the names of the festivals. I was even able to translate Neko's Gaelic pronunciation—"Sow-inn"—to actual spelling—"Samhain." Halloween. But I'd never actually paid attention to the specific witching days, never worried about when they hit the "real world" calendar.

Real world.

This *was* my real world now. I was a witch.

And I was going to be tested by my Coven, judged to see if I truly belonged as a new member. I thought about the magical runes and crystals lying in my basement, probably grown dusty, since I'd neglected them for a month or more, while I played with my still-unsuccessful water spell.

Where did the time go? And how was I going to get ready for my first encounter with the Coven, with Teresa

Alison Sidney? And what was I going to do once the Coven set an actual date for my testing?

Melissa might not have been privy to all of my witch-craft workings. She didn't know the feelings that grew inside me as I practiced my craft. She'd never understand the tremble of power as I worked a spell, the satisfying *snick* of release when my magic hit its target.

But she knew *me*. She recognized my fear. "It will all be fine," she said, topping off my glass and looking daggers at Neko, sending a sufficiently clear message that even he realized he should shut his mouth.

"But—" I said.

"You'll practice," she said.

"I don't—"

"You will," she affirmed.

"I've never—"

"No time like the present," she berated. "Or, more accurately, the future. You'll work with Neko and with David. You'll learn everything you need to know. And when you need a bit of support and reassurance, you'll swing by Cake Walk so that I can feed you and remind you of everything you *do* know."

She was so certain. So determined. There was no way that I could argue with her. She was my best friend, and she knew what was right.

I shrugged and stretched against the back of the couch, shoving my hands into my pockets to help ease the panic-kinks in my spine. My fingers brushed against the card that I had hidden away, the silver-edged message from Graeme Henderson. Acquisitions.

I felt the message like a gentle electric thrum, like the tension of static charge when you rub a balloon against a wool rug and then make your hair stand on end.

Friendship Test. Melissa was my best friend, and she would get me through my meeting with the Coven. Melissa, and Neko, and David.

A girl could hardly ask for a better support group.

Melissa plucked the remote from Neko's hand. "Oh well. We can hardly leave Victor Laszlo standing in the lurch, can we?" We watched the end of *Casablanca* without any further conversation, waiting until the final screen to shout out Rick's famous last words, all together, in mojito-lubricated unison: "Louie, I think this is the beginning of a beautiful friendship."

As I recited the line, my fingers drifted back to the card in my pocket. *Graeme,* I thought. And I let my mind wander over that British accent, that sly wink, and the beautiful…friendship that might await me when I phoned the number on the card. The possibility was almost enough to make me forget about my meeting with Teresa Alison Sidney and the Coven.

Almost.

But not quite.

I sat on the edge of my bed and stared at the phone. This was stupid. I'd made phone calls before. Thousands of them. Why should this one be any different? Why should it make my pulse pound? Make my tongue swell up? Make tremors march up and down my arms, like tiny electric soldiers trying to kick me into action?

Or maybe I was just hung over from mojito therapy the night before.

I wiped my hands against my jeans and reached out one more time for the small white business card. Graeme Henderson. Acquisitions.

This wasn't fair. I shouldn't have to make the phone call. He should have asked me for *my* phone number. *He* should have taken the risk.

But he had. He'd left his card, putting it right on the counter. He had made the first move.

So, really, it was like he had already asked me out, and all I had to do was pick up the phone and say yes. Right?

I palmed the card and leaned back against my headboard, hugging my pillow to my chest. Had I ever been the one to make the first move? Well, there had been that time in eighth grade, when I'd asked Adam Lehrer to the Sadie Hawkins dance. But that was hardly a date. I mean, there had been a dozen of us kids, all going to the dance together. We'd stood on separate sides of the gym and told nervous jokes with our friends, waiting until two hours had gone by before anyone was brave enough to take to the dance floor, and that was only because they played "Macarena," and we could pretend we didn't know each other while we flailed about on the basketball court.

No. I wasn't being fair to myself. I *had* asked Adam Lehrer to the dance. So what was I worried about? This should be old hat, right?

Of course, Adam Lehrer and I had been thirteen years old. And Adam had been a freakish six feet tall, even though he didn't weigh more than one hundred and thirty pounds. He wasn't about to say no to any girl who gave him the time of day. And I never actually *phoned* him for a date; I'd passed him a note in homeroom, asking him to check one box if his answer was yes, and another if his answer was no.

I was being ridiculous. I was a grown woman. I was a professional librarian. I was experienced, confident, capable. I was a *witch,* for heaven's sake.

I wasn't going to let one silly invention—the telephone—get in the way of my finding eternal happiness with the most gorgeous man I'd met since the I.B.

The Itinerant Bellyache. I'd pursued him, and look where that had gotten me. I'd even asked him up to Gran's farm, invited him to my family reunion, so that my humiliation could be placed on full display for everyone I knew and loved.

Wait. I'd asked the I.B., but only after he had invited me to lunch. He had asked me out first. He took the lead, and the relationship ended up in the toilet. There. The powers of the universe were clearly sending me a message. They were obviously demanding that I change my ways. Those who cannot remember the past are doomed to repeat it, and all that jazz.

I grabbed the phone and punched in the number before I could talk myself out of acting.

One ring.

I nearly hung up.

Two rings.

I caught my breath.

Three rings.

I started to compose a message for his answering machine, thought better of it, decided that I'd just throw away the card, that the universe was clearly reversing its original message. Now it was shrieking: Run! Run! Flee before it's too late!

Four—

"Henderson."

"Madison," I said, before I could stop myself.

I was such an idiot! He didn't even know my name. He was going to think that I was mocking him, just for answering his phone with a crisp, businesslike precision. "Jane

Madison here," I clarified, before he could hang up. "We met yesterday. At Cake Walk."

"Oh yes," he said, and I could hear him smile as he spoke. Yes. Hear him. Those perfect lips, curving around those flawless teeth. The British dentists' union should stage a protest—whoever maligned them in popular American media had clearly never met Graeme Henderson. He said, "The Lust girl."

"Er, yes," I said, and made a face I meant to be funny. I scowled when I realized that he couldn't see me, and then I felt even more stupid. My not-so-becoming flush was rising to my cheeks once again. No wonder I had sent Adam Lehrer a note in eighth grade—that communication was a thousand times easier than this one, even if I *had* needed to debate the size and shape of the boxes for him to check. Fortunately, Melissa had convinced me that heart-shaped boxes were Not Cool. "I wanted to follow up with you," I said to Graeme, clutching at straws to move this conversation forward. "To find out if the people at your dinner party enjoyed the dessert."

I was *not* going to say the word "lust." Wild horses couldn't make me say it.

"It was everything I'd been told it would be," he said. And then he lowered his voice and whispered, "And more."

Now he was definitely toying with me. He probably left his card on counters all across America. He lured poor unsuspecting shopgirls into thinking he was some harmless football-player frat boy from the Midwest, and then he dropped his sleek Acquisitions card, trolling to see just how many of them—of *us*—were foolish enough to phone him.

He probably had this whole call scripted. He already knew what he was going to say, how he was going to lure me into making more of a fool out of myself.

"Well good, then," I heard myself say in a tiny voice that might have traveled all the way from Mars. "Um, goodbye."

"Just a moment," he said, and my heart pounded so hard that I needed to open my mouth to take a breath. "Don't be so hasty." Hasty. Did Americans ever say *hasty?* It was a British word. Like naughty. I jerked my thoughts back from *that* precipice.

"I'm truly glad that you rang me up," he said. "I wanted to speak with you longer in your shop, but I was late to meet my friends."

"Actually, the bakery isn't mine."

"Oh?"

"It belongs to my best friend. I just cover for her sometimes. I work at the Peabridge Library, just a few blocks away. I'm a librarian." I heard the unwanted note of defensiveness creep into my voice. I'd learned to judge a lot about people from the way they responded to my job title. About fifty percent made "Marian the Librarian" jokes, apparently deluded into believing that they were the first people in the entire history of librarianship to make *The Music Man* connection. Another twenty-five percent immediately asked how long it had taken me to learn the Dewey Decimal System. I no longer had a civil answer for either group.

"Ah… 'My library was dukedom enough.'"

"Prospero!" I shouted. *"The Tempest."*

"Quite," he said, and now his amusement seemed warm,

friendly, including me in a select club—the cognoscenti, the literati, the something else extravagant that ended with -ti.

I started to make an excuse. "It's just that—"

He was already providing his own explanation, verbally waving off the quotation. "You know. The tedium of a classical education."

"I specialize in that tedium," I said, and then I grimaced. Tedium was not a word I wanted him to associate with me, in any way, shape, or form.

"So," he said, when the silence had stretched out just a little too long. "Is there a place where we could meet to exchange quips about the Bard? I can find out more about why a librarian offers up biscuits to the public during her spare time, and we could share a cup of coffee?"

I thought rapidly. "How about Bistro Francais? It's on M Street, in the center of Georgetown."

"Excellent." I could imagine him writing down the restaurant name in impeccable British penmanship. He didn't strike me as a BlackBerry sort of guy. He'd use a fountain pen, write on rich, creamy calendar pages. "There's one small hitch, though. My office is demanding beastly hours just now. Could we make this dessert coffee? Say on Wednesday night?"

Alarms went off inside my head. Office. Beastly hours. I'd heard excuses like that before. Excuses from a married pig of a man.

But, a little voice protested, struggling to be heard over the blaring alarms. Late hours are fine. Late hours are when a married man goes home to his wife and family. Beware the man who *keeps* you from his evenings and weekends and holidays.

"Wednesday night?" I said, and tried to sound as if I was paging through my very busy social calendar.

"Would half past nine be too late?"

Nine-thirty. We could chat for an hour or so, and I'd still be able to get home, get to bed, wake up on time for work. "That would be perfect," I said, fighting to balance my enthusiasm against my jaded disillusionment. Damn the I.B.! I refused to let the Incontinent Bogeyman interfere with my current plans.

I'm not quite sure what Graeme and I said to each other then, but I must have made perfectly normal "signing off" noises, because I was suddenly staring at a dead phone and a silver-lined card.

A dead phone, a silver-lined card, and the prospect of my first date since the Ill-bred Bête-Noire had poisoned my love life. I clutched my pillow to my face and squealed, trying to release some of the thrumming, paralyzing energy that rolled over me.

I had done it! I had made the phone call! I pounded my heels against my bed, inordinately pleased with my social bravery.

"Jane? Are you all right in there?"

Neko.

I sat up and placed the phone back on my nightstand, taking care to slip Graeme's card between my mattress and box spring. "I'm fine," I said. "Come in."

My door opened, and Neko poked his head around the corner. His gaze automatically darted toward my closet, to the small metal table that had hosted an aquarium until last October. The glance was so rapid that I would have missed it, if I hadn't been waiting. When Neko spoke, he'd carefully trained his face to impassivity. "David is waiting for you. He's in the basement."

My trusty warder.

He must have found out that Teresa Alison Sidney had summoned me. Neko would have kept him apprised of such a development, even if David's position as warder didn't grant him access to the information through other channels. I was a bit surprised that he hadn't awakened me at dawn, slave driver that he was.

"Thanks," I said to Neko, pausing only long enough to twitch my bedspread back into place. I glanced at the edge, envisioning my treasured card tucked safely away. I was pleased to see that nothing looked out of place. After all, a Friendship Test was a Friendship Test, and Melissa had asked me not to tell Neko about Graeme. Who was I to go back on my word? Besides, the prickly feeling at the back of my neck made me suspect that Neko would do *something* to ruin things with Graeme, if I gave him half a chance. My familiar and my love life were not a good mix.

Well, I thought, as I descended the stairs to the basement, time enough to think about my mysterious Englishman later. Now, I had to work. At least it was cool downstairs.

David was waiting for me by the book stand. "Good morning," he said. Somehow, he managed to convey that the morning had mostly fled toward noon, and that he assumed I had been lollygagging around—lollygagging!—rather than producing anything worthwhile in the witchcraft sense of the word.

For the most part, David and I had settled into an easy

relationship, a surprisingly straightforward give-and-take. Technically, David was my protector; his job was to keep me from hurting myself when I worked my magic or—more ominously—from being hurt by someone else. David, though, did far more. He had assumed the role of teacher, guiding me through using my powers, helping me learn more about the strange new world I'd discovered less than a year before.

When I got too stubborn, though, or David got too short-tempered, he threatened to stop teaching me. He told me that I needed to go to the Coven, to get an official instructor, a magical expert who could work with a witch as strong willed as I. Each time David threatened, however, we managed to make peace. I didn't like the idea of sharing my magical development with a stranger. I was proud of what I'd accomplished, but also embarrassed by the little things I hadn't quite managed to master. I should have had better control over my spell-working by now.

"Good morning," I said, doing my best to match his serious tone.

And then we engaged in the Greeting Ballet. We'd done this now countless times, every time David came to teach me, and it never became more graceful. If he were a friend of mine, I'd throw my arms around him and give him a quick hug. If he were a certain type of casual acquaintance (like Neko's main squeeze, Jacques), we would peck each other on both cheeks. If he were a work colleague, I'd extend my hand for a quick, hearty shake.

But he was all of those things. And none of them. And so we treated each other with proverbial kid gloves, stumbling into an awkward embrace that left both of us off balance. I tried to plant a quick kiss on his cheek and ended up grazing the air by his chin. He looked startled, and he pulled away, which caused *me* to pull away, backing into Neko.

As my familiar caught my elbow he shot me one of his wry, arched-eyebrow grins, and I bit back the first retort that came to mind. The last thing I needed was for Neko to make smart comebacks about my relationship with David. My awkward, undefined relationship with David. I brushed my hands through my hair and turned back to my warder. "Good morning," I said again, as if I could erase the entire embarrassing sequence from his memory and my own.

I crossed the room and collapsed onto the black leather couch. Neko's hot sweaty man-sex couch. No. I wasn't going to think about that.

David shoved his hands into his khaki pockets and jutted his almost-kissed chin toward the bookshelves. As I'd expected, he said, "I'm here to help you prepare for your Friday meeting with Teresa Alison Sidney."

"Does everyone call her that?" I asked, letting some of my anxiety spill over as annoyance.

"Teresa Alison Sidney?" He repeated himself. "That's her name."

"No, I mean, do they always use her first, middle and last name? I've only heard her referred to as 'Teresa Alison Sidney.' Never just Teresa. Never even Mrs. Sidney. Or Ms. Sidney, if that's what she prefers. Always the triple name."

Neko nodded, as if he agreed with me. He struck a pose and gushed to David, "She's right, you know. Teresa Alison

Sidney. Just like when you're seated next to a famous person at a banquet. David Hyde Pierce. You don't feel like you're allowed to address him by his first name, but you want to stake a claim that you're closer to him than 'Mr. Pierce.' So you spend the entire evening referring to him by all his names, and then, when you tell the story to friends, you have to go on that way, because that's the way you think of him. 'When I sat next to David Hyde Pierce…'"

I stared at Neko for a moment, wondering if he ever *had* sat next to David Hyde Pierce. Or maybe David Hyde Pierce was just the hero of the moment. Maybe Neko *dreamed* of sitting next to David Hyde Pierce. Or maybe he was only making a rhetorical point. I turned back to my David. "So, is that it? She's a famous person?"

"Well, she is that. At least within the Covens. She's headed up the Washington Coven for nearly twenty-five years. She's served three terms on Hecate's Court."

"How old *is* she?" I immediately aged *Whistler's Mother,* pushing her into her nineties, to the outer edges of frail existence.

He smirked. "Suffice to say, Teresa Alison Sidney got an early start on her career."

"Can you be a bit more specific? Is she in her sixties?" I redrew poor *Whistler's Mother* again, easing her wrinkles and giving her a red hat and a purple blouse to brighten her day.

"She's thirty-five."

"What?"

"She's thirty-five years old."

"But you just said she's headed the Coven for nearly twenty-five years."

"She has. She was something of a…prodigy. She's got strong powers, and she knows how to use them."

I swallowed hard. Thirty-five years old and the leader of the group of witches I aspired to join.

You know, I wouldn't have worried if she'd been ancient. We were all supposed to respect the elderly, offer them our seats on the subway, laugh at their jokes. I had almost managed to convince myself that being summoned in front of the Coven would be no worse than dropping in on Gran's Board meeting for the concert opera guild. I knew how to prove myself to people who were older than I was.

But thirty-five years old? That was younger than Clara! Younger than my own mother. Barely five years older than I was!

"Why didn't you tell me this before?"

Why didn't *I* tell you? David sounded exasperated. "I've been trying to tell you about the Coven for months. You're the one who always changes the topic of conversation."

"I don't change topics of conversation," I retorted. "Just the other day, at work, Evelyn told me that I have the most stick-to-it-iveness of any librarian at the Peabridge. She said she was impressed by my developing a lecture series, and she'd like to grow it into—"

David cocked his head to one side, sparing the half smile that I'd come to learn meant he was feeling quietly superior. "Not changing the topic of conversation?" he asked.

"No. I was about to come back to Teresa Alison Sidney. And her age."

David frowned. "Does that really matter?"

I looked down at my hands, realized that I had clenched

them into tight fists. Consciously, I took a deep breath and relaxed my claws. "No!" I said brightly. "Her age doesn't change anything at all!"

"Very well, then. We should get started."

"What, exactly, are we starting to do?"

David stood straighter. When he spoke, he used his "minister" tone, a deep, rumbling register that he saved for the most basic levels of my instruction. I imagined that this voice was the one he would use with preschoolers if he ever explained the ABCs, or with beginning library students when he set out the finer points of the Library of Congress classification scheme. Not that he ever taught anyone but me. Not that I knew about, anyway.

"This meeting with Teresa Alison Sidney is really just an introduction. She won't test you this time. You just have to offer up a suitable greeting."

"So, I need to learn the proper witchy handshake? Or is this more of a curtsy sort of thing?"

He swallowed as if bitter wormwood coated his tongue. "Actually, the curtsy isn't a bad analogy." He took a moment to study me, starting at the crown of my head and not stopping until he'd reached my toes. My toes, in their grungy sneakers. My toes that had not seen a pedicure in too many months to count. I tried to curl my feet under the front edge of the sofa. "This will be your introduction to magical society. Your coming-out party, if you will."

I laughed. "So, I'm going to wear a white dress and get someone to pile my hair on top of my head? I'm going to have to scare up an escort?"

"You've already got one of those." He settled his right

hand over his heart, as if he were about to recite the Pledge of Allegiance.

"You're kidding."

"I only wish that I was." Again, with that head-to-toe survey. "The Coven takes these things very seriously. I'm not nearly as concerned about what you'll wear, though, as I am about what you'll bring."

"Bring?"

"It's customary for a new witch to offer a gift to the leader of her Coven."

"And I'm guessing that a plate of Melissa's Peach Melba Tartlets won't get the job done."

"Hardly." David looked around the room. "You have to offer up something unique to you. Something that expresses your true nature."

It wasn't difficult to follow his logic.

"One of my books."

He nodded. "And you'll have to bind it up in magic."

"Gift wrap won't do? Even if I make a pretty bow and smother it in curling ribbon?"

He pursed his lips as he shook his head, and I knew that I was just asking questions to tweak him. To tweak him, and to smother the sudden pang of loss that I felt at the notion that someone—anyone—would get to keep one of my spell books. The books I'd discovered in the cottage basement when I'd moved in last year. How could I feel so possessive about things that I didn't even know existed a year ago?

I further delayed choosing one of my darlings for banishment by asking, "And what exactly do you mean by binding it up in magic?"

"Each witch presents things in different ways, ways unique to her powers and her temperament. If the element of Air spoke to you, for instance, you might surround your book in a miniature storm. You'd temper the winds, so that they could keep the book safe, and you'd train them so that they let one specific person—Teresa Alison Sidney—gain access."

It was my turn to purse my lips. I was hardly an expert on Air. In the past year, I'd harnessed it for a handful of spells, but it didn't sing to my powers; it didn't *speak* to me in any meaningful way. Just the same, I couldn't imagine weaving a magical box out of Water—not after my repeated failures with the kitchen-cleaning spell. And I was getting nowhere near Fire. Not with one of my precious books.

Even as I thought of all the magic that I couldn't work, that I *wouldn't* work, an idea took hold in my mind. I spun it about for a moment, testing it mentally, poking and prodding to see if I was an idiot, or merely an idealist. When I still didn't see any flaws, I dared to say, "Earth. Citrine."

David merely nodded as I walked over to the large box that held my crystals. I tried to brush dust off the lid without his noticing, and then I shifted the nested trays inside. I knew that I had three good examples of citrine. I liked its clear golden hue, and I was drawn to the steady warmth the stone emanated.

There! The three specimens that I remembered. One was small but expertly cut. Another was almost absurdly large, but a whisper of a flaw shimmered in its depths, black and jagged. The third, though, was perfect—large enough to be set in a ring, or to serve as an eye-catching center of a necklace. The stone covered the nail on my little finger.

I lifted it from its velvet-inlaid tray and turned it to catch the light. I could picture it centered above a book, spreading its crystalline power over the bound pages. *Generosity,* citrine said. *Prosperity.* Those were its ancient properties, its traditional symbolism. What could be more perfect as an offering to my new magical leader?

I turned to David and said, "Okay. Show me. Show me how to bind a book."

4

David looked at me critically, as if he thought I was not sincere in my enthusiasm for this latest chapter in my witchy education. I shrugged and said, "Seriously. Tell me how to start. I *want* to do this."

Still, he didn't respond. I squirmed a little under his attention, barely resisting the urge to raise my fingernails to my teeth, to gnaw away the edge of my nervousness. Fortunately, my Code Red nail polish saved me. It had taken me months to grow my nails long enough to warrant the expense of Lancôme. I wasn't going to suffer a setback just because David chose to play the part of inscrutable warder.

"All right," he said at last, and I wondered what sort of test I'd passed in *his* mind. "First things first. You need to choose a book. The binding that you create, the 'gift wrap,' will depend on the subject that you're covering."

I looked around my basement sanctuary. I could still remember shelving each of the books, creating order from the chaos, applying all of my librarian skills for good instead of for evil. I had been working to heal a broken heart that day—those four days, actually—and I still took pride in what I had achieved.

At the same time that I'd moved the books around physically, I had created a database, listing each one by title and subject matter, so that I could find them readily in a pinch. I was tempted to use my laptop now, to fire it up and browse through my records until I found the right gift.

Neko, though, threw the brakes on that train of thought. "Here's a good one! Teresa Alison Sidney should love this!"

I took the volume that he offered, a hefty book bound in crimson leather. Ornate gold letters were stamped on the cover: *On the Care and Feeding of Familiars*. The book was relatively new—it was printed rather than handwritten, and the pages were made out of heavy, rag-cotton paper instead of parchment. There was a simple table of contents at the front of the book, outlining chapters on Binding a Familiar to a Home, and Forcing a Familiar to Do Your Will in All Things, and Punishing a Willful Familiar.

Neko cocked his head at an appealing angle, looking up through his eyelashes with all the seductive aplomb of George Clooney accepting an Academy Award. He flashed me a brilliant smile, managing to convey that my happiness and satisfaction with his choice were the sole factors that motivated him to continue breathing.

"I don't think so," I said. "There's too much valuable information in that book for me to give it away. Besides," I said when Neko collapsed into a pouting heap, "I am certain that Teresa Alison Sidney's familiar would be too well mannered for her to ever need a book like that."

Neko grumbled and returned the crimson book to its shelf.

As I watched him scan the rest of my collection, working on some new ulterior motive, I tried to figure out a solution on my own. Teresa Alison Sidney truly wasn't likely to need a guide on controlling familiars. Nor would she need any of my numerous treatises on preliminary spells, or basic crystal-work, elementary rune-reading, or introductory hexes.

I shuddered to think about giving her anything that fluttered around the darker edges of magic. In the best case, she might use my gift to consolidate even more power over the Coven—and, by extension, over me. In the worst case, she might interpret my gift as a veiled threat. Besides, my collection had precious few resources on the bleaker side of my gifts, and I was loath to give away anything I might conceivably need in the future.

No. I needed to find the witchy equivalent of a coffee-table book. A grand volume that sang of riches, of largesse, one that collected fine pictures and minimal text. A book that evoked the spirit of being in another place, of living in another way. A book that Teresa Alison Sidney could display with pride, could invite other witches to peruse, could use to inspire admiration, and maybe just a hint of jealousy from all the members of her Coven who weren't lucky enough to own such a treasure themselves.

"I've got it!" I said. I crossed to the far wall and knelt in front of the lowest shelf on the bookcase. I ran my fingers along the spines of three giant volumes, each too large to stand upright anywhere else in the collection. The bottom one was the prize I sought.

I wrestled with it for a moment, fighting to free it from the weight of its cohorts. It was even larger than I remembered, and the cover was more spectacular. Green morocco leather stretched over thin wooden boards. It was stamped with an intricate design of pentagrams, circles and flames of spiritual fire. Decorative brass hinges cupped the spine, echoing the patterns from the book's cover. The hinges were matched by a metal hasp that held the book closed, protecting the treasures within. The brass devices had been charmed magically so that they never tarnished; even now, they gleamed like warm gold, whorls and fillips drawing the eye.

I levered the volume against my chest and staggered to my feet, taking care to set it gently on the book stand in the center of the room. David came to my side, automatically reaching out expectant fingers to touch the fine tooling on the leather cover. Even Neko decided to give up his pouting and show some interest.

"What's the title?" David asked, craning his neck to look around my familiar. There were no words on the spine or the cover.

I worked the be-spelled hasp, admiring the flawless mechanics as the volume sprang open. Perfect rag-cotton sheets were bound inside; the librarian in me knew that some skilled laborer had spent days creating the smooth writing surfaces. I turned to the title page and read aloud: *"An Illustrated History of Witches in the Mid-Atlantic Region, Comprising Maryland, Delaware, the Virginias, and the District of Columbia."*

I said to David, "It's local history. Especially appropriate for the Washington Coven."

David nodded, raising his eyebrows in appreciation at the lush, hand-colored illustrations that filled the pages. "It looks impressive. It's rare. It's highly unlikely that Teresa Alison Sidney has a copy in her own collection, at least not with all the plates tipped in. I think this is the perfect gift." Involuntarily, I grinned at the praise. "Now, for the wrapping, the binding you'll create. Go ahead and get the citrine."

I dug back in my box of crystals and extracted the stone, resisting the momentary urge to replace the perfect specimen with one of lesser value. If David was right—and I had no reason to think otherwise—if we truly were negotiating my debut in the professional and social world of witchcraft, I didn't dare cut a single corner.

The citrine was warm in my hand as I turned back to the book stand. Neko came to stand beside me, and I opened my hand so that he could see the crystal on my palm. He exhaled as he bent closer, almost shuddering with the force of his own breath, and when he inhaled, it sounded like a purr.

The stone glinted, catching every stray light in the room, mellowing it into a soothing glow before casting it back at the three of us. Without extending my senses, without drawing on a shred of my powers, I could feel the waves of emotion streaming off its cut surfaces—warmth, and calm and goodwill.

David moved to the far side of the book stand, pausing to nod when he was centered in front of me, in front of the heavy green-bound volume. "Excellent choice," he said, and the stone's warmth blended with his approval, washing over me like a chamomile-scented bath. He nodded, and then he said, "All right. Center yourself for your working."

I was familiar with the process. I'd done it often enough in the past ten months. Neko sidled closer; the heat of his body radiated against mine. I shifted the citrine to my left hand and folded my fingers around it. Forcing myself to concentrate, to shut out all conscious awareness of the two men in the room, I closed my eyes and took a deep breath.

It felt good to breathe so completely, to stretch my chest, to expand my lungs to their full capacity. It felt even better to exhale, to expel all of my stress, my tension, my worry about Teresa Alison Sidney. I repeated the breathing, again and again, each time pulling myself closer to the quiet core of my powers, to a place where I couldn't be worried by mundane details. My final exhalation was long and slow, controlled, emptying my body and my mind of everything that wasn't directly related to the spell I was about to cast.

"Very good," David said, and now he had set aside his minister's voice, using a whisper instead. A distant part of my mind noted his approval, beamed at his compliment, but I remained composed, poised on the magical edge of spellcraft. "Now offer up the purity of your thoughts."

I raised my right hand, letting it drift toward my face as if it were separate from the rest of my body. I touched my brow and felt my physical self settle a little deeper into the cavernous space of magic.

"And the purity of your speech." I touched my throat and sent myself deeper into trance.

"And the purity of your belief." I touched my heart.

I was deeper than I'd been in any of our training sessions, more calm, more poised. A tremendous well of magical power gaped beneath me, buoying me up as if I floated on a supersaturated saltwater sea. I knew that Neko stayed by my side. He was already serving as my familiar, gathering up my centering and reflecting it back at me. He deepened my trance, driving me further and further into my powers.

"Excellent," David whispered, and I knew that when I was through with this working, when I came back to myself, I would have to examine this feeling, this complacency, this totally enraptured sense of well-being. "Now. Center the citrine on the book."

I seemed to have developed special vision. Even with my eyes closed, I could see the stone precisely. I could measure the dimensions of the bound volume more accurately than any craftsman with a ruler, with a jeweler's calipers. A tendril of my powers drew from Neko's magnification; I confirmed that I understood the book, the stone. Filling my lungs again, I moved the citrine to its precise place, and when I set the crystal down, I exhaled until my fingers tingled.

The stone *fit* on the book. The moroccan leather reached up somehow, embraced the crystal, accepted it, melded with it. Intellectually, I knew that they remained separate, that they remained gold and green, stone and leather, mineral and animal, but my witchy senses told me that they had become more, that they had merged, that they had bonded. Next to me, Neko shivered, and I knew that he sensed what we had accomplished as well.

As did David. He nodded his approval and prompted,

"Take the power of the citrine, now, and bind it to the book. Meld it with the pages. Spread it through your gift."

I understood his words. I knew that I was deeply enthralled, that I was bound up in my powers, but I also knew I could ask a question without breaking that spell. "Am I trying to create a barrier?"

"You're creating a cover. A protective wrapper. Only you can decide what shape that cover will take. You can craft a shield that only Teresa Alison Sidney can penetrate, so that none of the other witches will know your gift. You can make a layer that is more welcoming, more open. You must decide what you want to say. What message you want to send to Teresa Alison Sidney. To the Coven."

What message *did* I want to send?

David had told me more than a little about the Washington Coven during our last year of training, even though I had shied away from the topic whenever possible. The Coven was the very core of witchcraft in our region. The women members—all witches were women, even if they relied on male warders for their protection—met regularly to educate one another on arcane practice, to learn new spells, new ways to harness the powers of runes and herbs and crystals.

The Coven also acted as a social center. Each woman could share the unalloyed joy of magic, the surge of energy that came from using her powers, and each member could commiserate on the frustrations—the spells that didn't work, the magic that could not be bridled.

The Washington Coven wove into a network of witches throughout the country, the world. The Coven gave its witches a spiritual home, an anchor. It gave them a place to belong, a place where they would be welcomed by sisters, no matter how odd—to a mundane eye—the magic they worked. Behind the Coven's walls, a woman could be sheltered, could blossom, could grow—with guidance and protection from others who had walked the same—or different—magical pathways.

But I had never been one to join clubs. In college, I had disliked the chummy exclusiveness of sororities, and I'd actively distrusted any group that required hazing to join. Or maybe that had only been my reaction because my first- and second-choice sororities wouldn't have me. In any case, David had made it clear multiple times: Witches belonged in covens. Witches were safest in covens. Witches learned more in covens.

So, how exactly should I present myself to Teresa Alison Sidney and the Washington Coven?

I could be brazen, showing off every last drop of my power and strength, pouring it into the citrine, over the book, building up an edifice that spoke of pride and power and arrogance.

I could be humble, submitting to the Coven completely, showing my figurative underbelly and asking for support and guidance, for protection.

I could be rebellious, mining the book with spikes of power, with jagged edges that reflected my refusal to submit to any will not my own.

Each image that rose in my mind was accompanied by a vision of the citrine's field. I could never change the stone's essential aura of generosity, of well-being. But I could groom it. I could shape it. I could craft it into whatever I wanted it to be.

Another deep breath, another gathering of my thoughts. More tendrils stretched toward Neko, reaching for his familiar-power, for his unique skill in magnifying and amplifying my own magic.

And then I shaped the citrine's bonds.

I felt as if I was organizing a miniature library. I could place each spark of power precisely, line up my witchery like books on a shelf. I could make every element straight, place every figurative spine in a precise spot meticulously measured from the front of each imagined shelf. I could shape the citrine like the most rigid of academic libraries, create an autocratic blanket of power that would stretch smooth and unbroken over the treasure of my book.

But I wasn't an orderly witch. I wasn't even and heavy, passive and calm.

By nature, I was a wilder person, a more tumultuous worker of magic. By comparison, I was a comfortable hometown bookstore more than an academic library. I was a series of rooms holding hidden treasures, nooks and crannies, where someone was likely to find an overpadded reading chair and a dozing marmalade cat. I was carefully controlled chaos, not perfect organization.

I laughed out loud as I shaped the citrine. I spread its force over the book like a bibliophile unpacking a treasure trove of boxes. I had *fun* at the edges, stacking new thoughts, new powers, new books into complex designs. I complemented the brass hinges, mirrored the metal lock. I thought of every bookstore I'd ever visited in my life,

every sudden discovery of a literary treasure, every seren-
dipitous find in a lifetime of browsing.

The citrine responded well to my lighthearted approach.
It captured my sense of goodwill, my hope, my optimism,
and let itself be shaped. I could not say how long I worked
with the stone, how many times I checked my design,
modified my wrapping.

But I knew when I was done. I knew when the package
said exactly what I wanted it to say. I knew when the *Illustrated History of Witches* had been transformed into something that was my unique offering, my special gift.

I opened my eyes at last. I saw Neko step away from me,
watched him shrug his shoulders, regain his own balance
and sense of self. I looked down at my gift, at what seemed
to be an ordinary green-bound book, with an ordinary
yellow stone sitting on its cover.

And then I looked at David.

He was staring at me. His lips were frozen in a bemused
smile; his eyes were locked on mine. He scarcely seemed
to acknowledge the book between us.

"What?" I said, and my voice was too loud for the room.

"Nothing," he said, but he didn't stop looking.

"Why are you staring at me that way?"

"You never fail to surprise me."

"What do you mean?"

"Let's just say that I don't think anyone has ever presented
Teresa Alison Sidney with a gift precisely like this one."

"What do you mean?" Suddenly, the goodwill from the
citrine dissipated, became a melody that I could remember
humming but couldn't sing out loud for the life of me. I

clutched the edges of the book, recognizing what I had created but suddenly doubting what I had done. "I should have gone with the library, right? I should have made it perfect."

"You did make it perfect," David said. "Perfect for you."

I didn't believe him, though. "It's not right, is it? I should do something else. Use my powers another way."

"I wouldn't let you, even if you tried."

"You're my warder! You'd have to!" Self-doubt sharpened my voice.

David only smiled. "Trust me. I know what's best for you here. What's best for your safety. What's best for your life as a witch."

"And this is best?" I felt like a child, like a little girl, suddenly unsure of herself in patent-leather Mary Janes and corded tights.

"This is best," David said. "The best that I can imagine you ever doing."

I tried to believe him, but I wished that I was meeting with Teresa Alison Sidney then. That very afternoon. I wasn't sure that I could stand to wait six long days.

Neko stepped forward, planting his hands on the book stand. "Well, *I* can't imagine going one more minute without something to eat. Preferably shrimp. With a side of crab salad."

I laughed unsteadily and let my familiar lead the way upstairs to the kitchen. I resisted the urge to look over my shoulder at the citrine-wrapped *Illustrated History of Witches*.

5

I stared balefully at the pile of clothes on my bed. I had come home from work at six o'clock and immediately discarded my layers of colonial clothing: hoops, jacket, petticoat, neck kerchief, sleeve ruffles. All were lying on top of my comforter, competing with each other to develop the deepest, most hard-to-press wrinkles.

On top of my costume lay dozens of other outfits—skirts, blouses, T-shirts, slacks—all in black. After all, black was basic. Black was dramatic. Black was sexy.

And I had enough to choose from. I had clingy black and sloppy black, goth black and elegant black, temptress black and too-fat black. I'd spent the evening combining separates that had no business being in the same closet together, much less on the same body. I'd dug out clothes that I hadn't worn since I'd last tried to drag Melissa to clubs, over a decade ago. I even tried the outfit that used to be my favorite one for work, before I was forced into the finest that Martha Washington had to offer.

Nothing was right for my date with Graeme Henderson. Nothing conveyed the energy that I wanted, the carefree, devil-may-care insouciance of a girl meeting a guy for late-night coffee.

(Who drank coffee at night, anyway? What sort of strange relationship disaster was I setting myself up for?)

Frustrated, I collapsed on my bed and stared at my nearly empty closet. If I were going to a formal dinner party, I was all set—I still had the emerald sheath dress that Neko had chosen for me last year, the one that was shot through with golden threads, the one that had made me feel like a princess at the Concert Opera Guild Harvest Gala. Somehow, though, I thought that was a bit much for a Wednesday-night get-together.

Green, though. A shot of color. Maybe that's where I was going wrong. Maybe I should look at the five percent of my wardrobe that *wasn't* black.

I tugged open my dresser drawers and dug to the bottom of a pile of T-shirts. (Yes, I needed four black ones. What girl didn't?) The tourmaline blue had been a gift from Melissa; I'd teased her at the time that she'd chosen it because it would look great on her. She hadn't appreciated my sense of humor.

I pulled the seamless garment over my head and checked in the mirror. It was streamlined, sleek. It looked as cool as the water in a swimming pool, promising a refreshing splash on a sweltering summer night.

And there. In my closet. A sapphire skirt. Now that I

thought about it, the skirt had also been a present from Melissa. Maybe she was sending me a message. Maybe she thought that I needed to change up my wardrobe a bit.

In this instance, though, I couldn't argue. The T and the skirt worked perfectly together. They combined to look cool and breezy, fresh. It seemed, in fact, that I'd simply reached for two garments readily at hand, tossing on any old thing, because what girl has time to fuss with getting dressed? No one would be able to tell that I had decimated my wardrobe to get to this point.

Next up: hair. I could take a quick shower and blow-dry my unruly auburn mop. Years of experience, though, told me that I'd be fighting fate. The dryer would take nearly half an hour, and my hair would frizz in the late-August heat within seconds of my stepping outside. I decided not to fight reality. A simple barrette would keep my mane off my neck.

I ducked into the bathroom and washed my face. Continuing my theme of summer simplicity I decided to do without a full makeup session. A bit of blush, a hint of indigo eye liner, a dash of lipstick.

Enough. This was a date. Not a marriage proposal. The paparazzi weren't going to be anywhere in sight.

I grabbed my clutch purse from my dresser and slipped into comfortable, flat sandals. Graeme Henderson might have been the most interesting man I'd met in months, but I wasn't going to waste the pain of high heels on him. Especially not when I was walking to the restaurant, walking over the scenic cobblestones that still lined many of Georgetown's streets.

I got to the front door before my plan fell apart.

"Sneaking out?" Neko chuckled from one of the hunter-green couches. I'd been so intent on leaving that I hadn't noticed him. Him, or Jacques.

"Not sneaking at all!" I said defensively, looking furtively at the door.

Neko had been resting his head in Jacques's lap, but now he scrambled upright. "Where are you going?"

"Out."

Neko pouted. "I bet you wouldn't answer your grand-mother that way."

"You'd lose your bet."

Jacques stepped in before Neko could complain again. "You look quite lovely thees evening, Jane." His accent was strong in the living room's dim light, and I smiled at the Gallic softening of my name, despite myself. What *did* that French hottie find in Neko? Especially given my familiar's rather, um, unorthodox housing arrangement and his invisible means of financial support? Oh well—the things we do for love. Or at least for strong, mutual physical attraction....

Jacques asked, "Who ees the lucky man?"

"Who says there's a lucky man?" I answered too quickly.

"Any man who will dine with you ees lucky. And at nine-thirty. I am turning you eento a proper French girl."

"It's not dinner," I said, although my stomach chose that moment to grumble and remind me that I hadn't actually eaten after work. "Just coffee. And dessert."

Neko pounced. "Food. Drink. It *is* a date, then. Where?"

"Bistro Francais," I said. After all, they'd get the infor-mation out of me eventually.

"Ah, *bon!*" Jacques exclaimed. "They are open until the

earliest hours of the morning. Perhaps Neko and me, we will come weeth you?" He nodded, as if this were the most brilliant idea he'd ever conceived. "We will join you there. Make sure that thees man you see ees a good one."

"No!"

I thought of the silver-lined card tucked beneath my mattress, the card that Melissa had made me promise to keep secret from Neko. Even greater than the promise, though, was my terror of the very real romantic damage my familiar could do if he put his mind to it. In fact, even if he didn't—Neko had a knack for saying precisely the wrong thing at the wrong time. Graeme would flee the bistro in short order if Neko had anything to do with orchestrating my love life.

My familiar hid a delicate yawn behind his hand. "Are you ashamed of us, Jane, or are you ashamed of your mystery man?"

I felt the walls closing in on me. But then, like a ray of sunshine slicing through a fog bank, I saw a way to escape. "If you must know, I'm meeting Melissa. She wanted to keep it secret. We're going to try the desserts at the Bistro, to see if there's anything she should duplicate for Cake Walk. We'll be there, sort of in disguise."

Both Neko and Jacques deflated at Melissa's name. After a moment's blessed silence, though, Neko twitched his nose, as if he could smell my lie. "Melissa? Sampling Bistro Francais at nine-thirty at night? Doesn't she have to be at her own bakery by four in the morning?"

"All the more reason—they'll never suspect their competition," I said, trying not to sound desperate. "Please,

Neko." I looked pointedly at Jacques. "The last thing I need is to have her angry, when she's trying to go unnoticed."

Jacques let out a long Gallic sigh, as if all the chateaux in France were weighing on his shoulders. "Poor Meleessa. I never meant…" He sighed again.

Neko stroked the poor Frenchman's hair, flashing a look to me that implied I had overstepped my bounds. "Go on, then," he grumbled. "Go enjoy your tarts."

I thought about challenging his tone, but I realized that I'd won the battle. Waggling my fingers in the guys' general direction, I ducked out the door, pulling it shut behind me.

Time was running short; I had to hurry through the heavy August night. The sun was still setting late; a faint hint of crimson afterglow remained in the sky. Despite the hour, heat shimmered off the sidewalk, and I wondered once again why our founding fathers had insisted on building their capital on a swamp.

When I was a block away from the Bistro, I stopped to catch my breath. I glanced at my watch—9:25. Perfect timing. I didn't want to get there too early, but I didn't want to be late. Receptive, I wanted to project. Open. But not eager. Not needy.

I resisted the urge to run my fingers through my hair. I even managed not to nibble at the nails on my right hand. I took three quick breaths to calm myself, and then I walked the last block to the restaurant.

*"Bonsoir, madame,"* the maître d' said, his accent challenging Jacques's for Continental grace.

"Um, hello." I said. "I'm meeting someone here, at nine-thirty."

"You are Meess Madison?" I nodded. "Right thees way."

Graeme stood as the maître d' escorted me to one of the booths in the back. The dining room was well lit, hardly a secret, romantic getaway, but Graeme had contrived to secure a quiet corner. Facing his movie-star good looks once again, I found my breath catching in my throat. His smile lit a tiny fire deep beneath my breastbone, and he said, "I'm so pleased that you could make it."

Before I had a chance to worry about how to greet him, he stepped closer and leaned down, kissing me lightly on my cheek. I breathed in the scent of him—fresh air, with just a hint of evergreen—cool and quiet on a summer night. His greeting was more intimate than a handshake, more alluring than Jacques's Continental two-cheek kiss. And it was infinitely more satisfying than the awkward dances I shared with David.

Graeme waved me to my seat, waiting until I was settled before he sat across from me. I cleared my throat and said, "I hope that you didn't have any trouble finding this place."

"None at all. I'm learning my way around."

"How long have you been in the States?"

"For quite a few years, actually. I'm based here now, although my business takes me back to London regularly."

I resisted the urge to fiddle with my silverware. Instead, I forced myself to look at him, to take in his open expression, the perfect bow of his lips. Maybe, just maybe, I could inoculate myself. If I stared at him long enough, often enough, I might become accustomed to his breathtaking appearance.

Yeah, right. Or maybe I'd just let the conversation lag so

completely that I'd be embarrassed to ever say anything else, to even try to get it moving once again. "Business!" I said, clutching at a conversational straw. "Your card said Acquisitions. Are you a lawyer?"

I caught my breath, waiting for the answer. Please-don't-be-a-lawyer. Please-don't-be-a-lawyer. Don't be anything like Scott Randall. Don't be anything like my failed romances of the past.

"Hardly." His eyebrows arched into an expression that would have been a sneer of disgust on a less refined face.

"I mean, a solicitor. Or a barrister. Or whatever they're called."

"They're called both, for somewhat different services. And I assure you, I stay as far away from the law as I possibly can."

I laughed at his rakish grin. "That makes you sound positively dangerous."

"I can be," he purred, and his smile was so intimate that I forgot to breathe.

*"Madame. Monsieur."* I jumped as a waiter made his presence known. The man wore a white apron, and he had a harried expression on his long, droopy face. "Will you be dining with us this evening?"

My belly reminded me that it had been sent to dress without any supper, but I firmly squelched a positive reply. Graeme said, "Just dessert, thank you."

The waiter barely stifled a sigh, but his eyes looked deeply pained. If he were an animal, I was certain he'd be a basset hound. A depressed one. "I'll bring the cart."

"Poor man," Graeme said as soon as the waiter was out

of earshot. "I didn't realize that the Hundred Acre Wood had shipped out poor Eeyore to wait tables at the Bistro Francais."

I laughed despite my nerves. "I suppose he was planning on earning a monster tip, hoping we'd order a five-course supper."

"Alas for him. But 'how shalt he hope for mercy, rendering none?'"

My jaw dropped. I mean, it was one thing for the man to know Prospero's line from *The Tempest;* the play was performed all the time. But *Merchant of Venice?* And then, to temper the knowledge of Shakespeare by mentioning my childhood favorite, sagging old Eeyore… My heart swelled inside my chest.

I was spared the need for a witty Elizabethan rejoinder because the basset hound returned with the dessert cart. We were treated to a desultory explanation of the treats— almond cake, baba au rhum, chocolate éclairs, a towering croquembouche, triplets of tiny fruit tarts, crème caramel, napoleons, Strasbourg cake, St. Tropez cake, profiteroles… I gained five pounds just listening to the list.

When the waiter finished his recitation, Graeme waved an inviting hand toward the cart. "What pleases you?" he asked.

Oh so many things, I thought.

Melissa had a long set of rules about foods to eat on dates. I needed to avoid anything that would squirt onto my clothes, anything that would leave seeds in my teeth, anything that would be difficult to cut on a slippery plate with the small fork that would likely be my only utensil. What did that leave? And what could I choose that wouldn't make me feel that I had betrayed Cake Walk?

Charmingly, Graeme misread my indecision. He said to the waiter, "Why don't you bring us a few things. The almond cake, and the chocolate éclair, profiteroles, and…?"

He quirked an eyebrow toward me. How did he maintain his quarterback physique, eating multiple desserts? I hadn't had any dinner, though, so I could splurge. Throwing Melissa's cautions to the winds, I said, "The fruit tarts!" They were likely to slip about when I tried to cut them into bites, and the berries posed a threat to my otherwise gleaming smile, but I was willing to live life dangerously.

"And the fruit tarts," Graeme told the hound. "And a decaffeinated coffee for me, with a Grand Marnier. Jane?"

"Decaf, also." The waiter nodded and started to wheel his cart away. "And a Baileys!" I called, abandoning the last of my common sense. He nodded and sighed, as if I had just sentenced his youngest child to a lifetime banishment in the barbarian wilds outside the city walls. I settled back in the booth. "Mmm," I said. "This is so decadent!"

"You see? Hardly the act of a barrister."

"That's right. But your card said 'Acquisitions.' What, exactly, do you acquire?"

"Whatever people need." He smiled easily. "It's like this. Say you read a magazine article, and it mentions a davenport owned by the Countess of Wessex. You decide that you can't live without that very furniture in your own parlor. I'm the man to find the piece for you. And I won't even tell the members of your bridge club where I found it. None of them will ever get the same piece."

I laughed, trying to picture myself bidding trump or half-trump or no-trump or whatever it is that bridge mavens bid. "I'm not exactly the bridge sort." I wasn't about to say that I had two *sofas,* instead of davenports, and I had a *living room* instead of a parlor.

"What, then? Your book club? Is that what all the librarians go in for these days?"

"I don't know about *all* the librarians, but I've been in a book club or two."

"So you could hire me to find a lamp, say, so that you could read great world literature in style. Or a tall-case clock, or whatnot."

"Acquisitions," I said, as if it made all the sense in the world.

"At your service." Graeme's smile blinded me.

The waiter chose that moment to return with our buffet of desserts. He put a large coffee press on the table and shook his head sadly before finding the energy to tamp down our decaffeinated grounds. He poured two cups and set our alcoholic chasers to one side. "Will there be anything else?" he said, and he sighed so deeply that I worried our profiteroles might blow onto the floor.

"Not at present," Graeme said, and then we were alone again. "Cheers!" my acquirer said, raising up his Grand Marnier. I scrambled for my cordial, touched glasses, and then watched him pour his into his coffee. I didn't know if the custom was British or Graeme's own, but my Baileys quickly met the same fate.

"So," Graeme said, when I had tasted the extremely satisfactory result. "You're a librarian who knows the Bard, and you help out friends in a bakery. What else should I know about you?"

What else? Well, I could tell him that I'd been raised by

my grandmother because my own mother didn't want anything to do with me after my fourth birthday. Hmm…not exactly an upbeat introduction. I could tell him about the last person I'd spoken to in London, my ex-fiancé who had broken my heart after twelve years of dating and the longest engagement known to man. Yeah, not a great conversation starter, either. I could fill him in on the I.B., and we could spend the rest of the evening coming up with more and more horrible meanings for the initials. Yeah. Right.

I needed something charming, something witty, something unique that would keep him here, chatting with me into the wee hours of the morning. I sipped my coffee, transferred a raspberry tart to my plate and said, "I'm a witch."

As soon as the words were out of my mouth, I couldn't believe I'd said them. I mean, it wasn't precisely a secret. David had never told me not to mention my powers. Nothing I'd read required me to take an oath of silence. If the Coven had rules, they'd never told me and, besides, I wasn't a member of the Coven yet.

But I could count on two hands the people who knew that I had magical powers. David. Neko. Melissa. My mother and grandmother. My grandmother's friend, Uncle George. The I.B.

There were likely others who suspected. My relatives in Connecticut had powers of their own to varying degrees, and they must have noticed the…odd…events surrounding the unmasking of the I.B.

But I had never told anyone before. I had never looked anyone in the eye and said, "I am a witch."

I waited for Graeme to laugh. I waited for him to look at his watch, to remember that he had somewhere else to be, to recall that he had promised to read the collected works of Dostoevsky to his Great-aunt Gertrude that night.

But he didn't.

Instead, he set his fork down, and he said solemnly, "There are Wyrd Women in my family, going back generations." Wyrd Women. Witches. "I don't know many of the details, but my da told me stories when I was a boy. Told me about what his mum could do, when she was angry."

"You believe me?" I was a little shocked.

He swallowed a bite of almond cake. "Why wouldn't I? What possible reason would you have to lie?"

To make myself more interesting. Because I'm a delusional madwoman. Because I'm an ax murderer, waiting to bewitch you into my bed and then do away with you under the light of the full moon.

"None, really," I said. My voice quirked on the second word, twisting into a semblance of a British accent, and I bit back a wince. I wasn't consciously trying to imitate him, it just happened. I rushed out more words, so that he wouldn't think I was mocking. "It's just so strange the way all this has happened. I haven't told anyone. It's not that I'm ashamed or anything, it's just that it's so bizarre, I'm afraid people will think I'm lying. That I'm making it all up."

"When you've seen as many odd things as I have in this world, you start believing more of what you're told."

"Odd things?"

"I'll tell you," he assured me. "But there's plenty of time

for that. You go first. I want to hear about how you became a witch."

And so I told him. Just like that. I told him about how the Peabridge had been on the edge of bankruptcy and my salary had been slashed, but I'd been permitted to move into my cottage on the library grounds as a sort of substitute for a full paycheck. I told him about finding a secret stash of witchcraft books in the basement—volumes that had been hidden away by a Washington witch named Hannah Osgood, decades before. I told him about finding a statue of a cat and reading a spell and awakening my familiar, Neko, entirely by accident. And I told him about how I had used my newfound witchcraft the year before, how I had poured my magical strength into crystals to help my grandmother recover from a nasty case of pneumonia.

I even told him about my crazy mother and her abilities with runes, her New Age insanity that had brought her hurtling from the so-called Vortex in Sedona, back into my life, even though I'd believed for years that she had died in a car crash when I was a child. (There hadn't been a car crash, I told him. Just a need to escape responsibility. I managed not to sound bitter when I said it. Or maybe that was the Baileys, coating the sounds of my words in my own ears.) I told him everything that I had learned about magic during the past ten months.

He was a wonderful listener. He asked enough questions to keep me going, enough to show that he was truly interested, but he never tried to change the topic of conversation. He never tried to steer me away from the odder bits of my story, the stranger aspects of my powers—crystals and runes and the specific spells that I had worked.

It felt wonderful to tell someone all of this, fantastic to share. I was grateful when Graeme caught the waiter's attention, when he signaled that we'd both have more coffee. When we'd finished that brew, along with additional supporting liqueurs, I finally looked at my watch.

"One o'clock!" I said. "I had no idea it was so late!"

"The restaurant stays open till four."

"I have to go, though! I have to work tomorrow. I mean, today!"

He smiled at my confusion, letting his grin grow into a laugh when I barely managed to fight off a yawn. "Yes, well. There is that." He got the waiter's attention and asked for the check before pulling out his money clip.

"But wait!" I said, pleasantly surprised again by that clip, by the very Britishness of it. "I never got to hear about the strange things you've seen."

"They'll keep. That is, if I may see you again?"

"Yes!" I could hardly believe that he thought he had to ask.

"Are you free Friday night?"

"Of course," I said, scarcely wasting a heartbeat to think that I should not admit to being available on a Friday, to having no pressing social plans.

Then I remembered. I *was* busy on Friday. Teresa Alison Sidney. "Oh. No." I hadn't gone so far as to tell him about my meeting with the Coven, and now I was overcome with self-consciousness. "I'm sorry. I do have other plans. Plans that I can't break."

He shrugged easily. "I'm afraid I have one of those business trips I mentioned coming up. I leave on Saturday for England, and I'll be gone for the entire week." I must have looked as crestfallen as I felt, because he grinned and said, "But perhaps the Saturday following?"

"Won't you have jet lag?"

"We seasoned travelers learn to cope."

"I'd love to see you, then."

"I'll ring you up that morning, and we can make plans."

And then he was helping me out of the booth. He was holding the door to the restaurant. He was stepping to the curb and raising a hand, summoning one of D.C.'s ubiquitous cabs. He was handing money to the driver, telling him to take me wherever I requested.

And then, just before he handed me into the car, he pulled me close. He tangled his fingers in my hair and set his lips on mine. His kiss was soft, gentle, tingling with potential. Before I could say anything, before I could respond, before I could rethink my need to be at work in a few short hours, he pulled away, helped me into the cab, closed the door and let me drive away.

I lay awake until dawn, watching my clock tick away seconds, minutes, hours—time that could have been spent much more pleasurably, if only I had responded faster to the promise of Graeme's kiss.

David shrugged as he completed his survey from the top of my purposely messy chignon to the soles of my practical sandals. Somehow, it had been much easier to prepare for meeting the Coven than it had been to get ready for dessert with Graeme.

Women. I knew what to wear for *them*.

I had pulled on a lightweight knit dress—black of course. Body skimming, but not skintight. Appropriate undergarments to avoid, ahem, the dreaded VPL. I didn't want to appear too severe, so I had accessorized with a necklace and earrings made out of fused glass. The jewelry reflected hints of lavender and crimson, with delicate sprays of emerald.

"Not too much?" I asked.

"I'm sure it's fine."

"You're sure? What does that mean?"

He shrugged. "It means that I don't spend a lot of time tracking women's fashion."

"Neko?" I wailed.

"Perfect, girlfriend." My familiar pursed his lips into a saucy kiss. "Trust me."

Trust him. Well, I did. At least in theory. But I still recognized the sparkling feeling in my fingertips as nervousness, and I reminded myself to take a few deep breaths. I turned back to plead with David. "Promise me that you'll stay with me, the whole time that we're there."

"I promise that you'll never be in danger." I was going to point out that there was a real difference between what I'd asked and what he'd offered, but he didn't give me a chance. "Okay," David said, brushing his hands together. "Let's go."

I realized that I'd overlooked a crucial detail. "The car!" I should have borrowed Gran's Lincoln Continental after work. I traveled by car so rarely that it had completely slipped my mind.

I glanced at my watch and swore to myself. Eleven o'clock. We'd really be pushing it, catching a cab and getting over to Gran's apartment building. I had keys to her car, though, and we could get into the garage easily enough. I just wasn't certain where Teresa Alison Sidney lived, how long it would take to get there. If the car failed to start (not that it ever had in the past), or if the gas tank was empty (even though I'd filled it two weeks before and Gran never drove), or if the garage gates refused to open…

"Relax," David said, producing a key ring from the interior pocket of his summer-weight suit. The silver fob was etched with an intricate torch.

"What's that?"

"My key ring."

"No." My exasperation was only partially based on my blossoming panic. "That design."

"Hecate's Torch? Symbol of witches everywhere?"

I *thought* I'd seen it before. It must be printed in some of the books downstairs. I let myself focus on the single silver key that dangled from the device, heavy and reassuring with its black plastic head.

"My car is out front," David said.

"*Your* car?" I was shocked. "How come I've never seen you drive a car before now?"

"'There are more things in heaven and earth,'" David said with a grin.

"If that's supposed to make me feel calmer, I'm not sure it's going to work." After all, what did I need with quotations from *Hamlet?* From a play where the main character sees ghosts, goes mad, and litters the stage with bodies before the end of the last act? "Relax," David said again. He spared an inquiring glance for Neko. "Ready?"

For answer, my familiar hefted the *Illustrated History of Witches.* I reached for it and said, "I'll carry it."

"It's my job," he said. "I serve you, remember?"

"That's the first time I've ever heard *you* say it out loud."

"You might want to mark today on your calendar, then. I'm not likely to repeat it, girlfriend." He stuck out his tongue and scampered to the door. Neither man spoke further as I secured the cottage, even when I double- and triple-checked the lock. I stopped walking when I got to the end of the garden path, turning around to look back at my home, at the building that had gotten me into the middle of all this witchcraft business in the first place.

Was it worth it? At the moment, I wasn't sure. I thought that I would choose a dozen first dates before I'd set myself up to meet a coven full of witches. Yeah, right. As if I had the choice to make.

When I got to the street, I was amazed by two facts. First, David had found a parking space directly in front of the Peabridge. In Georgetown, that alone practically required some working of magic.

Second, and even more shocking, was the car that waited for us. A Lexus. Black. With onyx leather that melted under the moonlight, and walnut trim that whispered old money.

David held the passenger door for me as Neko clambered into the backseat, grumbling about the indignity until David shot him a loaded glance. Neko settled the book carefully on the leather beside him, taking the opportunity to plant himself squarely in the center of the wide backseat. He bounced slightly as David pulled away from the curb, and I expected to hear him shout "Are we there yet?" at any moment.

When Neko failed to fill the silence, I asked, "Do you know where we're going?"

"Of course."

David handled the car expertly. While the streets of D.C. were never empty, traffic became lighter as we moved out of Georgetown, crossing the Key Bridge into Virginia and the western suburbs. I realized that we were heading into one of the toniest neighborhoods around, an area of estates that were set far apart, with long brick fences lining the roads, and wrought-iron gates that kept the riffraff from invading.

I wanted to ask David a hundred questions. Where exactly were we going? Who was waiting for us? How many women were in the Coven? What would happen once we arrived? How, exactly, was I supposed to prove myself, and what were the penalties if I failed?

I knew, though, that I'd get no further answers. David had already told me precisely what he thought I needed to know.

Just as the dashboard clock flashed eleven forty-five, David took a right turn off the winding road. He punched a secret code into a camouflaged control panel, and a wrought-iron gate the height of the Eiffel Tower swung open on silent hinges. We drove up the longest driveway I'd seen this side of *Gone with the Wind,* passing between sentinel ranks of oak trees. The car's high beams made eerie shadows on the trunks, and more than once I caught my breath, expecting some supernatural guardian to swoop down upon us.

I realized that my fingers were woven into a nervous clump, that I was rubbing my thumbs against each other like an obsessive maniac. Before David could issue another useless reminder for me to relax, I closed my eyes and took a trio of calming breaths. I leaned back in my seat and tried to imagine Neko standing by my side, tried to remember the feeling of his aura reflecting my own, his ability to mirror magical strength back to me, quietly, calmly.

My trick worked well enough that I was surprised when David braked to a stop. "Ready?" he asked.

My eyes sprang open. I was expecting to see Tara—massive columns, solid red brick, and a curving double staircase with servants at the ready. There might even be a barbecue out back, fragrant smoke rising from the grill as belles and beaux flirted with one another. A horse or two wouldn't be out of place, whickering friendly greetings and begging for sugar lumps. And come to think of it, a mint julep wouldn't be half-bad. Or a Baileys Irish Cream. With or without decaf coffee.

But I was completely wrong, so mistaken that all remnant flirty thoughts of Graeme and our mid-week decadent dessert outing fled from my mind.

Toto, we weren't near Tara anymore.

The house in front of me might have been designed by Frank Lloyd Wright, if he were in a particularly ostentatious mood. The walls were made of stone slivers, set without mortar to form horizontal patterns under the moonlight. I could make out windows high above us, arcane designs cut into their wooden frames. I could see two—no, three—chimneys, rising into the midnight darkness. A walkway led around to our right, hinting at a doorway that remained out of sight.

David led us down that path. I silently congratulated myself for choosing sandals, they were nearly silent on the flagstones, and I didn't need to worry about turning an ankle in the dark. Neko stuck close behind me; I could hear his breath catch as he shifted the heavy book in his arms.

When we rounded the corner, a low voice called, "Halt! Let all who would approach the Coven identify themselves and give good reason for their presence."

I blinked, and then I could make out a man in the shadows. A large man. A large man, wearing a dark cloak, despite the oppressive late-summer heat. A large man, wearing a cloak and holding a gleaming, naked sword.

I almost ran back to the car.

What had I been thinking? How had I let David drive me out here, miles from nowhere? Why hadn't I realized that I might become the victim of a strange, sword-wielding cult?

My story would be all over the newspapers and would fill the airwaves for weeks. Gran would put out a weeping appeal for my safe return. Even Clara would screw out a tear or two for the cameras. The tabloid press would interview my boss, who would say that she hadn't noticed anything unusual prior to my disappearance. They'd shove microphones in front of Melissa, who would push past the paparazzi to get inside Cake Walk, where she would grimly turn the sign to Walk On By in an attempt to free herself from the media circus.

"I am David Montrose, Warder of Hecate." David's voice resonated in the dark nook. He did not seem surprised by the man, did not seem the least bit startled by the sword. He intoned, "I bring with me a Daughter of Hecate, Jane Madison, who travels this path with her familiar."

"You may pass, Warder of Hecate." The man stepped aside, lowering his sword a fraction of an inch. "Welcome, Daughter of Hecate, and be honored in our safehold."

I expected David to step to one side (hopefully, the side between me and the glimmering sword.) I thought that he would be a gentleman and let me walk before him. Instead, he squared his shoulders and raised his chin, striding past the armed guardian with only the faintest of acknowledging nods.

As my warder stepped over the threshold and into the

house, a silver tracing flared up on the ground. A five-pointed star spread on either side of the door. It was surrounded by a perfect circle, a circle that shimmered with magical force. I knew immediately that the pentagram was a protective field, a barrier even stronger than the man with the sword.

David stepped through the glowing light, shuddering slightly until he reached the far side. He extended his hand, and I knew that I had no choice. He had brought me here because I had been summoned. He had told me that I would be safe.

I stepped over the threshold.

I felt the force field like an electric charge. It jolted up my neck, made me catch my breath, forced me to blink my eyes against a sudden light and then a crashing, terrifying darkness. Neko pressed close behind me, and I knew that he had passed through the pentagram as well.

He wasn't afraid, though. He was excited—alert and ready, attentive as he always was when we worked our magic. He was a cat, toying with a new mouse. He was *charged,* in his element.

I shook my head and followed David through the foyer and into the house.

The hallway opened onto the largest room I'd ever seen in a residence. The space was divided into a half-dozen conversation areas, elegant groupings of chairs and love seats (alas, no davenports belonging to the Countess of Wessex, as near as I could tell) that encouraged quiet, earnest discussion. A variety of tables was scattered about, sporting enough lamps to fill a showroom. All of the lightbulbs were subdued, as if the entire room was on a dimmer switch.

There must have been two dozen women present, all talking in voices low enough to match the lighting. I felt as if I had stumbled into a supersecret midnight meeting of the Junior League. Each woman looked more composed than the one before. There were a few girls, relative youngsters who looked as if they had only recently graduated college, but most had twenty or more years on me. Three women on the far side of the room looked like they'd be more in Gran's demographic.

No matter their ages, though, the witches looked fit and healthy. There was an air of determination about them, a razor-edged intensity that marked the multigenerational gathering as *special* in some indefinable way.

I'd been so confident in my black dress and my fused glass jewelry, but now I saw that cashmere and pearls would have been more appropriate. As if I owned cashmere. As if I owned pearls. I thought about hissing a rebuke to Neko for approving my outfit, but I knew this was neither the time nor the place.

In one cluster of women, a faint laugh rang out, and I wondered if I would ever get to hear the punch line. I caught a sudden gasp of surprise from another group, the universal sound of shocked gossip that begs for more details even as it warns away the impropriety of telling tales out of school.

A doorway arched to my immediate right, and I could hear a low hum of conversation emanating from behind an oak door. A low hum of *masculine* conversation—I immediately pictured an Edwardian smoking lounge, with well-dressed aristocrats cradling snifters of brandy as they pulled on fat cigars.

"David Montrose."

A woman materialized in front of us. Okay. I shouldn't say "materialized." It wasn't as if a fog swirled into the room and then a woman magically appeared. It wasn't like there was a flash of light and then she stepped forward. It wasn't *magical*.

Rather, she moved with perfect grace. Perfect grace and balance and…majesty. Instantly, I knew that this must be Teresa Alison Sidney. Her greeting to my warder toppled the entire room into silence.

"Coven Mother," David said, and he inclined his head in a gesture that would have been a bow in another age, in another land.

Coven Mother. Not that there was anything the least bit maternal about her.

Teresa Alison Sidney was the sum of all my nightmares from high school. I knew instinctively that she was one of the Popular Snobs; she'd *created* the cliques that the rest of us could only dream of joining.

She was tall, probably close to six feet, and slender, and she carried herself in a way that advertised the hours she spent at the gym. Her midnight hair fell straight around her face; its black depths gleamed blue in the dim light. It curled in a soft natural flip just above her shoulders, as if it had never heard of a breeze, or humidity, or any other summer challenge. I couldn't read the color of her eyes in the darkened room, but I would have given my eyeteeth if they weren't slate-gray.

She wore a perfectly tailored cashmere sweater—short sleeves in acknowledgment of the heat outside, but bloodred, as if we'd already moved the calendar forward to the heart of autumn. Her charcoal trousers must have had an invisible zipper on the side. They were impossibly slim and cut to exaggerate the length of her legs. She wore a single strand of pearls around her neck, and each earlobe was kissed by an unadorned milky sphere.

"Warder," the Coven Mother said, and the title made David stand a little straighter. "You may join the other men in the front room."

There was no question in her voice, no uncertainty. She was not asking David his preference or giving him any option. He was being ordered from my side, as certainly as if the Red Queen had shouted "Off with his head!"

Unable to stop myself, I reached toward him, brushing my fingers against his sleeve. He shook his head, once. "By your leave, Coven Mother," he said, nodding deeply before stalking away from Teresa Alison Sidney.

Away from me.

I watched him open the door to my right. There was a momentary pause in the male banter within, and then the noise swelled louder, all greetings and laughter and casual bonhomie. I swallowed hard and reminded myself that at least Neko had been permitted to stay with me.

Teresa Alison Sidney's smile was as perfectly manicured as the hand that she extended to me. Her fingers were cool in mine, sleek, as if she spent part of her life as a seal or a mermaid. "And you must be Jane Madison."

"Yes," I said. "Yes, Coven Mother." I answered her

perfect nightingale trill with a peacock screech. I knew that there was something else I should be saying, something else that I should do, but my mind was blank, numb. I wondered if I had lost some basic faculties when I crossed the silver pentagram into the room. Maybe some silent spell had stolen away my most basic social abilities.

I felt a jab in the small of my back and I took a half step forward. Even as I racked my brain for something to say there was another jab, a poke deeper into my spine. "Jane!"

The whisper broke my trance, and I half turned around. Neko was shoving the book toward me as if it were an infant needing a diaper change. I scowled, more embarrassed than ever by the awkward presentation of my gift. I should have wrapped it, no matter what David had said.

I turned back to Teresa Alison Sidney. "Coven Mother. I, um…I brought something for you. A small token of my respect."

She turned her head to a perfect angle, her lips twisting into the smallest of smiles. I dared to glance at Neko, steeling myself to take the heavy book from his arms. I forced myself not to picture dropping it, not to imagine the pages splayed and torn on the inlaid parquet floor, in case dreaming had the power to make it so in this strange place of witchy energy.

As soon as my fingers touched the citrine binding, though, a wave of calm washed over me. There was peace in the crystal, confidence. I remembered the power that I had felt when I bound the book. I threw my shoulders back and displayed the volume for all to see.

And I was rewarded with a collective gasp of awe from all the women in the room.

Even Teresa Alison Sidney, even the perfect Junior League matron, even she was surprised by the riches that I held. "For you," I said, as I extended my offering. "For you, Coven Mother."

She looked at me for a long moment, blatantly scanning my face for my intention. I hoped that she could see my earnest desire to fit in among my witchy sisters, to find the collective support that I'd never known in high school, in college, in any social aspect of my life. I hoped that she could tell I wanted to join this clique more than I'd ever wanted to join one before.

She glanced down at the volume and completed a tiny nod of recognition. The title might not be stamped upon the cover, but she knew the treasure that she held. I couldn't say whether she was able to divine the name by magic, or whether she had studied catalogs of valuable holdings in the past. She met my eyes, though, and said, "The *Illustrated History of Witches.*"

"I thought that you could make good use of it."

"I can indeed." She set her hands upon the green moroccan leather. "Citrine," she breathed. She closed her eyes and inhaled through her aquiline nose, drinking in the power of my binding.

Now, standing in this magnificent space, surrounded by a showroom of furniture and a gaggle of perfect women, I wasn't sure that I had made the right decision when I wrapped the crystal's power around the book. Maybe I should have been orderly. Maybe I should have been uniform. Maybe I should have followed the letter of the occult law, tamping down every single spark of individuality and creativity in my witchy soul as I bound the citrine to the *History.*

But I hadn't. And it was too late to make any changes now.

Teresa Alison Sidney looked at me with an expression that spoke volumes. I read her surprise at the binding I had chosen. She had clearly expected something more traditional—something more submissive, more humble. But I also read a flare of greed on her face—pleasure at the physical gift I'd given, certainly, but speculation about more. Speculation about the collection that nestled secure in my basement, even speculation about Neko. Somewhere, in the organized chaos of my citrine binding, Teresa Alison Sidney read her first taste of what I could bring to the Coven.

Or what they could take, if I failed to pass the admission test the Coven Mother set for me.

Teresa Alison Sidney said, "Thank you, Daughter of Hecate. Your offering to me, and to the Coven, through me, is most valued."

I bowed my head in reply, trying to imitate the precise angle that had symbolized David's proud humility. "Thank you, Coven Mother."

She pulled the book in closer to her side, balancing its substantial weight against her hip. Before it could become too heavy, though, or before—heavens forfend—it could crease her perfect trousers, a shadow glided up to her side. "Connie," she said, not even bothering to look at the newcomer. "Put this in the library."

Connie ignored the dismissive note of command, taking the volume as if it were a valuable crystal vase. She darted a glance at me and then licked her lips in quick agitation.

Like me, she was dressed all in black, and she seemed to disappear in the room's dim light, even when I looked directly at her. Her gaze skipped around, avoiding direct contact with any of the witches, and her nose twitched like a rabbit.

I felt Neko stifle a move toward her, and suddenly I understood. Connie was a familiar.

Just as Neko betrayed his feline roots, Connie expressed her own animal past—a rabbit, I realized, or I knew absolutely nothing about witchcraft. I darted my own quick glance around the room, and I saw that several of the women, several of the witches, had shadowy companions lurking silently by their sides. The familiars seemed to fade away in the room's darkness, almost becoming invisible beside their witches.

As Connie carried off my gift, Teresa Alison Sidney treated me to a slow smile. "Again," she said. "My thanks."

And then, a clock began to chime. All eyes in the room swung toward the corner, to the ornate tall-case clock. Witches and familiars, we all listened to the well-known Westminster sequence booming from the magnificent timepiece. After the song was done, there was a pause, long enough for me to measure the sudden, heightened tension, long enough for me to clench my fingers into fists. The tolling of the hours began—deep, sonorous tones. One… two…three…each note resonated through my body, winding me tighter, raising my expectations.

I realized that all of the women were responding to the clock in the same way, even Teresa Alison Sidney. Each of us clenched a little more as the clock counted off the hours, and when the twelfth note struck, every one of us was staring at the Coven Mother. Every one of us was waiting.

And Teresa Alison Sidney did not disappoint. "Welcome, sisters," she proclaimed, and her voice was even more resonant than it had been before—deeper, coated with more power. She traced a pentagram in the air. Everywhere her finger passed, a silver streak persisted. "Our midnight Coven is met."

The assembled witches repeated, "Our midnight Coven is met."

Teresa Alison Sidney raised her voice and intoned, "Let any who would betray us discover the true power of the Coven."

The witches took a step closer to their Mother and to me, and chanted all together, "So mote it be."

Teresa Alison Sidney lifted both hands into the air. "Let any who would harm us receive the true wrath of Hecate."

The witches took another step, and said in unison, "So mote it be."

"Let any who would wrong us know no end of earthly grief and loss."

The Coven surrounded the two of us. Neko poked me between my shoulder blades, and I joined in the chant. "So mote it be."

Teresa Alison Sidney looked pleased that I had found my voice, but she did not interrupt the ritual. "Hecate's Daughters, we gather this evening to celebrate our sisterhood. We gather in a circle. We gather in a pentagram of power."

Each of the witches stepped back, until they ringed the Coven Mother, Neko and me. Then, each woman traced her own circle in the air, followed by a personal star. I joined in, only a little behind the others. Neko leaned against my side as I moved my arm, and I felt him mirror back my magic, helping me find a steady flow as all my would-be sisters watched.

I wished that someone had given me a cue book before the stroke of midnight, so that I would know what was coming next.

The Coven Mother looked around our group, smiling benignly. "We are all sisters in the Coven. Let any who would speak to Hecate's Daughters do so now."

A woman stepped forward immediately. Clearly, her movement was expected; it was probably on the same page of the program as the pentagram tracing I had just missed. This witch was as poised as every other one in the room, as picture-perfect for the Junior League yearbook. Her chestnut hair was cut very short, covering her head like a spiky cap. Her eyebrows were plucked into surprised arches. Her face was tanned, golden, as if she had spent the better part of the summer lying out on a beach. Her lips gleamed in the dim room, and I wondered if she used gloss, or if she had just licked them.

"I would speak to my sisters, Coven Mother."

Teresa Alison Sidney smiled at the woman, and I immediately realized that the expression was different from every other one I'd seen inside this house. This smile was real. It was true. It was the sort of smile that I might share with Melissa—that I *would* share with Melissa, if I ever got a chance to tell her about this entire bizarre night.

"Yes, Haylee," the Coven Mother said. "Speak to your sisters."

Whatever friendly smile Haylee shared with Teresa Alison Sidney, she cast a harsher look at me. It wasn't angry, per se. It wasn't rude. It was *sharp*. Like a knife, cutting through to some essential core, Haylee cast a look at me, and then she said, "Coven Mother, there is a new witch among us. A sister who asks to join our circle."

"The circle is open to all of Hecate's Daughters."

"All of Hecate's Daughters must prove themselves to the Coven," Haylee said. She relished these words, thrived on them. I thought of my brief, unsuccessful experience rushing a sorority in college. Haylee was the membership chairman, pledge coordinator and social secretary, all rolled into one.

I pasted a smile on my face, trying desperately to remember that I was long out of college. I didn't need to worry about the silly social games of a bunch of party-hearty girls.

Neko brushed against my arm, though, and I realized that I *did* need to worry about these women. Like it or not, I was a witch, just like they were. I was a witch, and I needed my Coven. I needed the protection they could offer against arcane challenges. I needed the education they could provide, the wisdom gathered here in generations. But most of all, I needed their acceptance, their imprimatur, which would allow me to continue owning the treasures in my basement—the books and tools and Neko.

Teresa Alison Sidney was acknowledging Haylee's words. "It is true. Each of Hecate's Daughters must prove herself."

"The sisters have met, Coven Mother. We have determined a test for Jane Madison. We have decided what she must do to join our ranks."

Great. Now I was going to hear it. I could only hope that my initiation would be as easy as drinking a pitcher of hideous blue cocktails. Or wearing a toga for a week, pretending to be the slave for any of my so-called sisters. Or calling all the cute boys and asking them out to a party on behalf of the juniors and seniors.

Suddenly I remembered Neko's admonishment the week before, when he first told me that Teresa Alison Sidney had phoned. My initiation wasn't going to be over in a mere week. It wasn't going to cost me a handful of sleepless nights, a few hungover days. The witches would wait for a major festival. A major celebration.

I racked my brain, trying to calculate the next major event in the witch-bound year. We'd already celebrated Beltane; Ostara was long past.

Samhain.

Halloween. The traditional marking of the new year for witches, a celebration of change, of transition.

A little more than eight weeks away.

Teresa Alison Sidney's smile was slow, and I realized that she already knew what Haylee was going to say. She already knew the price for my entrance into the Coven. "Speak, Haylee. What have the sisters determined? How will Jane Madison prove her worthiness to join our ranks?"

Haylee's answering smile was almost feral. Something about her next words made her vicious. "She will set the centerstone, Coven Mother. When the sisters gather beneath the moon of Samhain, Jane Madison will set the centerstone for our new safehold."

7

I stood in the dimly lit kitchen, juggling a plate of finger sandwiches and a glass of punch, contemplating whether I could manage to slip a petit four onto my plate without collapsing my entire carefully balanced little world. It wasn't just the food that I worried about, of course. I was wondering about the witches who surrounded me.

Centerstone? Me? Just what the hell was I supposed to do to set a centerstone?

For the thousandth time, I glanced over my shoulder at the front room of the house, asking myself what the men were doing in there. Hadn't they heard the end of the witches' ritual? The loud crack of thunder, as Teresa Alison Sidney traced another pentagram in the air with her whole hand while she intoned, "So mote it be."?

None of the other witches seemed concerned that their warders were absent. In fact, none of the other witches even acknowledged the familiars slinking around the edges of the table. I had already shot Neko half a dozen glances, silently remonstrating with him that he was not allowed to eat the entire platter of tiny crab cakes, that he could not fill his teacup with cream, that the cream puffs had to be eaten in their entirety—white, fluffy filling *and* pastry.

I was scowling at him again, trying to get him to back away from the artful skewers of grilled shrimp, when Haylee stepped up to my side.

"No hard feelings, right?" she asked, extending her perfectly manicured hand and flashing me a smile. Now that she was no longer encircling me with ritual power, I could see that she was as thin as a model. Her collarbones stuck out with a vehemence that I'd never seen in person, only on the glossy cover of *Vogue*. I took her fingers as she said, "Haylee James."

"Jane Madison," I said, feeling slightly ridiculous. Every woman gathered around this midnight feast knew my name. I was the reason they had come. Me, and my new mission regarding their centerstone.

"I hope that you don't think I was calling you out, trying to give you any sort of special grief."

I had thought just that. I had thought that she enjoyed standing in the center of the circle of witches, that she'd taken pleasure in my flash of confusion, in my lack of understanding. I'd thought that I was transported back to the worst bits of elementary school, of high school, of college, and I had not appreciated the sensation that every other witch in the Coven knew what was going on while I was attempting to ad-lib from a very old, very outdated version of the play we had decided to stage.

"Of course not," I said, and I managed to smile.

Haylee reached past me and took one of the petit fours, popping it into her mouth without worrying about balancing a plate and a glass, without worrying about anything at all. When she had swallowed the morsel, she leaned closer and whispered conspiratorially, "Teri always does such a nice job with these get-togethers. Half the time, I think that's the only reason we let her be the Coven Mother."

Teri.

Teresa Alison Sidney, to me. Terrifyingly powerful, all-knowing leader of the Washington Coven, to me.

Teri, to Haylee.

I was up against more than the most popular girl in school, here. I was up against the entire Old Girls' Network.

Once again, I shot a glance toward the front room. Why hadn't David warned me about this? Why hadn't he told me who I'd be dealing with?

And then I thought, maybe he hadn't known.

Well, that was absurd. He'd been affiliated with the Coven his entire life. Warding was the family business, he'd told me. He'd even been drummed out of the warders corps, on a temporary basis, for breaching the witches' rules. He knew what was going on here. He had to.

If only I did.

Haylee flashed me a sympathetic smile. "It's all a bit overwhelming, isn't it?"

I tried to match the quirk of her lips, pretended for just a moment that I had her devil-may-care flair. I shrugged and attempted an airy "Just a bit."

"You'll get used to it."

"Really?" I realized how plaintive I sounded, and I hurried to cover my wistfulness. "It's just that I don't have any idea what's coming next. I don't know what people expect of me. What they want me to do."

What was I saying? Why was I talking to this woman? Had she cast some spell to make me confide in her?

As if to confirm that dark thought, Haylee raised a perfectly manicured finger to the base of her throat. I realized that she wore an ornament there, a delicate amulet that rested on a silver chain so slight that I could barely make it out in the dim light. I could not keep myself from stepping closer, from staring at the device.

A torch. The same torch that I had seen on David's key chain. "What is that?" I asked, before I could stop myself.

"This?" Haylee touched the jewelry again, and her voice conveyed a shrug, almost as if she were saying, *This old thing?* When I nodded, she said, "My Torch. The symbol that I've dedicated myself to Hecate." She looked around the room. "We all wear them. Teri presents them to us, when we're accepted into the Coven."

*Teri* again.

"Oh."

Well, that response made me sound absolutely brilliant. Like I was a shrewd judge of witchcraft. Or jewelry.

I must be even more tired than I'd thought. As soon as those words crossed my mind, a yawn began to grow at the back of my throat. I thought that I could hide it, that I could swallow it away, but I could tell from Haylee's arched eyebrows that I wasn't quite successful.

"I know," she said in a voice that wasn't quite sympathetic. "It's all strange when you're new to the Coven. Your mother certainly wasn't able to keep up with us."

"Clara?" My voice cracked with incredulity. When had Clara come to the Coven? When had she met the witches? And, far more importantly, why hadn't she said anything to me? "What happened with Clara?"

"Let's just say that she wasn't given any major assignment, shall we? No centerstones in *her* future. Poor thing'll be lucky if she learns how to read jade runes."

"She's actually quite skilled at jade runes!"

Why was I defending Clara? Well, it was one thing for *me* to challenge her, to say that she was a lousy witch and a worse mother. But I wasn't about to let a perfect stranger get in on the game.

"Really." I could tell that Haylee didn't believe me. "Well, I suppose we might have been mistaken. Some women are just so nervous when they come before the Coven. It didn't help that your mother was so worried about your grandmother. I don't think that either of them had stayed up past midnight in a long time."

Either of them. So Gran was in on the silent conspiracy as well. Anger rose up in my chest, competing incongruously with another yawn.

Apparently oblivious to my distress, Haylee went on, "I suppose it's *possible* that we all drew the wrong conclusion. We might have been thrown by neither of them having a familiar."

Well, of course, neither one had a familiar. Neither one had known she was a witch until I'd spilled the beans last year. And it wasn't as if Gran or Clara could have marched into Macy's to snatch up a magical helpmeet or two.

Familiars, I knew from my reading in the past year, were only created with the expense of a great deal of magical energy. When a particularly gifted witch died, she could encapsulate her power in an animal, feeding her spectral energy into its body, storing the raw stuff of magic for other witches to draw upon. Not every witch had a familiar—the valuable resources were generally allocated only to the powerful within any given Coven. So it wasn't at all surprising that Gran and Clara had no familiars.

As if on cue, Neko chose that moment to abandon his stalking of the food table. He materialized at my side like a ghost, licking his lips. I wondered how many treats he had stolen while I'd been talking to Haylee. Avoiding my dagger glance, Neko cocked his head to one side and scratched at his ear. I wouldn't have been surprised if he'd begun to whistle a tuneless little song—anything to make himself seem more innocent.

Apparently unaware of the tension sparking between Haylee and me, he asked, "Do you think that Teresa Alison Sidney will bring out any more of the salmon canapés?"

Haylee sniffed, and I immediately realized that she did not routinely speak to other witches' magical assistants. "Teri is not in the habit of providing extras for familiars." Again, I felt that strange instinct to defend someone close to me, to explain away Neko's hunger. "Especially now that people are heading home," Haylee added before I could speak.

I looked around, surprised to realize that there *were* fewer people in the room. The door to the men's club at the front of the house now stood open. While I couldn't see inside from my current angle, I could just make out the shadow of a familiar ducking inside and then, less than a minute later, re-emerge with a tall, sleek man.

The warder had clearly been summoned by the black-clad witch's servant. Confident and poised, the man crossed to Teresa Alison Sidney and bowed smoothly, raising her hand to his lips. She smiled tightly, expressing equal measures of satisfaction at the honor and world-weariness at the familiarity. The warder rose from his gesture and offered his arm to his witch, guiding her toward the door without a glance in my direction.

And suddenly, I knew that it was time for David to rescue me. It was time for him to make his obeisance before Teresa Alison Sidney, to say whatever needed to be said, to do whatever needed to be done. I was falling asleep on my feet, and the notion of waiting one more minute for my warder to appear was almost enough to bring me to tears. "Neko," I said, but he had already sensed my command; he was moving toward the far doorway.

I turned back to Haylee. "Thank you for your…conversation."

"I'm afraid that I've upset you. I didn't mean anything negative about your mother or your grandmother. It's just that they didn't have the power we were led to expect. Nothing at all like *yours*."

"No," I lied, and then I realized that she might think that I was agreeing with her assessment of my relatives' witchy abilities. My tongue seemed thick in my mouth as I hurried to clarify, "I'm not upset."

"Good." Haylee smiled and settled the fingers of one hand against the pulse point in my wrist, even as she once again touched the Torch that flickered against her throat. "Because I really do look forward to working with you. Maybe we could get together for coffee sometime. I do a lot of business with galleries in Georgetown—I'm an interior decorator."

I smiled at the vague invitation. Haylee wasn't actually so bad. She was reaching out to me. She was being sociable. She was welcoming me into the heart of the Coven, *assuming* that I would join the sisterhood, rather than betting against me. She was being a friend.

And if I had any doubt as to the goodwill behind her words, Haylee smiled winningly. "You know that you can ask me for help. With *anything*."

"Thank you," I said, and my response was made almost fervent by David's appearance in the doorway. I was scarcely aware of his steps across the room; I could barely watch him say his farewells. All I knew was that he settled his hand on my arm. I found myself stammering goodbye to Haylee, babbling something to a calm, collected Teresa Alison Sidney. I cut off yet another yawn as I glared at Neko, forcing him to come and stand by my side.

And then, finally, David guided me out the front door of that strange and mysterious house.

The pentagram across the threshold had faded away. As we walked into the wall of humid, late-summer air, I could sense the power that had once been housed in the doorway. Its living, electric thrill was gone, though. The man with the sword had departed as well, and I could not say that I was sorry to miss his shadowy threat.

I was suddenly so tired I could barely move.

I was so tired I did not bother to reprimand Neko as he hissed at another familiar, a birdlike man who hovered by his own mistress's car door, waiting for her to get settled before her warder turned his key in the ignition. I was so tired I didn't notice Neko opening the back door of David's car, ushering me onto the long, leather seat, making sure that my legs were inside before he closed the door and sat up front.

David was silent as he drove us home, retracing the tree-lined roads until we drove over the Key Bridge, working our way through Georgetown's cobbled streets. He again applied some warder's trick to find a parking space directly in front of the Peabridge. As David helped me to sit up, helped me to maneuver out the car door, onto the curb, onto the flagstone garden path, Neko skipped ahead.

My familiar opened our cottage door with his own key. He hovered in the living room, suddenly solicitous, but David shook his head. "I'll help her," he said. "Go to sleep." Neko shrugged before heading down to his basement lair.

"I'm fine," I said, but a yawn betrayed me, and I sounded like a cross child.

"It can be exhausting, entering a safehold for the first time."

"You could have warned me."

"No," he said seriously. "I couldn't. I wasn't allowed to. You needed to meet the Coven on your own. Those are the ancient ways."

He led me toward my moon-washed bedroom. I remembered the first time he had done this, the first night that I had ever stretched my powers beyond their natural strength. As if David had a cat's night vision, he removed my fused glass necklace, eased my earrings from my lobes. He loosened my hair from its precarious chignon.

In the past ten months, he'd had occasion to put me to bed a dozen times. He never took advantage of the situation, never brushed against me in a way that conveyed anything more than strictly professional interest.

Not that I wanted him to. He was my warder, not my boyfriend.

But I couldn't keep from leaning against him, couldn't help but turn my face toward his as he helped me out of my dress.

If he'd kissed me, I wouldn't complain. Hadn't complained, in fact, in the past, the one time he *had* kissed me. The one time he'd made my belly swoop lower with a sudden, gasping desire. The one time I'd tasted honest, magical potential on his lips.

What was I thinking?

He was my *warder.* And given my disastrous luck with men, I'd ruin everything if I ever thought of him as anything more than my magical protector. Besides, I was the recipient of a more recent kiss. Graeme Henderson's.

Against my better judgment, I giggled.

"What?" David asked, and I could hear patience in his voice as he waited for me to slip out of my bra. I turned away, suddenly shy in front of him.

"Nothing." But I giggled again, thinking of my secret romance. My Mystery Date, just like the ancient board game that Gran had bought for me when I was a kid. Graeme was no "Dud Date." That was for sure.

I was going to laugh again. Laugh out loud. For real. I had to think of something serious. Something scary. Something to keep from telling my romantic secret to my warder, who would likely never approve of the new man in my life. Of any man, distracting me from my studies. "Haylee," I blurted.

"What about her?" he said, easing my nightshirt over my head.

"She's strong." I took a few deep breaths, clearing my thoughts.

"Yes."

"Stronger than I am."

"Better trained," he said. There was something about his tone, something about the very careful placement of the words that cut through my suppressed laughter.

"But not stronger?" I slurred the last word. I might as well have drunk a pitcher of mojitos, for all the precision of my speech.

"No," he said. Again, I could hear there was a story there. There was something he wasn't telling me, something beneath his standard warder reserve.

"Teach me," I said suddenly.

"What?" His hands were gentle against my shoulders, but they were irresistible as he eased me back on my mattress. My pillow was like a cloud under my head, a cottony bridge to sleep.

"Teach me what Haylee knows. Help me to be a good witch, so that Teresa Alison Sidney likes me."

"Teresa Alison Sidney already likes you."

"Ha!" I sounded like a drunk now, and I wondered how my hand moved all by itself, how it stabbed the air.

"Well," he amended. "Teresa Alison Sidney respects you."

"Teri…" I whispered.

"What?"

"That's what Haylee calls her. Teri."

David pursed his lips in the silver moonlight. "Haylee's known her for a long time."

I clutched at his hand, pulled it close to my heart. I could feel the pulse beating through his wrists, beneath my gripping fingers, slow and steady and unexcitable. "Promise me," I said.

"Promise you what?" He might have been humoring a small child.

"Promise me that you'll teach me enough to impress Haylee. Enough to impress Tere—Teri."

He shook his head. "Jane. You can't learn magic just to impress someone. It's not a toy. Not an act. You should know that by now."

"Not just to impress her. Them." The popular girls. All of them. From college age to senior citizenship—all the Coven women who had gathered that night. I knew what I was trying to say; I just couldn't get the words out. "For the safehold. For the centerstone."

I could feel the tension in his hands, the wire-taut intensity that corded his wrists and set his shoulders. "Jane—"

"Promise. Promise that I'll be stronger than Haylee. I need that. Or I'll never pass."

He sighed, and I felt him give way. "I promise," he said.

I relaxed against my pillow, and my lips curled into a smile. It wasn't often that I won. Not often at all.

Even as I relished the victory, though, I remembered the man with the sword. I remembered the moonlight glinting on the naked blade, and the silver star that had flared up over the doorway. All that power, all that tradition… I had so much to learn.

Sudden tears rose in the back of my throat. I shuddered, afraid to look out the window. Afraid to see what might lurk in the shadows. Self-doubt. Or something worse. "What happens if I fail?" I asked.

"You won't."

"But if I do?"

David was silent for long enough that I almost drifted off to sleep. When he finally did answer, his words were hard, as sharp as the stone that made the walls of Teresa Alison Sidney's luxury home. "You know this. We've discussed it. Your collection is forfeit. The books, the crystals, the runes. Everything in the basement. They'll belong to the Coven."

Even in my exhaustion, my drunken fatigue, his words froze my heart as if I were hearing them for the first time. I had to force my lips to stretch around another question. "And Neko?"

"Gone."

"And you?" He refused to answer, only shaking his head in the moonlight. "David," I whispered. "Stay here tonight. Please."

He passed his hand over my forehead and smoothed back my hair. I closed my eyes, but I could not still my terrified shivering. "Sleep," he said.

"Here," I whispered, trying to pull urgency into the word, wrestling it free from my exhaustion. "Please," I said again.

"Sleep," he repeated. And then he took his hand from between mine.

I heard him tug at his shoelaces, heard his wingtips hit the floor. I felt him take off his suit jacket, remove his silken tie. There was a faint jangle as he emptied his pockets, the key to the amazing Lexus jostling with change on my nightstand.

I wanted to open my eyes. I wanted to see if he unbuttoned his shirt all the way or if he pulled it overhead. I wanted to watch him step out of his trousers, hang them neatly on my chair, settling them precisely so that they wouldn't wrinkle. I wanted to see if he wore boxers or briefs.

But I was too tired.

I felt him pull my sheet up over my shoulders, all the covers that I needed on a sultry night. I felt him lie down next to me, on top of the sheet. I felt him punch my extra pillow, wrestle it into a more comfortable shape. I felt him breathing beside me, slowly, deeply.

And his breath evened out my own. It calmed me. Soothed me.

And I slept.

I pushed my French toast around on my plate, using my fork to chase it into a puddle of maple syrup. My headache was pounding in time to the gospel music that echoed in the Corcoran Gallery's central courtyard. Clara had been responsible for choosing our brunch location this month.

Ordinarily, I would have been enchanted by my surroundings. The Corcoran's brunch offerings filled a dozen tables, with choices ranging from cold cereal to omelets made to order. One entire table was given over to fresh fruit, and another threatened to collapse under the weight of assorted desserts. A gospel choir enriched the air around us, the women singing loud enough to wake the dead.

Or to wake me, as the case might be.

I'd spent the entire day before—a perfect, work-free Saturday—sleeping off the aftereffects of my meeting with the Coven. David had left before I awoke. The only hints that he'd actually stayed the night were the impression of his head on my extra pillow and the faintest whiff of a woodsy scent that might have been soap, or maybe shampoo.

I'd gone back to bed and dozed away the afternoon, the evening and all of Saturday night. Even this morning, I'd tumbled out of bed only half an hour before I was supposed to meet my mother and grandmother at the museum. I'd cursed my way through a rapid face-washing and hair-brushing, and I'd pulled on a light khaki skirt with a sleeve-less blouse to match—twin concessions to Gran's dislike of my mostly black wardrobe. I suspected that the color washed out my cheeks; my green eyes would definitely have benefited from a careful application of mascara.

Clara's had.

Clara and I shared the same eyes. Even the manager had commented on that as she showed us to our table upon my belated arrival at the museum. "Mother Daughter Sunday, is it? Have a wonderful meal!"

Both Gran and Clara had descended on the food as if they expected never to eat again. Each of them had gone back for two additional helpings, while I was still trying to commit to my French toast. My stomach had rebelled at the thought of my customary Eggs Benedict (even now, the notion of runny yolks made me swallow hard), although I *had* managed to gnaw a few strips of bacon. The greasy salt tasted good to me, like hangover remedies should taste.

Not that I was actually hungover. I was just floored by witchcraft.

Gran came back from the dessert table, bearing a slice of cheesecake the size of the Flatiron Building. She graciously accepted a refill of her coffee from a passing waiter before she reached out to pat my arm. "Now tell us, dear. Where were you last night? Some exciting party, I hope?"

Sarah Smythe eternally hoped I'd attend exciting parties. That desire must have been the side effect of listening to me moan my way through junior high and high school. I could barely remember those long-ago weekends when an absent invitation to a make-out party drove me into the slough of despond. Or the pit of despair. Or whatever other deep, dank dungeon of misery I'd inhabited through my teens.

"Yes," Clara chimed in, as if there could be nothing more exciting than my nightlife. I had to hand it to her. She really *was* trying to make these monthly get-togethers a success. I'm sure she only meant the best as she added, "You *do* look a bit bedraggled this morning. You should have taken a moment to purify your aura—a lavender wash would do that for you, you know. Just a spritz of the essential oil in the steam from your shower—"

"I didn't have time for a shower," I said, cutting her off at the holistic wellness pass.

Gran's face creased into a frown. I wasn't sure if she was disturbed by my interrupting, or by my failing to bathe. "What did I tell you while you were growing up, dear? One quick shower, and you can conquer the world. Even when you have the flu, there's nothing better than hot water. Hot water, shampoo, a brisk rub with a facecloth. Far better than lying in bed for another few minutes of sleep."

"I met the Coven Friday night."

There. That cut short the Shower Rhapsody.

Gran darted a look at Clara. If I hadn't been watching closely, I might have missed it. I might not have recognized the conspiratorial gesture for what it was, an admission of guilt. Guilt and complicity.

"Coven?" Clara tried.

"Coven," I repeated grimly, as the "Rock of Ages" crumbled into gospel silence behind us. Diners' applause echoed off the marble walls, and I took advantage of the chaos to exclaim, "How could you have met them without telling me? I thought we were all in this together! Why is that so goddamned hard for the two of you to believe?"

All right. I had to admit that I thought the clapping would last a little longer. Or that my voice would be a little quieter. Or that the silence wouldn't echo quite so loudly after my last angry exclamation.

I felt the families on either side of us lean away, pretending overwhelming interest in their own desserts and coffee. A waiter scurried over and thrust a fresh cloth napkin into my hand, as if starch and cotton would bring me back to my senses. "Can I get you anything, madam?" he asked, and I heard his plea for me to lower my voice, to behave myself in this very proper public place.

"Just the check," I said, keeping my eyes on Clara.

Her choice of venue. Her turn to pay. She fumbled in her hippie backpack and pulled out a wallet, slipping her credit card to the nervously dancing waiter without meeting my gaze.

Gran, as always, attempted to smooth things over. "Jane, dear, it's not like we *intended* to go behind your back." Well, that protest was enough to release Clara from my glare—I turned my hot eyes onto my grandmother. She waved her fingers above her coffee cup, as if she were sprinkling invisible bread crumbs onto the surface. "We didn't choose to go there, dear. They summoned us. They made us meet them."

Clara nodded and said earnestly, "It was a month ago. When the moon was full. They brought us out to a house—it was way outside of the city, in Virginia."

Gran backed her up, as if she were suddenly compelled to tell the story, as if she needed to free herself from the memory. "They sent that nice man to drive us. I was so relieved—I never would have found the place on my own. And those narrow roads—I'm not even sure that the Lincoln could have made some of those turns. Best-looking car on the road, that's for sure, but it's not made for those little rustic byways."

Clara was preparing her next line of inane conciliatory babble, but the waiter returned with the credit card slip. He set it down on the table directly in front of Clara and handed her the pen, as if he were afraid that she might delay signing. He clearly did not want to chance another outburst from me. I resisted the urge to snarl at him, to curve my fingers into claws and lash out at his tuxedoed chest.

"Have a wonderful day, ladies," he said as Clara finished the formality of paying. "Enjoy the sunshine."

Sunshine. The calendar had slipped to September, but we were still going to melt as soon as we left the museum's air-conditioned cavern. I thought about asking the waiter for a few frosty bottles of water—he probably would have come up with them, if he'd thought it would get me away from the brunch any faster.

Soon enough, we were walking down the museum stairs,

past a pair of enormous bronze lions. I led the way through the noontime swamp, taking advantage of a green traffic light to cross the street and strike out across a dusty park.

I didn't really intend to get away from my family. If I'd wanted to do that, I could have outpaced them easily enough, left Clara caring for my grandmother as I strode off toward Pennsylvania Avenue.

No, I wanted to finish the conversation that I'd begun. I wanted to find out exactly what they knew and when they'd learned it. I wanted to know what the Coven had told them. And I wanted to know why they'd kept silent, why they'd left me to face the witches on my own.

Skirting a row of vans selling everything from hot dogs to fake FBI T-shirts, I collapsed onto a park bench, only to sigh with all the passion of an aggrieved teenager when I needed to shift over to make room for both of them.

"Don't you understand?" I finally said. "If I'd known that you'd already been out there, I could have been prepared. I wouldn't have felt quite so much like an idiot. I would have had a chance of making a good first impression."

"Oh, sweetheart," Gran rushed to assure me. "You always make a good first impression."

I resisted the urge to look back toward the Corcoran. I hadn't wowed them there.

At least Clara had the good sense to stay quiet. We both remembered what sort of impression I'd made on her when we first met. I'd practically fled Cake Walk, I'd been so eager to get away from my own mother.

I took a deep breath.

I was a librarian. My job was to research information and

communicate what I learned to patrons. I should be able to speak to my own grandmother, to my mother, and manage to keep a civil tone.

"Here's the thing," I said. "It was all so unnerving. I felt like they were all watching me. Testing me. It was like they spoke a language that I didn't know. It was frightening and embarrassing. And if I'd known that you two had already been out there, it wouldn't have been quite as—" I struggled for the right word and then gave up "—as bad as it was."

Clara shook her head. "Jeanette," she started to say, but then she caught herself. My mother was the only person who ever called me Jeanette. That had been my original name, before she hied off to Sedona, leaving me with my far more practical, down-to-earth grandmother, and the name I'd used for twenty-five years. Jane.

Jeanette still rang strangely in my ears—it was the name of an exotic French beauty. Or a pampered American schoolgirl. Not me. Never me.

Clara tried again. "I just don't understand what was so unnerving about the visit. You stay up late all the time so the midnight hour couldn't be the problem."

Gran chimed in. "And the women themselves, the—" She was actually having trouble bringing herself to say it. "The *witches*—they were absolutely charming. Why, that Teresa Alison Sidney couldn't have been nicer if she'd been serving on the board of the concert opera."

I wasted a moment trying to picture Teresa Alison Sidney among Gran's superannuated opera compatriots. The classiness of the image worked, but there was something else that just wasn't right. Teresa Alison Sidney was just too…hard.

Too driven. She had her own agenda, and she'd spare nothing—and no one—to achieve it.

Clara, though, was intent on building some new castle of camaraderie, picking up where Gran left off with the Washington Coven Pep Rally. "And after we got past the introductions, they were all quite welcoming. I was actually embarrassed that I didn't have anything to give them after they presented me with my brooch."

"Your brooch?"

Gran clicked her tongue at my incredulous tone, but I ignored her. Clara waved off my question. "Fine, fine, call it a pendant. I don't think that I'll ever wear mine on a chain, though. It's not really large enough to compete with my crystals. It'll do on a lapel, if I'm ever called back to the Coven again."

Chain? Lapel?

"What the hell are you talking about?" My question came out even sharper than I intended.

"Jane," Gran protested.

I forced myself to take a deep breath, closing my eyes so that I could count to five. The darkness behind my eyelids was crimson tinged; it dripped reminders of the headache that pulsed beneath my every thought. I tested my words in my own mind, tried them again, and when I was certain they wouldn't sound petulant, I said out loud, "I didn't get any jewelry."

"Well, isn't that odd?" Gran truly sounded perplexed. "We both got the same piece, your mother and me. It's shaped like a torch. They said it was a sign of the secret knowledge we possessed."

As soon as Gran said the word "torch" I could picture it. The brooch would have the same stylized flames that had kissed Haylee's throat, that had graced David's key chain. It would call out to me, summon my fingers to reach toward it, to try to touch it.

Why had they each received a pin, when I'd received nothing?

"I didn't get one," I mumbled, ashamed to meet their eyes.

"I'm sure there was a reason," Clara said after an uncomfortable pause. I knew that she was trying to make me feel better. But that didn't help. Not now. Not while I was sitting in the park, dropped again into all the strangeness of Friday night.

I didn't belong with the Coven. They didn't want me. They wanted my mother and my grandmother—even if they looked down on their ability—but they didn't want me. Not on a permanent basis.

"Your mother is absolutely correct," Gran said, reaching out and patting my hand, as if she were consoling me about something as unimportant as the bakery being out of chocolate cupcakes. "I'm sure there was some reason, but you shouldn't fret about it. I'm certain that they'll give you one the next time you go out there. Someone probably just forgot to have it ready, forgot to call the jeweler, or something like that."

Despite the heat, I shivered. "It's just that I'm frightened to see them again. To see that guy with the sword."

"Sword?" Clara and Gran asked at precisely the same moment, in exactly the same tone.

"What sword?" Clara elaborated.

I looked from one to the other, wondering if this was part of their being sworn into the sisterhood. Maybe they were supposed to pretend, to us outsiders. Maybe they were supposed to disclaim any concrete knowledge of what went on in the safehold. After all, if I didn't have a Torch pin, I could be anybody. I could be as dangerous to the Coven as…as any of the tourists who strode by our park bench.

But no. They weren't pretending. They weren't reciting lines that they'd been taught. Looking from my mother to my grandmother, I was willing to swear that neither of them had seen a sword the night they had visited the Washington Coven.

"There was a man outside the door when I was there," I said slowly. "A large man, wearing a cloak, like some sort of medieval nobleman. And in his hands, he held a sword." They stared at me as if I were speaking in tongues. "He had a sword," I insisted, "and he was guarding the safehold. Protecting all the witches."

Clara shook her head. "We certainly would have noticed, if there had been a knight standing in the doorway."

"Not *in* the doorway," I insisted. "Outside of it. The doorway itself was protected by the pentagram."

"Pentagram?" Gran might never have heard the word for all the shock in her voice.

"You didn't see that, either?" I couldn't keep disappointment from my tone. "It was etched in the air. It glowed silver when we entered, David and Neko and me."

"David and Neko!" Clara shook her head. "They let you go in with David and Neko?"

"Of course. David's my warder. And Neko's my familiar."

Gran clicked her tongue. "But it's not like there were any other men there. Not when we were there." Clara nodded in agreement.

"There had to be!" My exasperation began to flow over my determination to stay calm. "You said that someone drove you out there! What happened to him? Did he just melt into the ground when you arrived?"

"Now, dear, there's no reason to get nasty about this. We just didn't see what you did. Now, I'm sure that you'll get your Torch soon. In fact, as soon as I get home, I'll give you mine. You can return it when you get your own."

"No, Gran." I shook my head. "I can't take your pin." And somehow, I knew that I really couldn't. I knew that whatever magic rested in the emblem would object to my handling it. I couldn't explain how I knew that, or what it actually meant, but I was certain that there'd be no transferring of Torches from one woman of the Smythe-Madison clan to another.

Clara was staring into the middle distance. I could just make out her eyes behind her sunglasses, and I could tell that she wasn't blinking. "That man," she said, and it sounded like she was trying to remember an elusive lyric. "He picked us up at your Gran's apartment. He drove us out past Great Falls. He helped us out of the car…." She shook her head. "I can't remember anything else. It's as if he actually did disappear."

"But weren't there other warders? And familiars?"

"Not that I recall." Her tone was perplexed. "You'd think we would have noticed. After all, we've seen enough of your Neko."

So. No warders. No familiars. No sword. No pentagram.

There was a time, back when I was a teenager, when I had known that I knew more than Gran. I'd been certain that I was wise in the ways of the world, that I understood how people behaved, how systems functioned. I'd been exasperated with her failure to comprehend the subtle workings of the universe around us.

For example, she hadn't appreciated the importance of passing notes in algebra, even when Mrs. Hock had already issued me two warnings. She hadn't grasped the nuances of who phoned whom, and why I was devastated to be pruned from the after-school phone tree of one particularly snobby girl whose name I could no longer remember. She hadn't understood—hadn't lived and breathed and *known*—why it mattered that Karl Nelson had the locker next to mine but chose not to use it, preferring to lug around his books in a backpack all day, calling the burden "training" for the football season.

But Gran had learned a lot.

Somewhere after my high school years, while I was in college, or maybe even pursuing my useless Shakespeare degree, Gran had become a genius. She read nuances into my conversations; she *understood* my world and the people in it. She knew before I did that Scott Randall was a complete jerk. She would have warned me about the I.B., if I'd given her half a chance.

But now? Today? With respect to the Coven?

Gran had nothing. No knowledge. No skills. No witchy sensitivities whatsoever.

And, looking at Clara, I realized that she wasn't any

better off. Sure, she might have a deft hand with runes. But she thought she could read auras, and I'd never seen evidence of her having any true skill in that direction. She'd glanced through my spell books, but she quickly dismissed them, saying they bored her. She'd shrugged off my attempts to speak about potions, about charms.

I looked at my mother and my grandmother, and I realized a terrifying truth.

I knew more about witchcraft than they did. Than they ever would. I was going to be tested by the Coven in ways they could not imagine. Their failure to tell me about their visit to the safehold the month before had not been cruel. It had not been mean. It had not even been a petty oversight.

They honestly and completely didn't realize how important it might have been for me to know. They had no frame of reference.

And for the first time I could remember, I realized I was going to have to take my next step alone. Sure, Gran and Clara would love me. They would stand by me, at least as long as they were permitted to do so.

But there was no way they could help me. And when push came to shove, come the night of dedicating the centerstone, I was going to be truly alone. Truly abandoned by friends and family. And—worst of all—I didn't have the first idea about how to prepare for the working.

9

I stared into my bathroom mirror, making fish-faces to guarantee that my lipstick had not coated my teeth. I had almost reached the end of my tube of Pick-Me-Up Pink. It might be time to graduate—Nars's Fire Down Below had caught my eye the last time I was in Sephora. Sure it was red. Sure it was semi-matte. Sure it would make me look like a hooker if I applied too much.

But I was learning to control myself, learning to master the fine art of lipstick. And if I couldn't handle a grown-up shade of crimson, then how was I ever going to master an entire relationship?

Relationship. I rolled the word around on my tongue as I ran my fingers through my just-trimmed hair. Ever since the Implausible Boob, I'd dreaded the concept of a *relationship*. I wasn't ever going to get involved in a relationship more complicated than the one I had with my dry cleaner.

I was never going to put my heart on the line again, never going to let down my guard.

After all, I was a very busy woman. I had a library reference desk to manage. I had a grandmother to assist, a mother to get to know. I had a basement full of books about witchcraft, volume after volume after volume that shouted out in no uncertain leather-bound terms that I had better start preparing for setting the centerstone.

But now I'd met Graeme Henderson. I'd been invited out for a dream date, for coffee and dessert at the Bistro Francais. I'd shared my witchy secret with a normal, nonarcane man for the very first time without totally freaking him out.

I'd agreed to meet Graeme Henderson for a Saturday night date.

Not a weeknight. Not an evening when ordinary people might work late at the office, might be called out to a business dinner, to a team-building staff meeting, to some other excuse to avoid a wife.

Saturday.

Married men never made dates for Saturday.

The I.B. had avoided them like our Founding Fathers avoided British Redcoats in the woods. I had accepted any number of his inane excuses to avoid meeting me on a weekend. Now, with the wisdom of hindsight, I knew that he'd been saving his weekends for his wife. At the time, I'd accepted his busy social life as an indication that the Immoral Brigand was truly desirable, truly admirable, truly everything a girl could ask for in a man, and more.

Okay. So I'd been deluded. A crush will do that to you—especially one that's delivered with the full force of an anvil dropped from an open window, seven stories up. It was hardly *my* fault that I'd been designated to play the Coyote in the Road Runner cartoon of my life. Did anyone think that the Coyote really *wanted* to subject himself to the Acme Destruction Tool of the week?

I sighed. I might be on the road to recovery, but it still wasn't easy to accept a Saturday night date as "normal." My unease was only heightened by the fact that I had no idea what activity Graeme had in mind. He'd told me to dress comfortably, but he hadn't mentioned whether we'd be inside or outside.

Outside on a September night. A night in the swampland beloved of our forefathers, where mosquitoes grew to the size of aircraft carriers, at least until the first killing freeze.

I knew from long experience that I reacted poorly to mosquito bites. It wasn't so much that I swelled up when I was bitten. Rather, I developed great puffy welts that looked like globs of uncooked dough. Those bites itched like an entire forest of nettles, too; I couldn't keep from gouging red furrows into my flesh with my still-relatively-new-to-me fingernails.

And I was certain that every mosquito in the metro area would be attracted to me. A vitamin B-12 deficiency, my childhood pediatrician had diagnosed. My shampoo. My soap. My scintillating personality. I couldn't say why for sure, but I was an absolute magnet for mosquitoes.

Magic was no assistance. It was too difficult to craft a spell that would banish so many tiny lives—each beating mosquito heart (did mosquitoes even have hearts?) would require a separate focus of my witchy attention.

Alas, unsure of my destination for this Saturday night dream date, I did the only sane thing. I slathered my body from head to toe in Deep Woods Off! I protected my vulnerable flesh as if I were preparing for a jungle expedition. I poured lotion onto my arms and legs, rubbing it in with the vigor of the converted. I worked it between my toes, around my ankles. I even ran my fingers through my hair. I was determined not to become The Amazing Swollen Girl of Washington before the night was over.

Slathering completed, I tugged on my newest black T-shirt acquisition. This one was lightweight silk. Its fabric twisted across my chest, accenting my somewhat lacking cleavage with soft folds. The shirt's hem rode right on top of the waistband of my short black skirt. I twisted to look at my back end in the mirror—I thought the skirt was slimming, but what if that was only an optical illusion? What if that was only a side effect of my contorting in front of the mirror? What if my skirt was like television, and I secretly gained fifteen pounds just by closing up the side zipper?

I glanced at my watch. There was no time left to change. Besides, I'd already tried on everything else in my closet. Graeme Henderson might be murder on my psyche, but he was great for Goodwill Industries. Each date with him, I found another pile of clothes to pass on to the charity.

I grimaced and told myself that this dressing-for-dates thing would be a lot easier if there were just a uniform, like the costume that I wore for work. I tried to picture Graeme's surprise if I greeted him in an embroidered overdress and hoops. The confining outfits had certainly acted like catnip on the I.B.'s libido.

A sharp knock at the door interrupted bad memories of the Immature Baby and his strange attraction to my eighteenth-century attire. I offered up one more fish-face to appease the lipstick gods, and then I took a deep breath, bracing myself to answer the door.

And there was Graeme.

My heart started pounding against my silk T-shirt, and I wondered if he could hear it echo in my living room. He was more gorgeous than I remembered—that quarterback build, the perfect blond hair, those almost-too-light blue eyes, with all the intelligence and shrewd goodwill of a husky.

Without fully intending to, I stepped forward, greeting him with a quick pursing of my lips which he took only seconds to transform into a knee-buckling kiss. I was grateful for his arms around me, for the rigid structure of his fingers spread across my back. All of a sudden, the window unit air conditioner, which had done such a noble job keeping my cottage cool in the sticky September night, seemed to stop functioning. The heat of Graeme's greeting melted my spine, leaving me winded—and desperate for more.

When he pulled back infinitesimally, I gasped, "Good evening."

"Quite," he said, and I felt his gaze on my T-shirt like a physical thing.

I was about to invite him in. I was about to close the door behind us, lock out the heat, secure us in the air conditioner's chilly grasp. I was already calculating what refreshments I had in the refrigerator—a bottle of tonic water, some salty olives that Neko had dragged back from the gourmet grocery store, a jar of Marcona almonds from the same source.

Surely we could survive on cocktail fare for the rest of the night? Cocktail fare and love… Was I even thinking that thought?

He sighed with the regret of a man who must choose his grade-school daughter's princess birthday party over free tickets to the Super Bowl. (Not that he had a grade-school daughter. Not that he even knew the first thing about American football.) He said, "The car is waiting."

"Car?" I tried not to sound disappointed.

"Just a little something that I arranged for the evening."

Curiosity trumped my libido, and I reached for my house keys. Then, I let Graeme steer me down the path that cut through the garden. His fingers hovered just above the small of my back; I felt their heat through the sheer silk of my shirt. I imagined them touching my bare skin, imagined his palm flat against my spine. Once again, my breath caught in my throat, and I forced myself to offer up a little mind-clearing cough.

"Summer cold coming on?" he asked solicitously.

"No!" I sounded too anxious, and I lowered my voice by an octave. "Not at all. Just a tickle at the back of my throat. Maybe some pollen from the garden."

I—or he—was spared any more of my demented babble as we rounded the corner of the library. I looked out at the street and stopped dead.

A limousine. A jet-black limousine, stretching half the block, complete with liveried chauffeur. Automatically, I glanced at the license plate, expecting to see the H that indicated a rented car.

No H.

Someone owned this vehicle. "Is this yours?" I finally asked Graeme.

"Let's just say that it belongs to a friend of a friend."

I glanced down at my T-shirt and miniskirt, suddenly feeling underdressed for the evening. "I don't know," I said. "Maybe I should go back inside and put on—"

"Nonsense," Graeme interrupted me, settling a fever-spiking palm on my forearm. "The chauffeur is the one in uniform. We wear what we want. When we want."

I heard the promise purr at the back of his words, and I wondered exactly what proposition was curled inside his English accent. I scarcely had time to blush, though, before the chauffeur was holding the door for me.

I slid across a leather seat as smooth as polished stone but far more inviting. A bar occupied the space across from my knees, and a bottle of champagne glistened in its ice bucket. Two flutes glinted in the overhead light as Graeme joined me. The chauffeur made a short bow and closed the door. In moments, we were gliding through the Georgetown streets. For the second time in a week, I was being conveyed through Washington, D.C., in a luxury vehicle.

I took great pride in not owning a car. I was a city girl. I walked where I needed to go, or took the subway; I even knew the city's bus routes pretty well.

But much more of this fine driving, and I could be converted. I wasted a moment, remembering that my last car ride had taken me to a Coven meeting, that I'd come back from that session with a responsibility. I had no business being out and about on a date—I should be learning everything possible about setting the Coven's centerstone.

But Samhain was still seven weeks away.

And Graeme was beside me right now. And the limo's suspension was incredible—even the cobblestones seemed to melt to smoothness under the whisper-smooth tires.

"May I?" Graeme asked, gesturing toward the champagne.

"Please." I couldn't help but smile as he leaned forward. His movements were so confident, so spare. He poured with an expert twist of his wrist, capturing even the troublesome last drop on the bottle's lip. When he passed me my glass, I let my fingers slip against his, and I had to catch my breath against the confusing tremble of heat and cold.

"To the past and to the present," he said. And then, touching his glass to mine, he added, "And to the future."

"Past?" I asked, because I couldn't fold my mind around the word "future."

"I figured we'd take a night tour of the monuments. Your nation's past." Unbidden, I thought of the movie *No Way Out,* of Kevin Costner and Sean Young writhing their way around a midnight Washington while suggestive images of the Washington Monument's obelisk filled the screen. I glanced toward the front of our compartment, but the chauffeur had already raised the opaque window that separated us. Graeme and I were blessedly alone.

I needed to say something, to fill a silence that was rapidly becoming awkward. "I'd like that," I said. I lubricated my enthusiasm with a large mouthful of champagne. "Very much."

And so we became tourists. The nameless driver was an expert at his job. He wove his way through crowded streets, stopping at necessary traffic lights but never jarring us, never disturbing the cocoon that we wove for ourselves in the backseat. Graeme did his part as well—he kept my champagne flute full, and he produced a series of snackable tidbits, including a tiny crystal bowl of Marcona almonds that nearly set me to laughing, because they mimicked the love-nest fare I'd contemplated in the cottage.

D.C.'s night monuments never failed to disappoint—the white marble glinted beneath creamy lights, with tourists silhouetted against the stone as if they were placed by some exacting movie director. As we circled around the Greek temple of the Lincoln Memorial, Graeme reached out to tuck a strand of wayward hair behind my ear. "Are you up for a bit of a stroll?"

A stroll? Well, I'd rather stay here in our private air-conditioned retreat, truth be told. But that wasn't very sporting of me, was it? If the man had something else in mind, I should play along. Be more flexible. Even the thought of that word—flexible—made me blush. What was it about this guy? Why did I find him so compelling? I set down my glass with a firm nod. "Of course," I said.

Graeme smiled, and he rolled down the compartment window to speak with the chauffeur. In moments, we were walking around the Reflecting Pool, staring up at the Washington Monument. A pair of red lights blinked at the top, like benevolent eyes keeping watch over us.

He nodded toward the marble. "From here, it looks like the color changes partway up."

"Oh, it does," I said. "They worked on it for about a decade before they ran out of money. It just sat there, unfinished, for nearly twenty years, and when they started again, they took stone from a different quarry. They didn't set the aluminum cap until 1888."

"Aluminum?"

"Aluminium, I suppose you'd say. At the time, it cost as much as silver. But of course, it doesn't tarnish."

"Of course."

I winced at his droll tone and realized how much I'd been babbling. "I'm sorry," I said. "I sound like a textbook."

"You sound like a woman with a lot of facts at her fingertips. And *that* is a trait I find quite attractive."

Before I could figure out what to say to that, Graeme wove his fingers into mine. He started to wander toward one of the side paths, away from the well-lit Reflecting Pool. "Where are we going?" I asked, barely making the words audible above my pounding heart.

"I was certain that you could tell me," he said, smiling. "Isn't there some other monument over here? Something off the beaten path?"

"Constitution Gardens," I said, and then I bit my lip. All right. I *was* a librarian. I knew stuff. But did I have to show off that knowledge like some completely geeky teenage girl? I fought against the urge to tell Graeme about the Monument to the Signers of the Declaration of Independence, or the fact that the Gardens were land reclaimed from the Potomac River Tidal Basin, or any of the other dozen Happy Tourist Facts that sprang to my mind.

Instead, I let Graeme guide me to a wooden bench. "What are those lights over there?" He nodded toward a vague glow that lit the path ahead of us.

"The Vietnam Memorial," I said. Designed by Maya Lin, completed in 1982, droned the travelogue in my mind.

"Ah," he said. "What was the name of the woman who designed it?"

"Maya Lin," I said, trying to keep the note of surprise from my voice.

"And how long has it been there now?"

"Since 1982," I said, and my awe definitely flowed into my words.

He didn't care that I knew things. It didn't bother him that I had a stash of trivia tucked away, that I could call up a ridiculous number of facts and tidbits.

And as I relaxed into the curve of his arm, I wondered why I'd ever thought that it *would* matter. But that, at least, was easy to answer. Most guys didn't like to hang out with girls who knew more than they did. I'd spent a lifetime trying to hide the fact that I was smart, trying to disguise my memory, the bits and pieces I'd picked up as a librarian.

Even David Montrose wasn't thrilled with my know-it-all approach. Or at least so I sensed. I held back from him. I assumed the role of student, let him play the part of teacher. I gave in to him regularly, because that was how we related to each other. Those were our *jobs* with respect to each other. He taught. I learned.

I blinked as I became consciously aware of the things Graeme was doing with his fingertips on the back of my neck. The very stimulating things he was doing. The downright arousing things, as his lips moved toward my silk-wrapped cleavage.

Toward the cleavage I had liberally doused in chemical-tainted, mosquito–damning poison. "Wait!" I said.

"What?" He pulled back reluctantly.

I let my own fingers travel toward the neck of his white shirt. The cotton glimmered in the dim light, and I licked my lips nervously. At least there was no taste of Off! there. Who knows what this gorgeous man would think if I let him proceed? If I let him continue on the shimmering little journey of discovery that he'd commenced? What a way to kill a romance—literally, with poison.

I undid his top button. "Nothing," I said, aware that his exclamation was still hanging in the air. "I just thought that I should do a bit of the work." I added a taunting smile to my words.

He grinned back at me. "Work?"

"Work," I repeated, and then I shrugged. "Play. Whatever."

I kissed him, to keep the proverbial ball rolling forward. His fingers tangled in my hair, adding an urgency to my lips. I fumbled at another of his buttons, and another. I could see that my Englishman had a fine dusting of blond hair on his chest—not one of those movie-star smooth torsos that always reminded me of a boy. No. Graeme Henderson was a man. A man who was obviously eager for me to return to my ministrations.

Who was I to disobey? Without thinking, I hitched my skirt a little higher and eased onto Graeme's lap, facing him and the shadows of Constitution Gardens. His indrawn breath told me that my attention was more than welcome, that I had, indeed, made him forget my chemical-soaked skin. I leaned down, determined to continue my successful enterprise. Another button. Another. A tug to free his shirt from the waistband of his slacks.

I might have ignored the sound of a clearing throat. I had definitely overlooked the slap of feet against the blacktop path. But there was no way I could avoid the beam of a flashlight.

A flashlight that had all of the intensity of a *CSI* investigation. A flashlight that immediately picked out and broadcast the fact that my T-shirt had ridden up considerably higher than the waistband of my skirt. A flashlight that showed exactly what a remnant trail of Pick-Me-Up Pink looks like against pale English flesh, especially flesh that was framed by a tousled cotton shirt.

Graeme blinked and sat up straighter on the bench, holding me steady with one confident hand. "Is there a problem, Officer?"

Officer. Crap.

I jumped away from Graeme as if he were a lightning rod channeling an entire thunderstorm of electricity.

The policeman took advantage of the movement to shine his light directly into my eyes. "I was going to ask you the same question, sir." I could hear the smirk behind his words, an infuriating "just a joke between us boys" tone that made my blood boil. "We've had reports of certain…unsavory characters here in the park," the cop went on. "You can never be too careful."

I started to splutter a reply, but Graeme settled a soothing hand on my forearm. "I'm being careful enough, Officer."

I could swear the flashlight beam dipped lower, that the policeman made an entirely inappropriate inspection of Graeme's trousers. Or maybe that's where *my* eyes traveled. Oops.

"All the same," the policeman said. "The park isn't safe after dark. You two should move along."

We were being rousted by the D.C. police. We were being chivied along like vagrants. Herded up like street-walkers. Well, *I* was the one being treated like a street-walker. Graeme was just my unsuspecting john.

I started to protest, to ask if the park was closed yet, if it was technically after hours. I was going to demand a meeting with the cop's boss, with the sergeant, or whoever it was who took charge of these badge-toting, flashlight-wielding tyrants of the street.

But then I thought about riding in the back of a police car. A car that would almost definitely be lacking the smooth suspension of Graeme's limousine. A car that would certainly be in short supply of champagne and almonds, of the miniature chocolate truffles that I had glimpsed in the cabinet of culinary wonders.

And so I let myself be hustled out of Constitution Gardens. I let myself be marched back to the main path, to the uncomplimentary glare of streetlights. I let myself stand beside Graeme as the policeman waved a jaunty farewell, shaking his head as he left to search out other miscreants in the night.

I was too embarrassed to hear Graeme's parting words to Washington's finest. I didn't even feel Graeme's fingers on my elbow, guiding me back to the limo. I didn't see the chauffeur, standing at attention beside the sleek black door. I didn't taste the champagne that Graeme poured from a fresh bottle, didn't feel the tickle of the tiny bubbles at the back of my throat.

Instead, I sat on my half of the car seat, swaddled in my own private blanket of misery. I felt like a child caught stealing cookies from the cookie jar. I remembered the time that Gabriel Kahn had come over to study high school physics, and Gran had caught us necking on the living room sofa, our textbooks long forgotten.

Only when the limo pulled up in front of the Peabridge did I trust myself enough to speak. "Thank you for a lovely evening," I managed to say.

"Jane," Graeme said. "Don't be like this."

"Like what?" I started to ask, and I was horrified to hear tears behind my words.

"Hush," he said, and then he pulled me close to his lipstick-traced and now cotton-covered chest. I felt his arms around me, though, calm and soothing. He wasn't embarrassed. Or at least, he didn't act like he was.

I felt him brush his lips against the top of my head. My mosquito-lotioned hair. That was the problem. Deep Woods Off! had ruined everything. I pushed back from his chest enough that I could look into his eyes. "It wasn't like we were doing anything wrong," I said. I felt as if I was testing foreign waters, easing in with a toe before I dared to take a plunge.

"We're both consenting adults," he agreed.

"He didn't have to be so snide."

"He was likely jealous. Miserable sod."

We stared at each other for a long moment, and I realized that I could do the responsible thing. The adult thing. I could invite Graeme in, take a quick shower to remove the Off! from my tainted skin, and pick up right where we'd been interrupted.

But there was Neko to consider. Neko, and Jacques. I shuddered. There was also the fact that I had promised Melissa—*sworn* to my best friend—that I would keep this romance secret from my familiar.

Friendship Tests could be a bitch.

"I'm sorry," I said, at the same time I heard Graeme say exactly the same words.

He laughed, and he cupped his palm against my jaw. "Sometimes, when the moment's lost, you just have to let it go." He sighed as he traced my jaw with one blunt finger. My belly—or something lower—flipped over. "Promise me that you'll save next Saturday night for me. Let me make this up to you."

I looked around—at the limo, the champagne, the remnants of a perfect evening. I was acting like a spoiled brat. I shouldn't need Graeme to make anything up to me. If anything, I should be making things up to *him*.

Saturday night, he'd said. Just like a regular boyfriend. "I'd love that," I said.

He reached for the door handle. "Let me walk you to your door," he said.

"No!" I pictured Neko and Jacques, staring out the cottage windows. "No," I repeated in a slightly more sane voice. "I want to picture you here. Remember the good things about tonight." I leaned in and gave him one last kiss, a hint of what I wanted to make happen next Saturday night.

"Good things," he said with a smile, as he came up for air. And then he opened the door.

I was only a little embarrassed to find the chauffeur there, waiting patiently. Of course, he was waiting for me to emerge from the sex lair of the backseat. That was his job. He offered me the slightest bow as he handed me out of the car. "Good evening, madam," he said. He kept his eyes straight ahead, his demeanor as different from the cop's as any two men imaginable.

I forbade myself to look back as I walked down the garden path. Instead, I focused on slowing my breathing, on steadying my pounding pulse. I started to weave together the bits and pieces of my story, the tale I would need to tell as soon as the front door opened.

Earlier, in fact. Neko pounced on me from the front porch. "Where were you?" he asked.

"And who were you weeth?" Jacques added from his own darkened corner of the doorstep.

I wondered how long they'd taken to coordinate their interrogation, but I was suddenly inspired to answer with disarming truthfulness. I shivered a little, overcome by my daring. "I had a date," I said, breezily opening the door and letting all three of us into the living room.

"With who?" Neko cocked his head to one side, as if I were a mouse he might bat across the floor.

"Whom," I said, smiling sweetly.

"Whom," he growled, flexing his fingers like a predator's claws.

"Nate Poindexter," I said, tossing off the name as if I'd said it a million times. Where had *that* come from?

"Poindexter?" Neko asked.

Okay, maybe I shouldn't have chosen a surname that made me want to laugh. "Nate," I said firmly. "We went to high school together."

"High school?" Jacques asked, as if the notion of education were completely foreign to his French mind.

I reached back into my store of schoolgirl French and said, "*Lycee.* I ran into him the other day, just walking down the street in Georgetown. He's been living out in San Francisco, but he decided that D.C.'s really more his style."

"San Francisco?" Neko asked, making the name of the city sound like an accusation. Hmm. Maybe I shouldn't have chosen a gay stronghold. My familiar just might use that one against me. But not if I got him off track soon enough.

"Actually, Silicon Valley. Cupertino."

Neko nodded, storing away my words. He even stretched, working out every last kink in his seemingly elastic spine. "Where did you go tonight?"

"Morton's. For steak. Apparently no one serves red meat in California anymore."

Neko sniffed, and for just a moment, I wondered if he was trying to smell filet mignon on my breath. I wouldn't put it past the little sneak. Before I could come up with another lie to cover my meat-free evening, Neko shook his head. "What *are* you wearing, girlfriend? Eau de Pine-Sol?"

"It's not that bad!" I gasped.

"Not if industrial solvents turn you on." Neko made a face. I tried to remind myself that he had once been a cat. He was a magical familiar. His senses were more finely tuned than any true human's. They had to be.

"Enough," I said. "I'm going to bed. You boys keep the noise down."

They were quiet enough. But I tossed and turned for hours. Even after I took a quick, cool shower—enough to wash away the Deep Woods Off! And the lingering heat that Graeme had stirred inside me.

10

I looked up from the lectern, once again surprised by the number of people who were sitting in the Peabridge's conference room. "And so," I said, gesturing toward the screen behind me, which showed a hand-lettered surveyor's plat, "you can view our extensive collection of maps, study them like the founding fathers did in their endless attempts to resolve border disputes, determine effective trade routes, and ultimately break free from British control."

The applause was spontaneous, and I found myself surrounded by eager audience members as I turned off the microphone that was, incongruously, attached to my lace bodice. A middle-aged woman set a hand against her well-groomed silver bob as she said, "Thank you so much! These Monday sessions are the high point of my month."

I put on my best librarian smile. "They wouldn't be anything without people from the neighborhood joining us."

My words sounded fake in my own ears, but they seemed

to please the local matron. As I dug for something a little more sincere to deliver as a follow-up, I felt small hands tugging at my skirt.

"Now, Nicholas, you know that we don't do that."

Well, maybe Nicholas's mother knew that he wasn't supposed to tug on every last pleat in my colonial garment, but Nicholas himself seemed distinctly unaware of that fine point of etiquette. His toddler's cheeks were smeared with something that looked like strawberry jam, and his tousled hair screamed "Dennis the Menace." Especially the "menace" part.

I had noticed the kid during my presentation. He had taken advantage of the lowered lights and the quiet crowd to demand his sippy cup, and then had dropped the damn thing on the floor. Repeatedly. Despite his mother's stage whisper that he sit down. Despite the hissed complaints of other patrons. Despite my attempts to incinerate him with glares from the lectern.

His success at prying open the top of the supposedly-indestructible sippy cup and spilling the contents all over the conference room floor was merely an added benefit for those of us who got to maintain the Peabridge's space.

Now, Nicholas buried his face in my embroidered over-skirt. What sort of mother uses sticky peanut butter and jelly sandwiches as a (blatantly unsuccessful) quietness bribe? I could only hope that the library would consider my dry-cleaning bill a reimbursable business expense. Or maybe I could conjure up some sort of cleaning spell. There had to be something practical in all those books lining my basement walls.

Sometimes, I wondered why I had launched the Peabridge's program of community open houses on the second Monday of every month.

"That was excellent!"

I finally managed to extricate myself from Nicholas's unwelcome embrace as I turned toward my boss's voice. Evelyn was standing beside the lectern, resting her hands on the wooden surface as if she longed to take her own place on the podium. She was dressed in one of her boxiest suits, determined as ever to be a grand ambassador for the Peabridge. At least this ensemble featured a cool blue bouclé, a soothing complement to her graying hair. She generally favored muddy browns and acid greens, colors that competed violently against her complexion. I was afraid to rave about the improvement, though, lest she detect my criticism of her past sartorial splendor.

"Thanks," I said, gathering up my notes.

"Well, with ten of these under your belt, I have to say that you've really mastered the art of handling this audience."

I stood a little straighter. I *did* do a good job of finding topics that would interest our neighborhood scholars. And I managed to keep my training sessions light and informative.

"Stop it, you brat!" The shout came from the doorway, and I looked up just in time to see a linen skirt swirl over the threshold, flouncing toward the library's lobby. I wasn't surprised to see darling Nicholas standing in the aisle, scrunching up his face in preparation for a deafening bellow. I wondered what poor person he'd attacked. Then, I asked myself if I was a terrible human being for feeling grateful that the victim was not me.

I settled for making a face and cocking a half smile toward Evelyn. "Maybe we need to set an age limit on these things."

"And miss out on mothers in the neighborhood, who might not have any other way to get here without bringing the younger ones?"

The worst thing was, she was serious. And no self-respecting Nicholas-terror would ever think to harass *her*. She looked downright evil—like a fairy-tale witch, if I did say so myself. And every little child knew that it was a witch who captured Hansel and Gretel, who kept them in a cage and readied them for the oven.

Poor Evelyn. She didn't even get the benefits of magical powers, but she was stuck with the stereotype.

"I'd better get upstairs," I said. "Some of these people might need coffee to sustain them on their long walk home."

"There's the spirit," Evelyn said, and I thought that she was going to separate my shoulder as she clapped a pleased hand down on my colonial garment.

I wasn't actually all that eager to staff the coffee bar—I desperately wanted to work on a new research project I'd just begun, involving medical treatments developed in the colonies prior to the Revolution. No, lattes were not my friend, but I wasn't about to get stuck cleaning up Nicholas's sippy cup disaster.

The heat was forecast to break tomorrow, but it was still muggy enough outside to curtail the line of brewed espresso drinkers. At the beginning of the summer, Evelyn had tried setting up industrial-strength blenders to make überpriced coffee milk shakes for our patrons, but even her avarice needed to yield to the truth: we *were* a library. People expected some modicum of quiet on our premises. Ice cubes being ground for long, earsplitting minutes went too far.

And so I ended up just pouring a couple of iced coffees, and considered that I'd gotten off easy. In fact, I wouldn't mind the coffee bar at all, if I didn't need to waste time foaming milk and making complicated cappuccino orders. See? I wanted to say to Evelyn. I was willing to compromise. She wasn't interested in compromise, though. She wanted to maximize coffee-based income—a goal that increasingly conflicted with my desire to be a reference librarian.

I had just wiped down the counter and straightened the ever messy container of individually packaged sweeteners when a familiar voice said, "Is it possible to make a mocha over ice?"

"Mr. Potter!" I hurried around the counter to give the man a quick embrace. He spent a great deal of his time helping Gran with her concert opera work, but the Peabridge's guardian angel never failed to stop by the library for my Monday lectures. I hoped that he was pleased with them— it was his generous donation that made the extra sessions possible. The extra sessions, along with the cataloging work that continued downstairs, as we finally started to get our extensive collection under control.

He laughed at my attention, and I couldn't help but notice that he stood a little straighter when I stepped back. He even took a moment to smooth his nonexistent tie flat against his chest. If my eyes didn't deceive me, he actually sucked in his belly a bit, too. Sweet man.

As I moved behind the bar to make the coffee drink, I said, "And how is poor Beijing holding up under the summer heat?"

"Perfectly fine," Mr. Potter laughed. "That little shih tzu has the entire world wrapped around his paws. He has me trained to turn a fan on for him whenever I leave the house. We'll both be glad when the weather finally catches up with the calendar."

"But I'm sure that he repays your attention with flawless loyalty." Knowing Mr. Potter's sweet tooth, I held up the canister of whipped cream. He started to shake his head "no" but gave in to his true desire and held his fingers apart about an inch, to indicate a short dollop. I obliged, giving him the huge serving that I knew he really wanted.

"Loyalty." He shook his head. "I suppose that's what some might call it. I'd say he's just spoiled. But I worry enough about him that I take him with me when I travel. Like this weekend, when I drive to Pittsburgh for my brother's birthday party. We're going to a karaoke bar!"

"That should be fun." Not that I thought it would really be fun to drive all the way to Pittsburgh. With a yappy shih tzu in the car. To sing karaoke with a bunch of septuage-narians. I'd rather organize my crystal collection.

"Which brings me to the reason I stopped by."

I handed over the iced mocha and smiled inquiringly. Mr. Potter took a moment to sip the beverage and declare it "perfect" before he reached into the pocket of his sports shirt. He handed me a slender envelope, the type that looks like a birthday card with money from an elderly aunt. "Go ahead," he said. "Open it."

Puzzled, but excited like a little kid, I eased my finger under the flap. Two tickets were nestled inside. I fanned them out against the envelope and read, "Kennedy Center. *Romeo and Juliet.*" The date was for Saturday night.

"I was going to exchange them at the box office," Mr. Potter said. "But then I realized that I've seen enough Romeos and enough Juliets for a lifetime. Perhaps you can find someone to go with?"

Someone. Graeme.

All of a sudden, I remembered straddling his lap on the park bench, cringing before the intruding flashlight of Washington's finest. My cheeks became incandescent.

"Aha," Mr. Potter said. "I see that you have someone in mind."

I sighed. I'd have thought that my blushing circuits would be long-ago burned out. "I do," I said, all of a sudden too shy to mention Graeme by name. I could just picture Mr. Potter saying something to Gran, and then my trying to explain my stunning Englishman to my grandmother and mother both, maybe over another of our infamously strained get-to-know-each-other torture brunches. Better to keep my secret a while longer. Until I was certain that it would survive under the nuclear blast of my family's interest.

As I looked at the tickets, I realized I shouldn't be planning any dates around town. I should be thinking about the Coven, about setting the centerstone. I needed to start working on my magical test, or Samhain would arrive before I knew it.

But the Kennedy Center? And Romeo and Juliet? And Graeme? "Thank you, Mr. Potter! Thank you so much!"

"You'll have to tell me if the play's the thing, then," he said. "I'll be in Pittsburgh all next week, but when I get back, I'll want a full report!"

A full report. Well, he might not be getting that. Not if an evening of theater became as supercharged as a tourist turn about the monuments. "Absolutely," I lied.

I tried to wave off his money, but he insisted on paying for his iced mocha. "I have an interest in this library, you know. I'd never forgive myself if you went into the red because of caffeine fiends like me."

More like whipped cream fiends, I started to say, but I didn't want to risk hurting his feelings. I clutched the tickets to my chest. "Thank you, Mr. Potter! I really appreciate your thinking of me."

"Enjoy, Jane."

I watched as he walked across the lobby, taking the time to say goodbye to Evelyn. He would never get over the sorrow of being a widower, but the Peabridge had become something of a second home for him, and I was glad.

When he got to the library's glass double doors, he needed to shuffle left, then right, dancing to avoid a messenger bearing a huge vase of flowers. I shot a glance to Evelyn at the same time that she looked at me. Clearly, neither of us was expecting the delivery. Maybe Nancy, helping patrons check out books at the circulation desk? Or the cataloger, working downstairs?

The messenger approached the front desk, setting down the elaborate display and producing a clipboard. As Nancy signed for the arrangement, Evelyn and I both zeroed in, drawn like hummingbirds to crimson sugar-water.

Flowers exploded from the vase. There were tall stems of lilies in rich orange and yellow. Daisies brightened the arrangement, and baby's breath ghosted over broad leaves of greenery. A full dozen red roses were tucked into the explosion of color, their broad petals just beginning to open up.

A card peeked out from the midst of the arrangement, and my name was prominently displayed in bold Courier type.

Evelyn sighed. "They're yours." She waited for me to pluck the card from its plastic fork. My belly did a somersault, and I wished she would back away, let me read the card in peace.

*Thank you for an arresting Saturday night.*

And it was signed with the initial G.

Arresting. Well, not exactly. I mean, it wasn't as if we'd actually been dragged down to the police station. It wasn't like the policeman had read us our rights before whipping out his handcuffs.

Handcuffs. Maybe that was the image that got me. Or just the memory of the heat that had melted through my short skirt as I straddled Graeme's lap. Or the thought that I had been one of *those* women, the type that gets caught having sex in public. (Almost sex. Whatever.)

But suddenly, my cheeks were as dark as the roses.

"What does the card say?" Evelyn asked, holding out a hand as if she expected me to hand over the incriminating evidence.

"It's just a little joke," I said, trying to make an offhand shrug. "It wouldn't mean anything to you. I mean, um, to anyone. That is, anyone but me." I gathered up the huge display of flowers and hurried them back to the staff kitchen, where I made a great show of topping off the water in the vase and adding the powdered "life extender."

Don't bother talking to me, I tried to project. I'm much too busy to answer silly questions about flowers. About a card. About a man who would send an entire florist shop to a librarian he'd only met a couple of weeks before.

Fortunately, by the time I came back to my desk, Evelyn was involved in a discussion with Nicholas's mother. It looked like a heated confrontation, and I imagined that it involved the uncapped Magic Marker in Evelyn's hand. I didn't see immediate evidence of what Nicholas had ruined, but I didn't waste a lot of time looking.

Instead, I picked up my telephone handset and stared at the keypad.

I could picture Graeme's business card in my mind, even though it was safely tucked away beneath my mattress. The bold silver border glinted in my imagination, and I could see the strong font. His name. His phone number.

I punched in the digits before I could chicken out.

One ring.

Two.

"Henderson."

"Hi," I said. "It's me. Jane."

"Good afternoon," he said, his voice suddenly much warmer.

"The flowers are beautiful."

"I figured that I owed you something. It's not every evening that ends with such a…bang. Or shall I say, 'whimper.'"

I swallowed hard. And what was I supposed to say to that?

He went on, before I needed to improvise. "I would have sent them yesterday, but it was impossible to find a flower shop open on Sunday."

Besides, I thought, it was much more satisfying to receive

them at work. Even if the delivery *did* make my boss jealous. Especially if. "Graeme," I said. "I was wondering? If you were serious about next Saturday?"

"Quite." I thought I heard a smile behind his reply. Or maybe that was just the British accent.

"A friend just gave me tickets to *Romeo and Juliet*."

"'In fair Verona, where we lay our scene'?" he quoted from the play.

Be still my beating academic heart. "Verona, or the Kennedy Center. Whichever's closest."

"Shall I pick you up at your cottage, then? Before the show?"

I pictured the limousine and the champagne flutes. And the professionally blank face of the chauffeur, acting as if nothing untoward had happened on our previous outing. And Neko's boundless curiosity.

"No!" I gritted my teeth and looked down at my desk, certain that half the library would be glaring at me. I forced my voice into a more Peabridge-appropriate register. "I mean, I have something I need to do on Saturday afternoon. Can we meet at the theater? Maybe grab a nightcap afterward?"

"I'd love that." The simple way he said those three words tightened my chest so much that I couldn't breathe.

"Wonderful," I managed to say. I struggled to add something—anything—but I couldn't string three words together. At last I gasped, "There's someone coming up to the reference desk."

"You'd best go help them, then."

"Yes, I'd best."

But when I hung up the phone, there was no patron in front of me. Instead, there was only the massive bouquet of flowers. As I gazed at them, I convinced myself that I could see the rose petals stretching wider, reaching out to the mysteries of the world around them.

Perhaps I should learn a lesson from the natural world. Perhaps it was time for me to start reaching out. To start taking risks.

I hummed to myself as I straightened my desk and finished up my Monday shift.

11

I tried not to look forlornly at my wallet where it huddled on the countertop beside the half-full fifth of rum. It had cost me almost forty dollars to get Neko and Jacques out of the house, and if I'd had any more change available, they would have held out for that as well.

The trade-off had been worthwhile, though. I felt I hadn't seen Melissa in months; this was our first mojito therapy since the *Casablanca* get-together. It was only Wednesday night, but we were both free and eager to catch up on work lives, love lives, and other best friend details.

"What's that?" Melissa asked, pointing toward a smooth, egg-shaped stone on the kitchen table. It was blood-red, mottled with black splotches. The highly polished rock half filled the palm of her hand.

I shrugged. "I don't know. I mean, it's an egg, carved out of jasper. At least, I think it's jasper. That's what it looks like."

"What's it doing here?"

"I'm not sure. I found it on the porch when I stepped outside to get the newspaper this morning."

She laughed. "Are you in the habit of finding stone eggs on your porch?"

"You wouldn't believe half the things Neko drags home." I rolled my eyes.

"Um, yes. I would. What are you going to do with it?"

"I don't know." I watched Melissa rub her fingers against it, almost as if it was a worry stone. An involuntary shudder rippled down my spine. "Ugh. How can you stand doing that?"

She looked up, surprised. "What do you mean?"

"It's so rough. Doesn't it feel like sandpaper on your fingers?"

"What are you talking about? It's smooth as silk."

I shook my head. It had rasped against my hands when I picked it up. I'd considered throwing it directly into the bushes, but I'd worried about what havoc a contemporary jasper egg might wreak on an eighteenth-century garden. The last thing I needed was Evelyn complaining that I'd compromised the Peabridge grounds.

I'd originally set the egg aside, thinking I might add it to the collection of crystals down in the basement. The more I thought about that, though, the more it seemed like a bad idea. There was something…odd about the jasper egg. Something slightly off about it.

I shrugged. It was probably nothing more than the fact that the egg was a cheap, mass-produced souvenir, which wouldn't mix well with the witchy treasures in the basement. "It's yours if you want it. Just don't say that Neko never gave you anything."

Melissa stuck out her tongue, but she slipped the egg into her pocket. I maneuvered our tray of drinks and glasses into the living room.

"So? Which one was this?" I asked, folding myself onto a couch. As I poured a lime-rich cocktail into Melissa's chilled glass, I couldn't help but look at the giant display of flowers Graeme had sent me. They filled the coffee table, perfuming the room with the heavy scent of roses.

Melissa grimaced in partial reply to my question, but she consoled herself with a sip of minty comfort. *"Washington Today."*

As far as I was concerned, the *Washington Today* want ads were the weakest link in Melissa's dating scheme. Half of the men who advertised there were married and looking for a little action on the side. About half of *those* bothered to admit that level of commitment up front. Melissa had learned about the others by sad trial and error.

"Married?" I asked, thinking that we might as well get the disaster quickly out of the way.

"Oh no," she said. "Not currently."

"Not…currently?" That reply required my taking a healthy swallow of my own drink.

"He got married at the tender age of twenty-three. To his college sweetheart."

I made a face. "Let me guess. She broke his heart, and now he wishes that he had his college years back, so that he could sow those near-forgotten wild oats."

"Are you going to let me tell this story, or not?"

"Sorry!" I grinned and dodged a waving lily to select one of Neko's Marcona almonds from the pottery bowl on the table. Crunching the salty snack gave me greater satisfaction than usual. If my familiar was going to blackmail me into taking his boyfriend away from our shared premises, the least he could do was keep me from expiring from hunger.

Melissa ran a hand through her honey-colored hair and brought her feet up on the couch, sitting cross-legged like a preschooler at reading time. Her overalls settled into place like a child's favorite flannel nightgown, and I felt like we were staying up late at night at a slumber party. Another swallow of mojito, though, reminded me that I was a grown-up and slumber parties were a thing of the past. The distant past.

"Okay," Melissa said. "*Washington Today*. Married at twenty-three to college sweetheart. For the first time." She held up one finger. "Divorced her at the age of twenty-five. Married—" Another finger. "A woman he met in a bar, one week after he met her, because he thought he'd found true love. Had the marriage annulled six weeks later. Married—" Another finger. "College Girl again. Divorced her one year later. Married—" Another finger. "His secretary, because she loved him, despite having heard the sordid saga of his love life thus far. And, not surprisingly, divorced her. Spent two years in litigation over the resulting sexual harassment suit."

As Melissa extended her thumb, I said, "Married College Girl again."

"Bingo! Do I need to go on?"

"Where did the count end up?"

"Four weddings to College Girl. Three in-between girls. I was being auditioned for the role of number four."

"Any possibility there'd be a decent alimony settlement when you two break up?"

"With all those other hands in the pie? I'd probably need to sign a prenup a mile long. After all, he *is* a lawyer."

"What type of law?"

"What else? Divorce!" We clinked glasses on that one.

"Sorry to hear it," I said. "Don't you think it's time to give the *Washington Today* ads a rest?"

"And miss out on so many highly credentialed professionals? What sort of girl do you think I am?" At least she could laugh at herself. Ever a true-blue friend, she said, "But come on! Tell me about your date with Double-oh seven."

"Double-oh seven?"

"That's what I've been calling him in my own mind. I mean, he's got the accent and the glamour. He's got that slight air of mystery, luring you away from all you know and love." She gestured toward the flowers. "And he certainly knows how to get your attention."

"What do you mean?" A defensive edge sawed into my voice.

"Oh, don't worry. I totally understand," Melissa said, in a tone that implied she might not understand anything at all. "He's swept you off your feet. How could you possibly find time for a girlfriend, when you have *Graeme* waiting in the wings."

I started to protest, but then I realized she was right. I

hadn't stopped by Cake Walk in over two weeks. Was that possible? Even when I stopped to think about everything that had been going on—Graeme, the Coven, Family-Togetherness brunch with Gran and Clara—I was surprised at how much time had slipped away. Especially since I usually dropped in for at least one sugar fix a day. Graeme might be poison to my friendship, but he was working wonders on my waistline.

"I'm sorry," I said, and I let real remorse color my words. "I won't let it happen again."

"If you do, I'll have to cut you off. You know, never let you work the counter again. Never let you have first dibs on eligible bachelors looking for Lust."

I heard the tremor beneath her words, and I leaned forward to clink my glass against hers one more time. "That's a deal. Hey, are we all right about this?"

"Are we all right about your meeting Mr. Perfect while I'm left with the dating dregs?" For just a moment, her face looked pinched.

"Forget about Graeme for a moment," I said, wishing that I hadn't set my flowers right smack in the middle of the living room. "Are *you and I* all right? I mean, if neither of us ever saw another man for the rest of our lives, are we still going to be friends?"

Her laugh was more bitter than I expected. "We'll always be friends."

I needed to say something. Do something. Break the mood. "Rock, scissors, paper, for getting Neko's olives out of the kitchen."

It took her a moment, but then she counted to three,

tapping her right fist against her left palm. I chose paper, and she chose scissors. I was glad to let her win.

By the time I'd brought in the olives and refilled our glasses, Melissa had obviously decided to let her dark mood pass. "So," she said. "Tell me about your date. I really do want to know."

I wasted a minute, weighing whether she wanted me to tell the truth. What the hell, I decided. She was my best friend. I'd never lied to her before, and I certainly wasn't going to start now. Popping a stolen olive into my mouth, I launched into the sordid tale. By the time I got to the mosquito repellant, she was grinning, and when I described the obnoxious policeman, she was laughing out loud.

"I do not believe you!" she said. "You are such a skank!"

"It wasn't my fault!"

"And I'm sure that Neko totally agreed, when you dragged your sorry self home."

"I didn't tell Neko."

"What? You didn't tell His Nosy Highness?"

"I promised you that I wouldn't. Friendship Test, right?" The Friendship Test had become so automatic that I'd invented my long-lost high school love without blinking. Ah, the power of girlfriends… "Graeme's a secret, between the two of us."

She flashed me a grateful smile. "I wasn't sure that you remembered."

"I've got a crush," I said. "Not amnesia. I did have to invent a boyfriend, though—Nate Poindexter. How's that for romantic happily-ever-after?"

She laughed for real, then, and I knew that everything *would* be all right between us. Before we could say another word, there was a knock at the door. Melissa looked at me curiously, but I shrugged. I wasn't expecting anyone.

Anyone but my warder. I opened the door to a rather agitated David Montrose. "I don't know what they think they're doing—" he started, and then he realized Melissa was sitting on the couch.

"Hello there," she said wryly, saluting him with her mojito glass.

I knew my warder well enough to tell that he was silently counting to ten. Not because he had a problem with Melissa—they actually got along quite well. Rather, he'd clearly been expecting us to work together, to polish up some witchy routine, something he'd suddenly realized I needed to know about the centerstone. I could tell from the way his shoulders were set, from the way his jaw tightened when he looked at the fish-chased pitcher of drinks. Or maybe that was merely his taking in the floral display. "Who sent those?" he asked.

A strange shiver chose that moment to stalk my spine— once again the proverbial "someone walking across my grave." After the quickest of glances at Melissa, I said, "Nate. Nate Poindexter."

"Nate Poindexter?" David asked incredulously.

"He's a guy I went to high school with." I waved toward my best friend, expansive with the secret she and I were keeping. "*We* went to school with. He just moved back from Silicon Valley."

Melissa wiped her smirk clear before David turned on her. "Do you know this Nate? Does he send flowers to all his high school classmates?"

"I haven't seen him in years," Melissa said sweetly. "I hear that he's changed a lot in the last few years." She gave me a blatant wink.

I don't know if David accepted our ad lib, but he seemed unable to think of another probing question. "Mojito?" I asked.

"Might as well."

Well. That was interesting. David never joined my decompression sessions with Melissa. I felt a wave of foreboding as I wondered just what news he bore. Something bad enough to drive a warder to drink? I'd better make mine a double.

I caught Melissa's eye and then glanced toward the kitchen. "I'll get you a glass," Melissa said obediently, unfolding her legs from her half-lotus position.

"I'm sorry," I called after her retreating form. "There aren't any clean ones, so you'll have to rinse one from the counter." I knew Melissa would glance at my well-stocked cupboards, that she couldn't miss the glistening glassware. I also knew that she'd give David and me a chance to whisper a hurried conversation.

"What's wrong?" I asked.

He ran both hands through his hair, making the silver at his temples stand out more than usual. "The Coven wants to see you tomorrow."

A shard of ice shot through my belly, colder than any mojito in the world. "Why?"

"I don't know," he snapped. Before I could take offense, he sighed deeply and then repeated in a drawn-out voice, "I don't know."

"But I haven't done anything wrong!"

He must have heard the panic in my voice—I wasn't exactly subtle. I was running over everything I could remember from my other encounter with the witches. The man with the sword, the horrible feeling that I was back in high school, the desire to be friends with the women, and the fear that they would never accept me....

My apprehension broke David out of his own dark mood. "It'll be fine," he said. If I hadn't spent hours working with him, days, weeks, months learning everything that I could about witchcraft, I might have been fooled by the sudden steadiness of his words. He nodded once, as if cementing his certainty. "You have nothing to worry about."

"But—"

Uncharacteristically, he cut me off. "This is actually a *good* thing. The more that you get to know the Coven before you're tested, the better. We need to start focusing on setting the centerstone anyway. This will give you a chance to build allies, make friends."

As if on cue, Melissa returned with a suspiciously dry glass, which she hurriedly filled for David. "The almonds are great," she said, nodding toward the bowl. "And the olives are wonderful." David started to decline, and then she added, "They're Neko's, but we've appropriated them for tonight."

David shrugged and helped himself to a handful of nuts. Before I could pretend we had just been discussing something innocuous, the phone rang. I crossed the living room to answer it, taking a healthy swallow of my mojito along the way. "Hello?"

"Are there any policemen in the vicinity?"

"Oh!" Graeme.

Did David count? After all, he was my astral policeman. At least, he was my astral protector. I half turned toward the wall, as if David and Melissa might forget that I was present. I wondered if there was some way I could drop the name "Nate" into the conversation, without making Graeme think I'd gone nuts. Nothing came to mind. Realizing that approximately three centuries had passed since my startled exclamation, I painted a smile into my voice and said, "None in my current line of sight."

"Perfect." Graeme's voice was as smooth as the rose petals in the bouquet on the coffee table. "I should come over to visit, then. We could continue the conversation we started in the park, before your jackbooted thug interrupted."

"He wasn't mine!" I heard the giggle behind my voice, and I wondered what I must sound like to David and Melissa. I lowered my voice into a more austere register, and offered a silent prayer that the two of them would start to talk to each other, to cover my conversation with their own noise. "You must be mistaken, sir," I whispered.

"Sir?" Graeme repeated. "We're going to be formal now, are we? And here, I thought we'd moved beyond that."

I wanted to say something to assure him that his initial impressions were correct. I wanted to tell him that we had definitely moved, that we'd shifted light-years away from "sir." That, in fact, I wanted to banish "sir" from our vocabulary forever.

But I couldn't very well say that, could I? Not with an audience, suspiciously silent in the living room behind me?

Damn Melissa! Why didn't she start some conversation? Why didn't she distract David—after all, she was the one who had extracted the promise of secrecy from me!

I settled for, "There's a lot of territory to move through." I winced. Had I ever sounded this stupid before? If only Neko were here, he'd be babbling about something behind me, keeping the conversation flowing, if only to hear the beauty of his own voice.

God, things *had* gotten bad, if I was actually wishing for Neko's interference.

In the meantime, miraculously, Graeme was chuckling at my miserable attempt at humor. "I realized that after you spurned me—"

"I didn't—" I started, before I realized there was absolutely no way for me to finish that line—no way that was fit for public eavesdropping consumption. "Really. I didn't."

Another chuckle. Great. He thought I was playing games. Annoyed with myself, annoyed with the situation, I said, "What did you realize?"

"You never told me what time the play is on Saturday."

"Eight," I said, thinking that answer was cryptic enough to protect me from prying ears. I gritted my teeth. He could have looked up the time on the theater's Web site.

"I could have looked up the time on the theater's Web site," he said. What? Was he reading my mind now? Did he have some secret magical powers of his own that let him reach through the phone line and divine my every thought?

"But you didn't because…"

"Because I wanted to hear your voice." I felt a twinge inside me, a swooping shudder as he purred his response.

If I'd begged for a more romantic answer, I couldn't have found one. I wanted to slump against the wall, slide down to the floor with the phone still cradled against my shoulder, the perfect picture of the lovesick teenager I'd apparently become.

*Speak,* I reminded myself. *Say something, before he thinks that you've hung up.* "That's very kind of you to say," I finally responded, and I winced before the words were out of my mouth. I thought Gran might have hotter conversations with eighty-year-old Uncle George. Next, I'd be putting on a fake Southern accent and telling Graeme that I'd always depended on the kindness of strangers.

"'Kind' wasn't the emotion I was reaching for." I could picture his lips as he spoke, his strong chin, those tourmaline eyes…. I sighed. It always came back to the eyes. "Come on, Jane. Am I really not going to see you until Saturday night? Can't we have dinner together tomorrow?"

Was this really happening to me? Was the man of my dreams really begging me to dine with him? And what else did he have on the menu, besides food?

Of course, I couldn't. David was lurking right behind me. I knew that the Coven was a command performance.

But Graeme wanted me. He really wanted me. That should count for something in the Broken Heart Recovery Sweepstakes, shouldn't it?

"I'd love to," I said. Then I added hurriedly, before he could misconstrue my response, "I'd love to, but I can't."

"Can't," he wheeled. "Or won't?"

I was so bad at this. Here, I'd been all concerned about protecting my conversation with Graeme from David.

Now, I needed to figure out a way to beg off dinner with Graeme, without cluing him in to the whole Coven thing. I mean, it was one thing for him to know I was a witch. It was another for him to learn exactly when the Coven was meeting and why.

It could be dangerous for the other witches. That was why we all had warders, right? To keep us safe from random madmen, and people who just hated witches for no cause? Not that Graeme was mad. Or a witch-hater. Definitely not a witch-hater, if our dates and my flowers were anything to judge by.

"Can't," I said firmly.

He sighed, and then was silent for several heartbeats. When he spoke, his voice was so low that I had to hold my breath to hear him. "I don't know that I've ever anticipated a play, then, quite as much as I do this *Romeo and Juliet*."

"'Tis twenty years till then,'" I said, quoting one of Juliet's lines in the balcony scene. I gritted my teeth as soon as the words left my mouth. Melissa was almost certain to get the reference. Would David?

"'Sleep dwell upon thine eyes, peace in thy breast.'" Graeme didn't miss a beat providing Romeo's rejoinder. "'Would I were sleep and peace, so sweet to rest.'"

All right. Even if I was about to face the third degree from the world's most suspicious warder, it was worth it. Graeme seemed to have the entire balcony scene committed to memory—and he knew how to use it to best advantage.

"I'll see you on Saturday," I said softly. I hung up the phone, but left my fingers on the receiver, as if I could still sense Graeme there. I closed my eyes and let his whispered words linger, like bold wine on the back of my tongue.

"We haven't disappeared, you know."

David. And his tone was the height of warder haughtiness.

"I didn't think I'd be that lucky," I said, before I dared to turn around. "That was—" I cleared my throat "—Nate."

I was startled to see the jasper egg displayed on a handkerchief in the palm of David's hand. He looked so stern that I didn't bother spinning out another lie about my long-lost high school love. Instead, I cast a surprised look at Melissa. "So, I guess you decided you didn't want it after all?"

She frowned. "David sensed it. I mean, he knew I had it in my pocket."

I turned my attention to David and was startled to see the grimace on his face. "What?" I asked. "What is it?"

"Couldn't you feel it? Couldn't you sense the spell?"

"Spell? It's just a crappy souvenir. They sell them in one of the import stores down on M Street for tourists to bring home to their kids. My parents went to Washington, D.C., and all they brought me was this lousy egg."

"It's *jasper*." He almost hissed the word.

"I figured out that much. I was going to add it to my crystals, but it didn't seem right somehow."

"There's a reason for that. Jasper guards against witches. It has an affinity for keeping them at bay. For limiting their power. Your power." He extended the carved egg toward me, and I had to take a step back. Was that magic, emanating from the rock? Or was it my own apprehension?

"It felt rough to me," I said. "Prickly."

"Then you're stronger than the spell. Apparently much stronger. How did you say it got here?"

"I assumed Neko left it. He often leaves, um, things on the front porch." No reason to go into the decimation of the local mouse and vole population.

David shook his head grimly. "Neko would not get anywhere near this thing. Not voluntarily."

Melissa chimed in before I could say anything else. "Then who did leave it? Did they mean to hurt Jane?"

"I don't think so." David finally folded the handkerchief around the stone. I could breathe easier the moment it was out of my sight. "I suspect that they meant this to be a warning."

"A warning?" I repeated.

"Someone wants to put you on notice. They know that you're a witch, and they're watching you."

I rubbed the prickles from my arms. The egg had to be connected to the Coven in some way. No one had bothered leaving me jasper threats before Teresa Alison Sidney came into my life.

David interrupted my speculation. "I don't suppose you're going to tell me who that was on the phone?"

"I told you. It was Nate. He's not connected to the Coven." My words came out sharper than I'd intended. The jasper had unnerved me more than I cared to admit. I raised my hands, palms out, silently pleading for peace. "Look, it was nothing. Nothing you need to worry about, I promise." David still looked suspicious. "Please, can't we just forget about the phone call? The phone call, and the Coven, and everything else? At least until tomorrow?"

His gaze traveled from my exposed palms to my face. He looked into my eyes for long enough that I grew uncomfortable. What was Melissa going to think? She was standing right here, watching us have this bizarre conversation, this non-lover's quarrel.

I don't know what David read in my expression, but he finally exhaled, like a man resigning himself to a life without sex.

Now, wait. Why had I thought of *that* image? I should have just noted that he sighed, and left the modifiers to a tamer part of my brain, a part that hadn't recently been stirred by champagne and flowers and limousine rides around town.

"Fine," he said. "But we're going to need something more substantial than almonds and olives, if we're going to make another pitcher of mojitos."

David was going to drink the night away with Melissa and me? What *had* gotten into him? Was the jasper that much of a threat?

I couldn't bring myself to ask, though. Instead, I shrugged and included Melissa in my question. "Chinese?"

"Mu shu pork," she said, and I could tell she was trying to pretend that none of the other strange stuff had happened.

"Beef with broccoli," David added.

"Hunan chicken for me," I said. "And we might as well order the salt-and-pepper shrimp, or we'll never hear the end of it when Neko gets home."

By the time the delivery arrived, we were well on our way through the next pitcher of mojitos, and Graeme, Shakespeare, and prickly jasper souvenirs all seemed very far away.

12

We were gathered around my kitchen table—David, Neko and me. I had brought the mortar and pestle up from the basement and set them in the middle of some yellow-ish, greenish flowers. The leaves that surrounded the be-draggled blossoms were shaped a little like oak leaves. Their tops were smooth and dark green, but their bottoms were covered with a cottony fuzz.

Mugwort.

I'd walked by the plant for months, completely ignoring it as it grew waist high in the summer heat. The gardens behind the Peabridge included mugwort because it was used by colonial women as a cure for all sorts of problems—bad periods, unwanted pregnancies, stomach and liver parasites, pretty much anything that didn't respond to other medicine.

David had decided to feature it in an impromptu training session, filling the time before we headed out to the Coven. He was droning on in his best professorial mode. "You'll want to dry all the mugwort you can get hold of. It protects against bookworms—silverfish—that might try to eat their way through the collection downstairs. You'll use it a lot working with the Coven—it's one of the best herbs for cleaning magical implements."

"I make a big vat of mugwort tea and then do the dishes? Like I'm camping?"

I knew that he hated my being flippant about magic, but I was bored. We'd been at this training session ever since I came home from a full day's work at the library. Neither Neko nor I was at our best—too much MSG in last night's Chinese food accounted for my headache. I could only imagine the escapades that my familiar had engaged in the night before. David, of course, was thoroughly unruffled. He'd already drilled me on vervain (a defense against metal weapons), rosemary (protection against the evil eye), and radish (defense against scorpions). Yes. Radish. Scorpions.

I tried to remind myself that a warder's job was to protect his witch. It was only natural that my herbal training would focus on vegetation that would assist him in that duty. Nevertheless, I'd spent the entire evening listening to Simon and Garfunkel inside my head, repeating "Parsley, Sage, Rosemary and Thyme" over and over and over. If I heard about a cambric shirt one more time, I'd scream.

Neko took the opportunity of my minor rebellion to shudder delicately. "I am *so* not going camping," he said. I laughed out loud. The notion of my familiar's carefully gelled hair and immaculately groomed fingernails roughing it far from a mirror was so outrageous that even David had to smile.

"You shouldn't cross camping off your list so quickly,"

David said. "You'd be amazed at what you can find growing in the woods. Besides, mugwort makes a fine mosquito
repellant."

Now he told me. "And there are so many mosquitoes
inside the house right now," I said grumpily.

"I could open the door," Neko volunteered. "It wouldn't
take long for them to track *you* down." With friends like
that, who needed enemies—astral or not? I made a mental
note to forget tuna on my next three grocery runs.

"Seriously," I said to David. "Why are we spending so
much time on herbs? Doesn't it make sense for me to focus
on crystals? Or stonework? Something that will help with
setting the centerstone?"

"I can't think of anything that will help you more. You
already have an affinity for Earth—for stone. We established
that when you helped your grandmother months ago, using
the aventurine to heal her pneumonia. You've only added
to that knowledge in the months that have passed. Frankly,
the easiest thing about setting the centerstone will be handling the marble itself."

Marble. Of course. A stone known for strength, for
protection.

I flexed my fingers. "I don't know about that. I'm not
really in great shape. I don't spend my time moving large
quarry blocks around the house."

"You won't do the actual lifting. We warders will help
with that. Part of the ritual will involve introducing you to
all of the warders. If you pass the Coven's test, then all of
us will know you as a witch to be protected, a Daughter of
Hecate whom we are sworn to defend."

And if I failed… I knew the answer to that one, so I decided not to bring it up again. Instead, I focused on something I could learn, something I could control. I forced my voice to be light as I said, "So the marble isn't a problem, and setting it in place is trivial."

"So we might as well have some ice cream and take the rest of the night off," Neko proposed, only to face a glower from David.

I shook my head, shushing Neko as I recognized the method in my warder's madness. "So I might as well learn ways to strengthen the marble. To add to its inherent properties. All of the herbs that we talked about today will help protect the Coven, if I use them in conjunction with the marble."

"Precisely," David said, giving me one of his rare smiles.

"Scorpions?" Neko interrupted my moment of protégé bliss.

David gave me a quick look, but I could only shrug. Why *was* I concerned about scorpions? The Washington Coven's territory didn't exactly extend to the southwest.

David's expectant gaze grew more wooden, and I forced myself to venture an answer. "Because poisons can hide anywhere? Because a scorpion isn't necessarily a literal arthropod, but anything that lies in wait, ready to jump and poison."

"Exactly!" David's smile was as warm as a cup of mugwort tea, and nowhere near as bitter. I preened and shot my familiar a self-satisfied smile of my own. That pleasure was dissipated, though, when David glanced at his watch. "We should get moving," he said, "if we're going to get to Teresa Alison Sidney's on time."

I glanced out the window, where darkness had just fallen on the garden. "Isn't the Coven gathering at midnight?"

"Not tonight. Today isn't a formal working. Just an...organizational meeting. No need for the full ritual. And no need to stay up past midnight on a school night. The meeting starts at nine."

I glanced down at my clothes, wondering what I should wear.

"What are you looking at?" David asked.

"I'm just going to go change—"

"No."

I started to protest, to tell him that it would only take a minute, but I recognized implacable when I saw it on his face. "Let me just grab some earrings, at least."

He scowled but waved his hand. Neko started to follow me out of the kitchen. "Not you," David said to my familiar.

"I'm just going to help!"

"With your help, she'll try on half her closet, just to match the jewelry. 'Help' by cleaning up here."

Neko growled, but he stayed behind.

In my bedroom, I made short work of changing tops, forfeiting my casual T-shirt for a gauzy blouse. They were both black. I was pretty sure David wouldn't notice.

Then I turned to my dresser, where my favorite necklaces were tangled with my most frequently worn earrings. I immediately passed over the turquoise—too ethnic for the Coven crowd. The jet beads were too fussy. Gold hoops were just plain boring.

And then my eyes fell on my sodalite set. The deep blue stones were veined with white. The earrings were fashioned into miniature wands, elongated rods set in protective silver. The short necklace consisted of polished beads; it was just long enough to go around my throat.

Sodalite was known to enhance self-esteem. It gave its wearer confidence, the ability to think clearly and speak well. I couldn't imagine a better crutch as I went to face the Coven. I fastened the necklace around my throat, threaded the earrings through my lobes and returned to the kitchen.

David was not quite tapping his foot, but his impatience was evident. And he *did* notice the change in clothes. I'd been a fool to think that he'd overlook it—even if he was a guy. At least he didn't say anything out loud; he just let me read the disapproval across his face.

Meekly, I chivied Neko in front of us as we left the cottage. I shouldn't have been surprised to see the sleek Lexus sitting curbside, directly in front of the Peabridge. Warders didn't exactly have their own magic, but they could weave reality to meet their astral needs. Most of the time.

As we drove out to Teresa Alison Sidney's home, I tried to pay attention. David had explained during our afternoon session that the new safehold would be built on the Coven Mother's property. The home that I had visited had not been constructed specifically for witches; it had not been set on foundations poured to line up with the cardinal directions, aligned with the four essential elements.

The new safehold would be built on a plain between the current house and a creek. It would be the height of witchy luxury, harnessing the natural world to strengthen the workings of all the witches within its confines. The centerstone would be the core of those spells, the heart of the safehold's magic. It was important that I understood all the power that flowed there, all the ways that the land moved around the witches' chosen gathering place.

The suburbs of northern Virginia felt wilder than Georgetown, as if we had driven back to antebellum times, or earlier. I tried to center myself for our meeting, becoming consciously aware of the streams that we drove over, the folds of fertile land that spread out between country homes. The air was heavy and moist, promising a thunderstorm before morning.

By the time we arrived at Teresa Alison Sidney's, I was nearly in a trance. I don't know if I was reacting to a day full of library work followed by an evening of instruction or to the calming power of my sodalite jewelry, but I emerged from the Lexus feeling peaceful. Powerful. In control.

At least until I ventured past the man with the giant sword.

I had enough presence of mind to realize that this man was different from the one I'd seen on my other visit to the Coven. Somehow, that thought took away all of my poise, drained off all of my confidence. Every single woman inside had a magical warder. Every single woman knew more about the witchy sisterhood than I did. Every single woman was better trained than I.

With a sound that might have been a whimper, Neko moved closer to my side. David contrived to ignore both of us as he led the way past the guardian, completing the pentagram ritual at the doorway with a rigid formality.

Then, I was back with the Coven.

This time, David did not even wait to present himself to Teresa Alison Sidney. Instead, he moved immediately to the front room, opening the door and closing it behind himself before I realized that I was abandoned. Neko glanced around nervously, and if he'd still sported his feline tail, I knew it would have been lashing back and forth in anxiety.

I raised my chin, though, and stepped into the sprawling living room.

"Ah," Teresa Alison Sidney said, looking up from a trio of women. "Jane is finally here."

I started to protest. David had told me to arrive at nine, and it was not yet nine o'clock. I started to explain that it was a long way from my cottage to the safehold, that I didn't even live in Virginia.

Instead, I raised my fingers to my sodalite and took a deep, centering breath. What did it matter? I couldn't change things and arrive any earlier than I had. I met Teresa Alison Sidney's eyes and said, "Yes, Coven Mother."

It was just as well that I didn't waste any time arguing. As Teresa Alison Sidney gave me a frosty nod, the tall-case clock began to chime. As before, its deep, sonorous notes ensnared the witches. Even though no one moved, each woman appeared to stand more still in her place. Each seemed to listen to some distant memory, to gather together a force and energy that was based in the echoing chimes themselves.

When the clock died away, we went through the same ritual that we had done before. The Coven Mother traced a pentagram in the air, and each witch intoned, invoking protection against any who would betray us, any who would harm us, any who would wrong us. I totally nailed the "so mote it be's," blending with the group as if I'd been

working this magic for a lifetime. I traced my own pentagram in front of my face when we were through chanting,
and energy thrummed around me as the protective circle
sealed us off from the greater world.

Teresa Alison Sidney took a deep breath, as if she were
feeding from the eldritch power we had raised. Taking a
moment to look at each of us, she finally nodded toward
the couches. "Sit, sisters. Let us do the work of the Coven
with fairness and with speed. Let us listen to our sisters with
compassion and understanding. Let us join our powers
together to gain strength from each, to lend strength to all."

"So mote it be," the witches whispered as they followed
the Coven Mother's lead. I moved a little more slowly than
the others; they apparently had regular, expected seats
around the room. For a moment, I felt like a child playing
musical chairs—I was the odd man out. But then, Neko
nudged my elbow and directed me toward a Chippendale
chair that looked as if it had been dragged in from the
dining room.

I wasn't sure whether I should edge all the way back on
the slick, upholstered seat, or whether I should remain at
attention, pretending I was at a job interview. I brushed my
fingers against my sodalite beads and settled for ramrod
posture, but I let my spine touch the wooden back of the
chair. Neko folded himself at my feet.

Glancing to my left to see if the nearest witch had observed
my discomfort, I was surprised to discover Haylee James
sitting there. Her Hecate's Torch glittered at the base of her
throat, silent reminder of her membership in the Coven.

My initial reaction was to bristle—after all, she was the one who had set me my specific task, the one who had demanded that I set the centerstone for the new safehold. She was the person who had criticized Gran and Clara's powers, to my face. But she was also the first witch to reach out to me in friendship. I could still picture her right hand cupped around her Torch as she settled her left fingertips against my wrist, friendly, inclusive. Before I could smile at the memory, Teresa Alison Sidney called the meeting to order.

"Sisters, let us begin. Billie, why don't you start with your Treasurer's Report."

Treasurer's Report. Followed rapidly by the Building Fund Report, the Party Fund Report, and the Security Budget Report.

I was sitting in a shareholder's meeting for a witches' coven. I nearly fell out of my chair with surprise.

As my sister witches droned on and on about endless accounting details and the need for better management of time and money, I tried to figure out what I'd been expecting. A round-robin tournament of spell-casting, perhaps? A potluck of potions? Maybe an exchange of extra crystals, along with examples of how to use the magical stones?

A million hours into the meeting, Teresa Alison Sidney called on Haylee to make the report of the Gardening Committee.

Yes. The Gardening Committee. I felt that I should be dressed for Ascot, wearing colors like cerise and aqua. Haylee stood and cleared her throat.

"The Gardening Committee has been very busy," she said. She ruffled her spiky hair with her perfectly mani-cured fingers, and I was shocked to realize that she seemed nervous. How bizarre. The steady, cutthroat witch that I'd met at the midnight Coven couldn't possibly be upset by a report on rununcula.

She licked her lips and continued. "We've selected the plantings for the new safehold's borders, and we've reserved space in the greenhouse so that we can grow everything over the winter. As soon as we've moved beyond the risk of frost next spring, we'll be ready to give the new safehold complete herbal protection."

"And what did you decide on for the borders?" Teresa Alison Sidney asked. There was true warmth behind the question; the Coven Mother even smiled—a courtesy that she had not extended to any of the other reporting witches. I was reminded once again that Teresa Alison Sidney— Teri—and Haylee were old friends.

"We'll go with the traditional protective herbs—parsley, rosemary, an edging of houseleek."

I fought the urge to look toward the front room, where all the warders were gathered in their manly retreat. I wanted to ask how David had known that we witches would discuss herbs tonight, how he had known to train me in the ways of floral defense just that afternoon.

Instead, I nearly yelped as Neko dug his fingernails into my leg, making me focus on the question that Teresa Alison Sidney had just asked. "Does anyone have other suggestions for Haylee? Anything else that should be worked into the border? We're particularly interested in strengthening the power for the spring, when our new safehold will be most vulnerable."

"Radishes."

I heard my voice before I realized I had spoken. In fact, I was only certain that I'd said the word out loud when a score of witches turned to stare at me. I fought the urge to curl my fingers around my sodalite for comfort.

"Excuse me?" the Coven Mother said, and I squirmed like a schoolgirl.

Still, I caught Neko's minute nod. I took as deep a breath as I could manage, and I repeated, louder this time, "Radishes."

Teresa Alison Sidney's eyes narrowed, but another woman actually spoke. "Radishes would be wonderful if we're inviting people over for tea and watercress sandwiches."

By the time I tore my gaze away from the Coven Mother's smirking lips, I was unable to determine which of the women had been so sarcastic. I let my hand drift down to Neko; my fingers barely grazed his shoulder.

I don't know if he twitched slightly, or if his focusing ability channeled my own unschooled powers. Suddenly, though, I *knew* which sister had spoken. I turned to face the witch squarely, meeting her almond-shaped eyes without blinking. Her lined face showed a long lifetime spent acquiring a tan, and I wondered if she exposed herself to ultraviolet rays or just baked on some Florida beach in the off-season. Her tawny coloring was the perfect complement to her silver hair, and the velvet-wrapped headband that swept back her bangs made her look like the worst type of suburban grande dame.

Her cheeks flushed as I stared. I kept my voice level and said, "If you're wasting your radishes on sandwiches, then you're ignoring the full herbal power we witches can harness."

I put a slight emphasis on the word "we" and then thought about adding more. I considered saying that she might not have the ability to study herb-craft. I debated stating that only an idiot would be unaware of the powers of radishes.

But I remembered how often David had schooled me with a single apt sentence—not to mention the fact that I'd only learned about radishes that very evening. Despite Neko quivering beneath my fingertips, despite the pressure of all those eyes staring at me, despite my heart pounding against my rib cage so hard that I thought the warders in the front room might think I was an attacking warrior, I managed to say no more.

I could hear the pendulum swinging on the tall-case clock. I could hear Haylee James swallow beside me. I could hear Teresa Alison Sidney breathing.

At last, the Coven Mother said, "Where have you learned about radishes, Jane?"

"From Hannah Osgood's collection. From the books in my safekeeping." I set the words down carefully, trying not to boast about the materials, but conveying that I was in control of a great deal of witchy wealth. I tried not to think about the fact that all my wealth would pass from me if I failed to set the centerstone on Samhain.

Teresa Alison Sidney's eyes were even more intimidating than the matron's. But when she nodded, I knew I had won this round. "Radishes, then. We'll use them for edging, to bolster our protection in the spring.

I exhaled slowly, trying not to let anyone see how stressed I'd been. The rest of the meeting crept by—there were more reports from more committees. Neko curled up against my chair and—for all I could tell—fell asleep.

At last, the Coven Mother asked if there were any other matters to discuss. When no one responded, she stood and led us through the closing ritual, walking in a great circle around the room, gathering up the energy that we had laid out to protect us. She sketched a spectacular pentagram in the air, tracing silver light with her fingertips, and then she intoned, "So we were met, Daughters of Hecate. Go forth from this circle with peace in your heart. Go forth with the power of your sisterhood."

"We go forth," the women responded, and I remembered enough from my first visit to join them.

I waited until a thunderclap had echoed through the room and the silver light had faded before I dared to lean back in my chair, closing my eyes for just a moment. I wanted to rub my temples, to curl up and take a nap.

"Would you like some tea?" I heard from closer at hand than I expected. "No watercress sandwiches—with or without radishes—but there's some killer crab dip."

My eyes flew open, and I saw Haylee James, extending a cup and saucer like a formal peace offering. I took the caffeine gratefully but was unable to ignore Neko's anxious glance toward the serving table. "Go," I said to him. "But leave some for everyone else." I turned back to Haylee as Neko darted away. "Thank you."

"I'm sorry Kate was so nasty." Kate. She must be the matron. Haylee shrugged. "You've stirred up a lot of the Coven. Many witches thought they'd be asked to set the centerstone."

I smiled wanly. "I don't suppose I could forfeit the responsibility?"

"You don't mean that." She flashed me a toothy smile. "You'll do fine. Really." She sipped her own tea. "And radishes are an…interesting idea. Quaint, actually. A throwback to the herb gardens where so many Wyrd Women got their original powers."

"I know it sounds ridiculous—" I started to defend my knowledge, but another quick smile implied that Haylee thought no defense was necessary.

"Lots of plants have power." She shrugged. "That's why I like the Gardening Committee. There's so much history in what we do. Have you ever looked at medieval paintings? Or Renaissance, with all those flowers and herbs? Each one was supposed to protect the subject—and the artwork itself—with magical power."

I shook my head. "I don't think I'd recognize half the plants I've read about. I'm pretty good at things in the colonial era, but going that far back…"

"We should go down to the National Gallery of Art some time. We could compare notes from your colonial collection with the paintings there."

Her words were offhand, but I recognized the thrill that jolted through my belly. It was like being chosen for an elementary school kick-ball team. Or standing in the high school cafeteria, tray in hand, and seeing a friend wave toward a nearby seat. Or staying up until dawn, clutching pillows and eating nacho cheese Doritos and gossiping about all of the cute boys.

"I'd like that," I said.

"Oh, God!" she said. "I shouldn't have said anything! My schedule is *insane* for the next week, week and a half."

"That's right. You're an interior decorator, aren't you?"

"Yes, and I'm finishing up a kitchen renovation for a major client. Can you wait till a week from Sunday? We could get to the gallery at two and avoid the morning tourists?"

I nodded. "That would be wonderful."

Haylee matched my shy grin with another one of her stunning smiles. Her fingers flickered to the Hecate's Torch at her throat, as if she were grateful for my agreement. "Fantastic!"

Eager to continue the conversation, I nodded toward her Torch. "I can't wait until I have one of my own. Just hearing about Gran's the other day made me realize how much I want one. *Need* one. It was so hard not to accept Gran's as a gift! As *if* that would work for me!"

"As if," Haylee repeated, and she reached out to pat the back of my hand, making my fingers tingle as if she were sprinkling them with magical pixie dust. For just a moment, I thought that I must look ridiculous to her. I must seem petty, jealous of my weak witchy grandmother. What had even made me bring up Gran? There was no reason to dwell on the Coven's dismissive attitude about my distaff relations.

"It's normal for a witch to want a Torch," Haylee said. "Almost as normal as getting hungry at one of these meetings. How about another cup of tea?"

I laughed and offered to fetch drinks for both of us. Maybe this Coven thing was going to work out after all.

"Have another muffin, dear." Gran pushed the plate of lemon-poppyseed treats closer. I shifted a little on her kitchen chair, grateful that I hadn't yet donned the whalebone corset that would keep me sitting straight for the rest of the day.

Corsets. Whalebone. We *had* come a long way, baby.

Consciously deciding to celebrate my liberated sisters' battles, I helped myself to a second muffin. It was still warm from Gran's oven.

I'd been skipping enough desserts (I'd still been too busy to wander over to Cake Walk) to justify the additional breakfast. I even thought I might have dropped a couple of pounds. Before I knew it, I might start to look like the svelte Teresa Alison Sidney. Well, at least I might have a touch more confidence the next time I met with the Coven for committee reports. What more could a girl ask?

I reached for the butter—it would be rude not to celebrate

fresh-baked muffins, right? It wasn't every day that I got invited over to someone's house for a home-cooked meal.

Gran cleared her throat and said, "Your mother and I have been trying to figure out the best way to talk to you about something, and I've convinced Clara that we should just broach the topic instead of beating around the bush."

So much for the loving care of a home-cooked breakfast.

I should have realized this was something big. Something major enough to make Gran actually *leave* a message on my answering machine. When I'd returned from work last night, the light was flashing. Instead of the usual "Jane Madison's grandmother," Gran had actually steeled herself to say that she was expecting me for breakfast the following morning, that she wouldn't take no for an answer.

I pushed my plate back, ignoring an inviting trickle of melted butter over the crisp muffin crust. I tried to convince myself that I'd never been a big fan of lemon poppy-seed—the seeds always got stuck in my teeth. My stomach growled, though, as restless as my mind had suddenly become.

"Yes," I prompted, when no further confession seemed forthcoming.

"It's just that we've been worried about you. About us. It's been difficult enough for the three of us to get to know each other, and now…"

Irritation pricked at the back of my throat. I'd been a fool to think that Gran and I would chat like lighthearted friends. I should have realized I would end up sulking here like a sullen teenager. What *was* it about coming back to Gran's house that pushed me into this long-abandoned role?

"What have I done to upset Clara now?" I heard the obnoxious tone beneath my words, but I felt no need to modify it.

"Now, you shouldn't automatically blame your mother. I've been concerned, too."

"So, what? The two of you get together to talk about me when you don't have anything else to manipulate? Did you bake for Clara also? Set out the fine china, so that both of you could figure out exactly what I'm doing wrong, and how you want me to change?"

Okay. The vehemence of my tirade even surprised me. I mean, I'd come to realize during the past year that Clara *was* my grandmother's daughter. Gran was going to do everything that she could to help Clara on her quest to return to the normal world. Clara herself was trying—she *had* moved back to the D.C. area, leaving behind her meditation group and the Vortex near Sedona, and all the strange New Age concepts where she'd learned to express her true witchy nature.

But I really didn't want to feel any sympathy for Clara. Not now. Not this morning, when Gran was practically admitting that the two of them had been plotting against me.

Gran tsked and lifted the tea cozy to top off her cup of Earl Grey. She settled the quilted cover back over the china teapot before she met my eyes. "Make me a promise, Jane."

Gran and her promises. Over the years, I'd promised any number of outrageous things to ease her ever-more-bizarre fears. I'd sworn not to eat fugu the first time I'd gone to a sushi restaurant; Gran apparently thought that poisonous Japanese blowfish would be the only thing on the menu. I'd vowed not to go ice-skating on the Potomac during one of the rare winters when the river had frozen over—as if I'd ever consider taking my weak ankles out on the ice. I'd promised not to sneak into the National Zoo at night, and I'd even offered up a special, auxiliary oath not to try feeding the pandas—because they only *looked* like people in panda suits, and they were actually dangerous wild animals with claws and a temper to match Tyrannosaurus rex. And just last year I'd promised not to lick any toads—an oath that proved surprisingly challenging, in light of my more obscure witchcraft paraphernalia.

Gran had perfected her promise extraction, making each one seem simple and straightforward and logical, even as I rolled my eyes and gritted my teeth at the absurdity of her disaster scenarios. In all the years that Gran had raised me, she had never made me promise to refrain from doing one single thing that I was even remotely inclined to do. (Yes, there was that one unwelcome promise that she'd successfully extracted—my affirmative agreement to meet my mother—but when it came to *prohibiting* behavior, I'd always been secretly proud to have an unbroken record of control.)

So, I should just go ahead and agree. Forget to fight. Move on with my life.

I dug in my heels.

"What are you asking, Gran?"

She stopped fiddling and looked me straight in the eye. Uh-oh. This was going to be a doozy. "Stop seeing the Coven."

"What?"

"Don't see those women anymore. Clara and I don't think that they have your best interests at heart."

"Of course they don't have my best interests at heart!" I sighed in exasperation. "They're *witches*, Gran. They're a Coven. They're a sisterhood, banded together to protect the magical group, not the best interests of any single individual. And *definitely* not the interests of someone who is still an outsider, like me."

Gran blinked. I don't think she had expected me to agree with her. "Then why are you so intent on meeting them? On working with them?"

"I don't have a choice."

"You always have a choice."

I shook my head. "Not this time." I tried to think of how I could phrase this, how I could make Gran understand. "This isn't a group that I've chosen to belong to. It's not like the concert opera guild, or the Friends of the National Zoo. This is *more*. It's deeper. I was born a witch. It's in every fiber of my being."

"But you don't have to associate with those women!"

"I do, though." I clenched and unclenched my hands, frustrated by the search for appropriate words. "I've been trusted with great power. Now, I've got great responsibility."

Wonderful. I was reduced to quoting Spiderman to justify myself.

"Gran, I don't have to agree with everything they do. I don't have to be involved with every project they undertake. But I do have to work with them—or I'm going to be forced to work *against* them. They're the only game in town, quite literally. David says that there aren't any other witches in D.C., Maryland or Virginia. Teresa Alison Sidney is the strongest Coven Mother that any American coven has ever known, and her territory has grown as she has matured."

"That Teresa Alison Sidney—" Gran said, and she shook her head in disapproval.

"What, Gran? I thought you liked her?" Wasn't Gran the one who had been so enamored of the Coven Mother? Hadn't Gran contemplated inviting her to join the concert opera guild? What had changed?

Gran pursed her lips. "She was rude to me. And to your mother. You might not think that we care about this witch-craft nonsense, but we do, on some level. And we don't like to be made fools of in front of everyone."

Her voice was trembling. Tears had actually gathered in her eyes. My heart clenched, and I felt truly miserable, like I was leaving my family to seek my fortune, like I was turning my back on the woman who had raised me. "What happened, Gran?"

My question flustered her. She removed the cozy and lifted the china teapot, gently sloshing it from side to side to test how much water remained. "Do you want some more tea?"

"No, Gran." I waited for her to tell me.

"Now, you've let that muffin get cold. Let me pop it into the microwave, freshen it right up."

"No, thank you, Gran." I tried to keep an edge from my voice.

"Maybe you'd like some fruit? I've got some lovely pears—first ones of the season. Let me slice one for you."

I settled my hand on her wrist, keeping her from flying off to the kitchen counter. "Gran, what did the Coven do?"

She fretted at the edge of her napkin. "Clara got a phone call yesterday afternoon."

Yesterday. The day after the Coven's business meeting. "Who was it?"

"One of the witches. She didn't give her name, but her voice was older than Teresa Alison Sidney's."

"How did Clara even know it was someone from the Coven?"

"Who else begins a conversation, 'I speak as the messenger of Hecate'?"

Well, Gran had a point. I asked, "What else did she say?"

"She said the Coven had reconsidered. Teresa Alison Sidney had spoken. The witches decided to take back the jewelry that they gave us."

"The Torches?" I immediately thought of my conversation with Haylee. Had *I* said something to make the Coven act? But there had been no indication that my longing for Gran's Torch was anything out of the ordinary. Besides, the witch who had phoned couldn't even *be* Haylee. Not if her voice was old. And Clara had received the call. Not Gran. Not the grandmother I had inadvertently framed when I said I longed for a Torch.

No. I remembered Haylee's tingling fingers on my hand. Haylee was my friend. She would not turn the Coven against me. Against Gran and Clara.

Gran shook her head and sighed. "I mean, neither Clara nor I thought they were so important in the first place. You know that I was willing to give you mine."

"But they shouldn't just be able to ask for them back, for no reason. Did the witch give Clara any explanation at all?"

"She only said that the Coven had reconsidered. That the two of us aren't worthy of membership. That our powers aren't strong enough."

I went back over the secret meeting. Maybe this had nothing to do with me at all. Had there been any mention about rescinding membership? Had anyone said anything about getting back jewelry that had already been distributed? I could have missed the details, if they'd been buried in some committee report when my attention was wandering.

No. Gran and Clara's status with the Coven had not been part of the meeting. It must be separate. Personal.

But I still couldn't yield to Gran's request. This was one promise I just couldn't make. I took her right hand between both of mine, squelching a moment of surprise when I realized how thin her bones were, how papery her flesh had become. "Gran, I'm so sorry. But I can't promise. Not now. Let me try to make this right, from inside the Coven. Let me explain to them that they've been wrong."

Gran sighed. "Jane—"

"Gran, you have to let me go ahead with this. Once I'm in the Coven, I can learn things. And I can teach them, too. They were wrong to have treated you the way they did. They should have been more respectful. And once I'm inside the group, I can work to change that. I can work to build a group where all witches are welcome, even ones who—" I caught myself just in time, barely stumbling before I completed my sentence. "Even ones who are newly come to their powers." No reason to rub in Gran's and Clara's limited abilities.

Gran sat back in her chair. She took her eyeglasses from

the bridge of her nose, spending an inordinately long time polishing them against her apron. "It's just that I love you. *We* do, Clara and I, both. And we want what's right for you."

"I know that, Gran. I truly do." I leaned forward and kissed her cheek. "And now, what's right for me is that I get to work. Evelyn will kill me if I'm late."

Gran took a deep breath, and then she pushed herself up from the table. "Take her some muffins, dear. She'll forgive anything with a fresh-baked muffin on her desk."

Yeah. A fresh-baked muffin and a half caf, half decaf latte with an extra-large cap of whipped cream. I sighed and wrapped up a treat for my boss. After Gran walked me to her front door, I stopped with my hand on the shiny brass knob. "Are we all right about this? You and me? And Clara?"

"We'll be fine, Jane." Gran flashed me an unsteady smile. "We always will be."

The conversation bothered me as I walked all the way home. I could have taken a cab and saved some time, but I wanted a chance to think about what Gran had said. Besides, it had rained the night before, and the city streets shimmered with the first hint of true autumn chill. (And Gran was absolutely right about one thing—Evelyn *would* forgive my late arrival if I sweetened that news with a treat.)

Did I really want to be a member of a club that intimidated my closest family members? That invited people to join and then took away their membership on a whim? Did I want to be one of the Popular Snobs?

The problem was, every time I asked myself the question, the answer kept coming up yes. I could still feel the thrill of realizing that Haylee James was asking me to go to the National Gallery. (Me! Silly, new-witch, me!) My fingers tingled as if she were still touching me with her cool, steady hand.

And aside from the new friendship, I could remember the power I had felt at the midnight Coven, the silver-traced energy that bound the women together. There was strength in their rituals, traditions that gave them roots. My entire body could still remember the *pull* of the tall-case clock, the expectancy that grew out of its deep chimes.

A part of my witch's soul longed for that sense of togetherness, that bonding with others. I began to realize there was a reason that witches came together in covens. We *were* Wyrd Women. We did experience the world in strange ways. We needed to share those experiences with one another, order them, make sense out of them. We needed the sisterhood to sustain us.

By the time I got back to the Peabridge, it was already nine. I ducked into my cottage and donned my colonial attire in record time. I was still pinning my mobcap to my hair as I burst through the library's front doors.

Fortunately, Evelyn was away from her desk. I was able to slip the muffins onto her blotter without her ever being aware of my late arrival, using the treats to anchor a Post-it note saying that I'd brought them just for her. I powered up the coffee bar, grinding a batch of beans so that I was ready to greet the first customer of the day.

"Excellent!" my boss said, as she returned to the main reading room from the cataloging office downstairs. "It's a pleasure to see you so prompt and responsible."

At first, I thought she was mocking me, but a quick

glance at her close-set eyes convinced me that she really meant to deliver a compliment. I shrugged. "You know, anything for the Peabridge."

"That's the spirit!" Evelyn said. "Now, when you get a moment, come into my office, so that we can discuss your next Monday session."

For once, I was actually grateful to see a trio of customers approach, and I took my time brewing their complicated requests. I hadn't settled on a lecture topic yet: I'd been a little preoccupied the past two weeks.

Covens in colonial life, I thought, trying to generate a suitable subject.

Social hierarchies amid closed-membership eighteenth-century cabals.

Secret societies and the Founding Fathers.

Secret societies and the Founding Mothers. And daughters. And granddaughters.

I laced a mocha with whipped cream, nodding to myself. That was actually a possibility. Oh, not the secret society part. But mothers and daughters and the tug of filial duty through the ages. Evelyn would be sure to love the idea.

By the time I got back to my desk, even *I* was brimming with enthusiasm for my session topic. I could bring colonial mothers and daughters to life. I could present an interesting lecture about the pressures of multiple generations living and working in the same house, competing for respect in the same territory.

I sat down at my desk and smiled at the icon in the lower right corner that said new mail had arrived. My fingers moved automatically, clicking on the flashing yellow envelope.

To: Jane.Madison@peabridge.org
From: Warning@example.com
Subject: We Are Watching You
How much does the Coven mean to you? How much are you
willing to invest in their safehold? How much is the center-
stone really worth?

Beneath the words was a picture. A red jasper vase filled
the screen, black veins ugly against crimson stone. Four
sprigs of herbs were stuck in the vase, herbs as familiar to
me as Gran's battered copy of *Joy of Cooking*. Feathery dill.
Fennel, turned upside down, so that I could not miss its
branched white bulb. Oregano, with its simple, flat leaves.
Thyme, all woody stem and tiny, spiky leaves.

This time, I didn't need David to tell me I was being
warned. I didn't need my warder to recite medieval texts.
Dill, fennel, oregano, thyme. All were popular in contemporary cooking. All had survived to the twenty-first cen-
tury because people believed the herbs held extraordinary
properties. Lifesaving properties. The ability to stop a witch
in her tracks.

My hand shook as I forwarded the message to David and
then clicked on the delete icon. Someone did not want me
placing the Coven's centerstone. How far was he—or she—
willing to go to stop me?

14

I stared out at the Potomac River, trying to will my tears not to trickle down my cheeks. I could sense Graeme standing beside me, but I wasn't ready to look at him yet, wasn't ready to talk. Instead, the Kennedy Center fountains chimed away behind us, filling the silence with water sounds. Half the lights on the marble terrace had already been turned off; the huge entertainment complex was going to sleep now that its last evening performance was over.

How many productions of Romeo and Juliet had I seen in my lifetime? How many versions of the star-crossed lovers had I watched flit across a stage? How many times had I screamed inside my head, warning Juliet not to drink her potion, begging Romeo not to fall on his sword?

But tonight's show had been special. Well acted. Well designed. But something more than that—it had *moved* me. For the couple of hours that I had spent watching the play, I had forgotten that I was surrounded by red velvet and gilt lighting fixtures, that I had a library job to worry about, a coven to occupy my spare time.

The characters had lived and breathed and *been,* and now they weren't, and I could barely keep from sobbing as I stared out at the nighttime lights of Georgetown.

Graeme passed me an immaculate linen handkerchief and said, "They were wonderful, weren't they?"

"Yes," I managed, and then the tears did break loose, and I was looking away, trying not to let him see me act like a fool.

Maybe I was just overwhelmed by everything that was happening in my life—the Coven and its centerstone (which I still hadn't learned enough about), Gran and Clara and their demands that I back away from the witches, the Peabridge and the increasing hours that I spent brewing coffee when I should be researching colonial history...

Graeme...

He rested his hand against my back. I could feel the warmth of each finger as he set his palm between my shoulder blades. I was wearing a light cardigan sweater, emerald-green over my black sheath dress.

I resisted the urge to lean back, to feel the taut muscles of Graeme's chest, to fold myself inside his arms. If I let him touch me, I knew I would truly start sobbing like a child. I knew that I would turn to face him, and he would see mascara blobbing around my eyes like a raccoon mask, and he would realize that I was a sentimental fool, and he would be convinced that he wanted nothing more to do with this hysterical, gibbering woman.

Better to stare out at the water. Better to focus on the flickering lights and stopping the tears that leaked from my eyes. Better to wait until I could talk without sobbing, until I could force myself to be coherent.

"Do you know what gets me every time?" he asked, mercifully filling the conversational gap.

"Hmm?" I managed to make a questioning sound without actually shaping any words.

"The nurse." He shifted his weight, and the motion exposed my side to the steady breeze that blew off the river. Impossible as it was to believe, I was actually chilled out here on the marble patio. Every year, I thought we'd be doomed forever to eternal sweltering heat, and every year, I was surprised by the sudden autumn change in September's weather.

I rubbed my arms to tame the goose bumps that had sprung up under my sweater, and I asked, "The nurse?"

"She's the only person in the Capulet household who truly loves Juliet, who truly understands what Juliet is willing to do for her love. She's the only one who isn't surprised the morning after. But she's the only one who isn't allowed into the crypt at the end."

I sighed, thinking about the production we'd just seen, the actors ranged around the bodies. The young lovers had been so hopeful, so certain of themselves. Life—and love—could be so very unfair.

And that thought led me into very dark places. Places I didn't want to go—not with a gorgeous man standing by my side. A gorgeous man who was waiting patiently for me to recover from my morose sadness. Waiting patiently while I finished dabbing at my eyes with his handkerchief and hiding the mascara-streaked evidence inside my clenched fist.

Another gust of wind picked up off the Potomac and—despite my best intentions—my teeth started to chatter. "Come along now," Graeme said, his Britishness rising to the surface with more distinctiveness than I'd heard all evening. "Let's get you out of this weather."

"No!" I said, and then I realized that I sounded like a five-year-old spoiled brat. "I mean, it feels wonderful, after all the heat we've had. Do you mind very much staying a bit longer?"

Mind very much? I was starting to sound British again. I gritted my teeth. I hated the way I picked up other people's accents. I could watch a few episodes of *Upstairs, Downstairs* and sound like an English lass for hours. And watching an evening of Shakespeare didn't curb the tendency one bit.

Graeme didn't seem to notice. Instead, he smiled and slipped off his jacket, draping it over my shoulders with a protectiveness that made my heart skip a beat. A half-dozen beats. Nearly stop beating altogether.

Had any other man ever watched out for my comfort this way? Certainly not Scott, my former fiancé and philanderer extraordinaire. And the I.B.? It would never have crossed his Infantile Belittled mind to protect me.

"Mmm," I said, and then I *did* lean back against Graeme's chest. I let his arms fold around me, felt the warmth of his fingers spread like fans across my hip bones.

"I've been thinking," Graeme whispered, his lips close to my ear.

"Yes?" I managed to say, barely remembering that I needed to hold up some small part of the conversation.

"You're going to think that I'm daft."

What? *Graeme* had fears about what *I* would think? Me? The woman who bathed in Deep Woods Off! and then attracted the entirely unwelcome attention of the Park Police? The woman still recovering from *Romeo and Juliet,* like some lovesick teenager? "I doubt that," I said.

"It's just that you've told me about your…powers."

My belly went cold. Colder than the breeze off the river, colder than my memories of Scott and the I.B. How long had Graeme been thinking of me as "other," "different," "strange"?

"Yes." I pushed the one word past the lump that suddenly threatened to close my throat. I didn't want him to believe that I was some bizarre creature, something he couldn't relate to, couldn't speak to. Didn't want to spend time with.

"You've told me about them, but I've never seen you use them."

Yeah, like that had gone so well with men in the past. I thought of the Impressive Bother, and the times he'd seen me use my witchy attributes. The first occasion, in my cottage's kitchen, he'd been so unable to cope that he'd ascribed my magic to his own confused senses. And the last time, up at Gran's farm…well, there had been no confusion then. The Impetuous Blackguard had understood exactly what he was seeing. And he had been terrified.

With good cause, I might add.

Showing off my skills as a witch was not exactly at the top of any One Hundred Ways to Win the Man of Your Dreams list.

Of course, providing a small demonstration wasn't exactly forbidden, either.

"What are you saying, Graeme?"

His fingers clenched slightly, effortlessly, turning me around to face him. "I'm saying that I want to see you. I want to see what you can do. I told you about the women in my family, the powers that they've had. I want to see that power in you."

His blue eyes seemed silver in the shadows on the terrace. The lights were behind him, so that his face was carved in planes. I felt his urgency in his fingertips, sensed his earnestness in the heat that radiated from his chest.

"It's really not much to look at," I said, trying to make a joke of my supernatural powers.

"I want to look at it. I want to look at you."

Oh. My. God.

The heat in his words would have made me do just about anything. A striptease, here on the back porch of the Kennedy Center? No problem! Bring him home to my bed, ignoring the inquiring looks of my familiar and his lover? Hop on in! Present him to my grandmother, my mother and my best friend, and tell them that he was the man I was going to spend the rest of my life with, come hell or high water? Absolutely!

Oh. Wait. That last option wasn't really on the table. Yet.

"You want me to work a spell?"

"Just something small."

"Now?"

"Please." He made the request sound like an offer.

I licked my lips and looked out over the river. I'd spent so much time working with David, focusing on crystals and herbs, that I'd ignored the original aspect of my magic, the spells that I'd learned to work from the library in my basement.

I thought back to the endless rows of books that I had

cataloged, the pages and pages of magical words that I had examined, at least in passing. As the breeze picked up over the Potomac once again, I realized I had the perfect little working, ready at hand.

"I shouldn't do this sort of thing," I said, suddenly embarrassed.

"I won't tell if you don't tell." Graeme's white-toothed smile made me blush, as if he were promising to keep more secrets than my magic.

"It's just that I should have my familiar here. Or my warder."

He looked surprised. "I didn't mean to suggest anything inappropriate. If you're not allowed to use your powers without their permission…"

He trailed off, probably driven into silence by the angry set of my lips. Of course I was allowed to use my powers! David Montrose was not the boss of me. And Neko? He might think that he could run my life, but I was *his* master. Mistress. Whatever.

Neither David nor Neko could stop me from using my powers. At least with regard to something as minor as the spell I thought to work now. I mean, if I was going to try something *major*, like setting the centerstone, or something—well, of course, I'd expect my magical cohorts to be present for that.

But a few words, chanted on the nighttime breeze? I wouldn't ask permission to have a slice of cake for dessert. And I wasn't going to turn to David and Neko for something equally mundane.

I forced my frown into a smile. "No," I said sweetly. "I certainly don't need their permission. Watch this."

I *did* feel him watching. I felt his eyes as I turned back toward the river. I heard him catch his breath as I reached out for the essence of Water, the strength and power of the basic element that flowed past our marble perch. I imagined him stepping back in surprise as I raised my arms dramatically.

And there he was, behind me, catching his jacket before it slipped to the ground. "Damn!" I said. How could I have forgotten I had his coat draped around my shoulders? Why hadn't I realized what would happen as soon as I moved my arms? What sort of idiot witch was I? "I'm sorry," I said, my concentration shattered.

"No harm done at all." I heard the laughter beneath his words, good-natured humor meant to carry me along. He wasn't poking fun at me. He honestly meant for me to feel more comfortable. He held out the jacket as if it were a coronation robe. "Perhaps if you wear it properly?"

I smiled and accepted the offer. And then, before I could lose my nerve, I turned back to the river and closed my eyes, the better to concentrate. I touched my forehead, offering up the power of my thoughts. I touched my throat, the power of my words. I touched my heart, the power of my belief. And I said:

"Flowing water, flowing stream
Capture moonlight in a beam
Pass close to the quiet shore
Open up a magic door
Offer up your strength as heat
Beat back chill, cold breeze defeat
Let fast current turn to frost
Heat us, now that summer's lost."

I knew the spell was working even before I heard Graeme's indrawn breath. A suddenly warm breeze skirled off the Potomac, brushing my face like a promise of things to come. When I looked out at the water, I could see a silver path condensing all the way from the marble porch to Roosevelt Island in the middle of the river.

Anyone who happened to look down on the Potomac at that precise moment would have thought that the water was reflecting the moonlight. Reflecting with an odd precision perhaps, providing a cleaner line than expected, but reflecting, all the same.

I knew that the silver was not reflected light, though. The silver was ice. Rime settled on the water as I drew forth the river's warmth, as I created a silky summer breeze with magic.

I turned to Graeme, a smile broad across my lips. "And *that* is a little spell."

He was struck dumb by my working. I could see the surprise, flat across his face. What had he expected? Thunder? Lightning? Flashes of eternal hellfire spawned by my witchy demonstration?

"But…you…" He swallowed and tried again. "You stopped the flow of the entire river."

I frowned. I thought he would have missed that. "Only for a moment. I took too much water into the spell right at the start. As soon as I found the proper balance, I let the rest of it flow back."

"You let…" He stared at the silvery path in front of us. "That's ice, isn't it?"

"Ice. Frost. Whatever you want to call it. It's not that thick. It doesn't go down to the bottom of the riverbed."

"But you can keep it there, now. While we're talking?"

I'd left a tendril of my powers attached to the frozen streak across the water. In fact, my warm breeze did continue to blow, harvesting the river's power, draining the water's heat for our personal convenience. I shrugged. "It doesn't take much power to maintain. Casting the spell is the hard part."

"I see. I'd always thought…" He shook his head slowly. "But what do I know about magic, eh?"

"I should probably let it go. I wouldn't want to confuse any fish or anything."

"Oh! Yes! By all means!"

I closed my eyes and imagined the heat diffusing, sinking back into the river. I let the ice break up as quickly as it had developed. When I stared out at the river again, ordinary moonlight flickered over ordinary current.

"That was incredible," Graeme breathed.

"It was nothing," I said, embarrassed by his attention.

"No," he contradicted. "Truly. Thank you. Thank you for sharing that with me."

I don't know what it was about those words, but he made me feel…intimate. As if I had shown him something substantially more personal than a mild weather-working spell. I felt my blush heating my face, far more effectively than any magical breeze I'd pulled forth from the river.

Before I could say anything else, Graeme was kissing me. His embrace held all the urgency of our encounter on the park bench, all the heat of that fast-banked desire. His fingers tangled in the hair at the base of my neck, and I opened my lips, eager to get the full taste of him, the full feel of him.

And something jangled against my thigh.

Startled, I leaped back.

"It's nothing," he said. "Only my mobile." His cell phone. Apparently set on "wake the dead" for its vibration mode. "There," he said. "They've rung off."

I laughed nervously, but neither of us wasted time returning to where we'd left off. His knee forced its way between mine, and his arms closed around me, keeping me balanced, or at least on my feet, even as his lips began doing extremely unsteadying things to the base of my throat.

And his phone jangled again.

"Dammit!" he swore, slamming his hand into his pocket to pull out the offending appliance. He glanced at the number on the display screen and muttered something I didn't quite catch. "I'm sorry," he said curtly. "I'm going to have to take this."

He flipped the cell open and strode across the marble portico. The chilly natural breeze had returned from the river, blowing his words away from me so that I couldn't have eavesdropped if I'd wanted to.

*If* I'd wanted? Of course I'd wanted to.

I pulled his jacket closer and waited for him to finish his rather animated conversation. He ran his fingers through his hair twice. He shifted his weight from foot to foot, like a tiger preparing to pounce on some unsuspecting prey.

At last, he slammed the phone closed and turned to face me.

"I'm sorry," he said. His eyes were flashing anger more

than sorrow. I wondered who he'd been talking to, and I was glad—in a way—that I'd never know. He shoved the offending phone into his pocket with enough vehemence that I was afraid he'd rip out the seam. "I have to go."

"Go?" I was so surprised that I repeated the word like a mynah bird.

He shrugged angrily. "I have some work to do."

"Tonight?" I asked incredulously. "It's Saturday. And it's almost midnight."

"Eleven-thirty," he said, as if I'd really been asking the time.

"Whatever. Can't it wait till morning?"

He shook his head grimly. "No." And then he repeated, "I'm sorry." He put out his hand, cupping my cheek as if he truly wanted to continue the, um, conversation that we'd begun before we were so electronically interrupted. "Let me get you a taxi home."

I was so surprised that I let him lead me off the marble terrace. We passed through the now-darkened hallways of the Kennedy Center, moving among the last of the maintenance crews preparing the vast hall for its nighttime sleep. We walked out to the street, and Graeme managed to hail a cab instantly, applying the ancient masculine art of transportation management.

Just before he handed me into the backseat, he pulled me close for a kiss—a fiery kiss that almost made me moan like a silly heroine in a book. Then, he whispered against my ear, "I'll make this up to you. I promise."

And before I could say anything, he handed money to the driver and closed the door behind me. We pulled away from the curb, took the corner at a speed that would definitely not be deemed safe by the city's finest, and then Graeme was gone.

I gave my address to the driver and sank back into the seat.

Acquisitions. That's what his business card had said. What sort of acquisitions emergency happened at eleven-thirty on a Saturday night?

I tortured myself with scenarios until the driver pulled up outside my cottage. As I fit my key into the lock, my phone started ringing. I pushed my way into the living room, barely shoving the door closed behind me. Two rings. Three. I sprinted into the kitchen and grabbed the handset before the answering machine picked up.

"You've resolved the emergency faster than you thought, and you're ready to make it up to me now?" I remembered to smile as I spoke, so that Graeme would know I was only kidding, that I wasn't a screaming harpy, furious with a single change in plans.

"That was a very bad idea."

David.

Not Graeme. David. A shiver rippled down my spine.

I kicked off my heels and sank onto one of the kitchen chairs. "Oh. It's you."

"Yes, it's me." I heard his frustration, loud and clear. "What the hell were you doing at the Kennedy Center?"

"You don't have the right to spy on me like that!"

"I wasn't spying. You were broadcasting your location to anyone with the faintest hint of magical ability. What were you doing, working a spell in public? Trying to impress your Mr. Poindexter?"

I flushed at my dating subterfuge, but I wasn't about to

tell David Graeme's real name. Just the thought of sharing that confidence made me queasy. I swallowed my discomfort, letting it sharpen my words. "It wasn't anything major. I've been able to work that one for months. It was no big deal."

"Have you received any more e-mails, Jane? Any more 'gifts'?"

I never should have sent him the herb-o-gram. He was becoming completely paranoid. Now, thinking back to that e-mail, I was ready to laugh it away. Someone was playing a joke on me, trying to make me nervous. It was probably just a Coven thing, like a sorority sister being "kidnapped" from her dorm room on rush night.

"No," I answered David. "But if I had, you would be the first to know."

"I wish I believed you, Jane. Look, this is not a joke. If you expect to be ready to deal with the Coven on Samhain, we have to work every chance we get. You can't waste your energy on games."

I rubbed my face with a hand that still smelled of Graeme's cologne. Wistfulness actually stiffened my resolve. "David, I already told you, I'm not giving up my entire social life for the Coven. You and I are meeting, what? Tomorrow morning?"

"At seven."

I could have sworn that I'd agreed to nine. I never would have let him bully me into seven o'clock on a Sunday morning. "That's a little early, don't you think?"

"You know if I had my way, we'd have been working

tonight. And now you'll be drained of power, in addition to short on sleep."

"It wasn't anything major!"

"Is that what Nate Poindexter said?" He drew out the name, as if it were a grammar-school taunt. Next thing I knew, I'd be sitting in a tree, *K-I-S-S-I-N-G.*

"David, we have so been there. Done that. My personal life is my personal life."

"And that worked out so well for you last year, didn't it?"

"That's a terrible thing to say!" I was truly surprised. David was often pushy. Overprotective. But he rarely said things specifically designed to hurt my feelings. To make me remember just how foolish I had been, how irresponsibly I'd acted.

Now, he sighed. "Just be careful, Jane." A long silence stretched between us, as I tried to think of something to say, something that would tell him how much I had learned from the I.B., how different Graeme—er, Nate—was. "Just make sure you take care of yourself."

"I'm doing that, David," I said, suddenly certain that I had to end this phone call immediately. End it, or be sobbing into the phone. "You can be absolutely certain that I am doing that."

I hung up without saying anything else. As I stepped out of the kitchen, I caught a flash of movement as the door to the basement slipped closed. Great. Neko had overheard every word.

I stomped off to my bedroom, making every effort to send the echo of my footsteps thundering into the basement. I slammed the door closed, finding a little relief in the way the entire door frame shook.

As I threw myself onto my bed, I realized I was still wearing Graeme's jacket. I took it off and buried my face in the satin lining. I fell asleep breathing in his smell, telling myself that anyone could have a midnight occupational emergency. If it had been an omen, or a ruse, or a trick to break things off, then he would have demanded his coat back before sending me home. Right?

All night long, I dreamed of walking toward him, jacket extended, as my feet slipped and slid on a silvery strip of ice that never ended.

15

David nodded slowly as I let the last filaments of my cleansing spell dissipate from the air around us. "How did that feel?"

How did it feel? Like I was hefting the Capitol dome onto my shoulders. Like I was balancing the Washington Monument on my forehead, staggering to keep my footing. Like I was trying to drain the entire Reflecting Pool with a single bat of an eyelash.

"Fine," I said, managing a smile that I hoped did not look too fake. I let my fingers touch Neko's shoulder, and if he realized that I was stabilizing myself there, he didn't let on. "I think I'm getting the hang of this."

There was no way I was going to admit to my warder that his lesson had exhausted me. After all, what witch wanted to say she couldn't do something? Even something as apparently complicated as melding the edges of a centerstone, relying on herbal washes to blend together tiny striations in the rock's surface?

And I especially wasn't going to admit any weakness when I thought of what I was working toward. Membership in the Coven was one thing—one thing that had become increasingly important to me over the past month. I couldn't wait to take my permanent place with the women in Teresa Alison Sidney's circle.

But passing the Coven's test was more important than just my witchy social life. I needed to get into the Coven so that I could do something about Gran and Clara. And I needed to make sure that my books were not forfeit to the group, that Neko could not be claimed by a witch who might not indulge his…idiosyncrasies as much as I did.

Sometimes, I wondered if the Coven was worth all this. But then I remembered what I'd read, what David had taught me. The Coven was the center, the core. It helped its members, protected them against mundane authority. It was the very reason witchcraft had persisted through the ages, through the centuries of suspicion and persecution. The Coven was safety. The Coven was power. As a librarian and a student of colonial America, I could appreciate that the Coven was necessary.

Besides, I wouldn't have been so tired if David had given me a single day off in the past week. Ever since our midnight conversation about Graeme/Nate, he had insisted that we practice, making up lost time preparing for Samhain and the centerstone working. He'd even gone so far as to commandeer one of my lunch hours from the Peabridge.

I wasn't certain if he really wanted me to work on witchcraft that hard, or if he was trying to make it impossible for me to see Graeme/Nate. Just the thought of confronting him made me shiver with apprehension. In fact, he *had* kept me from seeing Graeme, even if that hadn't been his actual intent. I'd been reduced to a half-dozen flirtatious phone conversations as I tried to stifle unwanted yawns. I certainly didn't want to fall asleep on a date. Not with Graeme. Not with the man I was increasingly thinking of as my "boy-friend," even if we hadn't actually been in the same room for seven days.

I shook my head, dragging my thoughts back to my living room and witchcraft and herb-lore. I felt like I'd spent the entire morning lugging around a gigantic chunk of marble, lifting it like a free weight under the direction of the world's most sadistic personal trainer. (Neko assumed that role with more relish than I thought strictly appropri-ate. At one point, he had crouched in front of me and chanted, "*Channel* your energy. *Commit* yourself! You're not as weak as you think you are!" The effect was dimin-ished by his setting his hand against his hip like Richard Simmons's even more fey younger brother.)

In another reality—in the witchy one, the one that mattered to me more and more as we neared Samhain—I had enrobed my spectral powers around the energy of the marble, cloaking the stone with my unique astral signature. On that plane, no amount of taunting by my familiar or my warder could move me along. I succeeded on the basis of my own power, on the hard and fast limitations of my own strength.

When I washed the marble with a bath of radish tea, the stone *changed*. I didn't expect any scientist to be able to note the difference, but I could sense the transformation. I could tell that a bearer of poison (a scorpion, a liar, whatever) could not move past the invisible barrier I had created.

I sank back onto the hunter-green couch and sighed deeply, exhaling every pent breath that had haunted my lungs since David had arrived at the crack of dawn. I'd been expecting him, of course, and I had made a point to be ready when he arrived—pear oolong tea brewed, my hair pulled back into a serviceable ponytail, my T-shirt and jeans a testimony to my willingness to work.

I'll even admit to a certain sadistic pleasure as I threw open the door to the basement, slamming on the overhead light and calling out in a dulcet alto, "Neeeeko! David's here to see us!" I pretended not to hear Jacques grunting Gallic obscenities, and I ignored Neko's scowl as he climbed the stairs, pawing sleep from his eyes. I couldn't believe that Jacques tolerated the strangeness of Neko's life—the odd basement room, the lack of a traditional job. And yet the Frenchman seemed more devoted than ever. Could it be love?

I couldn't worry about my studies' effect on Neko's love life. After all, I was working on being the perfect witch. I was *not* going to listen to David go on and on about my own romance. I was not going to hear another lecture about jasper or herbs or any other threat to my witchy abilities. I was determined not to give David any excuse to criticize me.

Even if I *had* used a beginner's spell to banish my fatigue. Three times in the past week. Even if I *was* only pretending to be bright and perky and inquisitive on a Sunday morning when I would have much preferred to have crawled back under my comforter to sleep uninterrupted, dreaming of the incredible man who had kissed me an entire week before.

"Excellent, Jane," David said, and his praise jolted me back to the present, wiping a smile from the corners of my lips. "I have to admit that you've made major strides this week."

Pride burned off my pleasure at his compliment. "I'm not an idiot, you know."

He raised his hands, palms out, offering up a peaceful apology. "Why don't you just take my compliment at face value?" he asked reasonably, settling back on the couch. "So. I'd suggest that you take it easy this afternoon. You might be surprised by the power drain from this morning. I suggest that you read a book, take a nap. Eat a light supper and get a good night's sleep."

Neko nodded helpfully. "At least the museum café should have a light supper. They serve a lot of salmon. Will you bring me some salmon?"

"Crap!" I had completely forgotten I was supposed to meet Haylee James at the National Gallery of Art. Where had the week gone? Oh, that's right. I'd spent it with my warder and my familiar.

I glanced at my watch. It was twelve-thirty now. If I ate a quick lunch, I could still jump in the shower, dry my hair, throw on something elegantly casual and meet Haylee by two.

David shook his head.

"What?" I said.

"What do you and Nate have on the social calendar?"

"If you *must* know, I'm meeting Haylee James at the National Gallery of Art for a tour of their Renaissance collection."

"Haylee!" I don't think he would have been more surprised if I'd said I was meeting the president of France. He recovered quickly, though. "What could you possibly have in common with Haylee?"

"Aside from the fact that she's a witch? And part of Teresa Alison Sidney's Coven? And the only friend I have in the entire astral world?" I let the words drip with more sarcasm than a sixteen-year-old could muster when challenging her parents' most unfair edicts on curfew.

David didn't rise to my bait. His voice was deadly calm as he said, "Haylee James is not your friend."

"How can you say that? You've never even seen us together!"

"I know Haylee. And I know you. Friendship would be the last thing on Haylee's mind if she's making plans with you."

"That's a terrible thing to say!" And the more I thought about it, the worse it was. Was David saying I wasn't good enough to be friends with a witch as accomplished as Haylee? Or was he saying that she was too popular, too close to our Coven Mother to waste her time being friends with me? The options were opposing sides of the same coin, and I liked neither heads nor tails.

David grimaced. "Let's just leave it that Haylee has said far more terrible things about me in the past. Said and done."

"Aww," I said, irrationally stung. First, David was trying to keep me from seeing Graeme/Nate. Now, he was interfering with my hard-earned friendship. I mimicked the most annoying baby tone I could contrive. "Did Haywee huwt your widdle feewings?"

I heard Neko's jaw drop.

I had never challenged David so directly. He reacted to my ridicule instantly—his face snapped closed, and his jaw tightened like an iron brand. "Do *not* come to me when you have problems with Haylee James," he said, and his voice was so low that I had to lean forward to make out his words. "Do *not* expect me to clean up the mess you are making."

"Fine," I said. He didn't know that she was the only witch who talked to me at Coven gatherings. She was the only one of my so-called sisters who bothered to give me the time of day. He didn't know, because he abandoned me every time we entered Teresa Alison Sidney's home.

"Fine," he repeated. He waited a long moment, as if he thought I would take back my word, but then he shrugged. "And so we're done for the day."

I showed him to the door without making any attempt to smooth things over.

Okay. So, there was no time to dry my hair. But if I hurried, I could still take a shower. And I could eat the Triscuits as I hailed a cab to the museum. The soda? I was better off without it anyway.

But I got my soda later that afternoon.

Haylee and I had wandered through the Renaissance painting sections of the museum. I was astonished by the collection—I hadn't been to the National Gallery in over a decade. In fact, the last time I'd been there, I'd been on a school trip. The boys had stared at statues of naked babes, and the girls had made unkind comments about the dimensions of Rubens's models. I remembered standing in the rotunda, looking up at the statue of winged Mercury and wondering why no one ever sent *me* any secret message.

Well, I was long on secrets now.

"So?" Haylee asked, as we sipped Coca-Cola over tiny ice cubes in the museum café. We had poured our beverages from little glass bottles—the nostalgia component seemed almost enough to justify the four-dollar cost. A steady stream of museum visitors filed by the gelato bar, and I reminded myself that I did not need a cup of straccitella to make it through the day. "What did you think?"

"I think I have a lot to learn," I said. "I never realized how much information is…embedded in the world around me."

There were hints to our witchy powers buried everywhere in the museum. The marble columns that sheltered the artwork were only the first harbingers of magic, creating a protective arch around the space, around the temple of humankind's learning and accomplishments. I could sense further power in the flow of the Mercury fountain—in the round pool that centered the power of the museum's protective dome.

And the artwork! Sure, I'd put in my time learning to parse symbolism in paintings. I'd suffered through Art 101 in college, mastering basic vocabulary and belaboring the meaning of the open window behind Mona Lisa's shoulder. I'd served my sentence with Monet's water lilies and Dali's melting clocks.

But the paintings that Haylee had just shown me… I'd had no idea how much information was being conveyed in each and every brushstroke. "Just that peacock alone," I said. "I could spend days working out what the artist meant."

I was thinking of a round painting, one that had been created in Italy during the Renaissance and attributed to Fra Filippo Lippi. It was intended to be a presentation of the gifts of the Magi, the three wise kings adoring the Christ child. In the center of the panel, though, at the heart of the swirling imagery, a peacock stood on the roof of the manger.

I smiled at Haylee over my Coca-Cola. "I just can't get over how wrong I was. I don't know where I came up with the idea that the peacock was a vain bird, that it was silly because it showed off its tail." There was more, something I couldn't quite remember about the peacock. Something that lurked in the back of my mind, in my cluttered closet of academic knowledge.

"Oh, those stories *are* told. But that's because people are afraid of beauty." She said the words simply, as if she weren't aware of the effect her gamine hair and her high cheekbones had on half the men who walked by while we drank our soda. No, those men weren't *afraid* of beauty. They were attracted to it. Attracted to Haylee. She toyed with her Hecate's Torch, fingering the charm on its silver chain. My fingers tingled as if I was the one touching the token.

"People are afraid of the things that they don't understand," I said. "The things that they can't control."

Haylee's lips set in a grim line, and I had to lean closer to catch her words as she said, "That's why we witches get such bad press. Oh, we're amusing and fun at Halloween, when people can show us with warts on our noses and cobwebs in our hair. But ask about us at any other time of year, and you're likely to hear about the evil eye. Spells.

Charms. And witches burned at the stake for all the evil things we do."

Well. I hadn't expected the conversation to take quite so grim a turn. I cleared my throat and said, "The evil things we're *alleged* to do." I smiled, so that she'd know I wasn't chiding her. So that she'd know I was her friend. Or trying to be one.

She fiddled with the wrapper from her straw. "Alleged."

An uneasy silence pooled around us, spreading like a puddle of viscous tar. I reminded myself to breathe. To relax. To say something to break the dark flow of our conversation.

"Lovely weather we're having lately," I said, forcing a laugh so that she'd realize I was making a joke.

Haylee's eyes were dark, serious, as she asked, "Do you know how to change the weather?"

Immediately, I thought of standing on the Kennedy Center terrace with Graeme. I remembered the heat of his arms around me, the warm breeze that I had crafted, wafting off of the chilling river. I thought of the passion that had risen between us, the promise that had mounted until his cell phone had jangled us back to the real world.

"Um, I can work a few minor spells," I said.

Haylee must have seen my cheeks flush. She pounced like a peacock discovering the tastiest of wormy morsels in the gravel at its feet. "What?"

"What what?" I tried for humor, chiding myself for acting like I was thirteen years old.

"Why are you blushing?"

I shook the ice cubes in my glass, wishing that I knew a spell for making more Coke appear. For making minor earthquakes happen. For distracting a witch when she was hot on the scent of gossip. "It's nothing," I said.

"Your lips say 'nothing,' but your eyes say more, more." She laughed at her corny words, and I couldn't help but join her.

I stared at her Torch, unable to meet her gaze. "It's just this guy I met, a few weeks ago." She arched a perfect eyebrow but remained silent, forcing me to take a deep breath and continue. "We've only gone out a few times…"

Her smile was soft. "But you like him."

I let myself nod, and I finally looked away, shy. "A lot."

"Tell me all about him!"

Tell her about the cute boy I liked. That's what friends did, right? I would tell her, then she'd tell me about some guy she had met. We'd commiserate over past mistakes. We'd remind each other of the good things about guys, warn each other off about the bad things. Share and share alike. That's how girls made friends.

I thought of poor Melissa, with her parade of Mr. Wrongs. As miserable as those men had made her, they were one of the key reasons that she and I had bonded over the years, one of the reasons that we continued to get together for mojito therapy and commiseration. Except it had been ages since we'd managed to find time for cocktails and gossip. Almost two weeks had passed since that weird night that David had joined us, and it had been months since we'd spent time alone, just the two of us, catching up. I'd been too swamped.

"Go on!" Haylee pressed, leaning closer.

And so I did. I told her how Graeme had come into Cake Walk a month ago. How we had laughed about Almond

Lust. How he had left me his card. How we'd been on three dates, and each had left me a little more intrigued. Okay. A lot more intrigued. How we'd teased each other over the phone for the past week.

"He sounds like something," she said, when I trailed off.

"He is," I said, and I sighed. "If we could only keep from getting interrupted. Maybe I should wear sodalite the next time we get together."

"Sodalite?"

I heard David's voice in the back of my head, droning on in professorial authority, and I thought about the ancient guide to crystals that even now was opened on the book stand in my basement. "Sodium aluminum silicate chloride." I might as well have been speaking Greek, given Haylee's opaque expression. "It's a crystal that increases motivation. It gives confidence to the wearer, but can reach beyond that person. Maybe that's all that Graeme needs. Some clarity of vision, to keep us both on track."

"Clarity." Haylee said the word decisively. "Sodalite. Where *do* you learn this stuff?"

I was shocked. Didn't every witch know about crystals?

But of course they didn't. Most witches didn't have the hoard of books that I had in my basement. Most witches didn't have my librarian's compulsion to organize information, to pull together facts and details, to memorize, memorize, memorize. Haylee's strengths must lie elsewhere.

"I'm not sure where I picked that up," I said. "Just something I collected along the way, I guess."

"I'll have to remember it. And I'd love to learn more about crystals from you."

"Anytime!" I said, and I meant it. Here was a witch—an honest-to-goodness witch, and my first friend within the Coven. I would do almost anything to keep building our friendship.

Haylee glanced around us, and for the first time, I noticed that the café was emptying. She said, "Well, it looks like they're about to throw us out of here."

I frowned. "I wanted to go back through the painting galleries one more time."

"Not today." Haylee pushed back her chair. "You're not still thinking about that stupid bird, are you?"

"It's right on the tip of my tongue…"

"Peacocks," she said, and then started ticking points off as she slung her purse over her shoulder. "They're symbols in every major world culture. They represent the glorification of the soul. They stand for saints, because medieval people thought their flesh didn't rot."

"Their voice!" I finally remembered, as we walked out of the museum into the early autumn evening. "Hearing the peacock's cry is bad luck."

Haylee paused on the marble steps. "Isn't that owls? I heard the owl call my name?"

"Peacocks, too," I insisted. "That's what I've been trying to remember all afternoon."

"Well, at least we don't have to worry about accidentally overhearing one in the city."

"How did you know all the rest of that stuff?" I asked.

"I'm an interior designer, remember? You wouldn't believe the number of people who want to know the spiritual meaning of the things they put up on their walls."

I thought of Clara, and her obsession with harmonic New Age interpretations of every last thing around her. "Oh yes," I said. "I would."

We took another couple of minutes to chat about the paintings we'd seen, and then we promised that we'd get together again. Soon.

By the time I got home, I was exhausted. I might have impressed David by being ready for that morning's session, but I had definitely awakened too early. And invested too much energy into the centerstone training. I glanced around the living room, grateful to find that Neko was out, somewhere, presumably with Jacques.

Dinner was going to be a giant bowl of microwave popcorn.

I had already changed into my pajamas and burrowed my feet into my bunny slippers, when I realized that the message waiting light was flashing on my answering machine. I pressed the playback button and almost squealed when I recognized Graeme's voice.

"Hello there, Lady of the River. I hope you enjoyed the gallery with your friend. If memory serves, I still owe you from last week. I hope you'll let me make it up to you. Maybe you can even show me a little more of what you can do. Soonest, Jane."

Show him what I could do.

The notion excited me. I thought again of how I'd hidden my powers from the I.B., kept him from knowing the extent of my abilities until I needed to use my magic against him. The idea of being honest with Graeme filled me with a glow of happiness.

He knew about me. He understood. He was even more attracted to me because of who I was.

I knew I should play things cool. I should curl up on my couch and read a book, go to bed early, to prepare for my busy work week.

But I couldn't keep from dialing his phone number. The digits were now firmly memorized, burned deep enough that I no longer needed the silver-lined Acquisitions card. I caught my breath, ready to say something witty and entertaining, but the line went immediately to an answering machine.

He must be on the phone.

I tried back a few minutes later, and a few minutes after that. By then, my popcorn had gotten cold, and I realized I was too tired even for that snack of a dinner. I tried to reach Graeme one last time, but nearly broke my jaw biting back a yawn as his machine picked up yet again.

I should listen to the signs of the universe, I told myself. I could always reach Graeme in the morning. I should go to sleep.

And so I did.

Some mornings, even the coffee machine had it out to get me.

The first time I attempted to grind Colombia's finest, the grinder detached itself from the main machine, sending coffee dust into my eyes, ears and nose. When I finally stopped coughing, I wiped the tears from my cheeks, certain I was leaving behind prison-bars of mascara. Keeping Health Board regulations in mind, I cursed at the mess, ran downstairs to the restroom, cursed at the dim light, washed my face, cursed at the drying soap, rinsed my withering cheeks, cursed at the raspy towels, and then climbed the stairs to begin the process all over again.

The second batch of coffee stayed in the grinder—along with one of the blades, a screw, and a strange metal flange I'd never seen before. It took me the better part of half an hour to reassemble the machine. And, of course, I needed to curse, wash, curse, dry, curse, and start all over again.

By that time, I had already turned away three mothers and their precious children, a total of five brats—ahem, Junior Colonial Explorers—who had arrived early for my weekly American Family reading hour.

American Family had seemed like a brilliant idea when I'd first thought it up. I'd imagined sitting on the floor, surrounded by a circle of adoring fourth- and fifth-grade children who all longed to learn about the history of our country. I had pictured myself choosing favorites from my childhood, books that would stretch elementary school reading levels—*The Witch of Blackbird Pond, Johnny Tremain.* I could still remember laughing at Johnny's short temper, crying over our colonial battlefield losses, learning without ever realizing just how much history was being slipped into my daily entertainment quota.

Reality was a little different from my dreams.

First of all, I wasn't reading to ten-year-olds. They were all in school, of course.

No, I inevitably played hostess to a circle of toddlers, along with the occasional four- or five-year-old who was home sick from regular school. The neighborhood mothers all looked upon me as a free babysitting service; I had actually heard one shriek into her cell phone with unrestrained glee when she discovered the Peabridge's amazing community service.

Each week, the mothers collected their coffees (usually demanding an inordinate number of special requests—one pump of chocolate syrup rather than two, nutmeg sprinkled on top instead of cinnamon, anything to break the routine that just barely managed to keep me sane as I staffed

the coffee bar.) One woman, the bane of my barista existence, ordered skim milk in her drink and full-fat foam on
top. She acted as if I was attempting higher degrees of
murder when I got the order reversed. Twice.

Okay, I took pleasure wherever I could find it at the ever-
more-hated coffee bar. So, sue me.

Each week, the mothers lingered in the reference area
until they had all been served their caffeinated treasures.
Then, they retreated to the basement exhibit space, feigning
an unholy interest in whatever diaries we were highlight-
ing downstairs.

Downstairs. Where it was peaceful. Quiet. Child-free.

"Sit down, Jonathan!" I said for the seventh time in
ten minutes. "No one else can see the book if you're
standing up."

Jonathan finally obliged, crossing his chubby legs. I
smiled, pleased that I had finally gotten through to him.
He smiled back with his milky baby teeth, and then he
plunged his index finger into his nose. He cleared the
second knuckle easily, but I fought the urge to say anything.
After all, by the time I found a Kleenex and got him cleaned
up, there was no telling what the other kids would do.

As if on cue, three-year-old Kayla stood up and grabbed
at the crotch of her adorable corduroy pants. "Potty," she
said, groaning for emphasis.

The word inspired two of her classmates, who also began
clutching themselves and whining. Jonathan's younger
brother—what was his name? Aaron?—started to crawl
away from the group. His mother had promised me that he
wasn't ready to crawl yet. He'd only just mastered rolling

over two weeks before. (Yes, I had been thrilled to be the sole adult witness to *that* milestone, let me assure you.)

"Potty, potty, potty," Kayla chanted, turning the two syllables into an eloquent dissertation on struggle and deprivation, broken dreams and strangled futures.

I glanced toward the stairs, willing the mothers to return. Surely they were attuned to their own precious offsprings' needs. They must realize how much time had gone by. They had to require another freaking cappuccino, just to make it through the day!

Evelyn came out of her office, clearly distracted by the noise. She gave me a disapproving glance and then loomed over Kayla. "Young lady, we do not sing in the library."

Kayla burst into tears. As if on cue, the infant Aaron collapsed onto his belly, looking like a startled turtle for the split second before he added his own shriek to the fray. Jonathan continued excavating his right nostril as if he hadn't a care in the world, and the two other children resumed and amplified Kayla's chant.

Evelyn shot me an accusing glance. I smiled as sweetly as I could under the circumstances and said, "Their mothers are right downstairs. Do you want to get them, or should I?"

Evelyn spun on her heel, as if she couldn't leave the room fast enough. "Come on," I said to Kayla. "There's nothing to cry about."

"I'm afraid of w-w-witches!" she said.

I looked down at my pinafore, noticing a streak of coffee grounds that I'd somehow missed in my earlier disaster cleanup. "Me?"

"The witch!" Kayla said again with even greater

urgency, and she pointed after Evelyn's departing back. In fact, she inspired Jonathan to add his own slimy digit to the mix, and they repeated to each other, "The witch! The witch!"

"So, they've found out the truth."

Neko. I'd know his smug voice anywhere.

I turned to face him with a speed that might have been misconstrued as desperation. Momentary distraction was all that Aaron had been waiting for. "Stop that baby!" I cried as the infant started to race past my familiar. Neko looked down in horror, but it was Jacques who cornered the squirming child, trapping him between two wooden chairs.

"Kayla!" I shouted, loud enough that I shocked the girl into silence. "There isn't any witch."

"There isn't?" Neko asked, apparently unaware of the chaos that surrounded him. I shot him a look that threatened to jolt him back into his statue form.

"There isn't any witch," I said again. "The nice lady who went downstairs is a librarian. She works here just like I do."

Neko's mouth stretched into a precise O, and I saw him recognize the error in his ways. He turned to me and mouthed, *E-ve-lyn?*

I nodded grimly. Neko reached toward Kayla and patted her head with delicate fingertips, as if he feared contracting chicken pox—or some more horrific childhood scourge—from the contact. "You poor little girl. No wonder you were frightened."

I glared at my familiar and took advantage of a momentary lull in the cacophony to ask, "What do the two of you want?"

"We just woke up," Neko said, adding a delicate yawn to

illustrate his words, "and you were out of coffee at home. We thought we'd come over here and have you make us some."

"The coffee bar is closed during American Family hour."

Jacques looked at his wristwatch. "American Familee. Is over at eleven, no?"

"Yes." I glanced at the clock on the wall, thrilled to see that this week's purgatory had finally ended. "Yes, it is," I repeated with relish.

As if on cue, Kayla resumed her chant. "Potty, potty, potty." Neko jumped back as if she were threatening to steal one of his lives. Jacques took a moment to process what she was saying, and then he, too, took a large step away.

"You," I said, pointing to Neko. "Take those two by their hands. And you—" this time it was Jacques I pinned with my evil librarian eye "—pick up that baby. And Kayla, that is *enough!* Jonathan, come with me. We're going downstairs now."

Like the Pied Piper, I led the procession down the library stairs, trying to ignore the glares from the handful of patrons who were actually trying to get academic work done at the reference room reading tables.

Evelyn was the one who had created this problem, I tried to tell myself. Evelyn had turned the reading room into a café, complete with child care. Evelyn. Not me.

I scowled.

Neko seemed terrified to disobey me. He recognized the tone I'd used; he probably realized I was only a shade away from snapping out a magical word of power.

At the foot of the stairs, I found Evelyn chatting breezily with the mothers, laughing as one of them finished up a droll little tale about a family trip to Colonial Williamsburg. "Well," my boss said, fanning herself and exclaiming as if the patron were the most brilliant storyteller ever to grace the Peabridge halls. "How were *you* supposed to know that the cider was alcoholic?"

Kayla launched herself at her mother's knees, keening about her toileting needs. I accepted Evelyn's glare, considering it worthwhile to get rid of the child, even at the cost of some professional standing. I jutted my chin from Jacques to the well-coiffed mother of Jonathan and Aaron. I let my voice freeze as I said to her, "You'll be thrilled to know that Aaron has mastered crawling now."

She smiled like a grateful saint. "These mornings at the Peabridge do him so much good. You really should host American Family sessions every day."

"Every day?" Evelyn asked, as if the idea had never occurred to her.

"What?" I said quickly, hoping to dig out the idea before it could take root. "And lose out on them being so special?"

"Jane!" My name echoed in the stairwell, and I recognized the voice of Nancy, the circulation clerk. "Jane, we need you up here! There are some patrons who want coffee!"

What the hell? Who said that *I* was the only person who could make a fool out of myself at the coffee bar? When Evelyn had stumbled on the coffee brainstorm, she had intended all of us to learn how to grind the beans, how to foam the milk, how to make the endless variations on a steaming cup of joe. Somewhere along the way, though, I had been designated chief coffee-maker. And child wrangler. And bottle washer. It was a minor miracle that I even remembered how to use our online catalog.

"Excuse me," I said, barely keeping an edge of professionalism in my voice. "Jacques, you can hand Aaron over to Mrs. Duchamp now."

"Duchamp?" he repeated, perfecting the nasal pronunciation that I had merely attempted. "Madame Duchamp?" He squealed at the prospect of meeting a fellow countryman. Rolling my eyes, I left him and Neko to the joy of the Peabridge American Family community.

As I climbed the stairs, I watched my feet. The last thing I needed was to slip on the steps—my dignity had been injured enough by spending the morning babysitting. I smoothed my mobcap, making sure the muslin was still centered on my head. Wouldn't that be perfect if it slipped into someone's latte?

"Good morning."

My heart stopped. One moment, I was a harried librarian, wondering how I could move a coffee bar out of my library and into the nearest Starbucks, where it belonged. The next, I was a lovestruck woman, staring into all-too-familiar light blue eyes.

"Graeme," I said.

He smiled, obviously amused by the startled expression on my face.

"What are you doing here?" I whispered.

This wasn't right! He was part of my real life. My important life. The private life that I lived away from the Peabridge. I didn't want him here in the library, didn't want him to see me surrounded by screaming kids and temperamental coffee grinders. He was supposed to think of me as smooth and witty, urbane and experienced.

Yeah, right.

I yielded to the inevitable. "Can I make you a coffee?"

"I'm sorry," he said. "I shouldn't have come by. But I wanted to see you here. Where you work. It makes it easier for me to imagine you." He lowered his voice to a whisper so soft I couldn't hear his British accent. "To think about you when we're apart."

Could a girl make a coffee drink when her knees had melted? "It's fine," I managed to say. "I'm glad you came by. Even though there really isn't much to see."

He looked at my embroidered silk dress, and I imagined his fingers on my whalebone stays. "Oh, I think there's more here at the Peabridge than meets the eye."

Desperate to defeat the blush that was spreading up my neck, I said, "Please! What do you want to drink? I have to look like I'm working!"

He grinned wolfishly. "I'll have a mocha, then."

"A fine drink," another voice said. "My favorite, in fact."

"Mr. Potter," I said, recognizing the speaker before I could even turn around. "How was Pittsburgh?"

"Exhausting. But a mocha would be just the thing to pick me up. Little did I expect to find someone else ordering my drink." He laughed at his little joke.

"Oh!" I said. Graeme was standing patiently, as if he were accustomed to waiting for flighty women to remember to introduce their elders. "Mr. Potter! This is Graeme Henderson. Graeme, Mr. Potter gave me the tickets for *Romeo and Juliet.*"

Mr. Potter's smile was wide. "And I take it, you are the young man who escorted Jane to the performance?"

"Yes, sir," Graeme said, managing to connote a tiny half bow behind the two words. Something about the answer made him seem like a nobleman, a knight, a regal protector in shining armor.

I took a deep breath and moved behind the coffee counter. I contemplated harnessing some sort of spell to make the machinery function properly, but I couldn't figure out a way to mutter the words without being too obvious. And the way my day was going, I didn't have any confidence that my magic would work. I settled for crossing my fingers with all the passion of a third-grader hoping for a passing grade on a math test.

"And how was the production?" Mr. Potter asked.

I missed Graeme's reply as I poured milk into a stainless steel pitcher. Whatever he said, it clearly pleased Mr. Potter. Both men laughed, and Graeme started to describe the costumes for the ball scene in the first act.

The men's conversation was easy and smooth, and I relaxed enough to create two perfect mochas. I topped Mr. Potter's with extra whipped cream, just the way he liked it, and then I turned to Graeme. "Whipped cream? Er, chantilly?"

His smile was just sly enough to make my heart pound as he accepted a dollop.

I handed over both cups and was about to join the conversation about the Friar Lawrence scene, when I realized that disaster loomed.

Neko and Jacques must be close to finishing with the

American Family mothers. They'd come over to the coffee
bar when they were done. They'd get the drinks that had
lured them here in the first place. They'd stand at the
counter and ogle Graeme.

And Neko would ask me questions. Questions that I had
promised Melissa I wouldn't answer. Questions that I had
no intention of sharing with David Montrose or anyone
else involved in my witchy life. Worse yet, Neko would
jump to the conclusion that Graeme was "Nate," and I'd
be left making excuses to everyone, excuses that sounded
feeble even as I tested them in my own mind. I shivered,
suddenly chilled to the bone.

"Here!" I said, my voice a shade too shrill. "Mr. Potter,
you must be exhausted after your trip back from Pittsburgh! Why don't you sit down at the reference table!"

Graeme looked at me curiously, but he obligingly helped
our elderly library benefactor over to a seat. I managed to
arrange things so that Graeme's back was to the coffee bar,
so that Neko would not see anything suspicious when he
came upstairs.

Now, if I could just have Neko's and Jacques's drinks
waiting, I could get them out the door that much faster.
Neko was easy—steamed milk, with just the smallest drop
of coffee. Ecru, he preferred, he'd told me often enough.
Not beige. Not ivory.

And Jacques? He was getting a latte whether he wanted
one or not.

I made the drinks in record time, digging into my own
hidden colonial pocket to extract money for the cash
register. It was worth it, just to hurry them on their way.

Sure enough, Neko and Jacques accompanied the American Family mothers up the stairs. "Yes," Neko was saying. "A daily reading session does make sense to me. I'm certain that the children would get much more out of it." He smiled winningly and waggled his fingers at Kayla's mother as the entire troop of miscreants left the Peabridge.

Then, he pounced on the coffee bar.

"Here," I said, thrusting one cup into his hand and another into Jacques's. "Go ahead. Take them with you."

"It was cold downstairs," Neko complained. "We'll just sit down at that table in the sun, to warm up for a moment."

That table. Next to Graeme and Mr. Potter.

"No!" I shouted, and then I remembered that I worked in a library. "No," I repeated in a stage whisper. "Why don't you take your coffee outside and warm up there."

"Eet's too cold," Jacques said, stirring four packets of sugar into his latte. "The weather, eet has turned to autumn."

"Fine," I said, knowing better than to push the matter. "Stay inside." Before I could figure out some other way to speed up my familiar's departure, I saw Graeme push his chair back. As he started to stand, I said to Neko, "Wait here! I have to help a patron!"

I sailed across the room, grabbing the first book that came to hand. "Here!" I said, setting it down on the reading table between Graeme and Mr. Potter. Graeme had turned toward me as I approached, but I maneuvered myself into an awkward position toward the foot of the table, forcing him to turn away from the coffee bar. Away from Neko's curiosity. Safe from prying eyes. I took a seat, and Graeme sank back into his own chair.

"I thought you might be interested in this!" I said, glancing down to see which book I'd grabbed.

*Ports and Harbors of Colonial America.*

Mr. Potter looked up with a perplexed smile. "Why am I interested in ports, Jane?"

Why, indeed? I opened the book at random, hoping to find an intriguing map. "You were in the Merchant Marines, weren't you?"

"Me? With these eyes?" Mr. Potter laughed and waved a hand toward eyeglasses that would make Coke bottles seem fragile.

"I could swear that Uncle George said you'd served with them." Okay. So I was desperate. I could not let Graeme turn around, could not let him draw Neko's attention in any way.

Involuntarily, I glanced toward my familiar, only to find that he was staring at me intently. If he were still in his cat form, his tail would have twitched back and forth. He took a single step toward me, and I forced a bright smile. "Whoops! Another patron. I'll be back in a moment." Graeme started to stand again as I left, and I resisted the urge to press my fingers onto his shoulder. Neko would certainly notice that level of attention. "No, no," I said. "Don't get up!"

And then I was back with my familiar. "What?" I asked.

"I was just wondering?" He scuffed his shoe along the floor, looking for all the world like a schoolboy caught red-handed with the answer form for a multiple-choice test.

"Yes?" I wanted to glance toward Graeme, wanted to make sure there wasn't anything suspicious about him and Mr. Potter, anything that would make Neko question my personal dedication to that particular pair of patrons. No. I could not look. I could not turn.

"May I lick the pitcher?"

I glanced at the stainless steel container that I used for foaming milk. It had already been wiped spotless. "Neko!" I said in exasperation. "You shouldn't have done that! This isn't our own kitchen."

And then, like a nervous twitch, I couldn't help but look over my shoulder. Couldn't help but see Mr. Potter yawn and stretch and climb to his feet. I lunged forward, throwing myself into the space so that Neko could not look across the room.

"Jane, are you all right?" Jacques asked with Gallic solicitousness.

"You're acting strange," Neko said, much more frankly.

"I'm acting busy," I insisted. "I have library work to do."

Another quick glance—Mr. Potter was coming our way. For some reason, though, Graeme, was paging through the ports book, keeping his head lowered over the pages. Yes. There was some luck left in the world.

"No," Neko said. "I've seen busy. You're not busy at all."

I made myself look toward Evelyn's office. "I know whether I'm busy or not. Come on, you two. Get going."

"Jane," Mr. Potter said, and I was forced to turn around. "I must be going. Time to walk Beijing and read the newspaper. It was a pleasure meeting your young—"

"Yes," I interrupted loudly. "Yes, you *should* be getting home. Beijing needs you."

"Your young wh—" Neko started to ask, but I was already rushing Mr. Potter across the room.

"Have a wonderful day, Mr. Potter. And thanks again for the theater tickets. I'm glad you had a wonderful time in Pittsburgh!" And I finally hustled him out the door.

By the time I got back to the coffee bar, Neko was eyeing another stainless steel pitcher. I slapped the back of his wrist. "Out!" It would take me ages to sterilize the one he'd already defiled.

"What was that man saying? A pleasure meeting your young what?"

"A pleasure meeting my boss. Evelyn. The woman who will fire me, if she sees me spending more time talking to you."

Neko looked dubious, but Jacques chose that moment to reach out for my familiar's arm. "Let us go," he said. "Eet ees time to get to work."

Work? What did Jacques do? He always seemed available to lounge around the cottage with Neko. I wasn't about to look a gift Frenchman in the mouth, though.

"Goodbye," I said firmly. "And good riddance," I muttered under my breath as they finally left the Peabridge.

"Jane!" Evelyn stepped out of her office before I could cross the room and collapse on a chair next to Graeme. "Come in here for a moment. I think that the idea of expanding American Families is brilliant. Positively the best notion you've had all year."

I looked wildly toward Graeme. He had finally stood up and turned to face me. He must have understood my pantomimed frustration. He made a great show of shooting his cuff, glancing at his watch. He smiled slowly—sexily—and then he shrugged. *Later,* he mouthed.

And then he headed out the Peabridge doors.

Defeated, I slumped into Evelyn's office, determined to find an explanation for why I could not survive daily American Family sessions.

17

"I don't know how you do it," I said to Melissa, watching her swirl the foam on top of a customer's latte. With a few deft twists of her wrist, she created one of Cake Walk's trademarks—a perfect heart of layered white foam against the darker coffee base.

She reminded me of the clowns who created balloon animals at children's birthday parties. They could take one four-foot balloon and twist it into a Tyrannosaurus Rex. If I, on the other hand, attempted to do something as simple as a sword, I'd end up creating some phallic sculpture that would make a mother scream and demand that her child drop the so-called toy immediately.

Melissa handed off the latte and accepted a few dollars in exchange. As she rang up the sale, I took a delicate sip of my own tea—Earl Grey, in honor of the dank day outside. I stared out at the gloomy weather, grateful that

I'd taken a mental health day from the office. Some Fridays were meant to be spent away from work.

September had slipped into October and today's rain had been falling without a break, tugging leaves from the trees and melting them into a slippery mash on the sidewalks. The rain matched my mood.

I sighed and said, "Melissa, we need to talk."

Almost two weeks had passed since I had juggled patrons at the Peabridge. I'd invested a dozen more training sessions with David and Neko. I felt like I had memorized every book in my basement and worked the spells in at least half of them.

I'd only managed to see Graeme on one night, and then I'd practically fallen asleep over a late dinner and a single glass of burgundy at "our" restaurant, Bistro Francais. I probably would have embarrassed myself a few more times, but Graeme had announced that he had another business trip to London. He'd been gone for seven days, and I thought I might be going crazy. Our nightly phone conversations left me eager for his return, slated for next Wednesday night.

The spell-work was exhausting me. But I was equally worn down by the double life I was leading, the secrets that I was keeping—from Neko and David about Graeme. And from Graeme about the Coven. It was long past time to relieve some of that pressure. Long past time to be released from my Friendship Test. Hence, my mental health day and my presence in Cake Walk on a Friday afternoon.

"Sounds serious," Melissa said, unsuspecting. She frowned with a best friend's sympathy and leaned against the counter. Before I could dig up the words I needed, the front door opened.

Three women jostled into the store. Their cheeks were flushed, and their dripping hair was pulled back. Water pooled onto the floor from their running shoes. Melissa smiled automatically, as if to say that she could imagine nothing more fun than a Friday afternoon spent mopping up after her customers. With a rueful glance putting my intended conversation on hold, Melissa called out to the customers, "Nothing like an afternoon run to justify something from Cake Walk! What can I get you, ladies?"

Their orders bubbled up, and I watched Melissa handle both food and drink with an easy efficiency. She was *good* at what she did. Her coffee grinder never broke at crucial moments. It wouldn't dare, given the smooth control of her hands on the levers. The runners took their snacks and conquered a table, falling into over-oxygenated chatter about their workout.

"You were saying?" Melissa finally settled down, once again leaning against the counter.

I was saying. I sighed. I didn't want to confront my best friend, didn't want to seem as if I was valuing the man in my life more than her. I grimaced and looked over her shoulder at the calendar on the wall. There were lines of X's crossing off the days, the weeks, since I had last hung out at the shop. A twinge of guilt crinkled the skin around my eyes, especially when I saw two red X's in the mix.

Two more first dates. First dates that a best friend should have known about.

I nodded toward the wall. "What did I miss in the first-date department?"

Melissa shrugged. "Are you sure you want to know?"

"That doesn't sound good." Didn't sound good on a couple of levels, I thought. Melissa would already have gushed about complete romantic fulfillment, about pledging the rest of her life to some man of her dreams. More important, though, Melissa shouldn't worry about censoring herself, about telling me *anything* related to her dating life. After all, we were best friends.

So-called best friends. I guessed I'd been falling down in that department for a while.

"Come on," I said, suddenly afraid of the distance that was spreading between us. "What happened?"

I saw the precise instant that she decided to share with me, decided to overlook the evenings I'd spent with Graeme, the nights I'd spent under David's tutelage. Her smile was as warm as the ovens at the back of the shop. "Sequin?" she asked, nodding toward a large pottery plate of Ginger Sequin cookies.

She knew how much I loved them—they were as thin and crisp as sugar cookies, but the crystallized ginger on top gave them an added bite. Melissa didn't make them often: the dough was tender, and the finished cookies had an unfortunate tendency to break across the middle. Unfortunate, that was, for Cake Walk's bottom line. It was a downright boon to those of us who helped take care of the so-called culinary disasters.

I nodded, and Melissa produced a plate of "rejects" from beneath the counter. I smiled as crunchy ginger goodness melted over my tongue. "Thanks," I said. "Now come on. Spill. Who was the first guy?"

She sighed. "A Dedicated."

That would be Dedicated Metropolitan Singles. A group of unattached men and women who got together to do good deeds on a regular basis. The organizers of each project accepted volunteers, then distributed an e-mail list of names and numbers afterward, so that the workers could get in touch if they'd hit it off during the event.

Usually, Melissa's Dedicateds were earnest young men. Too earnest. Melissa had been lectured by a vegan for conducting the abattoir of her bakery, sacrificing all those eggs and pounds of butter that kept innocent chickens and cows in servitude. She had been bullied into writing large checks to several Dedicateds' favorite charities. She had been shamed into spending weekends patrolling local waterways, cleaning up other people's messes.

I wasn't a big fan of the Dedicateds, but I mustered a best-friend smile and asked, "So? Where did you go?"

"Dinner at Luna Grill, and a movie."

I smiled cautiously. "So far, so good."

"Oh, the dinner was fine. He ordered the pasta—with three toppings, so I knew he wasn't a tightwad. I had the veggie panini."

"Melissa," I said, using a mock-warning tone. She knew I wasn't interested in the menu.

"And then we went to the theater across the street. You know, the ones with screens as small as my television upstairs?"

"They're not that bad. What did you see?"

"We were there for that new documentary, the one about the crazy old man who built the Taj Mahal out in the Nevada desert?"

"The one who saved tin foil since he was a boy?"

"Yep." She nodded grimly, as if a mock Indian monument were the greatest threat to mankind's safety and peace of mind.

"I take it that the documentary was not well-done?"

"I wouldn't know. I couldn't see it. I spent the entire evening wrestling with the octopus sitting next to me. I mean, it's not like we're in junior high anymore. Sometimes a movie is just a movie, you know?"

I knew what she meant. And I also knew that the date hadn't been a complete disaster. It wasn't like the Dedicated had broken her heart. He had merely wasted her night. She clearly hadn't liked the guy from the get-go; I could tell from her halfhearted description of the date. When Melissa really liked a guy, her disaster stories were much more elaborate.

Once again, a pang of conscience tweaked the skin around my eyes. What sort of friend was I? I should be indignant on my best friend's behalf, even if her bad night out had not been the disaster of a dating lifetime.

Melissa spread her hands flat on the counter. "I'm about ready to do it," she said.

"Do what?"

"Become a nun."

"Weren't you raised Jewish?"

She snorted. "Jewish. Catholic. Whatever. I've got enough guilt for either. For both."

"What do you mean?"

She wouldn't meet my eyes. "I feel guilty about Cake Walk."

I was shocked. Melissa had never expressed the slightest hint of doubt about her bakery before. "What do you mean?"

She picked up a clean rag from the stainless steel sink and

ran it over the already spotless countertop. "I'm worried about it. About me. I'm afraid that I'm just indulging a hobby, when I should be working toward a career."

"A hobby? What are you talking about? Cake Walk is *amazing!*"

"I need to grow my business." She managed a tremulous smile, and I began to realize how much that admission had cost her. "I mean, I love what I'm doing here. I love running the shop and testing new recipes and stocking whatever *I* want to stock."

"But?"

"But it's not going to be enough in the long run. I need to expand."

"Open up another bakery?"

She shrugged. "Like I'm going to find the time to do that? The only reason I can make ends meet on the rent here is that I staff the place myself."

"So what's changed?"

This time, she *did* meet my eyes. "What if I don't find someone, Jane? What if I never meet the man of my so-called dreams?"

"What if you don't? What difference does a man make? You're running your own business, living your own life."

She sniffed. "That's easy for you to say. You've got Graeme. And even if things don't work out with him, you'll always have David and Neko."

There it was. The perfect window for me to address the Friendship Test. But I could hardly ignore the source of my best friend's distress. "Melissa! You're being ridiculous. You'll always have *me!*"

"You know that's not the same. And you're definitely not going to support me in my old age." She shook her head and tossed the rag back into the sink. She scored a perfect two points, but I don't think she really cared. "I need to save more, if I'm ever going to retire."

"Retire? Melissa you aren't even thirty yet!"

"If I'd gone to law school, I'd be a partner by now."

"Maybe. But you'd also be exhausted and miserable and you'd hate every moment of your life." I did some quick mental math. "And you'd most likely still be fighting to *make* partner. Working fifteen hours a day."

She looked around, taking in every corner of the funky little bakery. "Like I'm not doing that now?"

"Melissa, you're scaring me. I've never heard you talk like this before."

"I guess I've never been quite as tired of the dating scene before. Quite as ready to stop and admit that I probably will be on my own forever." She took a deep breath, and I watched her exhale slowly, like a yoga master. "Enough," she said. "We're not going to settle all my problems this afternoon. Why did you stop by? What did you want to talk about?"

Ach. This was so not a good time to bring up my successful dating life. I took a Sequin and crunched it methodically. Only after I had swallowed ginger-scented crumbs did I say, "Look, it's nothing. We can talk some other time."

"Ja-ane." She drew my name into two syllables, the familiar wheedling of a best friend.

I took a deep breath and braved her gaze. "I-need-your-permission-to-tell-Neko-about-Graeme."

"What?"

I forced myself to speak more slowly, to enunciate the words so that something other than a hummingbird could actually understand me. The effort made me shiver, a bone-deep trembling as if I'd been caught outside in a storm. "I need to tell Neko about Graeme. I've been going nuts, trying to keep them from finding out about each other, and it's just going to be worse when Graeme gets back from London on Wednesday."

"It was a Friendship Test!"

"It was. And I've kept it so far. But I think that this is something real, Melissa. I think Graeme's going to be around for a while. I've spoken to him every night that he's been away, but I can't keep hiding what's going on. Neko does live in my basement, you know."

Oh. Bad choice. Mentioning my basement had to conjure up a picture of the couch that my familiar slept on. My familiar and, often enough, his boyfriend du jour. Most recently, the Frenchman who had spurned Melissa for the tender mercies of a cat-man.

Before I could figure out a way to make my argument stronger, the door opened and Siamese twins walked in.

Oh. Wait. They weren't actually joined at the hip: they only looked like it. While Melissa waited to take their order, the pair of young Goths took a long minute to kiss, intent on raking each other's tattooed shoulders with their black-painted fingernails. The girl finally came up for air, and Melissa took advantage of the break in the action to say, "Can I get you anything?"

"Um, yeah," the guy said. "Two plain coffees."

"Sumatran Samba or Colombian Caramel Cream?"

The customers had a whispered conference, requiring much nuzzling and—I tried not to look—a quick dart of his tongue stud against her teeth. "One of each," came the guy's final answer.

"With lots of room for cream," the girl added helpfully.

Melissa nodded and poured two cups. The tough Goths proceeded to take them to the fixings bar at the end of the counter, adding enough milk and sugar to simulate coffee ice cream. Steaming coffee ice cream.

The rain chose that minute to pick up. Rather than risk their eye makeup running down their faces, the Goths huddled at a corner table, slurping their coffee like five-year-olds with glasses of chocolate milk.

Before I could resume my argument in favor of telling Neko about Graeme, the door opened again. I bit back an exasperated sigh and quenched another shiver. This was the bakery that Melissa worried wasn't busy enough? The newcomer was a regular; Melissa grabbed for a carryout cup before the guy had even reached the counter.

Money changed hands, and I cleared my throat, anxious to make my point before yet another customer could interrupt us. "It's just that I feel like I'm lying," I said, keeping my voice low enough that the Goths couldn't hear me. Not that they'd be listening all that carefully. They seemed intent on breaking whatever law of physics said that two bodies couldn't occupy the same point in space and time. I turned so I couldn't be distracted by their acrobatics. "Lying to Neko *and* lying to Graeme."

"'Lying' is a pretty strong word," Melissa said. I could see she intended to fight me on this. I should have waited to bring it up. The whole long-term life plan thing must really be bothering her. And the fact that Neko's current boyfriend was another stop on her long road of dating failure only heightened her resistance. I gritted my teeth. I was sorry about Jacques—I really was. And I was sorry about the octopus Dedicated, and sorry about every other bad date Melissa had ever suffered. But I didn't think it was fair for her to put the kibosh on my own happiness.

I opened my mouth to tell her so, but the damned bakery door opened yet again. As Melissa served up four Cinnamon Blondes to go, I held back a pointed comment about the bakery's constant patrons. When the harried young mother added the pasteboard box to her shopping bags, I almost offered to open her umbrella for her, to get her out of the shop and back into the rain. My fingers twitched, eager to turn the sign around on the door, change it from Walk On In to Walk On By.

Instead, I delved back into my argument, no, my *discussion* with Melissa. "It does feel like lying," I insisted. She continued to look unmoved. "I'm hiding a pretty essential truth. How would you feel if I hadn't told you about Graeme?"

"But you did tell me. You had to. I'm your best friend."

My sigh of exasperation threatened to burst into an angry shout as yet another crowd of customers came in. There were four this time, and each wanted a complicated coffee drink, along with one of Melissa's trademark sweets. As the inevitable clanging and banging began, I forced myself to stop thinking about the Friendship Test, to set aside my frustration with Melissa. Today just wasn't the day.

Besides, I had plenty of other things to worry about. I

glanced at her calendar again. October sixth. I had three and a half weeks left. Twenty-five days until Samhain. Until I was tested by the Coven. Of course, if I lost my books and Neko in the testing, then I'd hardly have to worry about divulging the secret identity of my boyfriend.

"There!" Melissa exclaimed, and I realized we were once again alone at the counter.

"What?" I looked over my shoulder.

"You were doing it again."

"Doing what?"

"Zoning out. Going somewhere. Dropping out."

I hunched my shoulders defensively. "I don't know what you're talking about."

"You get this look in your eyes. Like you're staring inside instead of outside."

I forced myself to smile. "No great inside/outside going on here. I'm just trying to enjoy a great cup of tea."

"You don't even like Earl Grey that much. Listen, you've got to stop dwelling on things."

She was one to talk. "I'm not dwelling!" I realized how loud my voice had gotten, and I glanced at the Goths. I was only marginally comforted by the fact that they were busy testing each other's tattoos for secret Braille messages.

"You *are* dwelling. You're stewing. Look. Keeping Graeme a secret from Neko is not that big of a deal. It's not like you and that cat-freak are lovers or anything."

"That's a terrible thing to say!"

This time, the Goths did look over their shoulders, staring at me as if I was a madwoman in some bizarre zoo. The boy whispered something to the girl, and she nuzzled his neck. By apparent mutual agreement, they gathered up their leather jackets and braved the great outdoors, leaving behind cups, stirrers and a litter of extra sugar packets.

Melissa clicked her tongue. "Come on," she said. "I didn't mean to hurt your feelings. It's just that you've become so distant. Sometimes I feel that if we didn't have the Friendship Test, we wouldn't have any friendship at all."

"I'm not distant. I've been busy!"

Melissa cocked one eyebrow at me—a gesture that always made me jealous, because I couldn't do it.

"I have been!" I said. "Nothing's changed between us. It's not like we've stopped being friends or anything. You're exaggerating, to justify your stupid test."

"All right," she said, spreading out a hand towel on the glass-fronted refrigerated case. "Tell me what I've got inside here."

"What?" Her question made no sense.

"Yeah. It's a Friday afternoon, and you've been standing here for over an hour. If you've paid any attention to me, to what's important to me, you'll have an idea of what I've got in the case."

I didn't have the slightest idea what was underneath the towel. "That's ridiculous," I said.

"Come on. Don't stall. You usually notice right off the bat."

"I've usually heard you talking about it, all week long."

"That's my point, exactly."

Oh.

I closed my eyes, trying to remember what I'd seen when I'd walked into the bakery. Nothing. I didn't have any image in my mind, no thoughts at all.

I thought about nudging behind the towel with my

witchcraft. I should be able to do *something.* Maybe a mirror spell, working off of the chrome finish on the sides of the refrigerated case...

I glanced at Melissa's set jaw, and I realized that using my powers would only make things worse. Well, I knew her repertoire. I could make a guess—an educated one. Like best friends make.

"Hazelnut Claires de la Lune, Latin Lemon Merengues and Savory Basil Crèmes."

"Wrong, wrong and wrong!" Melissa shook her finger at me with each incorrect guess. She was really angry. Really, truly hurt. And when she pulled back the towel, I began to understand why.

Devil's Nips—rum-drenched chocolate truffles.

Lime Stars—miniature key lime tarts, built on star-shaped pastry.

Mint Pillows—mint-infused meringue floating on a bed of homemade chocolate pudding.

Rum, lime and mint. The ingredients of mojitos, our bonding cocktail of choice.

Melissa's voice shook as she said, "The rum would have kept, but the limes were drying out. The oil in their rinds only last so long. And the mint was absolutely on its last legs."

"Oh, Melissa," I said, suddenly realizing how much I had missed our evenings together. How long had it been? Over three weeks.

And then, before I could justify everything I'd been doing, before I could explain about Haylee and Renaissance art and the Kennedy Center and the centerstone—

if I even *could* explain about the centerstone—the door to the bakery opened yet again.

This time, it was a mother with two adorable children, both under the age of five. Both barely able to see the baked riches spread out on the counter and in the glass case. Both afflicted with a terrible case of indecision, as they weighed the relative merits of Lemon Bears versus Chocolate Dreams, with the Mint Pillows thrown in for good, guilty measure.

I waited for the mother to chivy them along, but she seemed in no hurry. I waited for Melissa to make some excuse, so that she could at least turn back to me, at least acknowledge my awkward discomfort. I waited for the children to make up their minds—this wasn't the last time the two kids were ever going to eat!

And when another minute ticked by, and another, and another, I realized that I couldn't wait anymore. I couldn't stand there as if nothing was wrong. I couldn't hang out, and try to come up with an apology that would mean something.

I felt trapped. And that made me angry.

I shoved my tea mug back on the counter, and I gathered up my soggy umbrella. Melissa flashed me a "wait" look, but I only shrugged. What good would it do for me to wait? What could I really say, to justify myself? Why should I *have* to justify myself, when I had so many other things going on? And how the hell was Melissa worried about her long-term savings when she had so many customers that a friend couldn't get a word in edgewise?

When I got to the door, I turned back, but Melissa was smiling down at the indecisive little girl. The Devil's Nips glared at me from the refrigerated case, like baleful eyes witnessing my departure.

I stomped out onto the cobblestones, my feet slipping in the sodden remains of a pile of leaves. I cursed and forced myself to walk a little more gingerly. I had been right to leave. I needed a friend who had time to listen to *me*. Time to help. Not someone who sublimated her passive-aggressiveness into freaking baked goods.

I ducked into the lobby of the giant Barnes & Noble store on the corner. While my umbrella dripped onto my shoes, I reached deep in my purse, digging until I found my cell phone. I punched in Graeme's number, taking a perverse pleasure that I remembered the digits, that I didn't need to rely on the phone's memory. I didn't have any idea what time it was in London, but this was an emergency. I needed to hear his voice.

One ring. Two. Three. Four.

His answering machine. I swore under my breath and hung up. No reason to leave him a message. No reason to tell him I'd just had a fight with my best friend. A fight that she wasn't even fighting.

Before I flipped the phone closed, I got another idea. I scrolled back through recent calls I had placed. Sure enough, the number was still there, from when I had called to confirm our earlier meeting.

"Haylee?" I said when she answered on the second ring. "It's Jane. I know it's short notice, but I was wondering if you were free to join me for dinner tonight?"

Well, at least the rain had stopped falling.

Not that I could be certain, locked away in my basement, kept company by no one but my warder and my familiar. David had insisted that we extinguish the overhead lights for our all-day Saturday session—we needed to distance ourselves from the modern world and focus on ancient power. Blah, blah, blah.

We'd already burned through one set of six tapers, tall dripless candles that had been brand-new when we started. I had just replaced them in the matched silver candlesticks that were part of my collection of witchy books, magic wands and other artifacts. Part of the collection that would be forfeit to the Coven if I failed to set the centerstone.

Let's face it—I enjoyed a romantic candlelit dinner as much as the next girl, but this was a little ridiculous. There was nothing romantic about trying to read by candlelight. In fact, in the past several hours, I had gained a healthy respect for Abraham Lincoln. I wouldn't have lasted one week, doing school homework by firelight. Our former president suppos-edly made it through *years,* studying in his log cabin.

That was then. This was now. My fingers itched to turn on the Sylvania 60-watts above our head.

"You need to concentrate," David said.

"You've been saying that for hours," I groused. Neko winced and shifted a little farther away from me, as if he didn't want to be caught in the backlash of my warder's anger.

"You've needed to do it for hours." David sighed and pushed back from the table. "This isn't just some theoreti-cal study, you know. That jasper egg was real. That e-mail was a threat. You need to know how to defend yourself magically."

"I know," I said automatically. I wasn't going to tell him about the three other e-mail messages I'd received, all with similar pictures and messages. I knew that self-defense was important. I needed to learn how to protect myself from ghoulies and ghosties and long-legged beasties. And things that go bump in the night.

But really. How many consecutive hours could one girl spend studying?

My stomach rumbled, and I cringed with embarrass-ment. My lunchtime peanut butter and jelly sandwich seemed a long time ago. Even *if* I had eaten a huge dinner with Haylee the night before.

She had agreed to meet me for supper, and after a bit of back and forth, we'd decided to get together in the city. Between the rain and my nonconfrontation with Melissa, I was feeling deeply in need of comfort food, so we descended on Café La Ruche, a French bistro just off Georgetown's main street. I started with French onion soup and moved on to spicy lamb sausages, all served with fresh, crusty baguettes. There was no need to observe First Date Rules of dining decorum—it wasn't like I needed to worry about looking foolish as I struggled with strands of melted cheese from the soup. Or at least, I didn't worry very much.

Haylee and I weren't through talking when we finished our main courses, so we ordered dessert (chocolate mousse for her, a homemade apple dumpling for me, complete with caramel sauce and fresh whipped cream.) I actually found myself quite pleased with my ability to smother my sorrows in a blanket of fat.

I'd told Haylee about my spat with Melissa, and she'd confirmed that my bakery-obsessed friend was out of her mind. There was no need to expand a business that was so busy the owner couldn't find five minutes to converse with a friend.

Haylee had asked me about how things were going with Graeme. I told her that he was out of town, and that I was going a bit insane waiting for him to get back. She'd laughed knowingly. Sympathetically. No, *empathetically,* as if she knew how hard it was to wait for a loved one to return.

And there was something else.

Haylee taught me a new spell.

It had started as a joke. We'd wanted to linger at our table, long after ordinary customers would have paid their tabs and left. When the waiter came by to refill our mugs of tea for the fourth time, Haylee had touched his wrist with one of her long, perfectly manicured fingers, cupping her Torch with her other hand and muttering a few words under her breath. "We'll call you if we need you," she said.

I watched as he blinked, confused and unbalanced for just a moment. When he stepped back from our table, he stumbled, as if he'd been sleeping on his feet. Haylee repeated her touch and the hastily spoken spell when the hostess stopped by to see if we needed anything, and again when the manager drifted over to see why we were lingering for hours. Each person who approached us left with a dazed look and an inability to remember that we were sitting at the table.

Which wasn't a problem until we tried to pay our bill. I attempted to catch the waiter's eye, with no luck whatsoever. I waved to the hostess. I actually reached out to touch the manager's sleeve. At that last gesture, Haylee had laughed. "Don't worry," she'd said. "You can't reach them."

And we'd left—like high school kids skipping out on a meal of burgers and fries. I'd felt totally guilty but also strangely thrilled by the power. In fact, my fingers tingled when Haylee accidentally brushed against them, our hands meeting in mid-air after I tried to flag down the manager. "How long will they be like that?" I'd asked, before we parted ways by Haylee's Mini Cooper.

"Until I release the spell. I'll do it before I go to sleep tonight." I frowned, uncomfortable with the notion of shoplifting an evening's food and drink. Haylee's laugh was clear as the rain-freshened air. "Don't worry, silly. They'll be good as new in the morning."

I waved as she drove off, but then I sneaked back into the restaurant to leave some cash on our table. There'd been no need to sneak, though. No one noticed me at all, and our dishes were still sitting on the abandoned tabletop. I had sighed and told myself that someone would be able to notice the money in the morning.

"There," David said, jerking me back to the present. "You were doing it again."

Wasn't that exactly what Melissa had said the day before? "I was not." I sounded like a stubborn toddler, and I waited for David to dig in with a suitably immature "Was, too." Neko seemed to anticipate something equally sophisticated; his entire face tightened as if he'd received too many Botox injections.

Our brilliant banter was interrupted by a deep vibration, a thrum that shook the entire basement room. I glanced up nervously. "It must be raining again. Thunder."

Neko shook his head sharply, and I was reminded of a real cat's predatory concentration. He climbed to his feet and paced behind my chair, taking a couple of tight, controlled steps in each direction.

And then, I realized that the "thunder" had not stopped. The low growl continued, barely at the edge of my hearing. It sounded as if the entire house was humming, as if the stone foundation beneath the cottage was vibrating. The note was deep enough that I wasn't certain I could hear it with my ears, but my body had no doubt. I felt it in my bones.

And it was getting closer.

Or larger. Or louder. Or more ominous. Something.

I glanced at David, hoping he was ready to laugh off the vibrating threat. My warder, though, offered no hint of comfort.

Instead, he stood on the other side of the table. His feet were planted solidly on the ornate silk carpet; he looked as if he had coalesced from its swirling design. His hands hung loose at his sides, his fingers extended downward. I tried to tell myself that if we were in real danger, if something truly threatened us from the astral plane, he would clench his fingers into fists.

But then I realized that I'd never seen David make a fist. He channeled energy when he worked as a warder. He guided flows of power. He needed his hands relaxed, available to direct anything that came his way. Even when he had encountered the sword-wielding guard at the safehold, he had kept his body loose. Alert, but loose. Like he was now.

The noise—if it really was a noise—grew stronger. I could feel it now with my entire body, feel it the same way that my eyes saw, that my ears heard. It was oppressive and large, like a wave of power rolling over the house.

But it wasn't a wave. It didn't rise and fall back. It didn't ebb and flow.

It only grew stronger. Steadier. Pushing like a crowbar against a padlock hasp.

This was magic. Magic I had never seen before. Magic I could not measure, could not predict. I tried not to picture it as a wall of carved jasper, blood-red stone cut through with jagged black lines.

"Neko," I said, gesturing sharply. He quivered, but he obeyed, coming to stand by my left side. I settled my fingertips on his shoulder, leaning against him and immediately feeling the familiar augmentation as he bolstered my powers, as the lens of his inherent abilities mirrored my strength back on itself, focusing my magic desires, my goals.

I tried to distract the vibrating force, to change its direction, break its concentration. There wasn't anything to touch, but I raised my hands in front of me, splaying my fingers wide.

I could feel the pressure of the malevolent force, sense it with my body and my mind. I imagined my fingers pushing against it, forcing into a doughy solid. Not stone. Not jasper. Anything but jasper.

There was a familiarity about the energy, a vaguely discernible *recognition* that let me move into even closer contact. I melded with the wall of power more closely than I would have thought possible. It felt like a physical thing, an object I could push against, that I could move.

I glanced at Neko, making sure he was close enough for me to draw on. His almond eyes were huge in his face, and his cheeks were pale. He stared at me steadily, without blinking. It seemed that he had stopped breathing.

David, too, was completely still. Watchful. Ready. Waiting to see what I could do with my powers. Waiting for me to save us from whatever this strange attack might be.

I took three breaths to calm myself. I touched my forehead, to offer up the strength of my thoughts. I touched my throat, to offer up the power of my astral voice. I touched my heart, to offer up the devotion of my spirit. I took a deep breath, and I declaimed the words Haylee had whispered in the restaurant the night before:

Looking, thinking, sensing—be
Elsewhere, somewhere, someplace. Free
Your mind from what you see here,
Let your thoughts be empty, all clear.
Turn away.
Turn away.
Turn away.

There was a flash of darkness.

It was the same flare of power I'd experienced countless times in the past, but it seemed all the more dramatic for our surroundings. For just an instant, everything in the basement—the basement itself—disappeared. The six new-lit candles were sucked into darkness, even the orange after-glows of their wicks extinguished into nothingness.

There was darkness, but more than that. There was a complete and utter lack of sensation. My entire body ceased to be. I could not hear the sharp panting of my breath, feel the drumbeat of my heart. I could not smell the nervous perspiration that pricked beneath my arms, could not feel Neko's shoulder, could not see David's rigid warder body, interposed against the vibrating threat.

And then sensation flooded back, rushing in with a purity and a power that made me stagger. The candles guttered as if a tornado had passed overhead. My ears were filled with the sound of my own heart, galloping as if I'd just stumbled across the finish line of the Marine Corps Marathon. I tasted salt at the back of my throat, and I realized that I'd bitten my tongue.

The vibration was gone.

The oppressive force had dissipated, shattered into a million shards. I could sense their remnants, glimpse them from the edges of my witchy senses, like fog drifting away after sunrise. I struggled to gather up a handful, to study the ghostly remains, to figure out who had attacked us and why.

Before I could succeed, though, David stumbled and fell to his knees. He gripped his head with both hands and rocked back and forth. Even before I ran to his side, I could see he was trembling, shaking like a man caught in a fever.

"Oh my God," I said. "Neko! Turn on the lights!"

I blinked as the overhead bulbs burst on. David flinched and buried his face in his hands, moaning like the wind around an abandoned castle's towers. I gripped his wrists, held them tightly, willing strength and power and calm into my warder. Neko crouched beside us, glancing rapidly from my face to David's.

"David!" I said, desperately hoping he retained enough reason to answer me. "What should I do? How can I help you?"

"Wait. A. Minute." With a superhuman effort, he stiffened his fingers, raised them from his face. He let me move his hands into my lap, cradling them gently. His lips were gray; all the color had drained from his flesh, leaving terrifying, bruised-looking pools beneath his eyes. If I hadn't known better, I would have bet good money that he'd been ill for weeks, that he'd been recovering from the worst of the flu, bronchitis and pneumonia combined.

"Let's get you upstairs," I said matter-of-factly, needing to do something, anything, to set things to rights. "Neko, put his right arm around your shoulder."

I wouldn't have sounded so calm if I had realized what a task I proposed. One witch with no upper-body strength and a familiar who spent more time at a hair salon than at the gym were nearly outmatched by a fit, well-muscled warder. The diet books always said that muscle weighed more than fat, and David seemed determined to prove the rule.

I don't think we induced more than half a dozen bruises by knocking him against the stair railing on our way up. And his head was certainly already aching when Neko let it bang, hard, against the door frame. And he honestly wasn't any paler than he had been by the time we dropped him on the sofa, wrestled his shoes off, and manhandled his feet up onto the couch.

"Run downstairs and blow out the candles," I said to Neko. "I'm just going to get a damp towel from the kitchen."

By the time I returned with the towel in one hand and a glass of water in the other, David had pulled himself up into something resembling a sitting position. He winced as he leaned back against the sofa's arm, but I had to admit he looked better than he had in the awkward position Neko and I had managed. He took the glass of water and swallowed with painful-looking bobs of his throat, but he batted my hand away when I tried to wipe the towel across his face.

I could have persisted—I think I might have been able to do anything to his weakened body, even without bringing my powers into play. His lips, though, had begun to return to a remotely normal shade, and the green-blue shadow of veins had faded from his forehead. I decided that he was recovering, and I crouched back onto the edge of the coffee table.

"Thank you," I said, and my voice trembled as I thought of what might have happened downstairs. "Thank you for trying to fight that thing."

"What in the name of Hecate's own private hell did you do down there?"

Neko arrived at the top of the stairs just in time to hear the end of David's furious question. I wasn't surprised to see my familiar turn tail, pulling the basement door closed behind him.

Coward.

I tried to understand the venom in David's voice. I assumed he'd been frightened—if not as badly as I had been. I knew he was exhausted. I could only guess how much his body ached.

But anger? Outright, untamed rage?

"I was trying to save us?" I cursed inwardly when my answer came out sounding like a question.

"By using Dark Magic?"

"Dark—"

"What gives you the right to work a Will Breaking spell?"

"Will—"

"And how did you think I wouldn't notice, when it was directed against me?"

"Stop!" I said, as he pulled himself up straighter against the armrest. I could see he was only moving to expand his lungs, to get more volume so that he could continue his excoriation. "Just stop for one damned minute!" I said. Whether he heeded my demand, or was merely too weak to go on, I took full advantage of his silence. "Directed against *you?* I was fighting against that…that thing! That pressure! The jasper wall that was threatening all of us!"

And then I realized what was going on. I remembered David's stance as the thrumming power had approached. I remembered his legs spread wide, his back strong and straight. His hands hanging loosely at his sides, fingers extended. And I recalled the odd familiarity of the magic I'd opposed, the way I had seemed to know it, somehow, some way.

David had been working a spell.

He was a warder. He wasn't able to do much magic. But he had some at his disposal—he'd told me as much the first time we'd sat down to dinner to discuss the wonderful world of witchcraft. He could use magic to protect his ward, to protect *me.*

Usually, it was minor stuff—reading the auras of people around us, making sure they weren't plotting any unseemly attacks. He could light candles and extinguish them. I'd been the recipient of his headache-banishing spell several times, when I'd pushed my own powers beyond their natural scope.

But the thing that had threatened in the basement? That was an entirely new range of activities. That was completely beyond anything I'd seen from David before.

Without thinking, I threw the damp towel at him, hitting him square in the middle of his chest. He reacted slowly, and was left grasping for the cotton cloth as it slid onto the cushion of the couch. "You bastard!" I said. "*You* were the power! You were pretending to threaten me!"

"I had to do something." His words were nearly as heated as my own. "You weren't bothering to practice."

"I've had enough practice!"

"I decide when you've had enough practice. I'm the warder."

"And I'm the witch!" I sprang to my feet, began pacing between the coffee table and the front door. Dammit! He had really frightened me. He had really made me believe that something malevolent was after us, that something truly evil was converging on my cottage.

"Now that we've established our roles," he said, ignoring the furious glare I shot his way, "maybe you'll deign to tell me where you learned a spell that has been banned for public use?"

Haylee.

Haylee had taught me the illegal spell by working it on the unsuspecting staff at Café La Ruche. She hadn't *intended* to teach me: I had just observed. Apparently, I'd paid close enough attention to master the magic on my own.

Or *had* I mastered it?

Haylee's spell had certainly not had the same effect as mine. Everyone at the bistro had gone about their business physically unharmed, waiting on other tables, collecting other patrons' money. No one had been hurtled to the floor; no one had been left bruised and breathless.

"Who?" David said again, and I could measure his recovery by the amount of raw rage behind the word.

It wasn't Haylee's fault that my working was too powerful. It wasn't her responsibility that I threw my powers around. I couldn't give her up, when I was the one who had done something wrong. "It doesn't matter who," I said. And then, even though I knew it was dangerous to do so, I had to go on. "You shouldn't be angry. You should be proud of me."

"*Proud* of you?" I flinched at the volume of his roar, even as a tiny corner of my mind was relieved by his rapid recovery. Surely Neko could hear downstairs. My familiar would *have* to interrupt, if a life-and-death battle erupted up here. He would *need* to come to my rescue. Wouldn't he?

"Proud of me," I repeated, with a bit less confidence. In for a penny, in for a pound, I told myself. "We were working on self-defense, right? Well, I protected myself. I used my magic to keep myself safe. That's what you want, isn't it?"

"I *want* you to be able to go about in the world of witch-craft. I want you to be able to practice freely. Do you have any idea what would have happened, if I had not contained your brilliant little working? Do you have the faintest notion how quickly Hecate's Council would have swarmed here?"

The last smidgen of certainty drained from my mind. "H-Hecate's Council?"

David sighed. "Jane, there was enough power behind your spell to feel it from New York to Georgia."

"Georgia?" I couldn't think of anything else to say. Me? I had summoned that much force? With one little spell that I'd never even tried to cast before?

David struggled up to a full sitting position, and I winced with him as he rubbed the back of his neck. "You should know this by now," he said. "The Council monitors Dark Magic. There's a whole group of witches who watch specifically for breaks in expected power. Your little show would have been off the scale."

"And so you stopped it?"

"I absorbed it. As best I could. I broke it up, anyway. If anyone was already looking here, already focused on your house, they'd be able to see that something happened. But I was able to keep the energy from flowing out as one massive block. There will be ripples left around for days, though. I can't do anything about that."

"I'm sorry," I said, even though my words were inadequate. And I was. I truly was. If my spell had been as strong as David said—and I had no reason not to believe him—then he had been my lifesaver, keeping me safe from Council justice. I collapsed onto the other couch. "I thought that I was protecting us. Stopping that thing, whatever it was."

"You certainly did stop it." He managed a ghost of a smile. For the first time since coming upstairs, I took a deep breath. Everything was going to be all right. We *were* safe.

But that just made me return to my original question. "What was it? What did you summon?"

His skin returned to its normal tone, and I realized that he must be blushing. David Montrose. My warder. Blushing.

"What?" I pushed.

"It was nothing."

"I felt it. Don't tell *me* it was nothing."

"It was just…you."

"Me?"

"You." He started to shake his head, but winced before he truly got the motion going. "It was your stubbornness. Your refusal to work. Your rebellion. I gathered the energy and pushed it back at you."

My stomach dropped. "All of that was coming from me?"

Instead of answering, he closed his eyes and eased his head to the back of the couch. "I shouldn't have done it. I just wanted you to feel a touch of danger. A hint of what could be arrayed against you. Placing the centerstone isn't a game, Jane. It's the most serious working of magic. You're going to build a safe haven for witches, a protected place for generations of practitioners to come. You'll be vulnerable at that working. You can't take it lightly. And you'll have to be prepared for the worst."

I fought against the chilly finger of fear that traced my spine. I spluttered for something to say. "So, you think that *I* am the worst."

He smiled, even though he didn't lift his head. "I think that you are your own worst enemy. For now." Before I could muster a response, he did sit up, and he looked straight at me. "Jane. This is important. Who taught you the Will Breaking Spell?"

"No."

My fingers jangled, like limbs awakening from a sound sleep. I couldn't tell him. There must be some mistake. Something that *I* had done wrong. Haylee had never intended to teach me the spell. I must have twisted her working when I attempted to reproduce it on my own. After all, Teresa Alison Sidney certainly wouldn't let Haylee run around working Dark Magic. The strongest Coven Mother in recent history wasn't going to let her best friend violate the laws of Hecate's Council.

David's voice was persuasive. "Jane, if I'm going to keep you safe, I need to know."

For just a moment, I was thrown back in time. I was sixteen

years old and sitting on Gran's couch. I was explaining that she needed to give me the car keys, needed to trust me with her Lincoln so that Melissa and I could drive to a friend's party. I'd pulled out the big guns. "Gran," I had said. "You taught me everything I know. Now you have to trust me."

It had worked well enough then—Melissa and I went to the party, and I had drunk nothing stronger than water, afraid that even caffeine would rattle my nerves for the drive home.

Now, I looked David straight in the eye. "David," I said. "You taught me everything I know. Now you have to trust me."

It was a great line.

"Fine," he said at last. "I trust you. But don't do anything stupid, Jane."

"Stupid!" I managed to sound scandalized at the notion.

"Stupid," he repeated, and then he waved toward the table. "Could you get me another glass of water? And open up the basement door. Tell Neko it's safe to come out."

I did just that. And as I filled David's glass at the kitchen sink, I wondered what I was going to say to Haylee when I saw her again. And how long it would be before David left, so that I could call Graeme. Just to talk. Just to share the craziness of my witchy day. Like any friends did. Any good friends. I pasted a smile on my face and counted the days till Wednesday.

19

"Well, well, well," Gran said. "It's hard to believe that another month has gone by."

Clara joined in with, "And it's so nice that the city has finally cooled off."

Great. We were reduced to chatting about the weather. The weather and the calendar. Were those any conversational topics for grandmother, mother and daughter? For three generations of witches?

But that was the problem. We couldn't talk about witchcraft. Couldn't talk about the single most important thing in *my* life. Ever since Gran had asked me to abandon the Coven and I had refused, I had felt unable to mention anything to do with magic. Yet, as autumn gained its true grip on our shortening days, I felt I had fewer and fewer topics to share. Setting the centerstone always lurked at the back of my mind.

I certainly wasn't about to mention the telephone conversation I'd had with Graeme the night before, after David had finally left. After Neko had gone off with Jacques, intent on making the Gallant Gaul stop sulking about an entire day lost to witchy business.

I took a quick sip of my water, trying to keep a blush from stealing across my face. After all, it wasn't every evening that I threw myself across my couch, whispering into a portable telephone. It wasn't every evening that I could have written a letter to a porno Web site. "Dear Hotmamas.com: I never thought that I'd be the sort of girl to seduce a man over the telephone…" It wasn't every evening that I pleaded—begged—a man to catch a transoceanic flight and come up and see me some time.

Graeme had laughed—no, *chortled*—and told me that he couldn't break away. He was in the middle of a business deal. I could hear him typing away on a computer keyboard, hear the chime of incoming e-mail. When I'd complained that it was the middle of the night in London, that no sane man would be working, he had told me that just proved he was insane.

So, he wouldn't hop an earlier flight. But that hadn't stopped us from talking. And after a while, I didn't *want* him to appear on my doorstep. I would have been too embarrassed about some of the things I'd said.

No, I wasn't going to be repeating any of *that* conversation to the Smythe-Madison women. That really wasn't what our monthly bonding brunch was all about.

Before I could think of suitably neutral tinder to toss on our dying conversational embers, the waitress brought our meals. Luna Grill was known for its build-your-own omelet brunch—I'd been reminded of the restaurant when Melissa recounted her disastrous date with the Dedicated. Looking at our current plates, I couldn't imagine a clearer depiction of our personalities.

Gran had ordered the heart attack special: a three-egg omelet with ham, bacon, and sausage folded in, along with cheddar cheese. She had shrugged when she ordered, accepting my gaping disbelief with a gentle smile. "If cholesterol hasn't done me in yet, it's not going to get me now." I accepted her reasoning, especially since I knew she wouldn't eat more than a quarter of the thing before declaring herself full.

Clara was going through a vegetarian phase. It had to do with discovering the true balance of her Pisces nature, with recognizing complete respect for all living things. In fact, she had initially declared herself a vegan, but since she had no idea how to cook tofu, tempeh or beans (without the addition of a good piece of salty ham), she had retreated to a broader definition of spiritually healthful eating. Egg-white omelet for her, then, with spinach, mushrooms and sautéed bell peppers. I wanted to ask her if she could hear the vegetables weeping for their lost siblings, but I thought that might only increase the friction between us.

I had been looking forward to a good egg dish when I got to the restaurant, but my relatives had put me off my game. I'd decided to abandon omelets altogether and stick with my ongoing theme of comfort food. Therefore, I was feasting on French toast, with a gallon of maple syrup dumped on top and enough whipped cream to make butter superfluous. I had added a side of fresh fruit. After all, breakfast was the most important meal of the day.

Okay. So we'd finished with the calendar. With the weather. I couldn't talk about the Coven, and I wouldn't mention Graeme. What did that leave?

"Things have been busy at work," I said, promptly filling my mouth with a giant bite of maple-soaked bread to avoid any immediate need to reply to their inevitable questions.

"I wanted to stop by for your Monday lecture, but I got busy with opera things," Gran said. "Did I see that you were discussing mothers and daughters in colonial times?"

"Where did you see that?" I asked, surprised, and a little impressed that Gran stayed in the Peabridge intellectual loop.

"On the library's Web site, of course," Gran said, taking another dainty bite of her Lumberjack Special.

I almost choked on a strawberry. Gran? On the Internet?

"Don't look so surprised," she said. "You did set up my computer for me."

"I thought you just used it for e-mail."

"For e-mail. But when I get bored, I skate the Internet."

"Surf," I said.

"Surf. That's right." Gran nodded happily. "Have you ever heard of Wikipedia?"

"Um, yes," I said. Of course I'd heard of the online en-cyclopedia. I used it for quick reference checks all the time, even if I was wary about the legitimacy of some of the entries. Anyone could register to participate in the service, creating and editing information that everyone could search online for free.

"Your Uncle George showed me Wikipedia. I'm working on correcting some of the opera entries. Do you know that someone actually wrote that *Tosca* has *four* acts?"

Clara answered before I could. "Scandalous," she said. Her eyes met mine over her coffee cup, and I think we were both trying to keep from laughing. Sarah Smythe, Wikipedia editor. My grandmother never ceased to amaze me.

Gran didn't take the bait. Instead, she said to me, "I've been trying to get your mother involved. There are hundreds of entries about astrology. Someone should be paying attention to them, making sure they're accurate."

"And I'm just the person for the job," Clara said, clearly quoting Gran's recruitment speech as she pushed food around on her plate.

I asked, "Is there something wrong with your omelet?" If the kitchen had messed up, I wanted them to correct things—I felt responsible for the meal because it was my turn to pay.

"Oh, no." Clara sighed and speared a wilted leaf of spinach. "It's just that I don't really like vegetables in my eggs. Eggs cry out for cheese. And maybe a bit of ham."

She looked forlornly at Gran's omelet, and Gran obliged by pushing her plate across the table. "Help yourself, dear. I can't eat another bite."

I smiled. I'd known that Gran wouldn't get close to finishing her entire meal. Clara speared meat from Gran's plate and augmented her own breakfast, while Gran and I refrained from commenting on the shocking collapse of Piscean vegetarianism in our midst. In fact, I helped myself to a bite of the meaty omelet, mentally justifying that I had to balance my sweet breakfast plate with Gran's savory one.

Gran, undeterred from her earlier topic of conversation, said, "Clara, you *are* the person for the job. I can't imagine anyone with more knowledge than you about the signs of the Zodiac."

I sank back onto my wooden bench and glanced up at the mural of a sun painted on the opposite wall of the restaurant. He was smiling, and I couldn't help but think he approved of our conversation. All was right in this little world. Gran was meddling quietly in our lives, expressing her absolute certainty that Clara and I could both conquer whatever we had in front of us. And, if history was any guide, it was just about time for the spotlight to turn on me.

"And you, Jane," Gran said with perfect timing. "You should take a look at their article about coffee. I'm certain that you could add something, given your experience at the library."

Great. I wasn't seen as an expert on colonial history. Or even on clothing in eighteenth-century America. Nope. I was about to be crowned the best latte maker in Georgetown.

And I wasn't even that. Melissa could pour rings around me any day.

I wasn't going to go there. I wasn't going to mention Melissa, to let Gran and Clara sort through our little friendship wrinkle.

As if she were reading my mind, Clara chimed in. "You could ask Melissa, if you had any questions."

So much for that plan. I made my voice firm. "I have no intention of editing the coffee article. I drink tea." I took the opportunity to catch our waitress's eye, to solicit a new pot of hot water.

Clara dug in. "I'm just saying that between the two of

you, you have a lot of information. You and Melissa could work very well together."

"If we were speaking to each other."

Oh. I guess I really *did* want to talk about Melissa. Why did my conversations with Gran and Clara always steer toward whatever one thing I was absolutely, positively certain I didn't want to talk about?

Gran pounced. "You had a fight with Melissa?"

"Not so much a fight. Just a…gap."

"A gap?" Clara looked at me as if I was speaking a foreign language.

"We've both been busy," I said, after stabbing another bite of Gran's omelet, buying time for a reply. "She thinks that I'm too tied into…other things." No reason to drag Graeme into the fray. Clara would want to work up his star chart, and Gran would have us married off in a matter of hours.

"And you think?" Gran prompted.

"I think that if she has a problem, she should talk to me directly." I excavated another sliver of ham. "She avoids me, and then she tries to make me feel guilty. I think we just need some time apart from each other."

"It sounds to me," Clara said, fishing for the last piece of sausage on Gran's plate, "as if you need to spend more time *together.*"

"Ha," I said, without a trace of humor. "I don't think that's going to happen any time soon." I was determined to get the conversation away from my so-called best friend. "Anyway, no matter how you slice it, I'm not an expert on coffee. If I have one more fight with the stupid coffee grinder at work, I might walk out of the library altogether."

Gran clicked her tongue. "That doesn't sound like you, Jane. You love the Peabridge."

"But I hate what it's become. Or what I've become, working there. We're a victim of our own success. Evelyn's little coffee bar is so popular that I spend more time making fancy coffee drinks than I do researching colonial history."

"Maybe you need to get rid of the coffee drinks."

"Like Evelyn would ever go for that." Everything was so simple in Gran's world. She could just dust her hands and be free of any little problem, like coffee grounds, or steamed milk, or chocolate syrup, or whipped cream.

Clara chimed in, and I could tell she was trying to be reasonable, trying to act as peacemaker—a novel role for her. "Why did Evelyn put in the coffee bar in the first place?"

I decided to play along. "So that we could add money to the operations budget. It's amazing how much we make by offering overpriced caffeine. Starbucks has already done our job for us—they have everyone conditioned to spend four dollars on a cup of coffee. If we charge five, and offer the convenience of drinking it in the library, they're only too eager to pony up."

Gran nodded. "But what if you simplified things? Cut back to regular drip coffee? That would make things easier for you, wouldn't it?"

"Our profits would plummet. Even if we charged three dollars a cup, there just aren't enough takers to meet Evelyn's bottom line."

"But drip coffee and a sweet? A cookie or a brownie or something like that?"

It actually wasn't a bad idea. We'd even had a couple of patrons ask about scones or muffins to go with their ill-gotten coffee gains. And if I only needed to slam a brownie on a plate after I poured regular old coffee… "Where am I going to find the time to bake?" I argued.

Gran smiled. "It takes less than half an hour to make an entire tray of brownies. You know that. We made enough for school activities while you were growing up."

I glanced at Clara to see if the reference to my mother-deprived childhood rattled her. She was intent, though, on sneaking a strip of bacon from the ruins of Gran's omelet. Oblivious, Gran went on, "If you don't have time, I'm sure that Melissa can help you out."

"Melissa is the one who doesn't have the time," I said flatly.

"Well, I'm sure that you could manage without too much difficulty," Gran said.

A line of Shakespeare came to me, from the scrambled depth of my literary mind: *Thou art a mocker of my labour.* It was from *As You Like It,* said by Orlando. I didn't bother saying the words out loud—neither Gran nor Clara would have recognized it.

But maybe they weren't mocking. Maybe I *should* consider a little baking at home. The more I toyed with the idea, the more it made sense. If we could get five dollars for a cup of coffee, what would people pay for an ordinary brownie? A couple of chocolate chip cookies? I didn't have to produce anything as complicated as Cake Walk did.

Sure, we might lose a buck or two by dropping the ex-pensive lattes and cappuccinos, but we'd still make a relative fortune on drip coffee. And we'd make up the difference—and more—on baked goods, even after we paid for the ingredients.

If I were freed from the tyranny of foaming milk, I could return to my true love—working as a reference librarian. It was worth half an hour spent baking each night, if that meant I could work as a librarian during the day. I sat back on the bench, enamored with the notion of trading in my coffee bar apron.

Sure, there would be complications. Mr. Potter would have to give up his mocha—although I bet I could convince him to accept a shot of chocolate in a regular cup of coffee. And he really *should* be cutting back a bit on whipped cream.

And we'd have to limit the children's access to sugar. One cookie apiece, and only after the American Family sessions were over, with the little darlings back in their mothers' tender loving care.

I stared directly at Gran. "I know what you're doing."

"What do you mean?" If the Academy of Arts and Sciences had been meeting in Luna Grill right then, the award for Best Actress would have been snagged for the year.

"Gran, you're trying to make me forget about fighting with Melissa!"

"Make you? I can't make you do anything! Clara, do you think that I could make Jane do anything that she didn't already want to do?"

I saw the look of fake innocence that my grandmother cast toward her daughter, and I couldn't help but laugh. "Okay," I said. "I'll think about it. Brownies and cookies aren't a bad idea. Maybe we could start in November."

"November first," Gran said, as if we'd reached a firm

agreement. "Nothing like the start of a new month for a new venture."

The waitress came by to take our plates. I had left two slices of French toast. Clara had abandoned the vegetarian dregs of her omelet. But Gran's plate was completely clean, thanks to all of our help. The waitress gave my grandmother a new look of respect. "Can I get you ladies anything else? Dessert, maybe?"

Before anyone could decline, I said, "We'll see a menu, please." After all, brunch without dessert was…breakfast.

We ended up ordering one slice of apple pie and another of cherry. At the last minute, Gran broke down and ordered the special of the day, turtle cheesecake. The waitress shook her head in obvious amazement as she wandered back toward the kitchen.

Only after we were safely ensconced with enough calories to support an entire football team did I see another meaningful glance pass between Clara and my grandmother. Gran inclined her head once, silently issuing an invitation for Clara to speak.

When only silence followed, I said, "What?"

"What what?" Clara countered.

"What are you supposed to ask me? What are you afraid I'll get upset about?"

"I don't know—" she began, raising her hand to the kunzite crystal she had started wearing around her neck months ago. Kunzite. Unconditional love. Family harmony.

At least she was trying.

Gran cut in. "We wanted to ask you about the Coven. We wanted to ask you if you're continuing to see those women."

*Those women.* Gran made it sound like they were prostitutes. Or child-murderers. Or worse. (What was worse? I'm sure that suburban witches headed up some sort of nefarious list.)

I took a deep breath and held it for a count of five before daring to answer. "I have to, Gran. Clara. I'm one of them. And I'm setting the centerstone on Samhain."

"Samhain?" Gran asked.

"Halloween," Clara answered before I could. All her years with the New Age folks had served her well. She shook her head at me. "It's just that the Coven causes so many ripples in the ether."

Ripples in the ether? This was a new one, even for Clara. I tested my response in the silence of my own mind, measuring it twice before I dared to speak it aloud. "Ether? I'm not sure that I can sense the ether."

Nope. I didn't quite get the tone right. Clara's shoulders stiffened, and her lips pulled into a tight little frown. Gran leaped into the breach. "The ether doesn't matter, dear. We were just wondering if you're working with them. If they're being nice to you."

Ah…they wanted to know if my playdates were working out well. If anyone had pulled my hair, or told me I was fat, or twisted my name into a taunting playground chant. "Actually," I said, "I had a great dinner with one of them just the other night."

And we left without paying the bill, I didn't say. And she inadvertently taught me a Dark Magic spell that nearly knocked out my warder and made my familiar quiver in the basement with terror.

I rushed past those details. "I think that we're actually

becoming friends. We went to the National Gallery of Art a few weeks ago. Looked at the Renaissance paintings. I don't think that I've done that since I was in high school."

"That sounds lovely, dear," Gran said. I saw the look that she flashed Clara, the silent command to accept what I was saying, to support me.

Clara swallowed hard and asked, "What's her name? Your friend?"

"Haylee. Haylee James."

"Isn't she the one with the short hair?" Clara jumped on the recollection immediately. "The snooty one who's best friends with Teresa Alison Sidney?"

I stared at the jovial sun mural on the opposite wall and took another five-count. A slow one. "That would be her. She's actually been quite nice to me. The nicest of the bunch."

That's not saying much.

Okay, neither Gran nor Clara said the words out loud, but I could read their faces—printed in size forty-eight bold Times New Roman.

"Hey," I said, anxious to change the topic of conversation. This brunch had gone too well to be sacrificed to the Coven and its politics. "Did you know that in the Renaissance, the peacock was a symbol of saintly purity, because people thought the birds' flesh didn't rot?"

Clara took the conversational bait. "In Eastern art, peacocks counteract venom. The birds ate snakes, so they were thought to protect people from poison."

I actually beamed at her. She had given us a clear path out of the Coven discussion. "I've been learning a lot about antidotes lately," I said. "It's amazing the powers that people ascribe to different herbs. We might plant the Peabridge gardens differently next spring, to reflect some of the colonial beliefs that I've uncovered."

And that was it. We made it through the last of brunch without another uncomfortable silence. Neither Gran nor Clara asked anything else about Haylee, or Teresa Alison Sidney, or David, or Neko, or anything else witch-related.

When the waitress brought our bill, I slapped down my credit card. It was good to be able to treat when it was my turn, good to continue this newfound family tradition.

After the meal, I walked my grandmother and Clara to Gran's massive Lincoln. Clara opened up the driver's door, while I walked Gran around to the passenger seat. I put my fingers on the handle, but she stopped me by settling her palm against my cheek.

"Call Melissa, darling."

I glanced away. "I will."

"Good friends are hard to come by. We can't afford to let any of them slip away."

Unexpectedly, tears rose in the back of my throat. What was up with that? After a great morning, a fine breakfast and some good conversation, I was surprised to find myself on such an emotional edge. "I won't," I whispered.

Gran stretched up and kissed me on the cheek. "Promise me, Jane. Promise that you'll call her."

Another Gran promise. Well, she hadn't specified *when* I needed to call Melissa.

"I promise," I said.

I just wasn't ready yet. Besides, I wasn't even sure Melissa would have time to talk to me. Not with Cake Walk as busy as it was. The queasiness in the pit of my stomach had to be a reaction to French toast and omelets and dessert and cups and cups of tea. What else could make me feel so miserable as I walked away from the best-looking car on the road?

20

I glanced around the cottage one last time before answering the knock at the front door. It wouldn't do to keep Haylee waiting. Not when I had barely summoned the courage to invite her into my home. Not when I was hoping she would distract me from staring at the telephone, waiting for it to ring, waiting for Graeme to announce that he was home from his business trip. Not when I had spent an hour and a half straightening, neatening, getting everything in order.

If Melissa had been coming over, I wouldn't have cared. She'd seen me at my worst—dust bunnies under the bed, mascara streaks under my eyes, broken heart under fake smiles. But I hadn't spoken to Melissa since she'd brushed me off in the bakery. My promise to Gran niggled at the back of my mind, of course. I would keep it—eventually. When I had time.

"Haylee!" I said, throwing open the front door.

"Oh my," she said, stepping into my living room. "Isn't this *quaint*."

Quaint. Not a great word. She probably thought the place was tiny. Bizarre. Inconvenient. But as I looked around, I thought it looked like home. "I'm so glad you could come by," I said. "It's amazing how some evenings stretch out, with nothing to do."

"I'm glad you phoned," she said, with a confident smile that helped me forget that she probably had dozens of names on her dance card. After all, she was an accomplished witch and the best friend of Teresa Alison Sidney. Why *wouldn't* she have a million plans for a crisp autumn evening?

I made myself grin and say, "I was just going to mix some drinks. Come into the kitchen?"

"Can I help?"

"No!" This was ridiculous. I was as jumpy as if this was a date. I forced myself to take a calming breath. "I've got everything I need. Please. Just make yourself comfortable. Tell me what you did today."

Haylee obliged, sitting on one of my ladder-back chairs. She'd gone shopping that morning, she said, trying to find a little black dress for an evening wedding next month. She was looking for something velvet, something wintry, but something that would still be comfortable in an overheated ballroom.

I made polite listening noises as I went about my hostessing business. I found the fish-chased pitcher on the first try and almost yelped with success. What a great sign! Neko sometimes hid it, and I was reluctant to summon him upstairs, to beg for his help in any aspect of entertaining.

I reached underneath the sink, prowling through my stash of alcohol. There, toward the back, was my fifth of rum. About half a bottle was left. There was a two-liter bottle of soda water as well. Perfect. I looked calm, cool and collected. Organized. Prepared. Mojitos R Us, twinge of Melissa-guilt be damned.

And then, I opened the refrigerator.

I reached for the bowl of limes that I had left on the top shelf, but it was empty. No problem. I must have put them in one of the crisper drawers. I tugged open the fruit drawer and was greeted by one sickly lemon and some desiccated husks that might have been grapes in a former life.

Before I could question my sanity, I saw a single Corona beer, nesting in a cardboard six-pack container. Corona. Mexican beer. Most frequently served with a sturdy slice of lime. I grated my teeth and told myself that Neko would pay for his unsanctioned little Cinquo de Octubre celebration. Especially since it was already October 11.

Fine. We would have mojitos made with lemon instead of lime. A new drink. For my new friend. I reached to the back of the refrigerator, for the tall glass of water that was holding my mint and keeping it fresh.

No glass. No mint.

I had the presence of mind to wait until Haylee reached a breaking point in her story—she had found the dress she wanted, but she couldn't find the proper heels. Everything was four inches high and slutty; she was looking for two inches and seductive. I smiled and laughed and agreed that fashion designers hated women.

Then, I politely excused myself and marched to the basement stairs. I flipped the light switch on and off twice, an agreed signal that told Neko to get his paws off Jacques and prepare for me to descend the steps.

And when I reached the foot of the stairs, it was immediately clear what had happened to my mint. "What are you two doing?" I cried.

Their faces were covered with a bright green paste. They looked like creatures from the Scope lagoon—their hair was slicked back and their eyes peered out from identical pale white circles.

Jacques barely moved his lips as he answered me. "Mees Jane! We should have saved some of thee mask for you!"

Neko nodded in cautious agreement, tilting his head back to preserve his cosmetic application. "Jacques said that these mint facials would do wonders for our pores. I can feel everything tightening up!"

I wanted to tighten *him* up. Instead, I looked over at the book stand, at a precariously balanced cutting board strewn with denuded stems of mint, and a bowl rimmed with a hardening paste. At least they'd shifted my crystals handbook to one side, closing the cover to protect the valuable parchment pages from mint facials.

No time to argue. No time to rant. Haylee was waiting upstairs. "Did you save me anything at all?"

"I think there's still a beer left in the fridge," Neko said helpfully. "Beer is good at relaxing people. You look like you could use a good relaxation regimen."

I stalked upstairs before I could waste my time telling him what I thought of his "relaxation regimen."

I forced a smile at Haylee when I came back into the kitchen. "Sorry. I thought I had more mint downstairs."

"Oh! There's a basement in this place?"

"It's fully finished. That's where Hannah Osgood's books are. Neko stays down there, too."

She looked doubtful. "And Neko keeps a supply of mint?"

"No," I said ruefully. "Not tonight." I turned back to the counter. All right. I'd already decided to make a new drink for us—it was just going to be a little newer than I'd planned. Lemon. Rum. Soda. How bad could it be?

That bad.

Haylee smiled politely after she took her first sip. But then she set her glass down on the table. Firmly.

I tried mine, to figure out what was wrong.

Nothing—if you liked watery, fizzy rum. My single desiccated lemon had added no measurable flavor. I'd tried to compensate by pouring the rum with a heavy hand, and I'd dumped in a generous amount of sugar, but the result was a cloying mess.

"Well," I said. "At least we have something to eat." I extricated a plate of vegetables from the fridge, pleased that I had outsmarted my familiar by choosing something healthy. "We might as well go into the living room. Make ourselves comfortable."

And so we did. But I couldn't really *get* comfortable. I was nervous, afraid that I wouldn't seem witty enough, engaging enough, plain and simple *fun* enough for Haylee to bother wasting an evening in my company.

All of a sudden, I remembered Melissa's dating strategy, the Five Conversational Topics she cultivated before each blind encounter. I should have come up with a similar list for Haylee, fallback for conversational lulls like the one we were weathering.

Maybe those Lemon Monstrosities weren't so bad, I was beginning to think. At least they'd provide a little social lubrication. And then, the basement door opened.

*"Bueno sera, muchachas!"*

"What the—" I couldn't keep from exclaiming. The creatures that sashayed into the living room had some vague resemblance to Mexican peasants—they had huge sombreros and brightly colored blankets thrown over their shoulders. But they would only be cast as Mexican peasants in a gay porn film. One that put a premium on black silk shirts open to display waxed chests. And tight leather pants. And perfectly hydrated skin, with expertly relaxed pores. "Um, hello?" I managed to squeak.

*"Mi burro es muy perezoso,"* Neko enunciated carefully in a schoolboy Spanish accent.

*"Mi burro es su burro,"* Jacques confirmed.

"And where the hell are you going?" I asked, not at all certain that I wanted to know the answer.

"Julio is throwing a party," Neko said. "We're late. We missed the first three days."

"Days?" I asked, trying to rein in my shock.

"He's celebrating Juan Perón's birthday." When I just gaped, he continued, "Juan Perón? The little Mexican man who sells coffee? Think, Jane! Why else would we be drinking Mexican beer? And wearing sombreros? And serapes?" He trilled the *r* in the last word.

I somehow managed to form an answer. "Juan *Valdez*

sells coffee. And he's from Colombia. Juan Perón was from Argentina."

"Argentina?" Neko sounded scandalized.

I glanced at Haylee to see how she was handling this. She looked shocked, but I couldn't tell if she was overwhelmed by Neko's geographic ignorance, or if she was overcome by his sartorial splendor. I grimaced and said, "Juan was married to Eva." Blank stare from Neko, and a baffled shake of the head from Jacques. "Little Eva?" I prompted. "Evita?" And I braced myself for the inevitable connection.

"Don't cry for me, Argentina!" Neko belted out, with such enthusiasm that his sombrero tumbled to the floor.

"Argentina." I nodded.

"Do zey drink Corona een Argenteena?" Jacques asked.

"I suspect they will tonight." I shrugged. Nothing I said was going to change their costume. And at the tail end of a three-day birthday blast for a dead South American demagogue, who would care what country they represented? "Be careful, you two. Don't stay out too late."

"We weell go back to my apartment after zee party," Jacques said. "Julio leeves right upstairs."

Who was I to argue? I certainly didn't relish the thought of my noisy, inebriated familiar stumbling around the house at three in the morning. "Fine," I said, but then I tossed a last warning glance toward Neko. "Don't forget, though. David wants to work tomorrow afternoon. I'm leaving work a couple of hours early."

Neko tilted his sombrero to a more flattering angle. "Afternoon," he said. *"Noche."*

"No. *Tarde.* Afternoon. Don't keep us waiting."

Neko frowned for a moment, but then he seemed to remember his battle against unsightly facial lines. He swooped over to me and air-kissed both cheeks before he and Jacques tumbled out the front door.

As silence drifted back over the living room, I winced and turned to Haylee. She was staring at the door with a look that could only be horror. "That was your familiar, wasn't it?"

"Yes." I couldn't quite meet her eyes.

"And he goes about on his own?"

"I awakened him on a night of the full moon. I, um, didn't know any better at the time."

Her eyes narrowed for just a split second. "And that man with him?"

"Oh, that's Jacques. He's not magical. Just a friend."

"A…friend." She shook her head. I somehow suspected that Haylee's familiar lived a different life from Neko's. A very different life. Although he might not realize it, Neko had a highly vested interest in my succeeding with the centerstone.

"More carrots?" I asked brightly, desperate to change the topic.

Haylee shook her head again. "No. No more carrots." She finally pulled her gaze away from the front door. I hoped that she could forget the image of our twin Argentine-Colombian-Mexican peasants, debauching their way through the streets of Georgetown.

"Hey," she said at last. And her voice was the one that I remembered from Café La Ruche. Inviting. Gossipy. Friendly. "Tell me more about that guy you mentioned. What's his name? Graeme?"

I felt that giddy crush-rush, the breathless swell of excitement that came from talking about the cute boy in study hall, the handsome captain of the football team, the dream date for prom. "What about him?"

"Why do you like him so much? What makes him different from every other bad-date single guy in town?"

"I can't describe it." I shrugged and tried anyway. "When I'm with him, I have this feeling that he's paying attention to me. Like I'm as important to him as he is to me. Like he thinks about me, even when we're not together."

"Great," Haylee said, scrunching her pretty face into a comic nightmare. "So he's totally obsessed with you. Sounds like stalker-time to me."

I thought of my magic flowing across the Potomac, washing over Graeme and me after we had watched *Romeo and Juliet*. I remembered the safety I felt when I was with him, the enveloping calmness as he placed his arms around me. I felt the spark he raised, deep inside me, with the brush of a kiss on my lips, with the fire of his palm against the small of my back.

"This is different," I protested. "*More*. Not creepy. Besides, I haven't even seen him in a couple of weeks. He's been out of the country on business."

"When does he get back?"

Busted. "This afternoon, actually. At least he was supposed to."

"Then he hasn't called yet?"

"No. But I'm sure he's exhausted, with travel and everything."

Haylee nodded, and I thought she was going to let the topic drop. Then she asked, "Have you even seen his house?"

I was immediately defensive. "No."

"His office? Anything about his private life?"

She had no way of knowing she was touching one of my hottest buttons. The I.B. had kept his private life secret from me. Every aspect of it. Including his wife. I raised my chin defiantly and said, "He's told me *a lot* about his private life. Haylee, he says that women in his family were witches. He's not afraid of me. Not afraid of my powers. He *honors* me for my witchcraft."

"Honors you?" Her smile was sly, and the knowing look on her face made me blush. Before I could retort, she said, "Let's go."

"Where?"

"To Graeme's house."

"I don't even know where he lives!" I shrieked, forgetting the power of that confession.

"Are you saying that the Peabridge reference librarian can't locate a simple home address?"

"I'm saying—" But I stopped myself mid-sentence. I *did* want to find out where Graeme lived. I wanted to visit his house. I wanted to know more about him, to prove to Haylee—to myself—that he was the man for me. I pushed myself up from the couch's deep, comfortable cushions. "I'm saying," I repeated, "that going to Graeme's house is an excellent idea. Besides, I still have his jacket. From that night at the Kennedy Center."

"It's only polite to return things that don't belong to you," Haylee justified for me.

"Only polite," I agreed.

I don't know why tracking Graeme down suddenly

seemed like such a good idea. Maybe I was trying to impress Haylee. Maybe I was trying to convince myself—reassure myself that Graeme and I *did* have something special going on, something real. Maybe I was trying to exorcise the Insufficient Bad-boy once and for all.

Or maybe I was just desperate to get out of my "quaint" little cottage, with my boring plate of healthy vegetables, and my undrinkable pitcher of sugary rum and soda.

Before I knew it, I had fired up my computer and completed a quick Google search or three. Then, Haylee and I were in her Mini Cooper, driving to the Virginia suburbs, following directions from MapQuest. We were pulling up in front of a brick colonial, staring at its lush green lawn, its welcoming porch light, its stone walkway and late-blooming marigolds and flowerless clumps of day lilies.

Marigolds, I thought automatically, with an attention to detail that would no doubt thrill David Montrose. Useful for healing wounds and resolving stomach ailments. And for brewing into an aphrodisiac tea. And day lilies, I thought frantically, mentally steering away from aphrodisiacs. Good for treating wounds and burns and snake bites. And nervousness.

Not that there was anything to be nervous about. Nothing at all.

"Wait!" I cried, reaching out to touch Haylee's arm as she pulled up to the curb in front of the house.

She braked to a stop, then looked at me questioningly.

"Drive around the block!"

She smirked, but she obliged me. And then she complied with my request to park four houses away, so that we could casually walk past Graeme's front door, trying to catch a glimpse through his gauze-curtained windows. (No luck—the sheers were just heavy enough to keep us from seeing anything useful.) And she kept me company as we strolled down the block, trying to snag more of a view from the side of the house. (Still no luck—not enough space between buildings.) His backyard. (Yet more no luck—ditto.)

I thought about cajoling her into walking around the block, trying to count off the lots, to figure out which house backed on to Graeme's, which backyard would be even with his. Before I could even try, though, Haylee shook her head and walked up the stone path to the front door.

Just like that. Brazen. Confident. Like she owned the place.

She ignored my chittering excuses, waiting only long enough for me to fold Graeme's jacket over my arm and come stand beside her on the marble flagstone. Then, she raised the brass knocker (shaped like a perching gargoyle), and let it strike—once, twice, three times.

My throat went as dry as Neko's so-called wit. My heart was pounding so loudly in my ears that my entire body throbbed. I tried to remember why I had let Haylee drive me here, what I had thought to gain by hunting down Graeme in his home. His private home. His personal space. On his first night back in the country for nearly two weeks.

"This was a really bad idea," I whispered to Haylee.

She smiled at me, calm as the cloudless sky above us. "I think you'll be surprised."

Before I could swear off surprises, before I could vow to live a boring life forever, a life of humdrum, stultifying or-dinariness, the dead bolt whispered back. The doorknob turned. For the first time since our little field trip began,

I thought to push my hair out of my face, and I wondered what had possessed me to leave home without even the quickest foray into my stash of makeup.

"What—" Graeme's eyes fell on Haylee, and he looked surprised, shocked at this stranger standing on his front porch. She inclined her head toward me, and his gaze automatically followed. "Jane!" He glanced back and forth between us, rapidly processing what had to be an astonishing sight. His killer smile quickly banished any look of consternation. "And to what do I owe this pleasure?"

His accent seemed thicker in the evening air, and I felt my knees go trembly all over again. "Welcome home!" I said, realizing that both of them were waiting for me to say something. To *do* something. "Haylee and I were out, um, having dinner. We thought that we would just stop by and say hello. And I wanted to return your jacket. And welcome you back to town." Well, that sounded idiotic, even to me. To compensate, I thrust his coat toward him. "Here!" He took the garment reflexively.

"I didn't realize you had my address," he said. But he smiled when he said it. I had to hold on to the fact that he smiled.

"I'm a librarian," I said.

"How could I forget?" He extended a hand to Haylee. "Graeme Henderson," he said.

"Haylee James." She shook with the firm grasp of a business executive. "Pleased to meet you."

"The pleasure is all mine." He looked back at me before I could even think about being jealous, before I could contemplate what my hair would look like if it were cut as short and spiky as Haylee's. Or how my eyebrows would appear, if I plucked them so carefully. Or how my cheekbones might be coaxed out, with just the right combination of blush and toner.

"Where are my manners?" Graeme asked rhetorically. "Won't you come in?"

"We don't want to be any trouble," I said. But Haylee was already smiling her cool smile and striding into the foyer. It would have been rude not to follow her. Downright uncivilized.

"No," Graeme said. "No trouble. No trouble at all." He closed the door after us and gestured toward the living room. "I just finished unpacking upstairs. I was going to catch up on some work." He nodded in the general direction of an oversize rolltop desk. Spreadsheets drifted across the horizontal surface, an adding machine anchoring the paper storm. "'Day, night, hour, tide, time, work,'" Graeme quoted, crossing the room to pull down the rolltop and hide away his labor.

"'Play!'" I said, finishing off the quotation. I couldn't help but flash a triumphant smile toward Haylee. "It's a line from *Romeo and Juliet*," I explained.

"I see," she said. Her cool voice dampened a little of my enthusiasm. I caught her sideways glance toward Graeme, and I knew that she was measuring his blond good looks. I stood a little straighter.

Graeme, apparently oblivious to the inspection, waved us toward the couch. "Please. Have a seat. I'll just be a moment."

And he was good as his word. Haylee perched on one of the oversize armchairs, while I (exercising girlfriend's prerogative) actually sat on the couch. She and I managed to chat about the coffee-table book—*Washington D.C., Then and Now*—and she was just urging me to look up the Peabridge, to see if there were any photographs of my home, when Graeme returned with a serving tray.

"I trust you both drink red wine?" We nodded, and he made a little show of pulling the cork and pouring the pinot noir. He passed around a small plate of chocolates, and I selected a perfect truffle, pleased beyond all reason that my boyfriend—yes, I was feeling confident enough now to think the word—my *boyfriend* had such sophisticated treats ready and waiting for random visitors.

Graeme settled back onto the couch beside me, looking utterly comfortable and relaxed, as if madwomen showed up, unannounced, more evenings than not. "Sometimes," he said, "it's best to go with the simple pleasures in life."

I thought of my disastrous attempt at cocktails and nodded agreement.

"So, Haylee," he said, turning his attention to my friend. "I'm afraid I don't recall Jane telling me what you do."

He was right, of course. I hadn't mentioned her to Graeme, because I hadn't realized she was going to be important in my life. Going to be my strongest link to the Coven. Going to be my new best friend (at least until I kept my promise to Gran and ironed things out with Melissa.)

Haylee sipped from her wine before she answered. "I'm an interior designer," she said.

Graeme glanced around, as if seeing his own living room for the first time. "I'm embarrassed, then, to think of what you'd say about this place."

She laughed. "It's actually quite well done. Strong. Masculine. Except for that lamp, there." She pointed toward a rather delicate stained glass lamp sitting on a table in the corner. "It doesn't quite fit in with the rest of the place."

What an eye, I thought. I wondered what impression I'd made, with the eclectic collection in my cottage.

Graeme scowled at the lamp. "That thing. I'm keeping it for a friend."

"Ah. The hazards of friendship." Haylee raised her glass, as if she were toasting someone, or something. Before I could decide whether I should join in the toast (possibly implying that Graeme had bad taste in friends) or stay silent (letting Haylee take an odd, controlling hand in our conversation), my witchy new best friend changed the topic herself. "Your accent," she said to Graeme. "I can't quite place it. North of London, isn't it?"

Graeme nodded. "Cambridge. You've got a good ear." I wondered if I would ever be able to pick apart British accents so accurately.

And that led us into a discussion of travel. They were both much more worldly than I. I managed, though, to parlay my one trip to London into an entertaining tale about being lost in airports and missing not one, not two, but three different planes.

Hearing Graeme speak wistfully of home, I began to plot another trip to England. Perhaps I'd accompany him on his next business trip. We could go to Stratford, see William Shakespeare's birthplace for ourselves. Wander through towns that still had thatched roofs and Tudor half-timbering. Sit in a pub and eat steak-and-kidney pie.

Well, steak pie, anyway. I would pick out the kidneys.

All of a sudden, a clock chimed twelve from somewhere deep inside the house. I hadn't heard it earlier, but the deep, steady toll of the hour immediately made me think of Teresa Alison Sidney and the safehold, somewhere farther out in the Virginia suburbs. I darted a glance at Haylee, but she seemed not to make the same connection.

In fact, she seemed not to make any connection at all. She was stifling a yawn against the back of her teeth—a move made obvious by her thin, elegant bone structure. "I'm sorry," she said, when she realized both Graeme and I were staring at her. "I must be more tired than I thought."

I started to jump up. "*I'm* sorry! I'm so inconsiderate! And Graeme, you must be exhausted, after your trip!"

I wasn't quite sure how the night had gotten away from me, except that I was enjoying being with Graeme—with Graeme *and* Haylee—so much. I'd been mesmerized by the conversation—by Haylee's cool wit and by Graeme's charming… Charming everything.

Haylee shrugged. "I should drive you home and then get back out here."

"Out here?" I asked.

"I live in Arlington, too."

I was mortified. Here, it was a work night, and I would have Haylee ferrying me around for another hour, after I'd already kept all of us up too late. "Graeme," I said. "Let me just call a cab. Do you have a phone book?"

"We can do better than *that*." Again, that perfect Graeme smile. It made me shiver at the same time that it melted something deep inside me. "Why don't I give you a quick ride home?"

"I—" I couldn't even think of a lie. I wanted him to drive me home. I wanted him to do more than that.

Haylee must have sensed the meaning behind my hesitation. "Well," she said, giving in almost too quickly. "If you truly don't mind…"

Graeme glanced at me and closed his hand over mine. "I truly don't mind." He excused himself to get his car keys and Haylee took advantage of his absence to flash me a wicked grin. "You look *smitten,*" she said.

"I am," I confessed.

Graeme returned and made short work of turning out a couple of lights. He unlocked the front door and ushered us back into the brisk autumn night. My waist tingled where his fingertips brushed against me.

"Good night," Haylee said at the curb. "Don't do anything I wouldn't do." She winked and got inside her car.

We settled into Graeme's Audi, and I automatically pulled the seat belt across my chest. He turned the key and the motor purred to life. I leaned back against the headrest, taking a deep breath against a sudden surge of expectation.

No business meetings. No cell phones. No strange, last-minute interruptions.

Even with my eyes closed, I could hear the grin in Graeme's voice. "And what do you think she meant by that?"

"I have no idea," I said, managing a tone of perfect innocence.

His laugh was a throaty growl. I leaned forward, then, eager to be home. Eager to be parking in front of the Peabridge. Walking down the garden path. Fumbling for my house keys.

And then we were there.

I reached for the light switch. "We don't need the light," Graham whispered, centered in a pool of moonlight in my living room. His lips were already hot against my throat.

And he was right. We didn't.

21

When I woke, I lay in bed with my eyes closed, thinking that I was suspended in a magical sort of movie reality. Early-morning sunshine crept into my bedroom window, turning my eyelids crimson and warming my face like a honey bath. Every inch of my skin was aware of my cotton sheets; every pore seemed awakened and energized, freed from the tangle of my usual nightgown.

I remembered to listen for Graeme breathing beside me, but I could not hear him. Fighting a sickening swoop in my belly, I contrived to roll over, taking the top sheet with me. I took a deep breath to steady myself, and then I popped open my eyes.

Gone.

One quick glance confirmed that my clothes were strewn—strewn!—about the bedroom. So, I hadn't imagined that part of the previous evening's entertainment. But my dream date, my seductive Brit (who had kept up a steady purr of accented endearments through a level of activity that rapidly made me forget the entire English language) had disappeared.

I swore and kicked off the sheets.

I slashed my arms into the sleeves of my robe, cursing as the belt tangled around my waist. I was an idiot. A stupid, gullible idiot. Why had I let Graeme into the house? Why had I believed him when he whispered sweet nothings in my ear? Er, against the hollow of my throat? Okay, against every erogenous zone ever identified in any sex manual anywhere?

I blushed. I couldn't even blame alcohol. My one glass of pinot noir had worn off well before Graeme's clock struck midnight.

No. I had deluded myself. Once again. I had let myself believe that Graeme was the one, that he was the solution, the salve. I was such an idiot. Swearing at myself, I yanked open my bedroom door.

And my heart nearly stopped beating.

The door to the basement was open.

Surely, I would have heard Neko come home, drunk as he must have been on Mexican (or Colombian, or Argentinian) beer? He wouldn't have changed his plans to stay over at Jacques's place, anyway—not unless something had gone seriously wrong with the Frenchman.

"Neko?" I called downstairs, hating the tremulous note in my voice.

"Good morning."

Graeme. Answering immediately. Cheerfully.

Relief slammed into me so hard that I needed to grip

the door frame to keep from falling. "Good morning!" I cried, and then I hurtled down the steps.

He had pulled on the khakis he'd worn the night before, and his white cotton shirt was wrinkled. He looked adorably sloppy with the tails untucked, like an incorrigible little boy who'd had enough of fancy family affairs. His hair was rumpled as well, and—truth be told—I could make out a few lines of fatigue around his eyes.

Well, I wasn't at my freshest, either. It wasn't like either one of us had slept a great deal the night before. It took time to get used to another body in bed, to grow accustomed to sighs and snores and shiftings on a mattress. Not that I ever snored. Not me.

"Mmm," Graeme murmured, finally taking a step back. "I couldn't sleep any longer—jet lag—so I came down here."

"There really isn't much to see," I said. "That is, if you aren't a witch."

"Oh, I don't know." He reached around me to pick up the book he'd been reading. I could just make out the flowery script stamped in gold on the worn leather cover. *Love Spells That Work*. What had the boys been thinking when they left *that* around? "You've certainly cast a spell on me, Jane Madison."

I blushed, and I let him fold me back into his arms. Into his arms, and then on to the couch. He circled his fingers around my wrists, keeping me from undoing the buttons that marched down the long front of his shirt, his warm lips distracting me with memories from the night before.

I twisted on the couch to keep from slipping to the floor, and that's when I saw it.

On the book stand. In the center of the room.

A jasper necklace, entwined with sprigs of fading greenery.

"Stop!" I pushed Graeme off me with a vehemence that must have stunned him. He staggered to his feet, but I was already crossing the room, scarcely remembering to tug my robe back into place. My voice shook as I asked, "Did you put this here?"

Eyes widening, he glanced from the stone beads to my face. "What?"

"The necklace! The jasper! Did you put it there?"

"Why would I—? Jane, what's wrong?"

But it wasn't just the jasper. It wasn't just the threat of an anti-witchcraft necklace, or the herbs, which I could now identify as thyme and oregano, twined about the stone beads.

It was the book.

Or, more precisely, the *missing* book. My handbook on crystals was gone.

I wasted a moment looking for it, even though I was certain it had been on the stand just the night before. I had seen it beside Neko's mint concoction; I had specifically made sure that its parchment pages were safe from the cosmetic compound the boys had made.

"Did you move a book from here?"

Graeme was staring at me as if I had gone mad. "A book?"

"A leather-bound book. It was right here. On the stand. Where the necklace is now."

"The only book I touched was the love spell one. It was over there on the couch, draped over the arm. I was just going to close it, to protect the spine, and I started reading a few pages. But I didn't touch anything else. I *wouldn't* touch anything else." He reached out, closed his hands around my upper arms. "What, Jane? What is it?"

I barely whispered. "Someone broke in here. It must have been last night. After Haylee and I left to visit you. Someone broke in here and stole a book on crystals. And left…that." I pointed toward the necklace.

He followed my trembling finger and then turned me around so that I couldn't stare at the mottled blood-red stones. "What is it?" he asked urgently. "What does it mean?"

It meant that I was no longer safe in my own home. It meant that David had been right, that the risk was increasing as we got closer to Samhain. It meant that someone was working, harder than ever, to keep me from succeeding at setting the Coven's centerstone.

"It means that I have to call my warder."

"Your warder?" He sounded so completely confused that I was catapulted back to mundane reality. I realized that I must sound like a madwoman. Who worried about finding an unexpected necklace, or losing one little book? Who jumped to life-and-death conclusions on a morning when she should be stretching sex-sore muscles and contemplating breakfast in bed?

"I'm sorry, Graeme. This has to do with the Coven. With the witches I've told you about. Someone has broken in here and left that *thing*. It's a threat. A sign to witches that they aren't welcome. That they might come to harm."

"Do you…" He swallowed hard, then looked at me without flinching. "Do you want me to do something with it? Throw it away? Take it to the police?"

I shook my head. "The police would laugh you out of the station." I shivered, feeling sick in the pit of my stomach.

"Jane," Graeme said, and I felt the tiny hairs on his knuckles as he brushed the back of his hand against my cheek.

"It's all right," I said, but I was pretty sure I was trying to convince myself. Not Graeme. "Or, it will be. I need to get my warder here, now, though." I caught Graeme's hand in mine. "And I don't want him to see you. Not this morning. Not right now."

Graeme shook his head. "I want to help you."

"The biggest help is leaving. Don't make me explain to him why you're here."

His eyes widened. "Does your…warder keep you from seeing other men?"

I shook my head—a terse motion. An angry one. But I didn't even know who I was angry with. "No. It's not like that. But David thinks that I've made…poor choices before. I don't want to waste time explaining us, when we should focus on finding my book."

Graeme still looked uncertain, but he nodded, reaching out to pull me close to his chest. His arms felt like a solid wall around me. I longed to lean against him—to collapse against him—for a long, long time. His fingers strayed to the sash at my waist, and I finally had to close my hands over his. "Graeme…"

He pulled back, his rakish grin nearly stopping my heart. "Call me. Let me know what happens."

"You know I will."

And he was gone. Up the stairs. Out the door. Gone.

I knew what I had to do. I'd done it once before, in a

panic. Now, I measured out my power, poured it into a single steady stream of magic. *Neko,* I thought, broadcasting my power like a radio beacon. *Neko. I need you. Home. Now.* And for good measure, I included David in my transmission. After all, he'd sense the power I was spending. Better to invite him than have him show up unannounced.

Not that I'd done anything wrong. This time.

I closed my eyes, the better to concentrate. "Neko!"

"No need to shout." He stood in front of me, surveying the basement with the wariness of a hunter. Without his silly Mexican accessories, his leather pants and silk shirt seemed sleek, dangerous. His eyes darted to the corners of the room, and his nose twitched warily. I couldn't help but glance down at my robe, wondering just how much Neko could sense about my escapades the night before. If he glanced at the clothes thrown around my bedroom, he'd conclude that Nate Poindexter was one smooth operator.

I shivered and jerked my sash tighter. Neko was my familiar, not my jailer.

He found the necklace immediately. Stalking around the book stand, he eyed the jewelry from every angle, his nostrils twitching as he recognized the thyme and oregano. He reached out one hand, a frown marring his smooth features, and he started to breathe through his mouth—as if he could sense more that way. As if the very air in the room could tell him what had happened. Who had been here, invading our privacy. Our safety. Our home.

"What do you sense?" David's voice was quiet, but I could hear the urgency behind his question. I wasted a moment, wondering when I had become so accustomed to his presence that I did not flinch at his silent arrival.

Neko cast his head to one side. "Nothing particular."

"What does that mean?" prodded my warder.

"I can feel *you,*" Neko said, shoulders twitching in annoyance. "And Jane of course. And Jacques and me."

Jacques! Could he be the source of the eerie jasper warnings? That was absurd, though. He'd never shown the slightest interest in anything magical, and he'd certainly had ample opportunity, with all the time he spent at the cottage. He was interested in Neko's body and—just possibly—my familiar's mind (or at least his fashion sense.) But Jacques had nothing to do with the threat in my basement.

"And?" David prompted.

"And...the Coven."

I waited for him to elaborate, but I ultimately needed to prod. "The Coven?"

"I can sense them here." He moved his hand in the air above the necklace.

"All of them? Like they held a meeting here?" I could not picture all of those Junior League women crowded into my basement. Their warders would have needed to wait upstairs, maybe in my bedroom. Their familiars would have been painfully obvious, lurking in the shadows of my too-small basement room. They would all have been disappointed in the caliber of my refreshments, too, unless a pitcher of watered-down rum and a few dried-out vegetables on a platter were their idea of slumming fun.

"Of course not," Neko snorted, and my fantasy image

disappeared. "But there's a...dusting. Like talcum powder, settled from the air."

"How many were here?" David asked, his eyes darting around the room, as if he expected to find malefactors still lurking in the corners.

"One?" Neko said, but he made the statement a question.

"When?" David said.

"I can't tell." Neko twitched and shook his head in exasperation. "My mind knows that the jasper wasn't here when I left last night. But I can't sense how it actually got here. Something is blocking me."

I asked, "Could someone have made it materialize here? Without actually coming into the basement? And then have stolen my book?"

David's eyes narrowed. "It's possible, but that would take a tremendous energy drain. Most witches don't have anywhere near that level of skill, working with something as antithetical to their powers as jasper."

"But Teresa Alison Sidney—" I started to argue.

"Oh, Teresa Alison Sidney could do it." David nodded slowly. "She might be the only witch on the Eastern Seaboard who could."

I rubbed my arms with cold hands, my belly turning queasily at the notion that the Coven Mother herself might be stalking me. "But why would she?" I asked, not caring that my voice was tiny. "Why would she try to frighten me like this?"

David glanced at me and seemed to awaken from his own spell. Squaring his shoulders, he crossed the room and settled a handkerchief over the necklace and herbs. The oily discomfort in my gut eased as soon as they were out of sight, even though I knew that they were still present in the room. "That's the thing," David said. "I don't think that she is. There's no reason for her to intimidate you."

"But who…" I trailed off, realizing that if Teresa Alison Sidney hadn't made the jasper materialize, then someone actually *had* broken into my cottage.

"Were you home last night?" David asked.

I braced myself for his disapproval. "No."

Threading an even note of steel through his words, David said, "Where did you go?"

"Virginia," I hedged.

"To the Coven?" David's tone was disbelieving. "By yourself?"

"There are lots of other places in Virginia," I said. "Who says we had to go to the Coven?"

"Who's 'we'?"

My lips clamped shut. I felt like a teenager, caught sneaking out after curfew. Neko glanced between us and then said, "Haylee." He flashed me an apologetic smile, shrugging as if to say that his reply was all for the best.

"Haylee James!" David's surprise was explosive. And a tiny part of my brain was relieved that he was so upset about Haylee. I just might get away without needing to admit that I had brought a man home after my excursion to the wilds of Virginia. After all, David was my warder, not my father. He had no reason to police my romantic liaisons.

"She's my friend," I answered hotly.

"She is *not* your friend," David said.

"She's the only person in the Coven who has actually

reached out to me! She's the only one who acts like I might possibly be treated as an equal after Samhain!"

David's jaw tightened, and I knew from experience that he was barely restraining himself from making some unpleasant observation. He started three different sentences before he settled on, "Did Haylee come down here last night? Did she have any time alone with your collection?"

"Of course not! Neko and Jacques were here, getting ready for their party. Haylee and I left shortly after they did." I rolled my eyes. "David, Haylee wasn't alone in the cottage the entire time that she was here." I flattened my voice, making it absolutely clear that I would not tolerate more discussion about my only witchy friend. "It wasn't Haylee."

David sighed and ran a hand through his hair. That motion chilled me even more than the jasper necklace had. David only ran a hand through his hair when he was truly worried. When he actually believed that I was in danger. That something might go terribly wrong.

"I don't want you staying here." His tone was flat. Absolute. "Call Melissa. See if you can sleep at her place for a while. Just until after Samhain."

I shook my head, even before he was through issuing his command. "No."

"She's your best friend. She'll understand."

Right. We weren't even speaking to each other. She'd be just thrilled to have me sleeping on her couch, to have my colonial dresses filling her closet. And I'd have a grand time, shlepping up here to the Peabridge every morning, walking the streets like some Revolutionary War re-enactor. "She won't," I said. "You can't make me stay with Melissa."

David must have heard the adamance in my tone. "Then go to your grandmother."

I pictured my pink bedroom, complete with little corners of tape that had once held up posters of Kevin Costner and Andy Garcia. "I can't do that. Besides, how would I explain it to her? She'd worry herself sick."

"Jane—"

"David," I countered. "I'm not giving in to them, whoever they are. Let's just *say* that Neko's right." My familiar yelped indignantly, but I rolled forward without stopping. "Let's say that the warnings are from someone in the Coven. Someone who broke in after Haylee and I left last night. That person wants to set me off balance. She wants to keep me from centering on my witchcraft, from being ready on Samhain." I firmed my resolve and raised my voice. "But I won't give in. I've got to stay here, to study. To center myself. To learn everything I can."

"Jane—"

"David, I've got less than three weeks." I did some quick math. "Nineteen days to prove myself. Don't disrupt that time. Don't make me turn everything *else* in my life upside down when I should be focusing on magic!"

I could see he was wavering. He looked at the hundreds of books, at my container of crystals. He actually looked at me—for long enough that I started to feel uncomfortable.

"If I let you stay here…" I nodded, encouraging him. He kept his eyes on me and reached into his pocket before he said, "You have to promise me…"

He pulled out his key chain, cupping his Hecate's Torch in his palm. Both of us stared at the sleek silver lines, at the art deco design that seemed to glow with a light of its own. I realized once again how much I wanted to have my own Torch, how much I longed to be welcomed into the Coven, to have this testing and judging and suspicion behind me.

David reached some sort of conclusion in his own mind. He fumbled with the key chain for just a moment, and then he passed the Torch to me, slipping his liberated keys back into his pocket.

"I can't take that!"

"Yes, you can."

"But it's yours!"

"It's mine, and part of my warder's powers are linked to it. Enhanced by it. I can keep better track of you if you're wearing it. Put it on a silver chain, and keep it close to your heart."

I felt a blush flood my cheeks, and I tried one last time. "I'm not allowed to have a Torch until the Coven gives me my own."

"If you don't take this one now," David said evenly, "you might not last long enough for the Coven to give you your own."

I swallowed hard, unable to keep from looking at the now-hidden jasper necklace. Whatever bravado I had mustered to argue against moving in with Melissa, camping out at Gran's, I really *was* disturbed that someone had broken in the night before.

I closed my fingers over the Torch. I could sense David's presence in the metal amulet; I could feel his quiet, calm aura emanating from the silver. When Gran had offered me her Torch, weeks before, I had told her I couldn't take it; I had known that its magic would clash with my own.

I didn't feel that danger from my own warder's charm. It wasn't opposed to me. In fact, it felt as if it had already melded with my own magical abilities. "All right," I said.

David did not look happy, but he managed a nod. "Silver," he said. "Chain. Now."

I tried not to watch as he pocketed the jasper and the herbs. I did not breathe easily until I had his Torch around my neck, warming a spot above my fast-beating heart.

22

David sat back on my couch, the hunter-green fabric enveloping him like a cloak. He sighed like a man who had just finished consuming a porterhouse steak. With a loaded baked potato. Along with a bottle of aged cabernet. I wouldn't have been surprised to see him pat his belly in contentment. "Perfect," he said, favoring me with one of his rare grins. "I don't think we have anything left to review."

The past two and half weeks had flown by—the fastest eighteen days of my life. Things had gone smoothly—surprisingly smoothly.

I hadn't found a single jasper ornament anywhere in or around the house. While I *did* continue to receive e-mails from my anti-witch stalker, I'd been able to set up a filter program to block them from my computer screen. (After all, there weren't any work-related reasons for anyone to send me messages with the words "coven," "safehold," or "centerstone.")

I knew David remained wary, but he had not policed me unfairly. He'd probably been reassured when I'd committed to working with him on a daily basis. Tonight, though, was the first time I'd heard him express actual contentment with the progress that we'd made. I felt a bit like a lost little girl, uncertain about the kindly rescuer who was offering me a free ride home.

Even as Neko executed an elaborate, spine-twisting stretch, I asked, "Are you sure? I've still got fifteen minutes before I have to get back to the library."

While David glanced out the window toward the back of the Peabridge, Neko hissed his disapproval. My familiar was less than pleased with the amount of time we'd spent working, even if he understood exactly how much rode on my Samhain magic. "Why don't you astonish Evelyn?" David suggested. "Get back from your lunch hour on time for once."

I spluttered, but I could hardly come up with a snappy reply. In the past few weeks, I'd become an absolute star at stretching out my midday break. Anyone could tack on five or ten extra minutes by claiming to lose track of time, or blaming traffic, or complaining about slow service at a restaurant. But with the final phases of preparing for the centerstone working, I had routinely dragged lunch out to two hours.

I *had* tried to make up for my extravagant lunch hours by going in early. Not that I was hugely successful with that gambit. But it's the thought that counts. By good fortune, Evelyn had let slip the fact that she loved a shot of cinnamon syrup in her morning coffee. Like the wicked witch that I was, I'd used that knowledge to the utmost of my ability. Five minutes early, cinnamon syrup and a dollop of whipped cream served with a wink and a smile—so far, I'd had no problem finagling the extra time that I'd spent studying to set the centerstone.

But now David said that we were through. I couldn't believe him, couldn't accept that truth. "Shouldn't we go over the spells one more time?"

David shook his head. "You know them all by heart."

"How about reviewing the ingredients for the herbal wash?"

"You memorized them weeks ago."

"Practice casting a circle, for protection?"

"You can do that in your sleep. Have done, since the jasper necklace. Right?"

I nodded, crossing my fingers to exclude the evenings I'd spent with Graeme. I wasn't going to cast any circle that would keep *him* away from me.

David went on, obviously unaware of that little duplicity. "Besides, I'll be there. Me, and all the other warders. You don't need to worry about protection."

I couldn't believe what he was saying. I was ready. Me. To face the Coven and join with my sisters once and for all.

When I was in elementary school, I had dreamed of this moment. Not of joining a group of witches—I hadn't even known witches existed then, for real. But of joining the in group. The popular girls. The ones who were chosen first for the softball team, for homecoming court, for the dance team and all the other measures of popularity that we ate, drank and breathed every day of our fraught existence.

I had never been one of the popular girls. Sure, I had friends. I'd spent enough hours on the telephone to drive

Gran to distraction. I'd gone to my share of slumber
parties, and I could always find someone to hang out with
at the mall.

But I'd never been part of the inner circle. The special
core. The girls who set the trends and led the way and made
all of the rest of us jealous, no matter how much we'd protested to the contrary.

Now I was a little more than twenty-four hours away
from my first real chance to join that clique. Tomorrow
night, I would set the centerstone. Tomorrow night, I
would join the Coven that would support me and
comfort me for all the rest of my witchy life. If I succeeded, of course.

Without conscious thought, my fingers fiddled with
David's Hecate's Torch, which was hanging freely outside
my colonial shift. I'd grown accustomed to the soothing feel
of its sleek lines, its simple, swooping design. Soon, I'd
have my own.

When I did, I could use it to nudge the Coven in directions I thought worthwhile. Once I'd settled in, I could
question Gran's status, and Clara's. I could explore giving
them back their own Torches, working with them to build
their skills. It only seemed fair that they should have *some* place
in the Coven, even if it was around the edges. Not everyone
could be in the absolute center of the Popular Snobs.

I rubbed the Torch again and realized that I was putting
the magical cart before the enchanted horse.

I needed to set the centerstone before I started changing
the slightest direction of Teresa Alison Sidney's Coven.
David's eyes tracked my hand, and then he shook his head.

"I have to admit it," he said. "I didn't think you could make these lunchtime meetings work. But you were right."

"And?" I prompted, matching his slow smile with one of my own.

"And?" he asked, seeming confused.

"I was right, and…? You?"

He actually laughed. Out loud. Like an ordinary man, instead of a grouchy, hypersensitive warder. He truly *must* be pleased with my accomplishments. "I was wrong. You've been better prepared for our sessions than I could have dreamed. I can only imagine how hard you've been studying each night."

I cast a quick glance toward Neko, who could blow my cover with a single misplaced word. He tilted his head to one side, and his eyebrows raised in that way he had, just before he asked the most annoying questions in the world. The last thing I needed to hear now was some wry speculation about "Nate Poindexter."

I rushed out an explanation. "I told you before. This is important to me. The most important thing I've ever done. If I have to spend my nights preparing for our lunchtime sessions…"

David nodded, accepting my words at face value, but Neko piped up, "I can't believe you didn't need to spend every evening here, though. Studying the books in the basement."

I refused to glare at him—showing my anger would only tip my hand. Instead, I flashed a smile that was only a single shade too tight to be sweet. "I'm a librarian. I study best in a library. It's habit, I guess. It's much quieter, and there are *far* fewer distractions."

I gave a pointed glance to Neko's throat, and the gold links of the necklace that Jacques had given him only the night before. He had the good grace to blush and look away.

Distractions. If only they knew.

I shivered as I thought about how I had seen Graeme almost every evening since he'd returned from London. Some nights, he arrived at my doorstep holding a paper sack from Dean & Deluca; others, he treated me to one of my favorite Georgetown hot spots. Three different nights, he'd taken me out to his place in Virginia, where he'd wined me and dined me and had his wicked way with me.

Or I, with him. Whatever.

I much preferred the nights that he *didn't* actually appear on my doorstep. I was still perpetuating the Nate Poindexter charade—pure luck had intervened to keep Neko from meeting Graeme so far. Luck, and Jacques, who knew of more parties in the Washington, D.C., metro area than any other ten people I could name.

Not that I was ashamed of Graeme, of course.

It's just that I still felt obligated to Melissa, bound by her stupid Friendship Test. Old loyalties died hard. I'd kept my promise despite the fact that I hadn't spoken to her in over three weeks—the longest time we'd gone without communicating in all the years that we'd known each other.

I'd started to pick up the phone dozens of times, to just call her and make everything right. Every time I started to dial, though, I remembered the way she had dismissed my concerns. I thought about how she had paid attention to everyone in her bakery, reaching out to them, helping them, before she even considered reaching out to me.

I thought about her having a phone, too. She could have called *me* any time in the past almost-a-month. Told me about more of her disastrous dates. Asked for commiseration, for an alliance against the men who broke her heart.

Demanded it, even, with a Friendship Test.

(Okay. When I was honest with myself, I silently thanked her for helping me keep my love life secret. I could only imagine what my overprotective familiar and warder would say when they learned about the new man in my life. There'd be time enough to deal with *that* disaster after Samhain.)

Before I could dwell more on my distractions, the phone rang. Neko perked up and said, "Jane Madison's grandmother."

I gave him a dirty look. Yes, Gran had been calling a lot, and she always left the same message. She'd never trusted answering machines, and I'd always cooperated by calling her back promptly. I just hadn't had time in the past three weeks to listen to more demands, to make more promises.

As the phone made another insistent ring, David waved me toward the handset. I guess we really *were* through with my training. The notion still sat oddly in my mind, as I answered a cautious "Hello?"

"Jane!"

"Oh. Hello, Gran." I looked at Neko, wondering if he had truly known she was on the other end of the line. I didn't think that familiars could do that, but who could really say? He smiled innocently and resettled on the couch, folding his legs beside him like a proper Victorian lady at a picnic. He and David started talking in quiet tones, and

I took advantage of their conversation to concentrate on my grandmother.

"Jane, I am so glad that I caught you on your lunch break! It has been *ages* since we've talked. Didn't you get my messages?"

"Yes, Gran." I sighed. "I've been busy."

"Too busy to return a phone call?" she asked tartly.

I made a face, feeling like I was about five years old. "David and I have been working together. A lot."

Gran liked David. Invoking his name was usually enough to make her forget extracting another dozen promises from me. True to form, her voice softened, and she said, "Well, dear, I was only calling because I found a great recipe for you."

"Recipe?"

"Weren't you going to start baking for the library?" All of my grandmother's hurt feelings rushed back into her voice. So much for the magic elixir of David Montrose. "I could have sworn that you said you were going to start serving baked goods on the first of November. I wrote it down on my calendar. In peacock-blue."

Peacock-blue. Gran always marked special events in the bright shade—my birthday, hers, the opening night of the school play. How could a shade of ink make me feel like a kid caught writing on the walls? With crayon. After several warnings.

"Yes, Gran, you're right," I hastened to respond, even though I had completely forgotten about the bottomless pit that threatened to become the Peabridge Restaurant, with a mere side room of dingy books for the occasional well-fed researcher.

"Then don't you think you should practice? Bake one or two things now, so that you know what will work best? It's practically November, you know."

Damn. I was running out of time to launch my Freedom From Cappuccino campaign on the first. Well, I'd just have to get some baking done tonight. It would be soothing. Keep me from worrying about the Coven too much. What could be easier than whipping up a batch or two of brownies?

I took a deep breath. "So, Gran, what's the recipe that you have for me?"

"It's called Homemade Turkish Baklava with Rose Water and Pistachio Cream."

I felt ill just hearing the name. "Baklava?"

"Homemade!" Gran enthused. "It takes forty sheets of filo dough, can you believe that? And a cup of butter. And a cup and a half of walnuts. Lucky for you, there are plenty of nuts in the store now that it's autumn. It shouldn't take too long to shell them. You'll be able to save money that way. Help out the Peabridge's bottom line."

Yeah, there were plenty of nuts in the store, and another one on the other end of the phone. Did Gran really think I was going to turn my kitchen into a baklava factory? She had raised me—didn't she realize the disaster she was proposing? Me? Cook anything more compli-cated than hard-boiled eggs? "Um, Gran," I said, trying to break the news to her gently. "I was thinking of starting off with something easy. Like brownies, the way we talked about at brunch."

"But Clara was over here when I found the recipe! She agreed that it sounds wonderful. She even cast her runes when she got home, and they came up Jera, Perthro and Sowilo. It's destiny!"

I cast an exasperated look over at David and Neko, but they were carrying on a perfectly friendly conversation without me. There'd be no escape from that quarter. I scowled and said, "I'm afraid I'm not quite up on my rune interpretations just now, Gran."

She clicked her tongue at my smart tone. "Jera is based on the harvest, Clara says. And Perthro is a sign of the feminine. Sowilo is the sun." She waited for me to say something, then continued with a touch of exasperation, "You should use harvested grains to pursue the feminine tradition of baking. In a hot oven." When I remained silent, Gran said, "Sowilo?"

"Sun. Oven. I get it," I said. "Look, Gran. Pastry chefs spend years learning how to make things like baklava. I don't think that *Melissa* has even tried it."

Stupid. Stupid, stupid, stupid.

Sure enough, Gran swooped in for the kill. "Speaking of Melissa, have you phoned her yet?"

"I've been busy," I said through set teeth, and then I regrouped. "Gran, if I've been too busy to return your calls, then you know I've been too busy to talk to Melissa."

"It's just that you promised, Jane." She sounded utterly disappointed.

"Have I ever broken one of my promises?"

I could almost see her shaking her head. "No, dear."

"And I'm not going to start now." I glanced at my watch.

Two o'clock. I was due back at the library an hour ago. "I've got to run, Gran."

"Shall I send you my baklava recipe by e-mail?"

Cruelly, I pictured her typing in the entire thing, hunting and pecking for each honey-soaked letter. "Why don't I stop by and pick it up? Some time in the next few days?"

"But what will you do for November first?"

"Brownies, Gran. I'm going to bake brownies. According to all the etiquette books, baklava is the traditional pastry for the *second* week of a bakery's existence."

She actually laughed and hung up, without wringing out any more precious drops of guilt. When I turned around, Neko was staring at me with horror. "You're going to make baklava?"

My smile was sweeter than the most honey-drenched Turkish confection. With rose water. And pistachio cream. "Only if you and David are standing by to put out the fire and stop the floods and settle the earthquakes and handle every other natural disaster from the end of the world as we've known it."

I left the men to their own devices and headed back to the library. Evelyn was standing by my desk, tapping her shoe and staring at the clock on my computer. I followed her gaze and winced involuntarily. Two-fifteen. Whoops.

"Jane, could you come into my office?"

Good things never happened inside Evelyn's office. Well, except for when she offered me the cottage as a place to live. But I hadn't realized that was a good thing at the time. "Could I make you a latte first? We have a fresh bottle of cinnamon syrup."

"No."

One-word answer. That wasn't good. Not good at all.

She barely waited for me to sit down in the chair opposite her cluttered desk. "Jane, I can't help but notice that you've been taking very long lunch breaks."

"I can explain—"

"The Peabridge is an excellent institution of higher learning. Our patrons depend on us to be here when they have questions."

When they want coffee, I thought, but I knew better than to say that out loud. I took a deep breath. "Evelyn, I've been working on our new patron program."

"Patron program?" The fact that I had an explanation— any explanation—stopped her cold in her tracks. "What patron program?"

"The new baked goods. Remember? We're going to start serving them on November first?"

"Well, I knew that we were going to launch something, but I wasn't certain that we'd settled on the date."

"We have. Just today, I was speaking with a consultant about baklava. Homemade Turkish baklava with rose water and pistachio cream." I actually floated my hand in the air, adding a fillip to the pastry's name, elegant and yet familiar, as if I made it every day.

"Homemade—" Evelyn shook her head, like a terrier trying to fling dirt from its ears. "But wouldn't that be terribly sticky? We don't want to do anything that might endanger our collection."

What? Protect the books in our *library?* What a fantastic idea! I resisted the urge to look at the paper coffee cup in

Evelyn's trash can, at the film of foamed milk that could just as easily have spilled over our holdings. I feigned concern. "Well, if you think that baklava might be too much…"

"I'm sorry, Jane. I realize that you're putting a lot of hard work into this project. But I think we'd do better to stick with something simpler. Maybe brownies."

Ha! I shook my head mournfully. "I suppose I *can* find another use for all those pistachios."

"There!" she beamed. "You'll see. We both want what's best for the Peabridge."

And the funny thing was, she was right.

I tried not to let her see my relief as I walked back to my desk. Truth be told, I'd been afraid that she'd put me on probation—or worse. Now, all I had to do was make the revamped coffee bar a success.

No problem.

No problem at all, for a witch like me.

Twenty-four hours till Samhain, and I was pacing my kitchen like a madwoman.

I had pulled a dozen recipes for brownies off the Internet, and they all called for the same basic ingredients—butter, flour, eggs, sugar, chocolate.

I had scorched the butter for the first batch, melting it before I added anything else.

I had carefully measured the flour for the second batch, but neglected to remember that I was doubling the recipe until after the glop was baking in the oven.

I had broken eggshells into the third batch.

I had spilled way too much sugar into the fourth batch,

foolishly believing I could target a measuring cup held over a boiling saucepan of almost-batter.

I had turned the melted chocolate of the fifth batch into an acrid pool of charcoal-tinged glue.

And I had burned the sixth batch, leaving the perfect batter in my oven too long, forgetting that the damned thing always ran hot. Very hot. Inferno hot.

As the clock chimed midnight, I sent Neko and Jacques to the all-night grocery store for more ingredients, and I collapsed at the kitchen table to drown my sorrows in the last remnant of a bar of Ghirardelli. Who knew how long it would take for the boys to get back? And who knew how many more ways I could ruin a perfectly simple batch of brownies?

I wanted to call Graeme. But I was the one who had told *him* I needed the evening off. He had wheedled in that unbelievably seductive way of his, but I had held fast. I didn't want to chance staying up too late. Being too exhausted tomorrow. It really was for the best, I reminded myself for the thousandth time.

The knock, when it came, seemed to make the entire cottage shudder. After my heart had slithered down out of my throat, I darted to the front door, taking care to stay away from the windows.

Was this my jasper stalker? Had she realized I was alone and vulnerable, my trusty familiar scouting out grocery store aisles, with a robust, full-bodied distraction keeping him from hearing any frantic summons?

I closed my hand over David's Torch and looked out the peephole.

"Haylee!" I exclaimed, tugging open the door. "You scared me half to death!"

Her spiky hair was perfect—as ever—as she waltzed into my living room. She had draped a large cashmere scarf around her neck, flinging it over one shoulder with a perfect casual air. She sniffed as the door closed behind her, peering curiously at the disaster area in the kitchen.

I took advantage of her distraction to tuck David's Torch inside my blouse. No need for her to see his gift. No need for the Coven to question my right to wear the symbol.

"So you sacked the kitchen in the midst of your terror?"

"Oh," I said, smiling weakly. "I'm trying out some new recipes. For work."

"I knocked loudly because I thought you'd be downstairs. Studying."

I shrugged. "I don't think there's much more that I can cram in, in one night. I can either do the working, or I can't."

She laughed. "You know, I said almost exactly the same thing, the night before I was tested."

"What did they have you do?"

"I can't tell you. You aren't a member of the Coven yet. Teri would kill me if I shared our secrets with a stranger." She smiled, but the words made my cheeks flame. I'd been presumptuous in asking. I hated the reminder that I was *different*. *Other*. Not one of the cool kids.

Yet.

Haylee reached inside the pocket of her impossibly slender slacks. "I wanted to give you something."

"What?"

"It's passed through generations of women in my family.

My mother gave it to me, the night before I was tested."
My heart clenched at her words. Haylee was reaching out
to me. Like a…sister. A true friend. "I know that your
mother and grandmother won't be there tomorrow. That
must be hard for you—most witches can look around the
Coven and find at least one friendly face when they
complete their testing. I wanted you to be able to look at
this tomorrow, and to know that I was thinking of you.
That I've been thinking of you, ever since you first came
to the Coven."

She took her hand out of her pocket. I extended mine
without thinking, palm open. I met her eyes, matched my
lips to her smile. And she opened her fingers.

A silver ring.

A plain silver ring. No engraving, no stone, and not a
hint of tarnish. Absolutely no indication of its history or
its meaning.

I shuddered as I slipped it onto my finger. The cool
metal made my hand tingle, vibrate as if my flesh were
awakening for the very first time. It fit snugly, occupying
the place of an engagement ring on my right hand.
"Haylee," I said, imagining the strength of the witches who
had worn it before me.

"Good luck tomorrow," she said.

"I can't—" I started to protest.

"You can. And you will. Just look at it tomorrow night,
and remember." Before I could say anything else, she gave
me a quick, bony hug.

I asked, "Would you like to stay? Could I get you a drink?
A brownie? Um, after Neko gets back?"

"No thanks," she said, and I think I detected a tremor that had nothing to do with witchcraft or covens or magical family-history rings. She looked into the chaos of my kitchen, and once again fought valiantly to hide her dismay. "I really have to be going. And you should get some sleep."

"I will." Before she left, I held out my hand, fingers extended to best show off the ring. "Thanks, Haylee."

After I closed the door, I sank against it, letting my knees buckle and my back slide toward the floor. It was happening. It was really happening. By this time tomorrow, I was going to be in the Coven. Or out of it forever.

"Good riddance!" Neko said, slamming my front door. "They're all thieves! Vicious little thieves!"

"They're children," I said, stepping out of the bathroom. I had just fought, and lost, the fourth battle of the night against my hair. "They've been looking forward to Halloween for weeks. And they've probably been eating candy since they got home from school this afternoon. Cut them some slack."

"I'd cut them all sorts of slack, if they'd left a single Three Musketeers bar." Neko stared dolefully at the bowl of candy in his hands.

"You don't even like Three Musketeers," I reminded him.

"But Jacques does. I promised I'd save one for him."

"You should have taken it out before answering the door the first time." I returned to the mirror, tugging my hair out of its collapsing chignon and brushing furiously before starting again.

Secretly, I was pleased that we had paid off a handful of

trick-or-treaters. The year before, no one had dared walk through the library gardens to get to my cottage. I mused, "Of course, you can always try mugging some kids on the street. They're sure to have a few candy bars you can give your beau."

"I should just get some of that nasty peanut butter taffy, the stuff wrapped up in orange and black wax paper. Serve him right, for abandoning me to door duty tonight."

I shook my head. I had long since stopped marveling at Neko's awareness of mundane details in our modern world, things like rock-hard peanut butter Halloween taffy. I had to agree with his assessment of the revolting sweet. I had always pawned mine off on Gran. She, showing perfect unconditional love, had accepted it with a smile and a hug. Years later, I'd found out that she'd actually buried it deep in the trash can, so I'd never know she hated it as much as I did.

I eased a decorative chopstick into my thoroughly pinned chignon and reminded Neko, "Jacques wasn't the one who abandoned you tonight. You abandoned him. Remember?"

I could barely make out the words that Neko muttered under his breath—more common knowledge that he couldn't have absorbed when he was suspended in his cat statue form. And he hadn't learned it from me—I tried my best to avoid that type of language. I didn't always succeed, but I tried.

This time, I could empathize with Neko. Graeme had called me three times during the day, trying to convince me to change my mind and attend a Halloween party hosted by friends. Friends from work, he'd said, dangling a bait that I would have snatched up any other night of the year. Finally—the chance to meet his colleagues, to find out more about his "acquisitions," to learn juicy office tidbits about my amazing mystery boyfriend.

A fancy-dress party, he'd called it in his droll British way. Costumes, he'd meant. I'd begged him to tell me what he was going as, but he'd refused, teasing that I'd never know if I couldn't be bothered to join him.

My frustration had only mounted because I couldn't tell him what I was really doing. I couldn't endanger the Coven by advertising our working, by announcing to anyone— even to Graeme—that I was going to set the centerstone at midnight.

There'd be other parties, I tried to comfort myself. Maybe even more fancy dress. We could come up with costumes together—literary husbands and wives, musical lovers. Once I was officially in the Coven, everything in my life would fall back into its proper place.

I slid the second chopstick home and tried a tentative shake of my head. Everything stayed where it was supposed to, and I sighed in relief.

"So," I said, stepping back into the living room. "How do I look?"

Neko set his right hand on a jutting hip bone, taking time to scrutinize me from the crown of my chopsticked head to the toes of my practical pumps. I'd gone with black. Basic black—the heart and soul of my wardrobe, especially when I wasn't with Graeme.

My slacks were lightweight wool. They should provide protection against the cool nighttime breeze. I'd selected a silk blouse, one of the most demure garments I owned, with a placket that buttoned up to the neck. Fearing the midnight weather, and knowing that I did not want to be hampered by a coat, I'd added a wool sweater and taken care to smooth it evenly over my blouse.

I looked like a high-class cat burglar, ready to romp around on Riviera rooftops with Cary Grant. My only concession to color was the deep blue of my sodalite earrings and necklace. I had chosen them specially, valuing their ability to provide clear sight and confidence. I worried that I might need both before the night was done.

"Okay?" I asked.

"Perfect." I knew I should be pleased by Neko's approval, but his single word only made me more nervous. He never thought I was perfect. Anything but. He was obviously trying to calm me. To steady me. To help me through my testing with the Coven so that his own fate was secured.

Before I could demand an honest appraisal, there was another knock at the door. "I know, I know," Neko said, throwing open the door. "Trick or treat."

"Treat, thank you." David perused the bowl of candy, digging deep to see what we had available. "No Three Musketeers?" he asked, stepping into the living room and closing the door behind him.

"Not anymore," Neko said, and he sounded so doleful that I actually laughed.

"I'll buy you a Three Musketeers tomorrow," I promised. "A king-size bar, if you're good tonight."

"Oh, I'm good," he said, nodding vigorously. "I'm good *every* night."

"That's not what I meant!"

He winked at me slyly.

Okay. So he was only trying to cheer me up. To distract me. But I was enjoying the attention all the same.

"Are you ready?" David asked.

"Ready as I'll ever be." I looked around the room. "What am I forgetting?"

"I've already got the herbs in the car. And the silver flask of rainwater," David said. "You don't need anything else."

I'd given David a shopping list earlier in the day—most of the ingredients for my working were common enough, but I'd wanted to make sure there were no surprises. Neko's feelings had been hurt, until I'd tasked him with picking out the trick-or-treat candy. He didn't seem to realize it was one thing to select sugar infusions for costumed beggars— another thing entirely to determine my future with the Coven. My future and his.

"What should I do with this?" Neko asked, raising the almost-full bowl of candy.

"Just leave it on the doorstep. It's late for trick-or-treaters, but if anyone comes back here after we're gone, they're welcome to whatever they want to carry off."

That was the smartest move, I told myself. Otherwise, I'd be eating leftover candy for weeks. Who was I fooling? I'd eat it all in three days and then swear off sugar for the rest of the year. Or at least until the stores started stocking miniature candy bars wrapped in Christmas red and green.

David made short work of settling the three of us in his car. I tried to relax against the rich leather seats, forcing myself to take deep, calming breaths. David had a CD playing—piano music that was perfectly soothing and utterly boring. Chopin, maybe? Gran would know.

I settled back into the onyx leather and watched the roadside lights glint off the car's walnut trim. The Lexus seemed to pull us forward into the night with a magic of its own, silent, powerful. I imagined witches in ages past, riding horses to their safeholds. All of that equine energy, mastered by a couple of leather strips.... They were better women than I.

David's keys jangled softly as he changed lanes. Involuntarily, I settled my hand over my heart, pressing against his Torch, which I still wore. I closed my eyes and took another calming breath, and then I dared to ask, "Do you need it back?"

He glanced at me quickly before returning his attention to the road. "Only if you want me to take it. I don't want it to distract you during the working."

"I'm used to it now," I said.

"Then you can return it after you receive your own."

I smiled weakly. "You seem so confident."

"I've seen you work. I know how much time you've spent preparing for this. Our lunch meetings every day, your studying every night. You're ready."

Yeah, I wanted to say. Except I wasn't studying witchcraft at night. I shivered, despite my wool pants, as I thought about Graeme, wondering again what costume he'd chosen for his party.

Oh well. No reason to confess to David now. No reason to let him know that I was winging it more than he knew. Neko shifted in the backseat, but he kept silent. I whispered a quick prayer of gratitude for small mercies.

Before I was ready, we reached the long road that snaked

up to Teresa Alison Sidney's house. We had plenty of time, and David pulled off to the side, extinguishing his headlights and turning off the ignition key. His face was lit only by the moonlight that streamed through the oak trees.

"You remember the layout, don't you?"

I nodded. He had told me at least a dozen times. I said, "They've leveled the land near the creek bed. It's out the back door of the house, down a flagstone path. We won't be able to see the house once we get there."

"The foundation was poured two weeks ago. It's had plenty of time to cure."

I looked at him curiously. "Have you seen it, then?"

"Of course." He shrugged. "I needed to make sure that there wasn't anything…unexpected before the concrete was poured. All of the warders and I, we supervised clearing the land last month—Fire and Air and Water, of course."

Of course, I nodded to myself. How else would a witch prepare for her new home?

"It's ready for the centerstone," he said confidently. "Ready for you."

The engine ticked in the nighttime, cooling off as we waited. I took another deep breath, and this time I could smell the herbs in the cotton sack at my feet. Paper or plastic? I was certain the woman had asked David at the organic market. But the greenery was in natural cloth now, ready to play its part in the evening's magic.

"David?" I said.

He grunted a wordless reply.

"Thank you."

"For what?"

"For helping me. For having faith in me. For bringing me out here to the Coven in the first place."

"They didn't give me a lot of choice, did they?" He smiled wryly. "Don't worry. You'll do fine."

I thought back to the first night I'd met my warder. He had thoroughly intimidated me, swooping in like a madman, demanding to know what I was doing with my powers. Since then, our relationship had mellowed. Sure, he pushed me. Pulled me sometimes. Twisted me, even, into his version of what a witch should be, could be.

But underneath it all, I had come to know—come to *believe*—that he was there for me. Would always be there for me. He wouldn't let me go forward with this working if he thought there was a true risk of failure. A real possibility of losing Hannah Osgood's collection. Of forfeiting Neko.

I tried to bleed off some of my nervousness by drumming my fingers against the dashboard. The moonlight glinted off the silver ring that Haylee had given me the night before.

"What is that?" David had stiffened beside me.

"What?" His alarm startled me. "This? A ring."

"I can see that." His words were suddenly terse, tense, and if I didn't know better, I'd think that he was angry with me.

"It's okay," I said, realizing that he must suspect the jasper-stalker. "Haylee gave it to me last night."

"Take it off." Okay. He *was* angry with me.

"David, what is your problem with Haylee? She's the only woman in the Coven who's reached out to me, the only one to take the slightest step toward being my friend."

"Jane, how many times do I need to tell you that Haylee

is not your friend? Not last night, when she gave you that ring. And certainly not tonight. Not when you're about to set the centerstone."

I spread my palms against the walnut dashboard. Truth be told, I twisted my wrists a little, maximizing the milky sparkle of moonlight off the ring. "What happened between the two of you?"

"Nothing."

I heard Neko shift in the backseat, and I might have missed his smothered cough of disbelief if I hadn't been listening for it. I didn't bother looking at him: I knew he would never actually divulge David's secret. Instead, I clenched my ring-enhanced fingers into a fist and settled back in my seat, feeling every inch a spoiled, immovable brat.

"You have to tell me," I said, playing my hidden ace. "I'm going to see both of you at the working tonight. I'll be distracted if I don't know what's going on."

Actually, I wasn't just being manipulative. I was speaking the truth. I *would* be distracted. It was novel enough that David would actually be present at this working. This was the first time I would see any of the warders. They'd be a reminder that the magic I'd be working was dangerous—more dangerous than anything that had transpired in Teresa Alison Sidney's living room.

I'd never thought of myself as a Band-Aid rip-off girl. I'd always been the sort to take a long, luxurious bath, to soak off a bandage with the perfect combination of bubble bath and aromatherapy oil. But now, with both the Lexus engine and the clock ticking, approaching midnight on Samhain, it was time to rip away. Time to get to the heart of David's antipathy toward Haylee. Especially if it had any potential to spoil the looming magical working.

And he must have agreed. He took a deep breath and exhaled slowly, rubbing a hand from his forehead to his chin. He clenched both hands on the steering wheel, and then he collapsed back against his leather seat. Finally, he spoke.

"Haylee was my witch."

"What?" I couldn't believe I had heard him right.

"Haylee. The witch who terminated me two years ago. The one who gave me back to Hecate's Council." The one who had condemned him to a life as an administrative clerk. Until I'd found Neko. Until I'd opened up the Pandora's box of Hannah Osgood's collection. Until I'd summoned him back into the business of witchy protection.

"Why didn't you say anything?"

"What was I going to say, Jane? Don't be friends with the witch who was mean to me? Don't hang out with one of the bad girls?"

"Yes! If that's the way you felt, you should have told me. I'd still make my own decision—"

"Why am I not surprised by that?" he interrupted.

"I'd *still* make my own decision," I reiterated, "but at least I'd have all the facts in front of me."

"Well, now you do." He sounded like a stubborn little boy.

"And thanks for giving me plenty of time to think about them." I whined like a birthday girl, piqued that I hadn't received a rose on my slice of cake. I always could match him in stubbornness.

"Children, children," Neko chided helpfully from the backseat. "It's time to move along. The clock just rang half past eleven."

What clock? I wanted to snap, annoyed as much by my familiar's interruption as by his usage of the British phrase "half past." Graeme would have said half past. If he'd been with us.

But David didn't question Neko. He reached down and turned the ignition key, shoving the Lexus into gear.

I stared at the silver ring reflecting balefully on my finger. "I have to wear it now," I said, almost apologetically. "If you'd told me before… If I could have explained to Haylee… But if I just show up without it tonight, it would be like a slap in her face."

David didn't say anything. He just maneuvered the car down the rest of the long driveway. I stared out my window.

Haylee and David. Well, that explained why he'd been so set against our friendship from the get-go.

But it didn't explain Haylee staying silent on the topic. It didn't explain her never mentioning that she *knew* David, much less that they had worked together, in the intense intimacy of warder and witch. She should have said something to me. Should have filled me in a long time ago. Anger jangled my nerves, making my fingers feel as if I'd brushed them across a bed of nails.

My belly did a sick little flop as David braked to a halt.

"David?" I asked, before he had a chance to unbuckle his seat belt. "What happens if I fail?"

He shook his head, looking in his rearview mirror. Stress torqued his voice into an exasperated sigh. "You know all this. The Coven will take possession of Hannah Osgood's

books. The books and the crystals and all the other paraphernalia. Neko."

I shook my head impatiently. "No, I mean, when? Will
I just blink, and they'll all be gone?" I couldn't look in the
backseat, couldn't force myself to catch my familiar's eyes
in the midnight gloom. "Will Neko turn back to a statue
instantly?"

Predictably, Neko growled, but his aggression tapered off
to a high-pitched whine.

"Don't think about that," David said. "You're not going
to fail. You'll be fine."

I might have believed him if his face hadn't been carved
into stoic wooden planes. My fingers mechanically followed
his as he undid his seat belt, as he pushed open his door.

It took us almost fifteen minutes to walk to the site.
Neko carried the cotton bag of herbs and the silver flask
of rainwater, holding both close to his chest. A breeze had
picked up, sending ripples down my spine to match the
flossy clouds that scudded across the face of the moon. I
was glad I'd put on a sweater.

David took the lead, glancing warily to the left and right.
Neko stuck close by my side. I wasn't sure if he was seeking
comfort from me, or offering. It didn't really matter.

We crested a slight hill, and then we could see the foundation spread out below us. It looked white in the moonlight,
bleached, like driftwood abandoned on a beach. Or bone.

I forced my mind away from that thought.

The foundation was a simple rectangle, edges knife-
sharp from the wooden forms that had contained the
concrete pour. When I took a deep breath, I could still

smell the faintest tang of charcoal, aftermath of the warders preparing the site. My witchy senses tingled with the magic potential below me.

The magic potential, and the magic actual.

As we approached, two dozen shadows loomed out of the darkness. I started to clutch at David's arm, to call out a warning, but then I realized that each black shape represented a witch, a woman clad in a hooded cloak that covered her from head to toe. As if listening to a silent command, they ranged themselves around the foundation, close but not touching the soon-to-be sacred space.

Other shapes moved behind them—larger shadows, bulkier ones. I swallowed hard and reminded myself that each witch was protected by her warder. Each woman's personal guardian stood behind her, prepared to use whatever means were necessary to protect the magic working—the magic workers—on this eerie night of change and shifting potential.

David stopped when we were still several paces from the foundation. I started to direct a questioning look at him— I feared my voice would be too loud if I actually spoke— but then I saw a shimmer of silver light in front of us.

Silver light. Like the circle that had protected my first Coven meeting up at the house. I looked for a warder knight, for a liquid sword of symbolic and actual warding. I found more than I had bargained for.

Three steps to my right, suddenly visible against the inky darkness in a way that made me certain magic was afoot, was the tallest woman I had ever seen. She was clad in a silver robe that was held closed at her neck by a shimmering Hecate's Torch. Her hands were rigid in front of her, clutching the hilt of a broadsword. She stared over my head, past me, *through* me, gazing into the endless nighttime darkness. Without David saying a word, I knew I was looking at a member of Hecate's Council, at one of the elite arbiters of witchy justice.

David bowed low before her, with Neko and I following half a heartbeat behind. "Lady of the North!" he proclaimed, as if he were the chamberlain at Cinderella's ball. "Lady of Water! We welcome your protection on this Samhain night. We ask that you watch all that transpires here and find Jane Madison worthy of inclusion in the Washington Coven. We ask that you protect our workings and bless them in the name of our mother Hecate. We ask that you guide us and keep us, illuminating the night before us with the power of your Torch."

The woman took her time inclining her head, looking for all the world as if she had come to life from some magical silver coin. "Welcome, Warder Montrose. I hear your entreaty and agree to guard the workings of this night, as watcher of Water in Hecate's Council."

We bowed again, almost perfectly synchronized, and then Neko and I followed David one quarter of the way around the circle, crossing to the western edge of the foundation slab. A man stood there—clearly the equal to the Amazon warrior we had just left. He was a full head taller than I, and his arms looked as big around as my thighs. He wore a cloak, too, and his brooch glinted balefully under the moonlight.

David repeated his salute, directing his address to the Lord of Earth. The councilman accepted our bows, agreed to protect us, agreed to watch over the magic we were about to undertake, agreed as watcher of Earth in Hecate's Council.

The southern edge had another woman, Lady of Air, and the eastern edge was guarded by the Lord of Fire. He actually stepped back after agreeing to watch, and he swept his sword in a perfect arc, slicing open a doorway in the glowing silver ring. The hairs on my arms tingled as I stepped through, and I caught Neko swiping at his face, as if he were batting away the finest filaments of a spider's web.

David stepped onto the concrete foundation, keeping his back rigid as a soldier's when he turned to offer me a hand. Neko scrambled up under his own power, darting his eyes around the circle of witches, warders and watchers as we glided to the precise center of the foundation.

I swallowed nervously. This was it. Now or never. A dozen other clichés clattered inside my skull, like the slogans on overwrought inspirational posters.

There was a ripple across from me, and one of the witches stepped up to the foundation edge. She raised two hands to her cowl, paused for a single dramatic heartbeat before casting back her hood.

Teresa Alison Sidney. Coven Mother. The woman I most needed to please before the night was done.

"Greetings, Jane Madison." Her voice was low and resonant, saturated with absolute confidence. She was a witch who would never need sodalite. "The Coven welcomes you this Samhain night."

I bowed my head, trying to remember everything I'd read about ritual, about Samhain. All the appropriate witchy words had flown out of my head, though, and I had to settle for mundane ones. "Thank you." I cleared my throat, and repeated, "Thank you, Coven Mother."

"You see before you the centerstone of our safehold. You hold within you the power to set that stone. Do your working, Jane Madison, that all of us might see your worthiness to join our ranks, to be our sister, to enter into the heart of the Washington Coven."

Taking one step back, she returned to the circle she shared with the other witches. She raised her right hand, as if she were going to bless me, and all of a sudden, I could hear a clock chiming the change of hours.

It was the clock in the Coven Mother's living room, the clock that had initiated the other meetings I'd attended. I did not know what magic Teresa Alison Sidney harnessed to bring the sound to us in our moonlit field; I was not certain how my ears made out the complicated notes across the distance. But I heard the tolling of the hours as I had on that first night, the deep insistent bass of the chimes filling my bones, resonating every magical fiber in my body.

The witches around me felt it, too. I saw them stand straighter. They raised their hands to their own cowls. They lifted their faces to the moon.

And as the twelfth note echoed across the field, as Samhain dawned in the darkness, each woman in the circle cast back her hood.

Despite myself, I looked for Haylee. I was still unsettled by David's admission, newly uncertain about the woman's intentions. But she remained the closest thing to a friend that I had in the entire magical circle. Without conscious thought on my part, I rubbed the fingers of my left hand over her ring, tracing the unblemished silver as if it held all the answers, as if it could make everything right.

Maybe it was the ring that distracted me. Maybe it was a sudden gust of chilly October wind. Maybe it was the sound of the cotton bag of herbs, settling gently on the concrete at Neko's feet, or the tiny clank of the silver flask of rainwater.

But it took me a moment to realize that not only had the witches bared their faces, but their warders had revealed themselves as well. In my peripheral vision, I could see each man standing behind his witch, each protector, stalwart and solid. There were two dozen witches. Two dozen warders.

But only one face penetrated the sudden fog before my eyes. Haylee's warder. Standing tall, directly behind her. Left hand firm on the hilt of his magical sword.

Graeme Henderson.

24

I took three steps toward him, before I realized I was moving. My face betrayed me, breaking into a smile by force of habit before my brain could freeze it, shut it down, force it into stony disbelief.

Absurdly, the first thing I could say was, "Fancy dress party."

Graeme inclined his head, the moonlight turning his blond hair to silver. He grinned bashfully, like a child caught lying about playing in a backyard pond. "As fancy as they come."

There was a rustle among the witches, a shift as every woman looked from me to Graeme to Haylee. And back to me. I felt the weight of all their eyes, the force of recognition as they realized some unscripted drama was unfolding, some unexpected spice for the trickster night of Samhain.

I clutched at David's Torch through my sweater, willing myself to breathe. Breathe. Breathe. Think of something to say. Anything at all.

I could not look at Graeme. Could not face his perfect

smile, could not listen to the purr of his seductive accent. How many Fridays had he lurked outside of Cake Walk before he had approached me? How long had he waited to acquire a gullible witch, along with a few squares of Almond Lust? How many times had he teased me, trying to schedule dates that he *knew* conflicted with my Coven activities? Had he ever read a single one of Shakespeare's plays? Or had he merely used some warder's power to memorize the texts, to somehow protect his witch, advance her interests by applying clever quotations?

I felt sick to my stomach.

Avoiding his pale, pale eyes, I wasted a dozen heartbeats staring at the silver ring on my hand. What had Haylee said the night before? "I've been thinking of you, ever since you first came to the Coven."

She'd been thinking of me. Hating me. Manipulating me—from the very first moment we'd met. And she'd wanted me to know that tonight. Had given me the ring specifically so that her manipulation would unravel me now. She wanted to destroy me, ruin all that I had worked for. She wanted me to look on her gift and know that I had been betrayed, that I would never fit into her Coven, never belong. She wanted me to fail.

I tugged at the silver band, ignoring the pain as it caught against my knuckle. I ripped it off and tossed it toward her feet. It landed in the grass, and I hoped she would never find it, not even by the light of day. "You knew!" I said. "You've known all along!"

"What? That you were sleeping with my warder?" The anger in her voice sparked across the void between us.

Neko squeaked behind me. "Nate Poindexter is a warder?"

David glared him to silence before he said, "Haylee."

I had thought that David was commanding in the past. He had frightened me when he appeared on my doorstep on the proverbial dark and stormy night. He had intimidated me when I reported to study sessions too hungover or too tired to work effectively. But if he had ever directed that precise and deadly tone against me, I would have fallen to my knees in terror.

Haylee blanched.

Haylee blanched, and Graeme swooped to her side, making a show of settling his left hand on the hilt of his sword. How had I never realized he was left-handed? How many other details had I missed in the weeks I'd spent with him?

David did not spare the other warder a glance. "Your fight is with me, Haylee. You had no reason to bring Jane into this."

"I had every reason," she countered, and the tremolo in her voice might have been caused by the icy wind. "She doesn't belong here. She's an upstart and a rebel and she has no business joining the Coven."

At last, Teresa Alison Sidney broke out of her immobility. "Haylee, what have you done?"

My so-called friend dared to look away from David. "Teri! You know it isn't right! You know that I was supposed to set the centerstone!"

"The strongest witch among the Coven sisters sets the centerstone," Teresa Alison Sidney said. "That has been the way of all witches, since the first safehold was built."

"You promised!" Haylee's wail was like a knife scraping sideways on a pottery plate.

"The *Coven* chose," Teresa Alison Sidney insisted. "You agreed, as one of the sisters. All of you chose to test Jane first. When, er, *if* she fails, you'll be allowed to try. You, and anyone else who thinks she has the strength."

Haylee spluttered, and I realized I should be angry as well, furious that the Coven Mother considered my efforts likely to fail.

But I wasn't angry. I wasn't feeling much of anything. I was still reeling at the extent of Haylee's betrayal.

Without asking, I suddenly knew she was the one who had arranged Graeme's limousine for our tour of the Washington monuments. She had phoned him that night at the Kennedy Center, after I had worked my weather spell. After he had spied on my spell-casting technique, I realized. What had she gleaned from his report on my ability to manipulate the Potomac?

She had ordered him away from me that night, kept us apart. Because she could. Because she was a witch, and she could command her warder. Command him far more completely than she had ever succeeded in commanding David.

Had she sent him to London, then, to keep him even farther away? Had Graeme even *traveled* to London? I'd only contacted him on his cell phone. Perhaps he'd been sitting in his Arlington living room the entire time, just pretending to be in England.

And about that Arlington living room, about the night that Haylee had driven me to Virginia?

I closed my eyes, and I could see the look of surprise on Graeme's face when he'd opened his front door. I had thought that surprise was at seeing *me* on his doorstep, but

I'd been mistaken. He had not expected Haylee to lead me to his lair.

And yet, he'd adapted almost immediately. They had played out their scene like flawless actors. They had even chatted about his decor—interior design that Haylee had almost certainly done. He'd said he was keeping that stained glass lamp for a friend. A friend. I had no doubt the lamp belonged to Haylee.

And I had fallen for it. Fallen for him. I had let them fool me completely, let Graeme drive me home, take me to bed. And *Haylee* had let Graeme take me to bed then, too, because she had a larger plan.

*The jasper necklace.*

Graeme must have planted the jasper necklace—and stolen my book on crystals as well. While I slept the dissipated sleep of the sexually exhausted, he had wrapped the beads with thyme and oregano, harnessed the ancient protections against witches. Haylee would know them, of course. She would have mastered herbal knowledge as she chaired the Coven's Gardening Committee.

Graeme had pretended concern, but he'd left before David and Neko arrived—left at my own benighted urging, before they could recognize him. Graeme was the reason Neko had sensed the Coven around my book stand. Who knew what other arcane knowledge Graeme had uncovered in my basement? What other magical information he had taken from me, passed on to the true woman in his life.

To his witch. The witch that wanted to best me now, wanted me to fail at setting the centerstone so that she could show her own strength.

I clutched the sodalite around my neck, using its energy to focus the vision unfolding inside my mind. I stared into Graeme's pale, pale eyes, and I felt a now-familiar shiver up and down my spine. A shiver I had first felt in Cake Walk, when Graeme recited his "nursery rhyme." "Keep our secret, silent be. Speak to no man, not of me." His warder's spell. His harnessed magic that had prompted me to live by Melissa's mundane Friendship Test, that had asserted itself with shivering force each time I even considered revealing my acquaintance with Graeme to any man. To David. To Neko.

Protected by my bespelled silence, Graeme could easily have left the jasper egg on my doorstep as well. He could have sent the threatening e-mails, taking all the time he needed to compose Still Lifes with Jasper and Herbs, to photograph them and insert them into his anonymous electronic threats.

All so that I'd be frightened. Intimidated. So that I'd back down and leave the centerstone to Haylee. Or, at the very least, bungle the job so badly that she could step in and save the day—using my own knowledge against me.

I wanted to blame them. I wanted to appeal to the Coven, to have my so-called sisters rise up in my defense. I wanted my warder and my familiar to stand beside me, before the other witches, the other warders, the watchers of Hecate's Council, so that everyone would know that I had been wronged.

And yet a voice gnawed at the back of my brain. I had made this bed. I had accepted Melissa's juvenile Friendship Test. I had kept my relationship with Graeme secret, held it too close, treasured it too highly. I had let Graeme steal me away, package me up for Haylee to destroy. I'd been suckered by a smooth accent and a brilliant line, never even dreaming of harnessing my magical abilities to protect myself.

Grasping my sodalite, I could picture Graeme extracting his business card from his money clip. The silver clip. The clip formed in the shape of Hecate's Torch. Graeme had dared to reveal his alliance with the Coven on the first day we'd met, but I had been too ignorant to recognize the message.

I took a deep breath and forced myself to meet his eyes. "Acquisitions, Graeme?"

He shrugged. "It seemed appropriate at the time."

A flood of shame and rage and embarrassment turned my mouth to copper. I finally dared to glance around the circle, to see how the Coven was reacting. Some of the women were still shocked to silence by everything that had been revealed—they darted furtive glances between Haylee and me, between Graeme and David. Some of the women were actually smiling, as if they had purchased tickets for a show and were enjoying the main event. And a few had moved to Haylee's side, surrounding her with a coterie of female support.

The Popular Snobs banded together, of course. They supported one another against any threat to their social status, any possible upset of their social prestige.

The warders took their cue from their witches. Most managed a neutral watchful gaze without betraying any actual emotion. But a few cast admiring glances toward Graeme. I could imagine their locker-room chatter. "Way to go, man!" "You totally had her fooled!" "Score!"

And I realized I had lived this story before.

I'd been thirteen years old, attending my first boy-girl dance, celebrating some bar mitzvah at a downtown hotel. Brett Lindquist had asked me to dance. Brett Lindquist— the coolest boy in the entire school. I said yes before I could chicken out. Brett led me out on the dance floor and lurched from side to side, showing off the seventh-grade equivalent of killer moves.

And then I saw the other boys. One called out, "Way to go, Brett!" and another whistled. A third boy sauntered across the dance floor, not even pretending to boogie. He sidled up to Brett and said, "Okay, man. You win. We never thought you'd actually ask *that* one!" A flash of money changed hands, the boy made an oinking sound in my general direction, and Brett strutted off mid-lurch.

I'd run out of the ballroom and up the stairs, into a tiny phone booth. By the time Gran pulled into the circular driveway in front of the hotel, I was crying too hard to explain what had happened. I was only able to tell her about my humiliation after a restorative bowl of chocolate mint ice cream, complete with Hershey's syrup, canned whipped cream, and—the grandmotherly coup de grâce—a maraschino cherry.

Gran had marched over to her calendar and torn off the page for the entire month of September. She'd crumpled her careful handwriting, the immaculate peacock-blue script: Jane's First Dance Party. She'd tossed it in the garbage, and we'd never spoken about Brett Lindquist again.

Peacock-blue.

Like the peacock in the painting at the National Gallery of Art—the painting that Haylee had shown me, had explained to me. I had thought we were sharing something special there, building a bond. All the time, she'd been exploiting me, searching for signs of weakness, for ways to keep me from succeeding at my magical task. For ways of cementing her best-friend bonds to the Coven Mother.

And, as if I'd been struck by another wave, I realized that Haylee had charmed me as well. The tingle I had mistaken for excitement when she spoke to me at Coven meetings, the jangle in my fingers, my entire arm, when Haylee brushed against me as she worked her magic. Her Dark Magic. Her unsanctioned magic. Haylee had made me compliant. She had made me accept what she did. She had made me stupid, even as I had thought she was acting out of friendship, out of a desire to school a fellow witch.

But Haylee hadn't known everything. Clara had taught me more. Clara had told me about peacocks in *Eastern* art. She'd said that peacocks could counteract venom. They could face down snakes. Traitors.

I closed my eyes and took a centering breath, clutching at my deep blue sodalite beads for confidence. I focused on the image of Gran and Clara sitting across the brunch table from me. Sharing dessert with me. Sharing stories of their lives, their love, their hopes for me. Even when the Coven had slighted them.

I owed it to my mother and grandmother to finish this matter with the Coven. I needed to set the centerstone. Set the centerstone, and complete my working, and not let Haylee or Graeme defeat me. All this flashed through me in under a minute.

I exhaled slowly, and when I opened my eyes, I was surprised to see my breath fog on the air. "All right, David," I said, forcing my warder to look away from our betrayers. "Neko." My familiar edged closer. "It's time."

The centerstone sat in the middle of the foundation. It was perfectly round, about two feet across, solid marble. Tiny crystals sparkled in the flawless white. Despite everything—my anger, my embarrassment, my growing physical exhaustion—I could see that the centerstone was beautiful. "'By yond marble heaven,'" I whispered, quoting from *Othello*, "'In the due reverence of a sacred vow, I here engage my words.'"

David caught my meaning and nodded slightly. It was time. Time to pass my test, or leave the Coven forever.

I closed my eyes and took three deep breaths. I touched my forehead, my throat, my heart. When I reached out for the Samhain ritual words, they were easy to find, planted so firmly in my memory that I did not need to think, I did not need to worry. I knew them, and none of Haylee's calculations, none of Graeme's deceptions, could make me forget.

"Witches gather, warders too,
Ringing in a season new.
Join together for this working
Stand against the darkness, lurking.
Pure of faith and strong of heart,
Well-met sisters at the start
Know Samhain power's, Samhain's lore,
Driving through this Coven's core."

With the first words of my incantation, Teresa Alison Sidney swept up her arms, figuratively embracing all who stood around the concrete foundation edge. She clearly gained power from my words, weaving a bond between all of the assembled witches. Despite everything, my spell was working.

Neko stepped closer, bowing his head and huddling by my side. Heat radiated off his body, warming me back to life in the desert of the midnight chill. I rested my fingers on his shoulder, taking a moment to anchor myself against his sturdy strength.

And then I spoke to the centerstone.

"Heart of Stone!" I called to it, brushing my fingers over the flawless marble, relishing its solidity, its safety, its central core of Earth. It responded to its name, vibrating with a power that hummed through my sodalite necklace, whispered through the crystal wands of my earrings.

I raised my silver flask of rainwater high above my head, priming it with moonlight before sprinkling its Water across the perfect Earth circle. The Water added its own note to the stone's, a higher pitch, a perfect harmony that echoed in my mind. I helped the elements to meld, spreading my fingers wide, coaxing the Water to find the tiniest striations, the invisible gaps.

Only when the water shimmered like an unbroken pool of molten glass, only when Earth and Water were perfectly merged, was I satisfied. As if Neko could read my mind, he handed me the cotton bag of herbs.

I shook out the traditional vervain and rosemary, the radish that David had taught me about weeks before. I set them on the Water-melded Earth, arraying them across the marble in the complicated pattern of the rune othala, a diamond with two trailing legs. The symbol meant home and safety, security and abundance. The herbs added their own music to the working, a clamor of treble notes sparking off the harmony of Earth and Water.

Closing my eyes, I lifted my hands high above my head. I knew the motion would make David's Torch stand out against my sweater, would let every witch and warder and watcher who bothered to pay attention know that I was wearing a talisman not rightly my own. I did not care, though, as I invoked the power of Fire, the cleansing element, the element that sealed strength into the heart of the centerstone.

For just an instant, I contemplated letting my flame burn brighter. I could make it flare toward the watching Coven. I could force Graeme to push Haylee behind him; I could manipulate him into doing something that *I* wanted, that *I* desired.

Neko shifted beside me, though. As I pulled my strength around him, focused my energies through him, I knew that I'd be wrong to abuse my witchcraft for the petty purpose of revenge.

I bent my wrists and directed a burst of purifying flame at the centerstone.

The herbs shriveled to dust. The rainwater sizzled into nothingness. The marble glowed gold, revealing its stony core for a dozen heartbeats. The music surged in my mind, in my body, in my soul. And then it crashed to silence.

I summoned Air, to blow away the residue. Ash whipped into the night, leaving behind only the acrid memory of burnt offerings. My summoned wind flowed hot over the Coven, giving them a moment's release from the chill Samhain night. I released the last of the elements, let Air slip away.

The centerstone was ready. It was primed, and it was active, and it would serve as the protective base for the Coven for years to come.

"Now!" I cried, and my voice was as wild as a crow's.

David stepped forward. He had promised me, weeks ago, that I would not need to lift the centerstone, and he had not lied. A half-dozen warders jumped to his side, ranging about the marble with the precision of a military band. Graeme was no fool: he kept his distance. He stayed by Haylee's side.

David issued some silent command, and the warders moved as one, shifting the marble circle, easing it into the precise center of the foundation. I nodded when the placement was perfect, and the men stepped back.

It was simple enough to raise my hands one last time. Simple enough to measure the crystal power of the marble. Simple enough to meld that power to the complex mixture of the concrete, to the sand and gravel and cement that had been poured and hardened days before.

I closed my eyes to make the joining perfect, to feel that precise *ping* as the centerstone found its home. I breathed to steady myself. Once. Twice. Three times. Four.

When I opened my eyes, every witch was staring at me in awe. I wondered what they'd expected, what they'd figured I would do. If they'd thought I would succeed. If they'd hoped that I would fail.

I spread my hands over the charged marble. "The centerstone is set," I intoned.

"So mote it be." The witches answered as if we'd rehearsed a script for months.

"Let all who would stand against the Coven be turned away at the door."

"So mote it be." The warders joined in heartily.

"May Hecate be pleased by our working and look upon her daughters with joy."

"So mote it be." The watchers added their voices to the chorus, rocking the foundation with the power of their affirmation.

The air was filled with the tinkling sound of breaking glass, and a million silver shards rained down upon us. Witches exclaimed and warders swore, and the watchers stood like statues. I blinked, more to clear my mind than my eyes, and I realized that the Council's protective silver circle had been broken.

I reached out to capture a last glint of the spectral light. The motion set me off balance, though, and I would have fallen if David had not spun to my side, catching my arm with a confident iron hand. "Easy," he whispered. "Give yourself a moment to recover."

But I didn't have a moment.

Teresa stood before me. For the first time, I saw her as nothing more than an ordinary witch. A sister. An equal. "Jane Madison," she proclaimed, evoking immediate silence from the babbling group around us.

"Coven Mother."

"We welcome you into the Washington Coven. We are

honored to call you sister, and to have you stand inside our circle."

I forced my spine straight, taking my arm from my warder's grasp. "It's over then?"

"It is done."

"And the Coven waives its claim to the property of Hannah Osgood? You recognize that I am the rightful owner of all the books and crystals and magical wares located in my home?"

Teresa smiled calmly. "The Coven recognizes your right."

I pointed toward Neko. "And my familiar is bound to me, and me alone? The Coven stakes no claim?"

"The Coven has no right to your familiar." Teresa gestured up the hill, toward her unseen home. She dispensed with formality and said, "Come on, Jane. Let's go back to the house. There's plenty to eat and drink there, and we can get to know each other better."

I ran a quick mental tally. Books, crystals, familiar.

That left my warder. I took a step back, so that I could read David's face, stripped clean in the moonlight. We couldn't speak mind to mind. My powers did not stretch that far. But we knew each other. We had trained together. He had guided me, supported me, leaped to defend me when I'd been worst betrayed. I cocked my head at the slightest angle, asking a silent question.

Without hesitation, he nodded. Once. Firmly. Calmly.

I turned back to Teresa. "No."

"No?" She sounded like she'd never heard the word before.

"I won't be joining you tonight. Tonight, or any other time, actually."

"Not joining me? But you're one of us now. You set the centerstone. Surely you know what that means."

"That you've used me to complete your work? To secure your safety?"

Teresa looked hurt; her perfect lips pursed into a pout. "Jane, you're the strongest sister in the Coven. The strongest witch in Washington, except for me." She spared a tiny smile, and I knew I was supposed to feel privileged. Honored. Special. "Think of what we'll be able to do together. You and me, Jane, sharing our powers."

I looked from Teresa to Haylee to Graeme, and then to all the other magical folk. "Teri," I said, relishing my unauthorized use of her nickname, "there is no way in Hell I'm going to share any magical powers with you. I am not going to stand in your living room, eating and drinking like you're my new best friend. I'm not joining the Coven."

Now Teresa looked alarmed. "If this is about Haylee, you can be certain we'll address what she did. She had no right to try to sabotage your initiation."

"Teri!" Haylee exclaimed. She might have said more, but Graeme clamped his fingers tight around her arm.

Teresa gave her supposed best friend a dirty look, but then she addressed me with an honesty that would have been attractive a day before—weeks before, months before. "Jane, I'll admit that I asked Haylee to find out about your powers. The Coven needed to know your capabilities. Your interests. What you could share with us, once we welcomed you in." Teresa's eyes narrowed. "But I *never* told her to use her warder. I never authorized the sort of gaming, the manipulation…"

Haylee spluttered for words, jerking her arm out of Graeme's grasp.

I dragged my disgusted glance from all of them. "It's not really about Haylee. Not even about Graeme. It's about the Coven, Teri. It's about witches setting up cliques for themselves. Counting people out, instead of bringing them in. Cutting women off from power—any amount of power—instead of helping them to increase whatever they've got."

Teresa swallowed hard, but she managed a shaky smile. "Jane, if you're talking about your mother and grandmother, I'm sure that we can do something. Now that you're in the Coven, you and I can discuss their membership, just the two of us. I'm certain we can find a way to make everyone happy."

"That's just it," I said. "I'm already happy. And I have been all along, even without the Coven. I guess, *especially* without the Coven. Goodbye, Teri."

David and Neko caught their cues flawlessly. The three of us turned as one. We flowed up the hillside, past the gorgeous house, around to the waiting Lexus.

David opened the back door for me, and I remembered how I had collapsed after my first visit to the Coven. I recalled dozing on my way home, utterly drained, unable to sit up, to speak, to control myself in any way.

This time, though, I was energized. I had stood up to Teresa and gained strength, rather than lost it. "No," I said. "I'll sit up front."

I had walked away from the Popular Snobs. They had issued me an engraved invitation, and I had thrown it back in their faces. Me, the girl who always got the third out. The girl who Brett Lindquist asked to dance on a cruel-joke dare.

I didn't need them. I had set their centerstone, but I was ready to leave them to their petty games. I had won.

Neko waited until David started the car before he pouted. "Couldn't we have gone inside for just a moment? Just long enough to grab a tray of salmon canapés?"

Walk On In said the sign on the door.

But sometimes it wasn't that easy. I dragged my toes along the sidewalk, feeling as shy as a preschooler at her first playdate.

I'd awakened at five in the morning, stunningly refreshed for having had a total of three hours of sleep. My first thought, upon consciousness, wasn't about the Samhain working. It wasn't about the Coven, or about how I might live beside them as a lone witch. It wasn't about Haylee or Graeme or the cruel deception they'd played.

It was about brownies.

About six batches of burned and hopeless brownies—and the realization that I needed to have *something* for Peabridge patrons to eat when the library doors opened at nine. Either that, or I had to admit my irresponsibility to Evelyn.

Maybe I *had* managed to set the Coven's centerstone. I'd confronted the strongest witch on the Eastern Seaboard and told her I didn't want to play in her sandbox. I'd decided to stake a claim to an unknown, unknowable magical future.

But there was no way in hell I could face the ripped and filthy brownie recipe that was glued to my kitchen counter with egg white and melted chocolate goo.

It was long past time that I came to Cake Walk to make my amends. I shifted a bouquet from one hand to the other. I'd harvested the flowers from the Peabridge gardens—they'd be succumbing to a freeze in the next few weeks anyway. The bright crimson and yellow and orange seemed to glow from within.

Through the years, Melissa and I had joked that we should bring each other flowers on a very regular basis, because no man was likely to do so. I thought ruefully about the floral tribute that Graeme had sent me after our first "date." I had been so pleased. So totally and completely sucked in.

I'd been such an idiot.

Would Melissa laugh at me now? Would she throw the bouquet at my feet, tell me to take my crappy offering and go away? Would she say she didn't want to be friends anymore, that she was tired of investing more in our friendship than I did? Tired of someone who had thrown her over for a *guy*—and a lousy, lying scoundrel of a guy at that.

My stomach executed a queasy backflip, and I thought about just taking the flowers home. I could always call Melissa later. We could limp through a conversation on the phone, grimacing separately at the awkward silences. In fact, I could send her e-mail and avoid talking to her altogether! That way, I wouldn't interrupt her. I would be showing more respect for her. What did I think I was doing, anyway, showing up at the bakery first thing in the morning? That was her busiest time of day. If I took the flowers home, I was just being considerate. Very, very considerate.

I turned away and took a half-dozen steps before I realized I was being absurd. Melissa was my best friend—current spat be damned. Besides, she was my only hope, where emergency baked goods and the Peabridge were concerned. Before I could lose my nerve again, I marched into Cake Walk, tromped up to the counter and held out the flowers, as if they were the scepter to the throne of all England.

"'The quality of mercy is not strain'd,'" I quoted, hoping to prompt her into generous forgiveness.

"'It droppeth as the gentle rain from heaven,'" Melissa replied, as if we'd been conversing all morning. She didn't even bother to cite *Merchant of Venice* as the source of my brilliant conversational gambit. It felt great to be back in the comfortable territory of Shakespeare. Stable. Familiar. Completely, utterly geeky, the way that best friends can be.

She accepted the flowers and smiled appreciatively. It took one twist of her wrist for her to locate the best view of the bouquet, the perfect angle to display the riot of color. "Thanks," she said.

I took a deep breath. "I'm sorry I stomped out of here that day."

"It was more than a bit crazy. Good for business, but bad for carrying on any sort of conversation."

"I should have called."

"So should I."

"I've been thinking about you a lot."

She smiled. "Yeah. I've been thinking about you, too."

She lifted a heavy glass dome and placed a trio of Bunny Bites on a pottery plate. "Want to try my new tea? Apricot Darjeeling."

"Do you mind? I mean, do you have time?"

"Oh, we'll probably get interrupted."

"Well, so long as it's good for business," I said, and she laughed.

So, that was easier than I'd thought it would be. But that's what best friends were really all about, right? We could reveal our inner selves. Admit our shortcomings. Show up at the start of a workday with a handful of flowers and a few stalks of autumn berries, and all would be forgiven.

It took Melissa seconds to fill a pot of water, to add a handful of tea leaves. She took down a small tray and added my favorite pottery mug and a stainless steel tea strainer. I smiled as I took the tray from her, but I needed to catch a yawn against the back of my teeth.

"Tired?"

"I had a late night," I said. My understatement almost cracked me up. Maybe I was punchier than I thought.

"You'd feel better if you started the day with a few sun salutations."

"My back would never forgive me if I started the day with sun salutations."

She shook her head. "Yoga is good for you. You'll get better if you stick with it." I made a face, but she persisted. "They're having a special class at the studio this weekend. Hot yoga. They raise the temperature by ten degrees. It really increases the benefit of the workout. Come on…" she wheedled. "You know you want to go."

"I know I do *not* want to do anything of the sort."

"Rock, scissors, paper."

"Melissa!"

But she had already folded her own fingers into a loose fist. Why did I let myself get roped into this sort of thing? I matched her hands with my own and counted to two before casting paper. She threw rock. "Paper covers rock!" I shouted. No sweaty yoga for me. Not this weekend.

Before Melissa could demand a new contest, or best three out of five, or five out of seven, or whatever it would take for her to be declared torture mistress of my weak and out-of-shape body, I pushed ahead with the main reason for my visit. "Hey," I said, reaching casually for a Bunny Bite. "Gran and Clara had an idea."

Melissa leaned back against the sink, gracious in her momentary defeat. "Let me guess. They have more secret relatives stashed in a closet somewhere. They can't wait to introduce you to Great-Aunt Edna and her triplet of witchy daughters, and they think that Cake Walk would be the perfect meeting place?"

"Ha-ha. No. This idea concerns you a little more directly."

"I don't like the sound of that."

"No, it's not bad. Really." Enough. Time to forge ahead. What was the worst that would happen? Melissa would say no, and I'd be stuck taking a trip to the grocery store for gummy lumps of partially hydrogenated lard? I steeled myself and plunged into the entrepreneurial waters. "You know how things are crazy at the coffee counter at work? Well, Gran and Clara thought that you could help out there. We could cut back to serving just plain coffee, but we could sell Cake Walk pastries instead, to make up the difference. You know, lure patrons in with quality, rather than quantity of caffeine offerings. More profit for you. Less fuss for us."

"And we could all bask in the smiles of happy George-town matrons, strolling the streets and eating baked goods from the Peabridge to the canal." She completed my vision glibly, but I could see that the idea appealed to her.

I put on my best wheedling voice. "We could print up a sign, let people know that the pastries come from Cake Walk. We could even keep your business cards on the counter, so that people can contact you if they want to cater a party. It would be expanding your business, without ex-panding your business, if you know what I mean."

"It would be a lot of extra work," Melissa said, but her protest was halfhearted.

"Not for you! You would just make another tray or two of treats—send us a couple of samples from everything you've already made for the main shop." I shrugged, to convey just how easy this all would be. "I bet it wouldn't add half an hour to your day. If that."

"'Thou art a mocker of my labour.'"

I laughed, thinking back to brunch at Luna Grill, when I had thought the same quotation in response to Gran's sug-gestion. "Orlando," I said, rising to the Shakespearean chal-lenge. *As You Like It.* I bounced a little on the balls of my feet. "Come on. I'm serious. Let's try this."

Finally, Melissa nodded. "Okay. But let's call it a three-month trial. If the sales aren't worth it, or if it takes too much time…"

"Three months!" I toasted her with my tea mug, barely keeping milk-infused Apricot Darjeeling from sloshing onto my fingers.

"When were you thinking of starting?" she asked.

Oh. There was that little detail. I glanced at the cake plates filled with treats, the refrigerated glass cabinet already arrayed to seduce early-morning snackers. "Today?" I offered her my most winning smile.

"Jane!"

"I tried to do this on my own! Really! I was going to bake brownies, but they didn't really, well, they didn't quite turn out…."

She was laughing. My best friend was laughing at me. My best friend was leaning against the sink in her bakery, folding her arms across her chest, shaking her head and laughing at me. "Let me guess," she said when she could catch her breath. "You ruined three batches."

"Six," I said. "It might have been more, but I ran out of ingredients."

Before she could gloat, the door opened. Gran and Clara walked in.

"Oh!" Clara said, when I turned around to face them.

"Good morning, dear," Gran said, as if we met for Cake Walk tea and crumpets every morning.

"What are you guys doing here?" I asked.

Clara shuffled from one foot to the other, glancing from Melissa to me, not quite ready to answer. I took advantage of her silence to say, "See, Gran? I kept my promise."

"Of course you did, dear. It never crossed my mind for a moment that you would go back on your word."

I rolled my eyes.

Clara stepped forward and said, "Jane, your grand-mother phoned this morning. She was eating her corn-flakes when she looked at her calendar, and she saw that last night was Samhain."

"Your calendar had an entry for Samhain?" I asked in dis-belief. Mine didn't go beyond the Federal holidays.

"Of course not, dear," Gran said, shaking her head. "I *wrote* it there. Peacock-blue ink, you know. Because it was a special day for you. Er, night, I suppose."

My eyes welled up. "Gran—"

Melissa looked at me, obviously lost. "Samhain?"

"Halloween," I said, leaping back to the solid ground of bare facts. "Witches' Sabbath. The night I was supposed to be inducted into the Washington Coven."

"Oh!" Melissa said. "I didn't realize—what happened?"

"Let's just say, I'm not going to be attending any Coven meetings anytime soon."

"Oh, dear," Gran said, raising her hand to my cheek. "I'm so sorry. I think they were just being hard on you because they didn't like your mother and me. They had no right to make things so difficult for you."

She didn't know the half of it. And I didn't think I'd be telling her about Graeme and Haylee any time soon.

"No. It's okay. Really. And it wasn't about you. Not exactly." I smiled at all of them. "I did set the centerstone. But then I realized that I didn't want anything to do with the Coven. Not ever again. I was the one who chose to walk away."

Melissa nodded, accepting my words at face value. I suspected it would take Gran and Clara a little longer to come around, because they knew how important Teresa had seemed to me. How important I'd thought she was to my happiness. To my life.

Pouring a mug of hot water for Clara's tea and a cup of coffee for Gran, Melissa said, "I'm sure there's a connection here somehow, but I have to admit that I'm missing it. Gran realized that last night was Samhain, and so both of you came down to Cake Walk this morning…"

"Well," Clara said, selecting a tea bag from the astonishing array in Melissa's teak box. "We realized that Jane wouldn't have time to do any baking last night. We knew that she wouldn't be able to launch her new project at the Peabridge."

Gran straightened proudly. "So, we thought we'd come to Cake Walk to buy enough pastries to get the new program off on the right foot. I hope you don't mind, Jane. We only thought to tide you over until you have time to make the baklava."

"Baklava?" Melissa asked incredulously.

"Don't ask," I said. Before I could break the bad baklava news to Gran, the bakery door opened again.

"David!" Melissa exclaimed before I could turn around.

There he was. My warder. Looking none the worse for his long night's service and short night's sleep. "Good morning," he said, making one general nod, as if he had fully expected to find all of us gathered in the shop.

"Let me guess," Melissa said.

David said, "I knew that Jane needed something for the library, and I was certain she wouldn't have anything ready this morning."

"Now wait a minute!" I said. "Doesn't *anyone* think that I can bake a tray of brownies?"

"No!" they all said, in perfect unison.

As if on cue, Neko walked through the door.

"Oh," he said.

"Et tu, Brute?" I said, making Melissa smirk.

Neko looked over his shoulder, as if he expected someone else to be there, ready to receive my Shakespearean accusation of betrayal. Following his gaze to its logical extreme out the front window of the shop, I saw Jacques, huddling unhappily beneath an elm tree.

Melissa must have made the same extrapolation. Her jaw tightened for a heartbeat, and then she forced a smile. "Go ahead, Neko. Tell Jacques he can come inside."

I held up my hand. "Really? You don't have to do this."

"Yeah," she said. "I know." And then she busied herself pouring coffee for David and milk for Neko, and a steaming hot chocolate for the Frenchman who would never be her boyfriend. When all of us had our beverages firmly in hand, she began to fill two pasteboard boxes, selecting pastries that would keep well at the library, even if they sat on the counter for the better part of the day. Which they wouldn't. I was certain.

I took advantage of the hubbub to pull David over to the corner. "Thanks," I said, setting my tea mug on a table.

"All in a warder's job description."

"No," I said. "It isn't." I reached inside my sweater and pulled out the silver chain that still bore his Hecate's Torch. "I guess you'll be wanting this back."

"No," he said. "Not really." I looked at him quizzically,

and he shrugged. "It's a symbol of the Coven. It was given to me when I was selected to serve my first witch. Haylee."

I wove the silver chain between my fingers. "You could have told me, you know."

"No, I couldn't. Or at least there was no point in doing so." He shook his head. "Within the rules of the Coven, Haylee was absolutely within her rights, with regard to me. I disapproved of the way she used her powers. I thought that she was irresponsible, that she overstepped her bounds. But she was my *witch*. I was sworn to her. I didn't have the right to question her. There's no halfway point between a warder and a witch."

"That's idiotic."

"That's the Coven."

I longed to ask another question, but I wasn't sure how he would take it. Oh, hell. He'd stood by me through everything else. "And Graeme? Did he have a choice?"

David met my eyes, calmly. Dispassionately. "The same one I did. He had a choice, and he made it."

Absurdly, tears started to clog my throat. "I'm sorry," I said. "It's just that I thought…when I was with Graeme, I let myself believe…I didn't realize…"

"They were cruel," David said. "Haylee felt threatened by you, so they were very, very cruel."

"But what about me is so threatening?"

He smiled and shook his head. "You really don't get it, do you?"

"Get what?"

"Your powers. The breadth of them. The depth. Most witches are attuned to a single type of magic." He nodded toward Gran. "Crystals." And toward Clara. "Or runes. But you? You combine it all. You weave together crystals and runes and you bind them with spells. You toss in herb-lore like it's nothing. You call upon elemental magic as easily as you recite lines from Shakespeare. Jane, you heard Teresa Alison Sidney last night. The strongest witch beneath the Coven Mother sets the centerstone. And you're the strongest witch. By far."

I stared at him, not willing to accept his evaluation.

"Why didn't you say anything to me before? Tell me about my supposedly amazing powers?"

"What? And let you get lazy?"

I made a face. "Come on. I mean it. You should have let me know."

"My job is to protect you. But I also want you to be the best witch you can be. The strongest. The work you put in these past couple of months honed your powers. It let you see magical connections, links that you never imagined existed."

He was right, of course. Two months before, I would not have been able to summon the magic that set the centerstone, much less channel it in a specific direction, harness it to a particular purpose. David's plan had worked.

Still… "If I'm so strong, how did Graeme and Haylee work spells on me?"

"You had no idea they were allied against you. You never suspected that they'd try to snare you in magic. With your defenses down—absent—you didn't stand a chance. Any witch can be caught by surprise."

"Even Teresa?"

"Yes. Even Teresa." He started to say the rest of her name, but he caught himself. Old habits were hard to break.

"Am I stronger than she is?" I asked.

He made me meet his eyes after I asked the question. Made me admit, even silently, that I was comparing myself to the Coven Mother, measuring myself against her. I saw him consider lying, consider telling me something good, then something bad. In the end, though, he shrugged. "I don't know."

It was hard to admit ignorance. I had certainly learned *that* lesson in the past two months. I could only begin to tally up how much my ignorance had cost. If I had known my own strength, I would have had more confidence. I wouldn't have been so desperate for Teresa's approval. For Haylee's friendship. For Graeme's…for whatever I'd wanted from Graeme. (Sex? No, it had been more than that. Acceptance. Approval. Love.)

I shrugged. "You know I didn't mean to start all this."

"I know."

"I didn't mean to come between Teresa and Haylee."

"Things might have been different if Teresa ran a different sort of Coven. If you had had a different warder." He stared at the silver chain that was twined between my fingers, at the Torch that rested against my knuckles. "When Haylee dismissed me, I was persona non grata in the Coven. It's a hard life, Jane. It made me a hard person. It's not easy being out there on your own."

"But it's not impossible," I prompted.

"No. It's not impossible."

I squared my shoulders. "And this time, we'll be out there together."

"Together," he agreed.

I settled the silver chain around my neck, tucked the Torch inside my sweater. I might have walked away from the Coven, but I wasn't ready to give up the symbol. Yet.

"Jane!" Melissa called, and I turned to face the chattering group at the counter. "Everything's ready to go!"

I scrambled for my purse, fishing out my wallet. "How much?"

Melissa waved me off. "We might as well start an account, don't you think? Wouldn't that be best, for a long-term venture?"

"That would be perfect," I said. "Absolutely perfect."

I made my farewells quickly—I didn't want to ruin my new Peabridge initiative by arriving late, and I still needed to change into my colonial costume. As the bakery door closed behind me, Melissa was freshening cups all the way around. Neko was insisting that he needed more milk, but he could likely get by with the filling from a cream puff or two. Jacques was agreeing, with Gallic enthusiasm and slavish devotion. Gran was telling Melissa about the recipe for Homemade Turkish Baklava with Rose Water and Pistachio Cream, and Clara was reminding everyone that some of the world's greatest mystics came from Turkey.

But David walked beside me, carrying my pasteboard boxes in easy, companionable silence.

★ ★ ★ ★ ★

*There's one more adventure for Jane.*
*Don't miss MAGIC AND THE MODERN GIRL*
*October 2008*

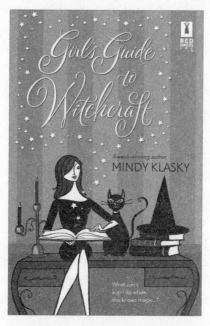

Isn't commitment what every girl dreams of?
Apparently not.

Maggie Hunter's boyfriend, Max, wants her to move in with him. But she's not certain she's ready to put all her eggs in one basket, or all her shoes in one closet!

As Maggie examines the relationships around her (her best friend Eloise can't get her boyfriend, Jake, to commit to an entire weekend with her, much less a joint lease) she realizes that she wants a man like Jake and Eloise wants a man like Max. Someone will have to make a switch—but who wants to mess with practically perfect?

## The Romancipation of Maggie Hunter

Available wherever trade paperback books are sold!

**RED DRESS INK**

™

www.RedDressInk.com

RDIJS89549TRR

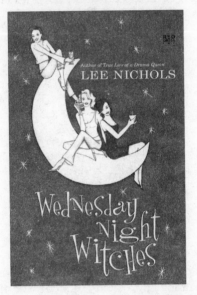